A.J. SCUDIERE

NIGHTSHADE

FORENSIC FBI FILES ✦ BOOK 7

THE CAMELOT GAMBIT

NightShade Forensic FBI Files: Garden of Bone

FIRST EDITION

"There are really just 2 types of readers—those who are fans of AJ Scudiere, and those who will be."

-Bill Salina, Reviewer, Amazon

For *The Shadow Constant*:

"The Shadow Constant by A.J. Scudiere was one of those novels I got wrapped up in quickly and had a hard time putting down."

-Thomas Duff, Reviewer, Amazon

For *Phoenix*:

"It's not a book you read and forget; this is a book you read and think about, again and again . . . everything that has happened in this book could be true. That's why it sticks in your mind and keeps coming back for rethought."

-Jo Ann Hakola, The Book Faerie

For *God's Eye*:

"I highly recommend it to anyone who enjoys reading - it's well-written and brilliantly characterized. I've read all of A.J.'s books and they just keep getting better."

-Katy Sozaeva, Reviewer, Amazon

For *Vengeance*:

"Vengeance is an attention-grabbing story that lovers of action-driven novels will fall hard for. I highly recommend it."

-Melissa Levine, Professional Reviewer

For *Resonance*:

"Resonance is an action-packed thriller, highly recommended. 5 stars."

-Midwest Book Review

An intellectual is a man who doesn't know how to park a bike.
—Agnew

1

"The body was clearly murdered," Donovan told her by way of greeting.

"It's good to see you, too." Eleri climbed into the car, glad to let him throw her bag into the trunk. "If it's clear, then this shouldn't be a case for *us*. Why are we even here?"

For a moment, she entertained the idea of turning around and going home. But right now, home was nowhere to be found.

"Because while our vic was obviously murdered, no one has any idea why, and there are no signs of *how* the murder was committed." Donovan was almost smiling at the bizarre case.

"Of course. What else could it be?" Eleri quipped as she let her head fall back against the passenger seat headrest. She was exhausted, and this one time she hadn't done all the required reading. She had little idea what she was walking into, only that she had no choice but to walk into it. "We're undercover, right?"

Donovan nodded and turned the steering wheel, hand over hand, as they passed street lamps with metal corn husk designs wrapped around them. *Yes,* Eleri thought, *they were definitely in Nebraska.*

She hadn't been undercover in—Jesus—*years,* and even then, it had only been for short, brief assignments. She had no idea how long she and Donovan would be here. "This murder is already going on six days old, isn't it?"

At forty-eight hours in, the window to solve a crime began

shrinking. Though the time frame wasn't the be-all, end-all that TV shows made it out to be, passing time did make things harder. This window was way past that. Though Donovan had gotten here two-and-a-half days before her and had already begun the investigation, he admitted he'd made no real headway.

That fact bothered Eleri as much as anything. Donovan was good. If he couldn't find a thread to pull, there probably weren't any. "I'm doing as well as I can, given that no one is supposed to know I'm actually a medical examiner. But yes, it's six days out and I don't have much."

His *I* would now become *we,* and Eleri was grateful they didn't have a second body—though, from the looks of it, they might soon get one.

Donovan took several turns, already at least a little familiar with the area, though the GPS talked him through the whole way. "We're actually heading to the morgue here in Lincoln first. The good news is, with Curie being so small and not having a morgue or a medical examiner of its own, we get to be here. That will, hopefully, be less obvious than trying to examine the murder in town."

She nodded, and then said, "Please don't hate me, but I did not read the case files on this one well enough." She'd been dealing with her sister's remains, the funeral service, and shaking the hands of family members she had not seen in years while they grieved the sister Eleri had grieved a decade ago. They all must have wondered why she was so emotionless and seemed to assume it was due to shock. They couldn't have been more wrong. Even so, it had been exhausting.

Eleri's plane had landed in Lincoln, Nebraska right on time, but Eleri already felt as though she were late. She'd stayed at home, at Patton Hall, only one day after her sister's funeral service. Eleri spent her week struggling to convince her mother of Emmaline's wishes without letting on that she'd been speaking to her sister for ten years after she'd disappeared. During the worst of their fights, Eleri had wondered if the storm that raged around the house had been nature's doing, or her own . . . *or her mother's*. Leaving had been a blessing.

But it seemed she'd buried one body, only to come here and deal with another. Both the death and the town of Curie were worthy of suspicion.

Donovan launched into what she'd missed while dealing with her family. "The deceased is Marat Rychenkov. Immigrant to the U.S. fifteen years ago, became a citizen ten years ago—which is fast. That's because he's a high-demand scientist—or he was, before he retired. As of right now, there's no clear reason for the murder, and it looks like a serial killing, though it's bizarre for a serial to go after such a prominent member of society."

"Prominent how?" Eleri asked as they wove their way through the town of Lincoln. "Prominent" could mean the mayor or the old guy who sat in front of the hardware store and waved hello to everyone. It really depended on the situation.

"As in: heading to work continually, always on time, interacting with a handful of other scientists in town, and generally being very well-liked. He was considered a contender for a Nobel."

Eleri blinked. That definitely counted as high profile.

"He wasn't missing twenty-four hours before the neighbors went over and picked their way through the lock," Donovan added as he aimed them toward the Regional CDC center. "We've got the body here because it gives us better access without raising suspicion."

Eleri raised an eyebrow. When being at the CDC was less suspicious, things were batshit. But she didn't say that out loud. Instead she asked, "What about the wife? And wait, he's got neighbors who can pick locks?"

"Wife was out of town visiting family. As to the lock picking, I wouldn't put anything past the residents of Curie. Apparently, three or four of them got together and hacked his computer-aided security system, to which he and his wife were known to change the code every week."

"Holy shit," Eleri muttered. She was not prepared for the town of Curie, Nebraska, and she knew it. What little she had read in the case files was bizarre.

Marshall Bennett, a billionaire businessman who was now eighty-six years old and supposedly retired, had spent the last several decades putting together what he considered a dream society. Apparently, Marshall had gotten tired of stupid people one day and decided he was going to build a town that had an IQ requirement. It had taken a decade for him to buy the land and gather the necessary permits. He'd searched out and hired the best city planners in the world and created the town from scratch out of cornfields in Nebraska. Nestled south of both Lincoln and Omaha, Curie was a marvel unto itself.

Eleri's head lolled toward Donovan. "So, I don't recall taking an IQ test to get into town."

Donovan laughed. "Westerfield said he faked ours."

"That's awesome," Eleri said. "What is the IQ requirement? Are we going to be the blazingly stupid ones who clearly cheated our way in? I mean, that might blow our cover."

"I don't think so. It's high, but I like to think we'd make it if we tried."

"I like that Westerfield didn't even give us a chance," she laughed. "Maybe he thinks we'd flunk."

Donovan laughed, too. "I automatically assumed it was just about expediency, but now that you put it that way . . . You're right, though. We have to be super smart just to fit in."

"Is that what you're finding from your first few days?"

"Absolutely. A few of them are disturbingly friendly."

"What does that mean?"

"Southern neighborhood type stuff. They see there's somebody in the new house, and they bring you a pie."

"You got pie?"

"Well, sure, but the pie is their own recipe. The crust has been cut into fractal patterns." He grinned. "No basket-weave crust in Curie!"

"Fractal patterns?" Eleri asked, stunned. She wasn't even sure how one would do that.

"Hey, when scientists bake, you get fractal-pattern pie. The neighbor on our right, LeDonRic, did not bake me a pie, but he has a Dalmatian named Lady Macbeth so he can open his door and yell, 'Out, out, damn spot,' every morning."

Eleri threw her head back and laughed again. She felt bad, given that she was here to examine a murder, but so far, Curie was sounding like a big batch of crazy. "And our cover?" she asked him.

"Still Donovan and Eleri, but with new last names."

Yes, she remembered that. "Good, because I'm not much of an actress. Professions are adjacent to our own, if I remember correctly." She was grateful when he nodded in response.

"I'm a research physician. You're a biodiversity specialist."

"Well, shit. I don't know enough about animals or plants."

"*Human* biodiversity."

She almost laughed again. She'd seen so much human biodiversity in this past handful of cases since she'd joined Nightshade, that she probably was an expert. "Okay, so we have a really smart town and a murder of a Nobel-worthy robotics specialist. What's so special about the murder?" She still hadn't read enough to wrap her head around why Westerfield had sent them out right away. *Why was this even a NightShade case?*

"The first issue," Donovan explained, "is the serial element."

"Okay. BAU?" she asked, knowing he would understand immediately that she was asking if the behavioral analysis unit had been contacted and if they'd managed to provide a profile.

He shook his head as he parked the car in the back lot of the CDC building. "That may be on you. They searched everything, but it doesn't match anything in the databases. And they're struggling to put together a profile without any reference data."

That's weird, Eleri thought. Serials operated from human urges—bad ones, but *human* ones. That this didn't resemble anything the BAU could put even a small tracer on was concerning. As she climbed out, she looked at him across the hood of the car, making sure first that no one was in earshot. "Is it . . . supernatural?"

But he shook his head no. They didn't speak about the case as they entered the building and he led her down through the twisted hallways to the morgue. She figured doctors had that ability, just like forensic scientists did, to find the morgue in any building they were in.

It was when he pulled the drawer open for the body that she finally understood why it was their case.

"I don't see *anything*."

"That's just it, El. You can see his hands and wrists were bound, but it looks like he just *died*."

2

Donovan parked his car in the garage of his "new home." Of course, it didn't belong to Donovan Heath, it belonged to Donovan Naman, a name he was relatively sure he was not going to remember very well. He knew the first time someone hollered out, "Dr. Naman, Dr. Naman!" as he walked down the street, he was going to have to remind himself to turn around and act like he belonged to the random sounds they were calling out. He did not see this going well.

The code to get into the house had been 1776, set by the real estate agent. He'd already changed it to 1492 out of spite. As they entered, he showed Eleri the code and how to activate it as he punched it in and opened the door from the garage into the laundry room/mudroom.

"Correct me if I'm wrong," Eleri said as she stepped into the building behind him, "but according to the stone sign at the neighborhood entry, we live in *Pythagoras Point*?"

Donovan nodded. "Just you wait, it gets nerdier."

"I'm not sure it can."

"In the Pythagoras neighborhood, all the houses are basically knockoffs of Frank Lloyd Wright and I. M. Pei," he said.

"Oh, you recognize the architectural stylings of I. M. Pei?" she asked.

"Oh God, no," Donovan replied. "My new neighbor . . ."

"*Our* new neighbor," she corrected, and he nodded.

"LeDonRic James informed me of the design styles."

"LeDonRic is the one with the Dalmatian named Lady Macbeth?" She seemed to be asking just to solidify it all in her mind. As though she was taking notes.

"Got it in one," Donovan said, smiling as he led her into the open space concept design.

"It's a really nice place." She looked at the high ceiling and up the modern-cut staircase. "Though I can't tell if it's a Pei or a Wright."

"Me neither. And the view sucks," he told her as they looked out the floor-to-ceiling glass windows onto the medium-sized backyard and wood fence blocking the houses behind it.

"Well, there wasn't much to expect," she said. "It's not like you can be on a hilltop and look at all the cornfields."

He laughed. They'd driven through plenty on the way over. Luckily, she'd arrived in the middle of the afternoon, and he'd even been able to take her to the roadside stand that sold *Lightning Tree Corn*, something he'd learned was a bit of a local delicacy and a Curie favorite.

Donovan set the corn onto the counter and helped Eleri carry her bags from the car. Their cover was that the house was Donovan's, that he had tested into Curie first, and that Eleri was an old friend living with him while she looked for a place of her own. They hadn't tried for anything more complex, like posing as a married couple—they couldn't pull it off. Siblings didn't work with their coloring. So Westerfield hadn't aimed for anything more than friends in a house. Apparently, even their boss was concerned about their acting ability. Eleri had lamented her poor skills earlier, and Donovan was convinced his own were worse.

"The problem with my cover story," he said, following her up the stairs with a duffle bag she'd brought as she dragged her small suitcase, bouncing up the carpeted staircase, "is that Westerfield saw fit to give me a job."

She stopped two steps above him, spun around and looked down on him for once. "You have a nine-to-five?"

"Not *that* bad. But I'm supposed to be a consultant at the hospital in Lincoln. *And* I'm on call at the local emergency clinic."

Eleri's eyes widened. "Did Westerfield just forget how long it's been since you've worked on a live patient?"

"I don't even know," Donovan said. "Westerfield says it's unlikely I'll get called. I'm just going to try not to kill anyone."

"Is that why the big textbooks are out on the table?"

He nodded. He'd been reading up. Next to the books, his computer was open to fifteen different sites as he'd downloaded article after article on the state of current ER triage and treatments. He'd closed the screen, but not the tabs. He was in the town of smart people, and his brain already hurt. After he'd helped settle her in the second bedroom, he showed her the room across the hall.

"I took the master bedroom because supposedly it's my house, and that seemed normal to me. So, you're in that room and I set up the smallest room remaining for the two of us to share as an office. We'll have to keep it closed up. If we have anyone over, no one can see what we've got in there."

Eleri nodded, understanding, as the darkness began to fall around the house. The time of day was always obvious with the large glass windows. Whatever the daylight was affected the interior.

She followed him back downstairs again as he explained, "There's pie on the counter, and I bought a handful of sandwich fixings and freezer meals."

"I'll probably start cooking for us," she said. "If I don't have a job, and I just have the one case to investigate, it makes sense that I would fix meals. Plus, I'm guessing getting out to the local grocery stores will help me get acquainted with people."

Donovan thought it sounded like a good idea—one that was going to get him fed better. He also thought it sounded like a good idea that he wasn't going to be the one to do it.

"We'll need to get your car," he said. "We've got a fake budget to 'buy' you one at a dealership outside of town." He'd used air quotes around the word buy, and Eleri understood they'd be meeting another agent who was handing over a thoroughly unmarked car.

"Is that the fractal pie?" Eleri asked as she peered at what was left from what he'd cut into the night before. "Is it apple, or is it some variant?"

"It's apple," he said. "When she brought it over, Maggie—LeDon-Ric's girlfriend—informed me that she liked to bring apple, as it was statistically the most commonly liked of pies and the least likely for someone to have an allergy to."

"Very statistically thoughtful," Eleri commented.

"Wait until you get a load of the high school," he said. He'd been confident that he'd grown up in some very poor neighborhoods with underfunded schools, but this place confirmed it. As soon as the words were out of his mouth, he realized Eleri may have gone to schools just as nice as the one here, though her family would have paid directly for her to go to them. She'd been raised in private school systems with twenty and even thirty-thousand dollar a year tuition, even at the elementary school level. So he shrugged, and she shrugged as well. They would check it out tomorrow.

"Should we do a nice little drive around town?" she asked.

"Yep." They needed to do it tomorrow, while it would still look acceptable for Donovan to be giving her tours.

She opened the fridge and peered inside, but apparently rejected his sandwich makings, because she closed the door without grabbing anything. "Is there ice cream?"

"You know there is."

"Vanilla?"

He only motioned her to open the freezer, and she immediately asked if he wanted a piece of pie as well. After a few moments of microwaving, they sat down at the table amidst all his textbooks, and he was grateful that while the back of the house was almost fully glass, the front was a little more conservative. It wouldn't help if the neighbors saw that he was reading medical manuals and not as competent at his job as perhaps he'd been sold to be.

She turned her plate from side to side, having put the ice cream next to the pie so she could examine the pattern of the crust. "It's really quite impressive. Do you think she made her own fractal-based cookie cutters?"

"Who knows? I think this particular fractal is a Dragon Curve." Donovan had yet to quite get a grasp on the people who lived in Curie. He wasn't sure how to make himself and Eleri blend in the way they needed to. They would have to get to know all the major players to find a killer. Still, he was discovering that, while he didn't fit in, the people who lived here seemed to fit together quite well. Whatever vision Marshall Bennett had for the town, he'd managed to put together a crew that appeared to be working.

The town was small, even by Nebraska standards, but Donovan had been impressed. The small size had made the residents notice a newcomer in their midst, although apparently, newcomers were a regular occurrence. The town was growing exponentially, and the residents were simply trying to keep up.

Donovan caught Eleri up between bites of what was truly a fantastic pie. Probably everything had been measured to a statistically perfect percentage. Perhaps she'd run a variety of taste tests. Having met Maggie, even only for a few minutes, and knowing she was friends with LeDonRic next door, Donovan was fairly certain that had to be the case.

He pointed out the side window, to where he hadn't yet closed the curtains for the night. "LeDonRic's lights are still on. There's always a light on. I don't think he sleeps."

"That's sometimes the case for highly intelligent people. They also tend to die younger, but it's not proven whether that's a lack of sleep issue or a lack of social support issue."

"Look at you, already trying to fit in!"

She wadded up her paper napkin and tossed it at him, missing by a wide enough margin to make him shake his head.

"So apparently," he told Eleri, "Marshall Bennett hand-picks the applicants that get in. Therefore, a certain score or higher on an IQ test is a requirement, but . . ."

Eleri seemed to catch on. "It's not entirely enough to get into town."

"Exactly. So," Donovan told her, noticing she was yawning and she would run out of steam soon. "So even though everyone here is smart, and everyone passed that threshold, Marshall Bennett let us in to examine this case—but he also, at some point, let in a murderer."

3

Eleri stood over the body of Marat Rychenkov the next morning. It was way too early to be at the CDC and in a morgue. But here she was, paper gown, hair cap, booties, and gloves. Aside from size, she and Donovan were indistinguishable. At least the smell didn't bother her.

The tour of town had been pushed to later in the afternoon, after both of them decided that coming back here and looking at the evidence head-on was their best first step. Eleri did not like what she saw, and she didn't like what Donovan had to say next, either.

"His wife is waiting on us. She wants to cremate him, or plant him in a tree, or something."

"Crap," Eleri muttered. The last thing they needed was pressure. After thoroughly examining the body, she still found no apparent cause of death, and when she asked Donovan, he'd only confirmed the same. She looked up at him. "There's not even a partial fingerprint! I mean, you did the same thing, right? Everybody's looked at him, his clothing, *everything*? With blacklight, with . . ."

"With every filter we have," Donovan continued for her. "There was not a hair found at the scene that doesn't immediately trace to a known person. The techs were good and found a handful. Most are Mr. Rychenkov and his wife, Johanna Schmitt. Others are for people that Schmitt confirmed had visited the home and were friends of the family. Those hairs were not found in other parts of the house where a guest might not have gone. Though the home was kept organized and relatively clean, there were no perfectly clean rooms—nothing that looked as though the killer had sterilized the place. There weren't even stray footprints on the carpeting. Basically, there's jack shit."

"There's no evidence of a fight or struggle," she said.

"There's no evidence of a *murder*," Donovan added, his frustration already clear.

He wasn't volunteering any sensory information, which probably meant he had nothing, but she asked anyway. "Do you smell anything?"

"No, nothing of value. By the time I got here, the body was old enough that I'd only find the most prominent clues. And there aren't any."

"Jeez." She pushed the word out through her teeth this time. "So what do we think happened? Or what crappy theories do you have?"

She picked up Rychenkov's nearest hand and rotated his arm from one side to another, checking the marks on his skin. The body, having been kept in cold storage for a handful of days, did not want to turn in a supple way. Still, she examined it carefully. "There are clear ligature marks on the wrists."

"And ankles," Donovan added, though she'd noticed that before.

"So what happens? This person comes in and—somehow without a fight—gets Rychenkov tied up. Rychenkov is married and appears to have no kinky lovers in the background—"

"Unless you count his research." Donovan grinned.

"What was he researching?"

"Robotics something. But Johanna—the wife—laughed when asked if he maybe had a lover. She said, 'His work.'"

Eleri nodded and turned back to the body. "So no lover, but he lets someone else tie him up and kill him in some unknown way. No real struggle until well after it's too late to fight back. Then the killer unties him and leaves the body there?"

"That's what it looks like," Donovan said.

They had looked at the body under lighting that would have illuminated bruising. He had a mark on his arm and another on his right ankle, but both were quite normal-looking. In fact, Eleri suspected there would be worse bruising found on her own skin at that moment if someone checked. She was pretty sure she'd run into the countertop in the kitchen this morning when she'd taken the turn too close.

Stepping back, Eleri peeled her gloves and smacked them hard into the nearest trash can. Perching her hands in fists at her hips, she paced a tight circle. "Okay, what if it's *not* a murder? What if he's having an affair, and somebody ties him up, and then he just dies? His lover freaks out, unties him, and runs scared. Why doesn't that work? What if this isn't a murder at all, and we don't need to be here, because it's just a weird, accidental death?"

"All right, three problems," Donovan said. "One, there's no cause of death still: no drugs and no wounds—obvious or not. The blood panel showed no protein markers from any kind of heart attack or even high cholesterol."

"Are you sure about the drugs?" she asked.

"I mean, I can't be positive, but nothing showed up on the tox screen, and the CDC here has tested for just about everything. I don't smell anything, and I sniffed his liver up close and personal," Donovan commented, as Eleri turned and noticed the Y incision on the front of the body. Then he dialed back a bit. "But that may be because the body isn't fresh."

"Two," Donovan continued, "there's no evidence at all of another person even being in the house. Why would a secret lover come over ready to leave *zero* evidence behind? Sexcapades tend to leave an abundance of evidence, not the opposite."

Didn't Eleri know that one from previous cases?

"And three, there are no external wounds. Plus, it looks like he *might* have suffocated."

"*What?*" Eleri turned sharply.

"Look at his nail beds. There's a tinge of blue. And some around his lips. But it's just a guess, as I didn't see the body until it was already old. Still, nothing else supports that. Nothing around his neck, not even the mild bruising one would see if there'd been a pillow over his face."

"So he just randomly suffocated in open air? *Sure.*" She plucked two more gloves from the nearby box and expertly slid them onto her hands. She turned Rychenkov's head from side to side, looking at his neck. "No marks, Donovan." She looked again at his chest. "The Y incision is in the way, but I don't see anything to indicate a hole in his lungs. Did his lungs collapse?"

Eleri knew the answer even before Donovan shook his head. If that had been the case, Donovan would have told her first. It would have been in the report. Unless they found something new this morning, it didn't exist. She looked back down at the neck and head again, pulling the eyelids up one more time.

"There's nothing. Not even petechial hemorrhaging," she added, noting the red blood vessels that tended to appear in the eyes when the oxygen was cut off, usually via strangulation.

"I know," Donovan replied.

"Blacklight?" she asked, and he quickly obliged. Though she knew Donovan had already done all of this himself, she just wanted to take her own look. Eleri was glad he didn't begrudge a second pair of eyes. She knew he was hoping she would get lucky and find something he hadn't. So far, she'd scored a big fat zero.

Eleri searched the whole body, including rolling Rychenkov over. She rolled the body using a technique of pulling one arm up and draping the other across the chest and pulling. Though Donovan offered to help, she refused. She wanted to see everything herself, not risking one of his gloved hands getting in the way and making her miss something.

Patiently, her partner continued to hold the blacklight on its stand and scan it over the body as she moved up and down, peering at anything that grabbed her attention. She noted the livor mortis—red and white coloring from where the body had cooled—all matched the initial reports. Nothing suspicious there. There was no evidence of anything trapped under the body and removed later, or even that he'd been rolled post-mortem. The coloring confirmed that the bindings had been removed soon after death, which was likely why the techs didn't find the bindings at the scene.

Donovan silently followed her from spot, to spot, to spot, and still, she found nothing.

Finally, she looked up and said, "Crap."

Donovan only shrugged at her. "I think this is why we're here."

"So the ME found nothing either?" The ME would have taken out each organ, weighed and tested it. She would have checked the contents of the stomach and looked for evidence of drugs, alcohol, or sex in the victim's last twenty-four to forty-eight hours.

"Neither the ME nor the CDC found anything. They're pretty

sure he suffocated, but . . . nothing. Well, the only clue is the ligature marks."

"Yeah," Eleri said. She frowned, thinking that one through, and assuming Donovan had once again already arrived at this. "So, if they tied him up, then . . ." She paused. "Okay, if they used something like a silk tie, you might not have seen the marks."

"This looks more like rope." Donovan's assessment agreed with hers. "Whoever was doing this wasn't being very kind."

"And it looks like he struggled a little bit, but only after he was tied up," Eleri said. "If he didn't want to be tied in the first place, there should be self-defense markings."

"Yes, so eventually he knew he was dying, or he knew something was wrong in some way."

She stopped and thought about it again, simply repeating what they already knew and hoping it triggered something. "But someone untied him. He wasn't found tied up."

"Nope," Donovan answered, holding up the folder and thumbing through the pages, reconfirming what they'd both already read.

Eleri wanted to put her hands on her head and pull at her hair, but one did not do that while still wearing the gloves she'd touched the body with. "So, he gets willingly tied up, and at some point along the way, discovers he doesn't like it, fights against it, dies, and then whoever it is removes the ties."

"Looks like," Donovan said.

She stared at the body for almost another fifteen minutes, eventually turning the blacklight off and on, pulling other color filters over, looking at it under red light, and checking carefully for things that Donovan may have missed, though she trusted that he hadn't. He had more senses than she did, flat out, and he hadn't caught anything.

Then, she asked something else. "When we were in the car with Darcelle, you said you could *smell* her fear, that she was really afraid. Do you smell any of that on him?"

Donovan only shrugged. "If he'd been brought to me fresh, maybe."

Shit, she thought again. Rychenkov's body had come here. He'd gone to the medical examiner. His clothes had been removed, and he'd been laid out on the table. His body had been cut open and cleaned, and it was only after the ME's office had worked it up that

Donovan had seen any of it. Eleri tilted her head. "What about his clothes?"

"Good call." They wouldn't have been laundered. They would have been saved as evidence. It took the two of them a good thirty minutes to get their hands on the clothing the man had been wearing. They pulled the items out, and Donovan took a sniff. "Shit," he muttered, and Eleri's heart sank.

"No fear?"

"A little," he said, "but not overwhelming, not like Darcelle was in the car when she was panicked. Not like the fear somebody has when their life is threatened."

Eleri swore to herself under her breath. Eventually, after putting the evidence back in the bag and restoring it and the body, she said to Donovan, "If we can't figure out *how*, then we have to figure out *why*."

"I know, and I want to get into the house and examine the crime scene."

"But," Eleri picked up the sentence, "his wife still lives there."

"Then I guess we're going to have to break in," he said.

4

When they finished—or effectively gave up—at the CDC, Donovan drove Eleri around the streets of Curie. Though it was in fact a sightseeing event to help her become familiar with the place, they had also agreed that they would drive by the home of Rychenkov and his wife, Johanna Schmitt, in an attempt to see how they might possibly break in and check out the scene. Without being able to flip open an FBI badge and demand a way in, illegal entry might be their only option to get what they needed.

Donovan watched as Eleri's head swiveled one way then another as they drove past the various points of interest in town. Though the types of places were normal—grocery stores, restaurants, grid-style streets—nothing about Curie was average. Donovan had already survived these eye-opening moments.

He pointed to the street sign at an intersection and waited for her reaction. Instead of using letters and numbers for the main grid, Bennett had laid the town out with famous scientists running north/south and the cross streets sporting periodic table elements.

While they sat at the light, Eleri read their green intersection signs and commented to Donovan, "We're at the corner of Tesla and Mercury."

Donovan nodded with a grin. The standard green street sign didn't even say the word "Mercury," it just had the two letters "Hg." It was assumed that everyone in this town would know what that meant.

"Are the elements in order?" she asked.

"Nope," Donovan answered. "They go out from the middle. Carbon runs through the center of town. It seems to be their main street."

"That actually makes sense," Eleri commented, though she was still looking out the window like a newbie tourist.

"From there, the main section of town uses the first several rows of the periodic table, but after that, it appears they picked favorites. They don't seem to have a hundred plus east-west streets."

She was shaking her head, but still hadn't looked at him. There was too much to take in.

"Check this." He pointed as he took a soft left onto a cross street that ran at an angle through the grid.

"Copernicus Way?" she asked.

"Absolutely. One of the locals told me it was because Copernicus was always at odds with everything else. So they made him the slant street."

He took that street for a while, angling back toward the middle of Curie. They needed to head to the other side of town anyway, where Rychenkov and Schmitt had their home. As they approached the middle of town, Donovan went around the traffic circle that marked the center several times, so Eleri could scope it out. She had to lean over to see out his window. Copernicus Circle had a central sculpture that rose out of a well-tended garden bed. Rotating slowly around a thin central pillar with a huge sun model on the top, all eight planets and Pluto circled with traffic.

"Oh my god," she commented. "They got the moons around Jupiter and the rings on Saturn."

"And," Donovan commented, "having looked at this several times, I'm pretty confident that—though it moves quickly—the planets move in proportional rotation to each other."

"Of course they do. We're in Curie, where there's an IQ requirement to become a resident," Eleri said even as she blinked at the sculpture. It was a work of art.

"Of course they do," he replied with a smile before taking his exit and continuing on Copernicus Way to the other side. He pointed to things they passed. To one side was the small grocery store that he liked, not quite a standard big box store—though he hadn't found any of those here. He didn't know if it was because the place wasn't big enough or if the residents were too green or too conscientious to let a behemoth in, but if he wanted a Walmart, he'd have to go into Lincoln.

"But," he said, "when I went into that grocery—Food for Thought—the people talked to me. The workers were polite enough, maybe a bit standoffish—but the other shoppers tried to say hello. So, I figured that might be a good place if you're going to go try to casually meet people and get any ideas what the town is really like."

"It's *weird*," she volunteered right away. "And super nerdy." But she nodded and waited until he pointed out the next sight.

"If you go down Boron Street all the way to the end . . ."—he heard her snicker again at the use of elements for cross streets, but continued—"No, it gets better. There's an entire Hobbit neighborhood."

"What? Take me there. Take me there now!" Eleri practically clapped her hands and bounced in her seat. For a moment, Donovan thought she might not believe him, but then he realized the woman who thought a grocery called "Food for Thought" was nerdy was disturbingly excited about a neighborhood of Hobbit houses. Though they were supposed to be solving a case, the town wasn't huge enough to get them too far off track, and part of their job was to learn their way around. So he took the turn and headed straight down Boron.

They passed a small theater that had only two screens, but at least was showing current movies. There was a bowling alley with arcade games, and he commented as they passed it. "If you go over to Carbon Street," he said, pointing in the general direction, "there's a really great restaurant. It's called *The Atomic Diner*. They have wonderful food, and there's a coffee shop next door."

"Excellent."

"It's called The *Up N Atom*."

"A-T-O-M?" she asked.

"Of course," they replied together.

"I'll take you by for coffee on the way back so you can see exactly where that is and maybe even go hang out. You can get online and pretend you're applying for jobs tomorrow, to get to know some other people. It's in a pretty different location from the grocery store, and I'm hoping we'll get different crowds there."

She nodded, apparently once again having been reminded that they actually had a case. They drove through the Hobbit neighborhood, appropriately named The Shire, both of them looking out the window like kids. Though he'd seen it before, he was still in awe at the little houses with the round doors and windows, all mounded under the dirt. Though he could have neighborhood-gawked for much longer, he pulled them out of the subdivision and took a left-hand turn. "I think LeDonRic's girlfriend Maggie lives in there."

"Are all the houses in subdivisions?" Eleri was frowning but she hadn't looked away from the small homes.

"Everything I've seen is. Remember, this isn't an organically grown town with settlers picking the best spot to farm the land and open a saloon. This town was designed from scratch. Apparently, even most of the people who specialize in that only do growth plans for existing cities or design hypothetical places. Bennett bought up the land through his own funding and grants and laid it all out. So I think, yes, all the homes are in named subdivisions. At least they didn't build to the trends of today."

"True," she commented absently because she was looking at a veterinarian's office they passed. *Long in Tooth and Claw*. It made Donovan wonder what they would do with him. "I guess a Hobbit home will never be 'so seventies' or such."

He headed for the Schmitt home where Rychenkov had lived. "This is our problem," he said pointing into the next subdivision.

"C'thulhu Heights?" she asked. "Our problem is in a place called C'thulhu Heights?"

"I told you, Eleri, it is a town for smart people, and Bennett did his research. He had all these things on deck before he laid the asphalt on Carbon Street. He had people lined up to live here five years before the town was built. They passed their IQ tests and paid their down payments, and apparently, they voted this stuff in. He named it Curie, but the town legend . . ."

"There's a town *legend*? Of C'thulhu? The town is only ten years old!" she protested.

"No, there's a *legend* like a map's key to the town. It's posted downtown, if you go into the library."

"Holy shit," she said.

"I know, but the people voted on the Shire, and Pythagoras Point."

"And C'thulhu Heights," she added.

"Exactly. Here's the problem with C'thulhu Heights: The houses are all stone."

As he drove into the neighborhood, she looked. Unfortunately, it was a neighborhood much like theirs. The houses on adjoining streets had relatively small yards separated by fences. They were made of stone that bounced sound and showed off intruders. "Fuck," she said.

"Exactly. I've been trying to figure out how to get into the house so that we can check out the crime scene." Basically, they were driving around the neighborhood and casing the place like criminals while waving like new friends to the people they saw.

"Do you know anyone who lives adjacent to the house?" she asked.

"Unfortunately, not close enough—not anyone that I'm supposed to know, anyway. I mean, I have a couple files."

"So no one we can stop and talk to, no one's house we can go into, get a lay of the land?"

He shook his head. It sucked. He'd thought the same things. It seemed, after working a handful of cases together, they were starting to think alike. He wasn't sure if that was a good thing or not, but it wasn't anything he could fix right now, and this case was on deck. "If we go in at night, she'll be there. As best I can tell without looking like a *bona fide* stalker, she's at home every night, in bed."

"So we need to get in during the day," Eleri said.

"Exactly."

"Is she at work, or is she at home on leave?"

"I don't even know. She was at home one time I came by, and I'm trying to get a bead on her, but there's only Wade here helping us. Westerfield couldn't bring in a whole crew. Wade arrived the day before I did, and Westerfield managed to install him in a house in this neighborhood, so that helps us. But the only house that was available for him was four streets over."

"Too far," Eleri commented.

"I know." Donovan shrugged. "And with the fences the way they are, we can't climb over them, because we'd have to go through another house to get into their backyard to climb over it. Which leaves us clearly sneaking through someone's yard."

Eleri had seen the aerial of the plot, Donovan knew. There was no real alternate way into the house. They would most likely have to go through the front door.

They took a turn and drove around the neighborhood, eventually coming up to the door of Wade's house, although Donovan didn't stop or slow down. They couldn't act as though they knew Wade—not unless something changed on their cover. Wade was here as Dr. Wade Duncan and was teaching one class a day at the high school. Westerfield had worked with Bennett to install Wade in a class that it was hoped would give him access to the parents most likely on the suspect list. It was a long shot, but cover was necessary.

"So the trick," Eleri told him as she finally turned and faced him, "is that we have to get her to let us in."

5

Eleri was up the next morning and on the job, though the job itself was odd. Her first task was heading out to the sidewalk as though she were checking the mail, to make herself visible to her neighbors. She'd aimed for an optimal time to run into someone. Though she could have gone through the garage to get to her car, she headed down the front walk, grabbed the two pieces of junk mail, and slowly meandered up the flagstone walkway.

She saw a woman who must be Maggie at the next house, knocking on the neighbor's door. Eleri waved, and the woman waved back. Eleri tried to look as though she didn't already have a dossier on as many townspeople as she did. It was hard keeping straight what she was allowed to know and what she wasn't.

"Hi. Are you new?" The woman had stopped knocking and was calling out to her.

"Yes. My name's Eleri." She paused for a moment as she forgot what her last name was supposed to be. Quickly, it came back to her that it was "Miller," but that had been a stupid gaffe. Luckily, she left it at "Eleri" and it didn't seem out of place. She waited until the other woman offered up, "I'm Maggie."

"Oh, you're the one who made us that amazing apple pie, with the fractal design on the top." She couldn't help but grin and was grateful that her undercover job mostly allowed her to be herself—with the exception of trying to remember that her last name was now Miller.

"Oh, I'm glad you liked it," Maggie said, now making her way across the lawn as there was no fencing or shrubs that separated the houses. The grass in the subdivision was very un-Frank Lloyd Wright, who tended to build houses into the landscape rather than on top of it. Eleri had no idea if the yard maybe resembled the works of I. M. Pei. The flagstone walkways cut the center of each lawn, heading straight up to the front steps, and Maggie was at a perpendicular, heading straight through the sod while Eleri stepped out to meet her.

"I grow the apples myself." Maggie smiled, and Eleri wanted to reply, "Of course you do," but figured that was not appropriate right now. Maggie was the norm here, and Eleri was not.

"What varieties are they?" She wondered if she should have said “varietals,” as she did not know her proper apple terminology, but she let it stand, and Maggie didn't seem offended.

"I use a mix. I have one tree of each of several of my favorites. My Fujis didn't come in well this year, but that may be because my beehive caught something last fall, and I put a new hive of bees in the year before. Anyway," Maggie seemed to notice that she'd wandered off into her own thought process and brought herself back on track, "the pie was a split of two-thirds Galas and one-third Grannies."

"You've got quite a set of varieties. Is it an orchard?"

"Oh, it's not really an *orchard,* but I also have peaches and pears if you want anything. And I have a wonderful Chinese Bing cherry tree."

There was something in the way she said “orchard" that made Eleri wonder, but she was still grinning.

"Oh my god." Maggie threw her hands up as though she'd forgotten something. “I'm not completely crazy, I'm a botanist."

"Oh," Eleri replied, thinking that that at least helped explain Maggie's obsession with having a variety of trees. "Where do you live that you have so many trees? I don't think there's enough space in Donovan's backyard for that much." She'd remembered at the last moment to say “Donovan's backyard," as it was technically supposed to be his house and not hers.

"Oh, I'm in The Shire, and we don't have any real land there, either. I did once try to grow blackberry bushes *on top* of my house, but they didn't ever take well enough to fruit," she mused. "I have a plot of land that's supported by grant money for my experiments, and

I'm growing a lot of it there. I try not to tell my grant providers that I'm sneaking some of the apples for pies."

Eleri hoped her grin stayed in place. She was wondering what kind of experiments Maggie was running on these apples that she'd seen fit to put into her pies. Instead of asking what kinds of pesticides or apple-squirrel hybrids she might have been fed, Eleri aimed for simple. "What else do you grow?"

"Mostly marijuana," Maggie said, as though that were just the normal thing to say.

"Oh, and that's your research?" Eleri worked to keep a straight face.

"Yes," Maggie said, "but I'm actually not allowed to speak about the details. I'm sorry. I'm not trying to be rude."

Eleri almost laughed out loud, as if Maggie was rude not explaining to her whatever marijuana *varietals* she was growing on what seemed to be a government grant. Those grants were hard to get, Eleri understood. "Well, it sounds like interesting work." It was the best she could come up with to say, and Maggie headed back toward the other house as LeDonRic appeared in the now open front door.

Eleri waved at him too, and Maggie made a formal introduction. The man was close to seven feet tall, looming over them both as he approached. His skin was a deep shade of ebony and his smile was warm enough that it made her wish that she wasn't deceiving him, even about something as simple as her last name and her ultimate profession. Eleri wanted to ask him if maybe he had gotten an apple pie as well, but she was now wondering if maybe the pie tasted so good because Maggie might have slipped some weed into it.

"Maggie was telling me about her apples and the pie," Eleri said, by way of continuing the conversation.

LeDonRic put his arm around the smaller woman, and the familiarity of the gesture made it appear that Donovan was right about the two of them being a couple. Eleri filed that bit of knowledge away.

"Don't let her fool you." He leaned in close, and whispered as though it were a secret, "She's one of the world's premier marijuana botanists."

Of course she is, Eleri thought. Even with her cover profession, she was going to be the oddball out, merely a biodiversity specialist. She needed to be the world's leading expert in something to fit in here, she thought.

After telling both of them that it was nice to meet them, she watched as they walked away, heading down the street hand-in-hand to wherever they were going. *Good,* she thought, *one-and-a-half days in, and she was at least getting some part of the job done.*

She still had no freaking idea how Marat Rychenkov had been murdered, though she did firmly believe he had been. She was no closer to the *why* of it either, but at least she was starting to get to know the town's residents.

Heading into the garage next, she started Phase Two of her morning and climbed into "her car" and headed out. Donovan's car was still in its space as he'd slept in late this morning, supposedly to work a late shift consulting in Lincoln this evening. She wasn't sure how that would play out, if any of the neighbors would notice the discrepancies they were surely creating.

The same concern held true for the car they'd picked up for her yesterday. They were to act as though they had just bought it, and it even sported a decal from a dealer in Lincoln. The car itself would hold up to scrutiny, but Eleri and Donovan only would until someone asked specific questions. She couldn't answer which salesperson she'd bought the car from, or even what the dealership looked like, or who'd helped sign the paperwork. It would have been better to claim they'd gotten it from a dealer in Omaha. Fewer people would have likely been familiar with the dealership, as Omaha was simply farther away. Given the conversation she'd just had with her two neighbors, she didn't put it past these people to figure out what she was, or that she hadn't been gone long enough to get to Lincoln and buy a car and get back. She would have to hope nobody asked.

Doing as Donovan suggested, she headed down Carbon Street and over to the *Up N Atom,* where she stepped into line to order a frothy coffee and quickly discovered that nothing in Curie was safe from the smart people getting their hands on it. She'd eavesdropped as several people placed their orders in front of her, which helped, but she was still woefully underprepared.

She listened as the man in front of her became gently pendantic, correcting his adorable barista from listing the sizes as "Veni, Vidi, and Vici" with the hard V sound and pronouncing them with the—albeit correct—W sound of Latin. When the barista turned away, he then uttered another word which Eleri believed sounded like Latin, though she couldn't be sure. His tone and expression did make her confident it was a swear.

As she stepped up to the counter, she pointed up to the sign and ordered a "Caffeinator." Eleri chose the Vidi option, saying it "Widi" with the Latin pronunciation. She did not want the other patrons correcting her, but she froze when the bored barista rattled off the next question. "Type Two or Ant Killer?"

"I'm sorry. I don't understand." Eleri looked at the signs for help, but it wasn't there.

The woman behind her in line stepped up even with her and gestured to Eleri, "May I?"

"Oh God, please help."

"We were all new here once, too. I'm Kaya Mazur, and 'Type Two' refers to cane sugar and 'Ant Killer' means you want aspartame, artificial sweetener."

"Oh! That actually makes sense." But Eleri was almost laughing too hard to tell them she preferred hers as "Type Two."

"I recommend a shot of 'Climate Change.'" Kaya was now stepping up to the register beside her and rattling off a list of seeming nonsense that she and the barista both clearly understood.

"What's that?" Eleri had to ask, as her adorable but maybe not Curie-IQ-worthy barista just smiled at her.

"It's a shot of extra chocolate from a rare cacao bean that's slowly going extinct as the temperature climbs."

"Wow, apart from the obvious side of impending doom, it sounds great." She was grinning though and so was Kaya. Another new friend. *Check.* She told her barista to add the Climate Change, and then thanked the woman beside her for her help.

Kaya waved goodbye and headed to the other side of the shop to wait for her order while Eleri moved toward the tables and settled herself in the corner with her laptop. She positioned herself in an attempt to be open to conversation while still keeping people from seeing what she was looking up. No one needed to see that she was scanning information Marshall Bennett had sent to her and Donovan about the town.

When her name was called, she picked up the coffee from a different barista at the other end of the counter. This one was not as young, maybe in her early thirties. Maybe she'd moved here as an adult, but had the baristas all passed the IQ test? It seemed the job couldn't pay enough or be mentally challenging enough for anyone who had.

Eleri was suddenly very curious who made the tacos, who stocked the grocery store shelves, and who took out the trash. Surely, Maggie and her new neighbor LeDonRic were not the ones doing that—and would the people who did have passed Bennett's requirements?

Back at the table, she opened her computer and began reading the details. Curie's IQ requirement made her blink; it was *that high*. Bennett was gunning for the best of the best. Eleri found he also wasn't using the standard Stanford-Binet test, which was good. That test was racially biased, among other things. As she glanced through the test questions, she blinked at the difficulty level.

On top of all the testing, there was an application. It was almost as bad as getting into college, maybe worse. Though hers and Donovan's applications had been greenlit by Bennett through the FBI, had she been required to fill it out, she wasn't sure she would have qualified.

The details interested her the most. One spouse could get in with the requisite high IQ and their spouse could come in at a lower entry level. That helped. She'd wondered how would that work if one spouse qualified but the other didn't. The children didn't have to test if both of the parents passed the first mark. However, if one of the parents was at the lower rating, the children would have to take their own entry testing. The schools reserved the right to hold them back a grade if they weren't keeping up, even though they might have been fine in a normal public school system.

Shit, Eleri thought, *even the kids were expected to be geniuses here.* Then again, Donovan had showed her the high school, and it gleamed like the top of the Chrysler Building. She was afraid to know what she would find them studying if she went inside. Hell, Wade was teaching their physics classes.

After a few more minutes of scouring the documents and legalese, she discovered a key piece of the puzzle: people could come into Curie to work during the day. There was no curfew, but they could not own a house or rent an apartment without the IQ test and Bennett's approval. Her barista probably had not passed the test.

She called Donovan. "Donovan, we have to get Bennett to go through all the applications and tell us if there are any he doesn't specifically remember admitting. And we need to find out if anyone is living here without official permission."

The more she looked through it, the more Eleri became convinced Bennett's application process was faulty. There were enough people in Curie that some could have cheated their way in without him noticing. The application and the IQ requirement and Bennett's need for approval was a breeding ground for motive.

6

When Eleri arrived back at the house after spending the morning at the *Up N Atom,* her immediate plan was to dive into the fridge and build herself a sandwich. However, despite her caffeine and sugar high from two frothy coffees and a pastry, she didn't aim for the food.

Donovan was at the table, his head almost in his hands, looking dead in the water. Heading toward him, she asked what was going on.

"We can't figure out the murder, so we have to figure out *why* Rychenkov was killed. I have *nothing* on the why. Nothing!"

Somehow this didn't surprise Eleri. She wanted to help but could also feel her blood sugar bottoming out.

"Want a sandwich?" She tried to speak the words over the sound of her stomach growling.

"Please, anything." He hadn't lifted his face out of his hands.

She knew him. She knew what he ate, and she knew how much he ate. So she dove into the fridge while he spoke and began pulling out all the pieces she needed. She was organizing the sauces and knives to bring to the table for them when he started talking again. Listening while she worked, she stacked the meats and cheeses.

"Here's what I have so far, and it's basically worth jack shit as far as I can tell . . ." Donovan warned her before launching into his information. "Rychenkov was a robotics expert. He worked for Boeing for four-plus decades and then retired."

"So he was in his seventies? He didn't look like he was in his seventies." Eleri forced herself to put the bread away, but she stuck a slice of turkey into her mouth so she wouldn't pass out.

"Oh no," Donovan said. "He began working for Boeing when he was fifteen."

"Of course he did," Eleri replied, and realized she was going to have to stop doing that before she said it out loud to someone like Maggie or LeDonRic next door. "Go on."

"So he was in his fifties when he left," Donovan added, which more closely matched what Eleri had seen of the body.

"And he was retired?" she asked.

"He had retirement payouts from Boeing, and he'd apparently sold several other ideas and was a consultant in a think tank."

"And his wife Johanna Schmitt also had income," Eleri filled in.

"Right. She had money of her own."

"What does she do?"

"She's a programmer with an electrical engineering background. She holds several patents. And that's it," Donovan said.

"Sure, just a handful of patents!" Eleri would have waved her hand around but it was holding a plate with sandwiches on it. "What do you mean *that's it*?"

"They've lived in Curie for five years. He's continued to have an income from various grants, so he's clearly working on something, but I can't figure out *who* he's working with or on *what*."

She went for the obvious questions as she headed back into the kitchen area for drinks. At least the open design made this easy. "Who did Rychenkov meet with? Who did he spend his time with? Where did he go often? Can we look at the police files?"

"That's just it. The police, specifically the forensics team, did not perform the best assessment of the case."

"Why not?" Eleri asked, "Everyone's so smart here."

"Well, as smart as they are, they didn't figure out he was murdered until they got him to the ME's office. The ME only found it because of the lack of an obvious cause of death. Natural causes didn't suffice, not on a man so young. A heart attack would have created a chemical signal. So that's ruled out. He had no unknown diseases ravaging his body while no one paid attention. He was in great health. And he's too young to have his heart simply stop beating. Even if it had been a freak MI, like I said, there were no chemical signals, and his heart was healthy. So no one even knew it was a murder until the ME in Lincoln sent him to the CDC because of the lack of evidence. The oddity of the case apparently triggered the CDC call to the FBI, which got Westerfield involved."

"So all of that domino-effected after the crime scene was already processed," Eleri said.

"Exactly. The death investigator came in from Lincoln, but the death investigator is apparently no Curie resident."

Eleri understood. She took the first bite of her sandwich and felt her blood sugar respond. She almost let out an audible sigh.

"There are two forensic techs here," Donovan said, "and they could go in and they could collect evidence. They're the ones that got the hair from the room later, and luckily Mrs. Schmitt hadn't cleaned or vacuumed because she was, well, grieving."

"Understood," Eleri said. "So we have two forensic techs we can use and we have a police department that didn't or couldn't collect enough evidence."

"And we want to get in the house ourselves," Donovan added.

Eleri looked up and saw a good half of his first sandwich was already gone. His eating speed always amazed her. "Bennett got us the police files, right?" Eleri asked.

"He did, and that's part of what I've been looking at. But the investigating officers didn't ask who Rychenkov was associating with. They didn't even know to ask questions. It looked like an unfortunate and sudden death. If it hadn't been for his age, they still wouldn't know," Donovan said.

"Then what's the problem?" Eleri asked. "We need to get in and get these questions asked."

"Right, *that's exactly* the problem," Donovan said. "How do we go to Johanna Schmitt and ask her who her husband was involved with without revealing what we're really doing here? By the same token, we can ask the forensic techs to go back, but we're going to have to trigger *someone*. Someone will know who we are and what we are really doing here. Every link in a cover story is a point of failure."

Eleri knew that one from experience, too.

Donovan continued, "Now, Bennett knows who we are, so maybe Bennett can ask the police force to ask the forensic tech to do a follow up. But my concern is the quality of information that we want is going to get lost going through a chain like that—and honestly, I'd rather have eyes on it myself."

With a sigh, Donovan tipped his head back as though it had simply fallen, as though he was at a complete loss, and Eleri understood. They'd always been operating as FBI agents before, and now being stuck with a cover to maintain was doubly difficult.

"I was thinking about that." Eleri set her sandwich down for a moment and tapped her fingers on the table. "We might be able to get into the house as techs."

"Sure, but if we go in as techs, we actually have to do the tech work, because Johanna Schmitt will be there watching us."

"So how do we get her out of the house?" Eleri asked. "Does she know Wade? As long as we don't openly interact with Wade, we can communicate with him, right?"

"Yes," Donovan said, "that's the one upside here. We just can't act in public as though we know him or get caught on the phone with him or anything like that."

"Okay. Can we get Wade to get her out of the house? Then we go to the house dressed like techs."

"Which works fine," Donovan said, "until somebody recognizes us. You're a biodiversity specialist and I'm a research physician. So there's no reason for us to be in that house. No good one. We'd need to think of a reason for *us* to be in the house. Then we could go in and it wouldn't matter if we were recognized."

Eleri took a deep breath. "She has a new breed of cockroach?" She suggested with a shrug of her shoulders.

Donovan laughed. "You're a *human* biodiversity specialist."

"Well, that's monkey balls." She took another bite of the sandwich as consolation. He was right, this was hard. She was used to flashing her badge and walking in.

"Another downside," he said, "is the size of the town. Everyone does seem to know each other, and that's a problem."

"The whole *Nebraska Nice* thing?" Eleri asked. It was a phrase used around the state. They prided themselves on being polite. "Seems to be a thing, even though most of these people are transplants." Eleri looked at him. "I noticed a lot of people here are foreign—immigrants, I would guess."

Donovan nodded. "That's something I learned the other day, too. Apparently, Nebraska opened their doors wide a good couple of decades ago. There are huge immigrant populations, not like what you would expect to find in such a rural state so far from the southern borders. But there are clear cultural neighborhoods in Omaha and some in Lincoln as well."

"Interesting. So, our scientists come here, and Nebraska's very welcoming to immigrants, and Curie is very welcoming to smart people."

"That's our other problem," Donovan lamented. "I mean, we could dress up like cable workers, and if we could get someone to let us in . . . but then we'd want somebody else to get her out of the house so we could examine everything. Who would leave the cable workers unattended?"

"We'd have to have someone she trusted stay behind with us. But someone we trusted not to tell what was happening. Which breaks cover for someone again." She threw her head back. "Oh my God, I am totally spitballing here."

Even with that, Donovan had another problem to throw out. "There's still the issue that someone might recognize us. They would want to know why the new people are going into her house like they're working on her cable . . . and the people here are smart enough that they *will* recognize us."

"I don't know," Eleri shrugged. "Some smart people have terrible facial recognition."

"It doesn't matter," Donovan corrected. "We only need one person good enough to point a finger at us and we're done."

Eleri took a moment to be grateful she had not been given a new first name, or a profession she was going to struggle to keep up with, since she wasn't even undercover in a general population. She was having to fool the best of the best.

Eleri ate in silence and polished off her sandwich before she had a better idea. "Let's get Bennett to take her out for the afternoon. He has to have told a secretary or assistant of his about us already. So that's not a cover break. Then we put on our best disguises and don't get ourselves busted. We can do this."

7

Donovan pulled the bill of his hat low. Being undercover was a bitch. He was in a coverall and a baseball cap—two things that definitively did not say "Donovan Heath." But that was the whole point, wasn't it? So he was wearing a cap that felt unusual on his head and was borrowed from the local power company. He and Eleri had talked Bennett into not getting a fake company name embroidered on anything. It would be noticed here.

The coverall had been hard enough to find in his size. Thank God there was an FBI branch nearby, and they kept things like that handy. As much as it wasn't his usual wear, it also wasn't Eleri's. He was chalking that up to being a good thing. Even as he stood on the front porch ready to knock and get let in, he thought the size difference between himself and Eleri might be enough to get them recognized. Her hair was pulled up and tucked under her hat, and his hope was that no one even recognized she was female. It would help throw anyone who noticed off their scent.

As per the plan they'd worked out, Bennett had come and spoken to Johanna Schmitt just a little while earlier. He'd brought his assistant, Kate, with him to the home and she'd graciously volunteered to welcome visitors and accept casseroles for Mrs. Schmitt while Bennett took the widow out of the house. Donovan didn't know what Bennett had done to get her out, but he was grateful.

Marshall Bennett was possibly more determined than they were to get the murder solved. He did not like crime marring his perfect town. Curie was his dream, and the death of Marat Rychenkov was his blackest mark.

The door opened and it was Kate who now greeted Eleri and Donovan at the door as though she were the homeowner. It was not a perfect setup, but it had its advantages. Anyone who asked Johanna Schmitt about it would get the answer that yes, Kate was supposed to be there, and she was supposed to let people in.

On the other hand, Donovan still worried that he and Eleri were too recognizable, that they were not good actors, that the residents of Curie were smart enough to figure it all out. As of right now Bennett believed only Mrs. Schmitt and a handful of the police knew Rychenkov had been murdered at all. He desperately wanted to keep it that way. The founder's willingness to dive in made Donovan think the case wasn't really NightShade worthy in the first place, but that Bennett had pulled expensive strings to get the FBI undercover in his town.

"Hello, we're here to check the electrical outlets in the house," Donovan said to Kate as was their plan.

"Of course, come on in. Mrs. Schmitt isn't here right now, but I'll be happy to help out." Kate stepped back and waved them in with a smile and a gesture grand enough to be seen from across the street. Once they were inside, she turned to them. "Marshall told me I'm to assist you in any way I can. If that means staying out of the way, or stalling people at the door, or cleaning, that's what I'll do. Just tell me."

"Thank you," Donovan nodded. "But right now, we're just inspecting."

He liked Kate, but they'd had to blow their cover with her to get in. However, chances were good that—as she was Bennett's assistant—she'd already known Rychenkov's death wasn't an accident and that there were FBI agents in town dealing with the case.

Adding to his mental list, Donovan decided he had to get the names of the people who knew about the murder, or at least the ones who were supposed to. If none of them was the murderer, then there was at least one more person who knew. If he and Eleri could figure that out, they would be miles ahead.

Once inside, as Kate stepped out of the way, Donovan and Eleri got to work. They'd been carrying toolboxes, but now they opened them and carefully laid out the forensic equipment they'd packed inside. They had cameras, rulers, line tapes, levels, fingerprint-lifting kits, an ionic print lifter, and more.

Donovan looked up at Kate and made his request. "I hate to ask this, but if you could go behind us and clean up anything that's out of the norm, that would give us the opportunity to get more done—and to make a quick escape if they come back unexpectedly."

"That's not a problem." Kate offered a smile, but he couldn't quite tell if it was genuine or not. "And don't worry. I'll know before Marshall gets back. I have him on a tracker." She held up her phone and Donovan almost laughed at her glee. He wondered if Marshall knew his assistant was tracking him. "As long as Johanna Schmitt doesn't ditch him and flee home, we're good."

Hopefully, the widow Schmitt would not know her home had been inspected by FBI agents.

"This way," Donovan said, and the three of them headed back toward the bedroom. "Has Mrs. Schmitt been sleeping here?" he turned and asked Kate, though Kate had no idea. Of course, she wouldn't. It made no sense that she would, but he felt the need to ask just in case.

"This," Eleri finally spoke up as she pointed to the bed, "was where he was found."

"Okay. Let's figure out how he was tied down first." Donovan went to work, immediately plucking at the covers, looking at the headboard. It was a nice, carved wood, but it was a solid piece. There was no place to tie a victim to, not really.

Eleri looked at Donovan and managed to say what he was thinking. "The livor mortis suggested his hands had been down by his side, his legs probably not spread-eagle. So he wasn't splayed out across the bed, more just tied down so as not to move. Which is weird."

Dropping down on her hands and knees, she immediately began checking under the bed. After shining her flashlight here and there for a moment, she reached a hand up. "Hand me my camera, Donovan, please."

He could only hope she'd found something. He only had to wait a minute.

"Look."

He couldn't get his larger frame down under the bed quite as easily as she had, but he tried.

Pointing to a mark in the wood, she directed him to look at the slat that ran across the bottom of the mattress frame. "This looks relatively new."

He pointed to a spot where it had a small chunk out of it. "Maybe, but it's nothing big. It could have been made by somebody running into it."

"Yeah, but if you ran a human leg into it, you wouldn't do *that*. This mark would come from something more solid. The gouge doesn't look like it's from anything sharp." She was examining the damage as she spoke. "I don't see evidence of a corner, but it's small. If we can find anything corresponding, maybe we'll have something."

"Given how he was tied down, and that there's nowhere to tie him to, my guess would be a hook," he said. It always felt weird to suggest how he would have tied someone up, slashed their throat, or stabbed them. But Eleri thought nothing of it other than to evaluate the idea itself. Immediately, she got down ever lower, trying to get her head under the edge of the bed. But the gap was too narrow.

"No one's crawling under here to hide out," she said.

"Nope. Hold on." He went into the toolbox and pulled out a small mirror. It took a few minutes to work the logistics, but they did find a corresponding scrape on the underside of the wood slat. All right, maybe she was onto something.

He headed around to the opposite side of the bed and looked there, too. Though he couldn't confirm the two marks were the same, there was another mark. He'd found a small, roundish dent, also on the back side of the wood, and another corresponding divot on the front.

"I don't even know what that would be from," she said.

"I do—the hook from a bungee cord."

"What?"

"They've got small hooks—one inch across?—at the end, usually with a rubber stopper. They're probably about the right size to go around this wood, not entirely, which is why it's got the dot in the back and the rub spot on the front corner."

"Oh. But he wasn't tied up with bungees."

"No, it would mean he was tied up with rope, and then the rope was attached to the bungee, and the bungee hooked to the bed."

"Seems pretty far-fetched."

"I agree, but it's what we've got." As silly as it was, it was clear the vic had been tied up. He'd been restrained enough to damage his skin, so he'd pulled against the rope—which meant the rope was attached enough to not give way. And there was nothing here to tie rope to.

They headed to the foot of the bed and discovered similar markings there. "These marks look like the hooks scooted a little in between tugs . . . as though he moved his feet around trying to get loose, probably."

"Wait," Eleri said, and headed back to the side of the bed and pointed downward. "Look. If these are the marks we think they are, then look. Look where they are."

Donovan looked, but he didn't see anything. They were right in the middle of the bed. That's when he understood. "So the perp tied him down with his hands in the middle of the bed, but it looks like they were relatively flat."

"Right, they weren't up over his head. He wasn't even overly restrained."

Donovan pushed her aside for a moment. Rychenkov had been relatively tall, thus Donovan was the better stand-in. He laid down on the bed for a moment, wondering what evidence he was leaving behind. Then he had a better thought.

"Wait." Donovan sat up and called out, "Kate, can you come in here?" Then he motioned for her to take his place. He hated lying in someone else's bed, or asking an assistant to do it, but he needed to see what had happened.

"Are you serious?" Kate asked.

"We're trying to solve a murder."

"All right, then." Bennett's assistant clearly didn't like it much either, but she lay down on the bed.

"In the middle," Eleri said. It was only a queen, and so the middle wasn't too far from the sides. Kate lay there for a moment, arms crossed on her chest, until Donovan and Eleri gave her more specific instructions. "Feet here." She was wearing a skirt and seemed a little self-conscious about it. Donovan wanted to mention that he was a doctor but didn't think that would play well.

Still, as he went to the foot of the bed and looked at the marks on the bottom, he had Eleri attempt to line Kate up to the position the body would have been in. When they looked at it, they discovered his arms were indeed down at his side. If the marks were right, that was the only option.

"Who does that?" Eleri said. "Why would his arms be down at his side? That's a terrible restraint method."

"Yeah." Even Kate was getting into it now. "When you tie someone's arms over their head, or tie their wrists together . . . Were his wrists tied together?"

"There's no evidence that they were bound together," Eleri replied. "They appear to be individually wrapped at the wrist."

But Donovan only stood there and stared. There was something about it, something about the hands being at the side and him still not getting loose, that began to touch an idea at the back of his brain.

8

Eleri headed down the front walkway again the next morning. It was a little later today and Donovan was already gone. She hadn't slept well after their talk last night about the Rychenkov-Schmitt home.

"Did you get anything—any impressions? Images?—as you touched it?" her partner had asked.

And that was the bitch of it. "I touched everything!" she told him. "I left fingerprints all over that room." She couldn't get an image through gloves. She needed skin contact . . . or she had. "I didn't get anything."

Donovan had only nodded and turned the conversation to what they had found, but the issue had picked at Eleri all night. Was she *broken*? She'd thought she was getting better at this. But she hadn't seen Emmaline since she left New Orleans with her sister's bones in a box. And now she wasn't able to get a sensation off of anything. Not even a glimpse of a scene or an emotion from the Rychenkov-Schmitt home.

She hadn't told Donovan how much it was bothering her, or that it had interfered with her sleep. He'd headed out the door to Lincoln. He would go to the CDC building to take one last look at Rychenkov's body.

Donovan was supposed to be consulting at the local walk-in clinic; however, he'd left town in hopes that he wouldn't be called.

The problem with all their "cover" was pretty much the same: he could say he was at the hospital in Lincoln, but anyone who questioned him would know that he wasn't producing the correct answers.

They had both been through training for this in the FBI. They'd learned how to fake names, provide bad descriptions, look up information that could be confirmed and mix it in with more that couldn't. In most places, you could make up a name, say you consulted with Dr. So-and-so or went into the office over on that street with the grocery and the laundromat. In most places, an agent could fudge it, even more than a little. Eleri just didn't believe she could put any of that past the residents of Curie.

Every interaction she'd had only solidified that concern. She now pulled the mail out again, having let it sit overnight so she could do exactly this. As she did, she saw Maggie walking up the front steps next door, exactly as she'd hoped. Someone to talk to. Maggie waved at her, only this time, the door opened before she reached it. It was LeDonRic who opened the door first, not making his girlfriend knock.

Before Eleri could even say hello, she realized he had appeared at his front door in a full medieval knight suit of armor.

Eleri felt her mouth fall open as he clanked his way out onto the small landing, sword hanging by his side, face shield raised, a wide grin splashed across his lips. He looked as though he'd just stepped out of the past. If Eleri didn't recognize him, she might have questioned things. The only really anomaly was the Dalmatian on a leash at his side.

Maggie scurried up the front walk and took the leash from his less-than-reactive fingers. "I've got her. You go, play with your friends, Sir Mix-a-Lot."

"I'm not Sir Mix-A-Lot!" But there was no real anger behind his protest.

Maggie wasn't even paying attention to him anymore as she turned toward Eleri and waved again briefly before she noticed the look on Eleri's face. Bringing the dog over, she started to make conversation. Eleri tried to close her jaw.

When she was standing by Eleri, with Lady MacBeth sitting quietly by her side—totally unaffected by any of it—she said, "He's larping."

Eleri still had nothing. She shook her head indicating she didn't understand.

"L-A-R-P," Maggie said. "Live action role play. He's meeting up with a bunch of his other friends who will also be dressed in knight-wear."

"Is that legit?" Eleri asked, pointing to the large knight as he clanked his way down the sidewalk.

"It is. You have no idea how long he looked for an actual suit of armor that fit him. Or how much he's invested in this. He had it re-fitted a little bit to accommodate his height, but he had a historical expert come in and do the adjusting for him."

"And there's a whole group of them?" Eleri asked as the dog sniffed around her ankles and made a circle. Eleri just hoped Lady Macbeth wasn't going to lift her leg and pee on her shoes. Though seriously, the dog seemed the most normal of the three.

"Yes, about ten of them," Maggie said, turning to stand beside Eleri, watching her boyfriend clank down the street. "It's just like that around here. Curie has a golf course, but it's more likely to be used for larpers than golfers."

"So while he's off fighting foes of yore, you're taking the dog for the day?" Eleri asked, still trying to get her disbelieving ducks in a row.

"Yeah, I take my pig into work sometimes and—"

"You have a pig?" Eleri interrupted, not on her A-game this morning.

"A little miniature."

"I though miniatures weren't a real thing." Eleri frowned. "Something about recessive genes."

"Right! You can breed them with the possibility of them staying miniature, but it's still not widely accepted that breeders can guarantee a small pig will stay small," Maggie explained. "But some of them do. I was prepared to have a six-hundred-pound behemoth in my house, but she stayed little."

"That makes sense," Eleri said. She'd heard of such things and the issue with selling online pigs or even in person as miniature when they often didn't stay that way. And she was grateful to sound intelligent in front of Maggie-the-Pot-and-Apple-Botanist.

"Do you want to meet her?" Maggie asked. "I mean, I don't know what you're doing today. But if you want, you can come to work with me."

Eleri was not used to such forward invitations. As an FBI agent, she was usually investigating someone and no one invited her along on outings. "I can just come to work with you?" Eleri asked, as though the day couldn't get any weirder before ten a.m.

"I can get you a guest pass. You can come on to the grounds. I'll show off my research and you can ask me questions that will spark new research! I mean, how many times do you get to see legal government-sponsored marijuana fields?"

"It does sound interesting." And Eleri thought, *This is what she had come for.* She had no idea if Maggie was the culprit or involved in Rychenkov's murder in any way. But making friends and getting to know the people who lived in Curie was the best way to gather information. Clearly, they did not expect this murder to be solved quickly.

"What do I need? When would we leave?"

Maggie offered up several options and seemed open to anything. Mostly she just seemed more than happy to share her pot-growing expertise with the world at large. After a few minutes working out logistics, Eleri headed back inside the angular house, changed into more sensible shoes, and hopped into her car to follow Maggie and Lady Macbeth out to the pot fields. Apparently, having a dog and a pig on your grant-funded farm was not a big deal.

As Eleri pulled up beside her in the parking lot, Maggie popped out of her car and headed over to the passenger side where she opened the back seat and undid two separate harnesses.

"Oh, my God," Eleri said, "your pig is adorable."

"Eleri meet Atinlay."

"Atinlay?" Eleri asked wanting to be sure she'd heard correctly.

"Give it a minute. You'll get it." Eleri assumed she was right. And as Maggie let both of them down onto the ground, the two animals appeared to be the best of friends. Eleri decided to do what she needed and start asking questions. So she tossed the first one out like a softball as she followed Maggie into the building, "So are you and LeDonRic an item?"

"Yes, very much so."

"But you don't live together?"

"No. We *should,*" Maggie said. "We're clearly wasting rent. But I have a Hobbit house in The Shire. I live on Aragorn Way. And I don't know if you've paid much attention to my boyfriend, but he does not fit well into a Hobbit house."

Eleri was laughing as Maggie opened the front door for her.

But Maggie was still going on. "And I have a *Hobbit house!* I'm not willing to give it up for some cubist monstrosity. We're going to have to eventually find something that suits us both. But I live in *The Shire*!"

Eleri laughed again, though she did understand. For someone who was a *Lord of the Rings* fan, a house in The Shire had to be a huge win. People had gone as far as New Zealand to see Hobbit houses or to stay in one. So having one here in Curie, Nebraska surely was quite the coup. Marshall Bennett had not been wrong picking out his neighborhoods and laying out the geek bait.

They headed through a lobby where people greeted the animals before they greeted Maggie most of the time.

"Hey, Atinlay!" one of the men crouched down and rubbed the spotted pink pig's head, much to the piggy's delight. Lady Macbeth stood patiently and waited her turn. All of this occurred while Maggie set Eleri up with a badge.

The badge was for *Eleri Miller*. She'd pulled out a driver's license to match the name and showed it to the guard at the building. It still felt weird. Weird enough that she almost signed in by writing Eames across the line. *I suck at being undercover.* It had been so long since she'd been trained or even worked this way.

Her acting/signature must have been good enough, because she was allowed to follow Maggie on a tour of the place. Eleri used the opportunity for the part she was good at: talking casually while they walked, extracting information without her target knowing it.

Though she hated thinking of Maggie as a "target," that's exactly what she was. Eleri didn't know yet that Maggie wasn't their killer. However, she would have put money on it that her new friend wasn't. The upside of all this was that Curie was a small town. Maggie had been here almost since the day Bennett had cut the ribbon and let the first moving trucks come in. So it was plausible that Maggie knew a lot of what was going on.

The trick of subtle interrogation was, Eleri had learned, not to bring up the subject. Or if you did, it had to be so artful that it slid neatly into the conversation, which meant she had to be on her toes and wait until the setup came around.

Luckily, in the meantime, pot farming was fantastically interesting. Maggie had seventeen different varieties growing in different rows. She explained how she was testing whether she could crosspollinate them, create new varieties with higher or lower content of THC. She was operating in conjunction with a small, Japanese pharmaceutical company that was doing a corresponding study on their own soil.

While Maggie was being asked a question by one of the techs working the plants, she handed Eleri a basket. Clearly, Eleri was not her first visitor, because she'd been neatly packed up and sent to pick apples, pears, and more while Maggie talked business. While Eleri wanted to listen in, it would be too obvious, and she was faced with a fall harvest that was far too bountiful for even the workers here to begin to eat all of it.

Maggie said they bagged a lot of the extra produce and hung the bags out in front of the building where people could pick up what they wanted. Eleri now had a heavy bag of incredibly fresh fruit. She'd been on the tour for almost an hour when Maggie's phone rang.

"Hello. Yes. No." Maggie held up a finger indicating Eleri should wait, and then said, "Can you give me a minute? This is my friend, Johanna."

Eleri, desperately trying not to let her reaction show, felt her back stiffen. Could it be Johanna Schmitt? As she listened in, she hoped so. Westerfield had found them an empty house, but he'd also tried to position both them and Wade in places that would yield the most information. Maybe he'd hit a jackpot.

When Maggie hung up, she looked disturbed.

Eleri took the opening. "Are you okay?"

"Her husband died last week and there's no cause of death. But . . ." Maggie took a gulp, then turned her attention from the middle space directly onto Eleri. "You're a type of human physiologist, right?"

Eleri nodded, wondering what was coming next.

It was a jackpot.

"Well, maybe you can help, because Johanna thinks her husband was murdered."

9

As Eleri came back down the stairs and into the main room of the house, she found Donovan sitting at the table. He'd not been at the CDC very long, and she had to believe that was because there wasn't anything more to find on Marat Rychenkov's body. Still, both of them had held out hope and had signed the order to hang onto the body for a while longer the first time. Even Eleri wanted to believe they'd just get an impulse and find the magic test. It had not happened, though Donovan had been unable to resist looking just one more time.

As he glanced up, he told her, "I gave up. I signed the order."

"For?"

"To let Marat Rychenkov's body be released to his wife. I expect him to be cremated, given what Johanna Schmitt stated in her requests. So everything will disappear. We've gotten all the evidence we can off him . . . or at least I hope we have. I honestly can't make any reasonable argument that we're going to find more if we keep him longer. His wife already has to be suspicious."

"Yeah, about that," Eleri said, leaning on the back of a chair "She is."

"She *is*? And you found this out how?"

"By doing my job," Eleri said. Noticing his frown, she commented, "What? Remember, it's a good thing."

It meant Eleri was doing her job and doing it well. Donovan

supposedly had an actual job, but Eleri was in town “visiting” and “looking for work.” Her role allowed her a slightly greater level of freedom than he and Wade had, but also more pressure to ferret out information.

She'd been heading out every day trying to make friends and find what she could. She was going to feel people out. She'd been here just a few days and already managed a little of it. “It means Westerfield put us in the right house. He used what little evidence there was and he used it well. I’m in the right spot. I’m making the right friends.”

“Good,” Donovan grumbled, “because I’m striking out, and it’s frustrating as hell.”

Eleri wanted to remind him that he wasn’t failing, but she’d been there, too. She always felt like nothing was working until it came together and they hit that critical mass necessary to see the connections. She was opening her mouth to say so, but Donovan beat her to it. "So, what do you mean Johanna Schmitt is suspicious?"

"Well, I was out this morning," Eleri told him, "with Maggie and Lady Macbeth from next door."

"The dog?"

"Yes, and Maggie’s miniature pig."

"She has a *pig*?"

"She has a pig. Named Atinlay." She pronounced the odd name the way Maggie had, with the stress on the “At.”

Donovan threw his head back and laughed. “Oh, man . . .” He gulped the words out between guffaws. “I have had such a shitty morning. But that is gold! We are up to our eyeballs in an unsolvable murder and now the wife is suspicious of it . . .” he gulped for more air, “But Maggie has a pig named Atinlay!”

"What's so funny?" Eleri asked. "I don't get it."

"What do you mean you don't get it?"

"So, Maggie said the pig was named Atinlay and I looked at her weird, and she said, 'You'll get it later'."

"Oh, you don’t get it." Donovan was still laughing, even as the expression crossed his face, understanding why she was not bellowing her laughter along with him. “Maggie has an *ig-pay*. Named *Atin-lay*."

"Ig-pay Atin-lay," Eleri sighed in near pain. "Oh my god. Her pig is named *Atinlay*. I can't *even* with this place."

"I can't either, but apparently all of our *'can't even'ing* isn’t helping, because there's still a murder to solve. And this person is probably way too smart to be caught."

"Well," Eleri said, trying to come to terms with that, "not every case gets closed."

"Good God. I don't want it to be *this* one."

"You and me both."

"So tell me how this all works," he said, once he was done wiping the tears from his eyes over the name of Maggie's pig.

"Apparently, Maggie and Johanna are friends. Maggie had a project a couple of years ago, and she'd asked Johanna to do some programming and engineering for her. I got her to talk about Marat —about *why* Johanna might think someone would do that. She said Johanna talked about Marat doing some robotics work to try and make a sniffer or design a harvester for the marijuana. That kind of thing. So Maggie knew Marat, too, and she and Johanna are at least friends."

"I think you're right." Donovan leaned back in his chair, his expression serious again. "I think a lot of people in this town are friendly enough that we can see some links. Which hopefully will work in our favor."

"So far, so good. Anyway, Johanna calls her and says she thinks her husband was murdered. And Maggie passes this on to me, because I heard her side of the phone conversation, and because I have a human physiology background. She thought I might have ideas that the ME didn't." Eleri sighed. Boy, had Maggie hit the nail on the head without knowing it.

Donovan was sitting up straight. Eleri finally stepped away from the back of the chair, pulled it out, and sat down into it so they could have a serious, face-to-face conversation. "Tell me why Johanna thinks this," he said.

"First off, the body has been kept too long for a standard death. She's smart enough to have figured out that the seven days that he has been on hold—and no one will give her a satisfactory reason why—is suspicious. She is well aware that he's far too young to have died of natural causes or old age. And she kept requesting a cause of death, but the medical examiner won't give her one. In fact, it was listed in the examination as 'incomplete' until two days ago. Johanna finally got the report sent to her and saw the ME had ultimately listed the cause of death as 'none'."

"Shit," Donovan said. Eleri knew he'd seen that listing on the original paperwork, but neither of them had known the medical examiner was going to eventually sign off on it and hand it back to Mrs. Schmitt that way.

"Fuck," he muttered, his hands coming back up to his face.

"I know. Honestly, an ME can get away with handing that to most people. But I suspect these people are going through each other's ashes and find the pacemaker or the bone chip or the filling, and say, 'This isn't my spouse.'"

Donovan nodded in agreement. The residents of Curie were smart and curious, and Eleri was coming to the conclusion that they were going to keep the case from ever getting closed.

Just then, they heard a loud crash from outside the house. Both of them jumped reflexively and rushed to the front window. The square nature of the house and orthogonal lines of the neighborhood made it virtually impossible to see what was going on next door without actually going out the front. They had barely glanced out the window before realizing they couldn't see anything. Both of them bolted toward the front door.

Eleri and Donovan ended up standing on the front steps of Donovan's porch and watching as LeDonRic James clanked his way up the front walkway, still in his full suit of medieval armor. The noise might have been lessened had another person not been clanking along behind him, also in full metal regalia. The two were arguing, hands waving as best they could while covered in curved metal. Their voices rang tinny through the helmets, even though the face guards were flipped up.

Three young women trailed along behind, though two were on their phones and all three seemed uninterested in the argument in front of them.

Donovan and Eleri waved and listened in.

LeDonRic turned to the shorter knight and declared, "I had the sword made to order. The details are correct."

The second, shorter knight replied quickly, "No, they're not. The scrollwork that you requested on the handle did not originate until at least one hundred and fifty years after the era that the suit is from."

"Suits of this general design existed for over five hundred years. They were around long enough to overlap the distinct style of scrollwork that I chose," LeDonRic replied.

In fascination, Eleri watched one of the nerdiest arguments she'd ever witnessed, though she had to admit she'd been part of a good number of nerdy arguments herself over the years. However, she was not a history geek, and while she was just barely keeping up, she couldn't contribute.

"The era of that armor design ends well before the scrollwork era begins. I'm telling you, you don't have historical accuracy."

"And *you* do?" LeDonRic replied. Eleri began to catch on that the person arguing with him was probably a teenager.

"I'm not aiming for historical accuracy," LeDonRic's companion said. "I was aiming for fun. *You're* the one who claimed you were historically accurate when you're not."

It was then the two of them turned slowly and paid attention to their inattentive audience. The girls had at least laughed along and were now occasionally interjecting information. Two of them had their phones up close to their faces and seemed to be looking up the information to support different sides of the argument.

"I can't find scrollwork from that era," one said.

"I'm looking up the hilts of swords. I thought that might be a better search." They weren't as uninterested as they had appeared at first glance.

With a sigh, LeDonRic noticed Eleri and Donovan watching his little gaggle of kids having their tiff. He turned to the two of them and offered a smile. "Allow me to make introductions."

Eleri smiled, but had a question first. "It's barely three o'clock. Aren't these guys supposed to be in school?"

"School's out early on Wednesday afternoons," one of the young women happily informed her. She had long, dark, curly hair and, on closer inspection, looked a lot like LeDonRic. Eleri was suddenly wondering if he had a daughter. It would explain the kids following him home.

"It's Club Day," one of the other girls said. She had long blond curls and was tall and thin, willowy even. She was going to grow into that, Eleri thought, unable to ignore the shape of the girl's cheekbones and the long length of her femurs. That kind of assessment just went with the territory of being a forensic scientist. *Not a wolf,* was the next thought that passed through her head.

The boy pulled off his helmet with a few more clanks, and LeDonRic continued with introductions. "This is Emersyn and

Madisyn," he said, pointing over the heads of the two young women who were as dark skinned as him. Wide smiles abounded as they waved.

"We're his nieces," said the one who'd just been introduced as Emersyn, as though she needed to explain these things. She looked younger than Madisyn. "It's Emersyn with a Y. Madisyn with a Y, too," she said. And Eleri wondered why the clarification was necessary.

"These two are their friends, the twins." LeDonRic waved his hands over the heads of the two children who did not look genetically related to him, although Eleri was personally aware that color could be deceiving in that regard.

She raised an eyebrow wondering if "the twins" was enough of an introduction, but LeDonRic grinned and named them as he pointed. "This is Joule and Cage."

It was Emersyn who piped up again, "Joule is J-O-U-L-E."

Eleri nodded. "Good to know." She turned back toward the blond girl. "Like a unit of energy?"

"Uh-huh. My parents are physicists," she said. "And my brother is a complete nerd."

Cage elbowed her in the ribs in response. But with the full metal gear on, it gave her a little more of a shove than he might have intended. She made a face behind his back which went fully unnoticed, because in his gear, he was unable to turn around and see it, not quickly enough anyway.

It was Cage who turned to the newcomers, smiled, and asked if either of them had any knowledge of the scrollwork on the hilts of swords from various historical eras. When both Eleri and Donovan shook their heads *no,* he thanked them and proceeded to clank his way inside the house behind LeDonRic. The teens waved and followed their leader inside.

Eleri and Donovan headed back into their own place with stunned looks on their faces. "Well," Eleri said, "I thought this place was nerdy, but I stand corrected. That was well beyond nerdy. Those were the high school kids." She caught the expression on Donovan's face and asked, "What?"

"I wonder if they beat up the jocks?" he asked. She wanted to laugh, though he seemed to have asked it in all seriousness.

She pulled out her chair and plopped down. Despite the interruption, she still had information to share with him. "I was telling you that Johanna Schmitt suspects her husband was murdered. But—before we were interrupted—I was getting ready to tell you that she also seemed to think someone had been in her home . . . and that they'd been looking for something."

10

Donovan spent the next morning on the computer, waiting for Wade to call him back. Wade's mobility as an investigator was hampered by his cover as a high school physics teacher. Though he was some level of adjunct and only taught the first period of each morning, he also wound up with papers to grade, the occasional teacher meeting to attend, and a variety of general to-do lists that came with the position.

Donovan lamented that Westerfield had seen fit to give them real jobs. He'd told his boss about it during the call the day before. In response, Westerfield had pointed out, "You don't have a *real* job. You have a very small portion of what appears to be a real job. I couldn't have three of you going into town and not having employment at all. You've met the people. Are they as bad as I suspect?"

"Worse," Donovan said, though he wouldn't have called it *bad*. "They were having an argument over historical eras and accuracies regarding the hilt of a sword yesterday. And," he'd reported, "they already seemed to have figured out that there was a murder. We're not able to keep that under wraps."

"Was that on you?" Westerfield asked, straightforward, and Donovan was grateful to be able to answer with a clear, "No."

Westerfield had asked only a few more questions before letting them go. But, probably as planned, the questions were lingering in Donovan's brain even now.

His phone rang, and he was glad to see only the letter "W" appear in bold across his screen. It was the way he'd listed Wade. He'd removed the name and picture he had used before, in hopes that if anybody found the phone, they wouldn't know that he was communicating with someone else in town. He would have to remember to put the settings back when the assignment was done.

"Hey. Everything okay? Have you figured out anything?" Donovan, for all he had learned, still had no connections and he had his fingers crossed that Wade did.

"Man, this case is for shit," Wade sighed out the words, dashing his colleague's hopes. Though they'd talked a few times since Donovan arrived in town, they still hadn't been able to put together much in the way of evidence or even pertinent information.

Wade had only arrived one day before Donovan. He'd used his time to get established, talk to the kids, and take over the class he was teaching—in addition to doing his actual work as an FBI agent. He was also trying to meet with the parents under the guise of being a new teacher learning about his students. It was time-consuming, but Wade was using it to his advantage, trying to suss out information.

"Okay, let's just trade what we have?" Donovan felt himself put a question mark on the end of his request. He hadn't intended it to be that way, but he was starting to think it was appropriate at the end of everything he said. For all the information he'd gathered—and it was a lot—it still felt like he held one to three pieces from each of five hundred different puzzles.

"Sounds good," Wade replied with a tone that let Donovan know he was feeling the same. He launched into what he'd gathered. "I've now managed to meet the vast majority of the parents, and no one seems to think anything of Rychenkov. It hasn't been easy working a murder into the conversation, but he did do special teaching days here, so that helps."

Donovan thought that might have been part of Westerfield's master plan and why Wade was in the high school.

"Everyone's worried about their kid's physics grade and college applications, which I don't know anything about, so I'm a shitty teacher that way."

"Nah, you're good at the rest of it," Donovan said. "Besides, you're only there one term, one class each day."

"Yeah. It's not enough kids, and yet it's too many," Wade said. "It's definitely too many."

Donovan had to laugh at that.

Wade went on, "Westerfield helped Bennett pull some strings and get me kids whose parents specifically should be the ones who interacted with Rychenkov, but it's still not yielding much of anything."

When Donovan only *Hmphed* in response, Wade said, "Tell me what you came up with, and I can let you know if it matches any of my kids' parents. If it does, I can create problems with class or assignments that will get me back into contact with them."

It was a good plan, Donovan thought, *if only there were connections.* "All right, I've been going through phone records. I've been looking at the police logs. Rychenkov and Schmitt had a land line in their home. He was apparently a little bit old-school. Between the land line and his cell, he often talked to Suzie Carmen, who's a doctor over at the pediatric office. She and he must have discussed quite a bit— I have no idea about what, but the length of the phone calls and the odd times during the day, when she would be at work, made me wonder a little bit. Especially since Rychenkov has no kids, and thus should have no familial or professional need for a pediatrician."

"Okay," Wade said. "Let me see if I have one of her kids . . . No."

Donovan tried the next name "He's also spoken to a Kaya Mazur on her cell, and he's called the home line for the Mazur family. She is a physicist. So's the husband—Nate. I could see a physicist and a robotics specialist having work-type conversations, but I have no idea what those calls were about, either. Honestly, this is just what we're looking at. We have no idea if there are or were any affairs going on or anything like that."

"We need to get to Mrs. Schmitt," Wade said, abruptly changing the topic.

"I was thinking the same thing, though I'm trying to figure out how to do that without revealing that we're FBI, and I can't think of anything that won't. I think we're going to have to talk to her openly," Donovan told him.

"We have to get that processed through Westerfield first."

"Story for another day. When Eleri gets in, we'll take a look at how to do it and whether or not we should."

"Sounds like a plan," he said. Though Wade seemed to support him, that also meant he didn't have a better idea.

Donovan continued down his list of names. "I also have Jivika Das."

"Wait, go back," Wade replied. "I have two kids. I have a Joule and a Faraday, set of twins, Mazur."

"Yes, that's them. I met them yesterday. Wait? Faraday? I met someone named *Cage*," Donovan said. "Oh my God. His name is Faraday . . . and they call him Cage. Never mind. I get it." Then he proceeded to tell Wade about Cage being in full knight's regalia. "They're the ones who were arguing about historic eras."

"Okay, good. So we have at least established a small loop with Rychenkov in it and people we can question. What else?"

Donovan listed three more names, only one of whom had a kid in Wade's class. Those got notes, and Wade began trying to determine what kind of project he could dream up that would put him back in touch with the parents.

"Who do *you* have?" Wade countered. "What kids do you have who might loop back to Rychenkov that I can check out?"

Consulting his list again, Donovan said, "I have a Madisyn James. Yes. She's my neighbor LeDonRic's niece, but I don't know . . ."

"Her father," Wade filled in, "is Marshawn James, LeDonRic's brother."

"What does he do?"

"He's an inventor of sorts. Most of his money comes from a sponge he invented, some new material. He's created a handful of cell phone apps, several of which have been pulled by the stores—"

"Why?" Donovan interjected, curious.

"Seems the apps themselves were fine and legal but could be used by kids inappropriately. Something like that. He also has a new-use patent on the workings from a coffeemaker . . . I haven't followed it further than that." Wade let the story trail off, and Donovan made a quick note.

Then Wade moved to the next name on his list. "Jeren Waits. He's a foster kid. He lives with a family over in the Shire, green people, do-gooders. Not much money, lots of heart, as far as I can tell."

Donovan added to the list, both the kid's name and the foster parents'.

"What if we're on the wrong track?" he asked Wade. "What if it's not work related? What if Rychenkov was killed from a love affair gone wrong? Or he overheard a Mafia hit, or something like that?"

"I don't even know how to find that out. I don't see anyone on here that he might or might not be having an affair with. I mean, it could be *anyone,* so we need to start asking the coworkers. This shit's tough undercover. I'm not inserted directly into a position to ask these questions."

"There was no position to take. Our vic didn't have a job he went to every day or even a club he attended regularly. I mean, unless you're going to live in his house as the butler, there's nowhere to go to get to know the people who knew him."

"True," Wade said. "Maybe you and Eleri can figure it out. If Rychenkov was having an affair, that's probably the first place to look."

"I don't know," Donovan said. "I mean, an affair makes sense —*someone* got him tied down to the bed—but it's not enough. What we really need to know is if there was any evidence that he'd ever been tied down before. This is a very different case if bondage was a normal activity for him."

Wade sighed. While Donovan wished his friend and fellow agent would jump in with a brilliant deduction, at least it was a relief to know he wasn't the only one floundering. "Nobody's found any evidence of that."

"Again, I say we blow our cover to Mrs. Schmitt."

"I think you're right," Wade said. "I have to go make class assignments now. I think Westerfield thought this was going to be easy, giving me one class per day, but it's not. I'm telling you, these kids are absorbing everything I'm throwing at them. I'm about to get into quantum mechanics, and just see if maybe I can stump one of those little suckers for once."

Donovan laughed. "If you're up for it, and if Eleri is, as soon as she gets home, I'm going to call Westerfield. I can't say I'm looking forward to it, but I believe with Mrs. Schmitt's understanding that her husband was murdered, it's time for us to go in and ask her the right questions more directly."

"I think you're right," Wade said, "and I'm glad *you're* calling Westerfield on that one—and not me."

Donovan understood. No one wanted to call Westerfield for this kind of thing.

11

Donovan stood on the front step of the Rychenkov-Schmitt home for the second time. Only this time, he was there as himself. Or mostly as himself—he was after all, in town as Dr. Donovan Naman.

He startled when a sweet voice called from behind him. "Hello, Dr. Miller, Dr. Naman," and he didn't catch that the name was his for a moment.

Neither did Eleri. Nudging his partner, he turned to see the young woman they'd met the day before.

"Hi," he replied and waved back, his voice a little too high-pitched. Her name was *Joule,* he remembered. The other young woman spelling the kids' names for him had actually been a boon to help him remember them all.

"Are you visiting Mrs. Schmitt?" she asked.

"Mm-hmm." He nodded, wondering why the girl was asking. He and Eleri were obviously waiting at the front door, but Joule only nodded and waved as she headed toward a house caddy-corner across the street. Did Joule and the Mazur family live so close to the murdered man?

He didn't get a chance to think about it as the door swung open and pulled his attention back to the house. Mrs. Schmitt gently greeted the two strangers on her doorstep.

"Hello." Though Donovan and Eleri knew many things about her, and even had been inside her home before, they had not yet officially met. According to Mrs. Schmitt, they knew nothing of each other, so he tried to approach the situation as if he were a stranger at her door and saw that Eleri was doing much the same.

"Hello, Mrs. Schmitt," Eleri said. "My name is Eleri Miller, and this is my colleague and friend, Dr. Donovan Naman."

Johanna Schmitt merely nodded at them. Though her face appeared curious about them, her hand lay by her side, her fingers curled into a fist, letting Donovan know she wasn't quite as relaxed as she appeared.

"I would love if you could let us in for just a moment," Eleri continued in her sweetest voice. "We're new in town. We live next to, we believe, a friend of yours, LeDonRic James. He's friends with your neighbor across the street, Joule—the Mazurs." Eleri motioned over her shoulder, as though a reference to a kid in high school was going to make Mrs. Schmitt feel better. If the woman was concerned that her husband had been murdered, that connection wouldn't make things any better.

Eleri continued, "His girlfriend, Maggie, is apparently a friend of yours, too, a good friend."

As Donovan watched, he saw that Eleri had gone too far. Johanna looked even warier now.

"Please," Eleri said, and Donovan decided to let her do the talking. He wouldn't be any better at this than she was, and Mrs. Schmitt was already on edge. "I'd like to not do this on your porch. We're trying to keep things quiet, but if you will let us into your home, we'll show you . . ."

Not the right words, he thought. They could easily be interpreted as her saying they didn't want to murder the woman in broad daylight, but in the dark interior of her own home.

"Don't wait, El," he said as he reached into his back pocket and pulled out his wallet with his FBI badge in it. Without flipping it open, as one normally would do, he simply handed the closed wallet to Mrs. Schmitt. He offered a simple instruction that he hoped would set her at ease or at least as comfortable as a widow who believed her husband was murdered and no one was investigating it could feel.

"Take this, step away from the door, and open it and look at it, please, he said calmly. "If you want, you can look up the number for the local FBI branch and call it in to check on all the information."

She did as he requested, stepping just out of the light as she flipped his wallet open and looked at the badge. Her discretion meant that no one could walk by and see what was in his wallet which would have completely blown their cover.

"My partner has one, too," he offered. "We will gladly hand it over when we get inside. We just don't want your neighbors to know who we are or why we're here."

He watched as Mrs. Schmitt broke, ever-so-slightly. Though she covered it well, for a moment her hand went to her mouth and he saw her fight back tears. She had to understand that their presence meant her suspicions were more accurate than she'd wanted to believe. Slowly, she pulled herself together.

"Come in," she said, smart enough not to hand the badge back to him until she'd gotten them inside and the door closed. She looked out with a smile plastered on her face and waved to Joule across the street. The girl had arrived at her front door and was turning the key to let herself in as Mrs. Schmitt waved to her.

"You know Joule?" Donovan asked.

"Oh, yes! Sweet kids. Joule and her brother Faraday, they come over here a lot. My husband loved working with them."

"Faraday?" Eleri asked.

"Cage. He usually goes by Cage. His parents were both physicists, and named the kids physics terms, and they thought Faraday Cage was funny or cute, I guess." She confirmed what he and Wade had come up with when they were talking earlier. The smile on her face said she liked the twins. "Those two are wonderful smart-asses, too. So sharp. People around here, they're weird. That's why my husband and I fit in. The Mazurs have been here since just about the time the town was founded, my husband and I not so long. We don't have any kids of our own, and Joule and Faraday are just . . . Well, they're great." She sniffed then, just a little. "Faraday is going to be one of the pallbearers at my husband's funeral tomorrow."

"Yes," Donovan said, nodding as the door clicked shut behind them. He put his hand out to request his badge back and watched as Eleri flipped her own open. Mrs. Schmitt, no dummy at all, carefully inspected the shield and the ID card.

"Those are not the last names you gave me."

"We're undercover." He'd gotten permission from Westerfield to say exactly this, though the conversation had been arduous and unpleasant for him. He suspected it had been for Westerfield, as well, but it had gotten them here.

"Would you like to sit down?" she asked. "I have tea, some high-end sodas, ice water."

Donovan was about to refuse, but Eleri touched his arm to stay him and said, "I would love a soda, if you have something not diet."

"I do," she replied. Donovan felt Eleri use the back of her hand to tap him on the wrist.

"I'd love a water."

Eleri was right. The more they put the woman in her comfort zone, the better off they'd be, and getting drinks for guests was clearly something that she was used to doing. It was only a moment before Johanna Schmitt had them all seated at the dining room table. A small, round affair, it held four chairs—the one empty seat seemed telling.

Mrs. Schmitt did not beat around the bush. "You're here because you think I'm right. I think my husband was murdered."

Donovan only nodded. "You're aware his body went from the morgue in Lincoln to the CDC?"

She nodded. "They told me they were just testing him, and that it all came back negative, but I don't believe it."

"That part, at least, is correct," Donovan said, glad he'd been authorized to tell this woman everything they knew about her husband. He figured she would want to know how he was qualified to tell her what was in the report and why it was right. "I'm a former medical examiner who's now an agent with the FBI."

She nodded, seeming to have fully bought into the badges, which was a good thing. Since she was the only person who knew who they were, she was going to be their only link to straightforward information. They needed her to be willing to give them everything she possibly could, even the things she didn't know she was handing over.

"We appreciate your cooperation," Eleri said, placing one hand flat on the table in front of her, almost as a half-gesture of peace. Had she known the woman better, she might have placed her hand on top of Mrs. Schmitt's. "Your cooperation will help us do our best to solve this."

A lone tear leaked out of Mrs. Schmitt's eye. "But you're telling me the toxicology screens came back negative. So what could it be?"

"That was actually what alerted the CDC to the problem. There's no chemical indication of a heart attack, no sign of aneurism whatsoever, and while it's plausible that he might have simply dropped dead . . ."— Donovan hated the term, but truly, other than "he just gave up," there was no good medical terminology for it—"It's not likely at all. However, the ligature marks on his wrists and ankles make it look like a murder."

"How was he killed?" she asked, aiming straight for all the smart questions.

"That's the problem," Eleri said. "We truly don't know. Are you willing to hear all of this?"

Donovan thought it was smart of Eleri to ask. He hadn't thought of it. He had just started talking about her husband's corpse during their interview. He watched as Johanna Schmitt got herself together and nodded.

"It appears he was bound," Eleri said, "but that there was no struggle." She gently handed over as many of the details of the case as they had.

Mrs. Schmitt agreed with everything, listening as they rattled off all the numbers. She asked for clarification on very little of it. It was then that Donovan asked, "Can you tell us what made you suspect your husband was murdered?"

"The same things," she said. "He's too young. He's been working on a project he hasn't even told me about." That perked Donovan's ears up. "And someone has been in my house."

"We were here a while ago," he explained. He hated having to admit what they'd done, but it was better she know the murderer wasn't casing her. "We gained access because we needed to check the scene for evidence."

"Did you find anything?"

He shook his head, though that wasn't fully true, and their evidence didn't really make sense. He told her about the marks on the bed.

"I don't think we even own rope or bungee cords. I mean, maybe one or two in the trunk of the car?" She was shaking her head and trying to think. "I have a garage full of old motherboards and soldering tools. We have spools of fine wire and an oscilloscope with dials, because Marat didn't like the advanced software that smoothed the curves. He wanted to see them as they were." Johanna Schmitt took a deep breath, probably to stop herself from bursting into tears. "But no rope or bungees."

Then she looked up. "When else did you come?"

"Just the once, two days ago," Donovan replied, as though having the FBI rifle through your personal things without your consent was better if they'd only done it once.

"Well, then I was right." She looked back and forth between them, her eyes wide. "Because someone has come into my home and gone through my things several times before that."

12

Eleri stared at Johanna Schmitt. "You think people were in your house *several times*?"

She wished she had brought a notebook. They'd come in for a casual conversation, to establish who they really were and lay out the ground rules of what Mrs. Schmitt could and couldn't share. Eleri had not been prepared for this.

"What is it they were looking for?" she asked, knowing it was likely a dumb question. But every now and then, someone knew and would actually tell them what the searcher had been after. Johanna Schmitt did no such thing.

Instead, she countered with a question of her own. "What did *you* look for?"

"We checked the scene of the crime," Donovan said.

"My bedroom?"

They were both forced to nod for the sake of honesty. It sucked. Eleri felt bad admitting they'd violated her privacy, but it was part of the job. "Please accept our apologies. I am aware we invaded your space. We are trying to solve your husband's murder, though."

Johanna Schmitt stiffened for a moment, and then as Eleri watched, her shoulders and her back softened. "I'm grateful that somebody understands that he was killed. And I'm grateful that someone of your caliber is trying to solve the case."

Eleri was starting to wonder how well her caliber held up in a town like Curie, where everyone was only of the highest caliber, but she didn't mention that to Mrs. Schmitt.

She let Donovan clarify, "We came in through the front door. Mr. Bennett's assistant, Kate, was left here to greet people including us," Donovan said. "She let us in, and we checked out the bedroom."

"Did you find anything?"

"Just the bungee-cord marks." Donovan looked to Eleri for a moment, and she offered a slight nod. She was still bitter. She'd touched everything and not gotten the slightest zing of information or feeling from any of it.

When he opened his mouth to ask another question, she put her hand out, motioning for Donovan to stop while she spoke to Mrs. Schmitt. "I apologize. We got a little bit out of order. We do need to make it clear that you are not to tell anyone what our real names are or what our real purpose is here."

Johanna Schmitt nodded. "Of course. I fully understand."

"We feel, and our SAC—our Special Agent in Charge—feels, that this is the best way to solve your husband's murder. We would have come in openly if we'd thought that would work better."

"I understand," she repeated, as though she were anxious to skim through the list of what she could and couldn't say and get back to the actual solving of her husband's murder.

"The second problem with having told you," Eleri continued, ignoring Johanna's eagerness for information, "is that you appear to already feel better knowing that we're on the case. You can't convey that to any of your friends. I've met several of them, and they'll pick up on it."

That, at least, made Johanna nod as though she hadn't quite thought of that possibility before. "Yes. I've mentioned it to Maggie. So what you're suggesting is that in my interactions with Maggie, I need to continue to act frustrated."

Eleri nodded. "In your interactions with *everyone*. Your reactions need to be as similar as possible to what they were before you found out. I have no idea what your acting abilities are, but the more you try, the better it'll be. Your convincing performance will make it much easier for us to investigate, hopefully without the *killer* knowing who we are, or even that he or she is under suspicion."

Johanna looked aside for a moment, and then looked back at them. "I assume this means I am not a suspect."

Eleri had to go the legal route. "You have not yet been ruled out, no."

"Interesting." Then she looked up with a shrug. "Investigate away. I'm sure you'll rule me out soon enough."

Though Eleri didn't say it, Johanna's very willingness to deal with them made her less of a suspect than she might otherwise have been. The twist here was that this was Curie, Nebraska, and everyone was smart enough to know that telling the FBI to thoroughly investigate you was the best way to look innocent. The spouse was usually number one on the suspect list, but for whatever reason, Eleri's gut was telling her this time that Johanna Schmitt hadn't committed murder. She was convinced that it wasn't Maggie Wells, either.

Without saying so, but acting as though the legalese had been fully gotten out of the way, Mrs. Schmitt turned back to Donovan. "So exactly what did you find in my bedroom?"

"Just the marks on the bed, and that's it. There wasn't anything else we were able to find."

"And that's part of the problem," Eleri added. "So, we believe we have a better understanding of how he was tied to the bed, but we have no understanding of what that means. That's why we needed to talk to you."

"So what happens now?"

"We ask you every question in the book, and hopefully, you answer us as honestly as you can."

Mrs. Schmitt took a moment to gather herself, but her words said something different. "If this helps find my husband's killer, and if it stops my home from getting invaded and checked, then I will give you everything I have."

Eleri tilted her head at the woman. "You don't seem as concerned as I would expect about the fact that someone came into your home."

Johanna just shrugged again. "If my husband was killed, I don't think they'll come after me. We work in entirely different fields. I'm armed, and I . . . I almost *hope* they come back, so I can catch them. It's a good thing, right? The more they come back, the more evidence we get?"

Eleri couldn't fault that line of thinking. Most people would be afraid, but everyone in Curie had to be taken with a grain of salt. Johanna appeared more logical than emotional, and though her reaction wasn't perfectly normal, it didn't seem too strange, in her case. Eleri nodded. Johanna wasn't wrong.

"All right." Donovan's tone said they were getting down to brass tacks. "Do you have dates for when you think someone came into your home and do you have any idea what they looked at?"

Johanna smiled at them as though they were soft in the head. But her words said, "Hold on."

Eleri looked at Donovan as Mrs. Schmitt stood up, leaving her glass of water on the table and exiting the room. She had no idea what the woman was doing and decided to look around the house while they waited.

This home was designed differently than the one she and Donovan had. All of the main areas appeared to be downstairs—yet Mrs. Schmitt headed upstairs. Eleri wondered if she was going up to the bedroom, or perhaps to one of what had appeared to be his-and-hers offices during their first, cursory tour.

It took only a moment for Johanna to return. Though the couple was in their fifties, they were certainly well within their youth still. Though Mrs. Schmitt, who dressed in cardigans and skirts that appeared to be from a bygone era, was nevertheless clearly in the prime of her own health.

She nearly skipped back down the stairs and, with some fanfare, smacked a notebook onto the table. Bound with black tape along the spine, it looked like an old-style composition book—not the new back-to-school variety. Donovan blinked and said, "Lab notebook."

"Of course." Johanna pushed the book into the space between the two agents. Though the cover was black and white with Rorschach-style splotches, the notebook bore no markings by Mrs. Schmitt on the front of it. After a quick glance asking if she could look inside, Mrs. Schmitt nodded and motioned for Eleri to go ahead.

The book was thick and puffy, *probably with added pieces or excessive highlights,* Eleri thought as she flipped to the front page. On it, she saw a date, eight days ago.

"The day after your husband's murder?" Eleri asked, because the page detailed several items in the home that Mrs. Schmitt thought had been messed with.

"Yes. That was the first visit. Turn the page."

Sure enough, Johanna had printed and taped photographs to the next two pages. They matched the listed items from the page before, although Eleri didn't see anything unusual in the pictures, and she said so.

"That's the problem. Nothing looks unusual, but it is different from how I left it."

"How?" Eleri asked.

"This," Mrs. Schmitt said, pointing. "This is out of alignment. I *always* square up my edges. And this," she said, tapping on another taped-in photo, "is not where I left it. I left it on the counter, I'm absolutely sure, but it was over more to the right. It was in front of the spices."

"So they looked in your kitchen, and they looked in your office?"

"On the first day. The second time," she continued, reaching out and flipping the page to a new list, "They looked in my bedroom . . . and I *think* they got under the bed. My shoes were a little out of whack, too."

"Are your shoes normally perfectly aligned as well?" Eleri asked, looking at a picture of a jumble of shoes, which weren't even really in pairs.

Mrs. Schmitt looked downward for a moment. "Unfortunately, no. The way I treat my data and the way I treat my clothing is not exactly the same."

Eleri wanted to laugh, but the gravity of the situation held her back. She turned the page again. This time, she saw pictures of Marat Rychenkov's office.

It seemed, during the first break-in, the criminal had checked to be sure they hadn't left anything behind. The kitchen had been examined because the intruder would want to be sure no evidence was left behind. He—or she—had likely been in there while meeting with Rychenkov before killing him. But on the second visit? Their killer had begun looking for something specific.

13

Donovan pulled out his tablet and scrolled through the pictures he'd taken. He glanced across their dinner table at Eleri then said, with a heart-felt sigh, "I really don't like pictures."

She just raised one eyebrow at him. He knew she probably hated crime-scene pictures worse than he did. The photos never caught what it was like to stand in the middle of the wreckage. He couldn't turn his head and get a different angle, and he couldn't carefully look under anything. Sadly, right now, all he had were pictures.

He'd been flummoxed. Mrs. Schmitt kept a lab notebook and carefully recorded all the things in her house that she thought had been moved. She did seem to fully understand that if she was wrong, the notebook would be used as evidence that she was going crazy. Despite the fact that her notebook wasn't much evidence at all, Donovan didn't think she was wrong.

He had been surprised by her apparent nonchalance that her home was getting repeatedly invaded. But she was so damn logical that it began to make sense.

"Whoever it is has been very careful to come here when I'm not home," she'd said. "They don't want to hurt me, and besides, I'm armed. If they keep coming back, I can catch them." Her words made sense, even if the emotional tone seemed a bit off. Donovan had to remind himself that everyone grieved differently.

If they allowed for her cold logic and operated under the assumption that all Mrs. Schmitt's notes were correct, then whoever had been in her house had been inside repeatedly and had been looking at a variety of different things. Did that mean they killed Marat Rychenkov but didn't even know what they were after?

The information from the notebook had also led Eleri to an interesting question when they'd been sitting at the table. She'd asked Johanna, "What else is in the house? What *hasn't* been touched? Which rooms *weren't* searched?"

Seemingly happy to now have federal help in hunting her husband's killer, Mrs. Schmitt popped up from the table. "Do you want a tour?"

They'd followed from room to room, taking notes while Donovan battled his expectations. He'd been prepared for a wary witness. Most people didn't welcome a friendly FBI agent when he showed up on their doorstep. Most didn't answer every question with precision and volunteer even more details.

Maybe Johanna Schmitt had thought she was going crazy. Maybe she thought all the little things that had been moved were things she'd done in her own grief. She'd even said at one point, "I considered that I so desperately wanted to believe he was murdered, that I couldn't accept the fact that nature is random and cruel. But I guess it's not. Well, nature *is* random and cruel, but that's not what happened here, is it? My husband *was* murdered."

The woman had needed no further comforting after she heard a few facts. And they'd gotten the full tour. He'd seen the kitchen, in which Johanna said only a few things looked a little "bumped," except perhaps the junk drawer, which she thought had been pawed through.

Eleri had pulled all the drawers open for further inspection. Johanna swore the others were untouched and, as neat as they were, it should have been easy to see. With the "junk drawer," it was impossible to tell. Donovan couldn't imagine what a killer might want with old-looking rubber bands, binder clips, random business cards, three deceased cell phones—one with a cracked face that would never get used again—and more.

"They were Marat's," Mrs. Schmitt said. He'd not let her throw them out when he was alive, insisting that he might need a part here or there for something, or that the old phone could be used to dial 9-1-1. Now that her husband was gone, she said, she should throw them out—but she couldn't, because now they were ties back to the man she'd lost.

Donovan understood. Of the very few things he'd carried from house to house growing up, the one he'd always made sure he had was his mother's scarf. She'd wrapped it around his neck, telling him to stay warm the night she died. He'd carried the scarf everywhere now, including all the way to South Carolina where, as an adult, he'd finally stayed put. He didn't fault Johanna Schmitt one bit for keeping broken cell phones.

The family had three bedrooms upstairs. The master bedroom was slightly larger (though not unnervingly so) than the other two, which she and her husband had used as offices. Both offices had been searched, she'd said, though at separate times.

She'd found that interesting. Donovan did, too. He didn't openly agree at the time, but now, sitting at the table, he said to Eleri, "Whoever is getting into her house has relatively easy access. It means they have the code key or an override or something."

Eleri sighed. "I didn't want to mention it. But I'd be surprised if she hadn't already figured that out. I'm guessing she's sleeping with a baseball bat already."

"Or a home-made taser," Donovan countered. She'd said she was *armed,* and a baseball bat was way too low-tech for someone of Johanna's skill.

"Do you think they hacked her lock system?" Eleri asked. "She has that same kind of coding system that we see on so many of the houses here."

That was a mistake, Donovan thought, *giving all the residents the same kind of system.* The FBI was aware it was a problem in housing subdivisions that were getting high-tech. If everyone had the same kind of lock, it was easy to figure out how to hack your neighbor. Johanna was using her tech, and she should have picked her own lock system. He agreed with Eleri. "That was my guess too."

Eleri and Donovan had looked through both the offices in the house, trying to find information. The problem was, they'd found an overabundance of it. Just like his wife, Marat Rychenkov seemed to keep records of almost everything. They hadn't wanted to move any of it, afraid that if they did, they would alert whoever was coming into the home that Johanna Schmitt was onto them. As Mrs. Schmitt had stated, she had not done anything to let her friends or the general public know about the intruder before she had told Maggie.

She'd only told Maggie because she'd had two more instances, close together, and she was starting to get worried. Unknown to her, one invasion had turned out to be Eleri and Donovan, but another had happened the night before, which was when her office had been searched. The intruder had searched Marat's office first.

During the tour he and Eleri had been given, Donovan had also followed the two women into the garage, which apparently was not where one parked the car. It was where Marat Rychenkov did much of his robotics work.

Donovan had admired all the various work tables, tools, and rows of robots before he uttered, "Holy shit, Eleri."

Only after the words came out of this mouth did he realize it was an inappropriate thing to say to the widow of the murdered man. He turned toward Johanna. “I’m sorry.”

She shook her head. “I’ll take it as a compliment. Marat was brilliant. These are just his ‘toys’.”

Three oscilloscopes sat on the counter, old-school-style instruments with dials rather than touch-pad buttons, just as Mrs. Schmitt had said. Motherboards were filed in cabinets with upright slots, the kind that usually kept china plates in their proper places. Horizontal racks, which Donovan was certain were the same kind as in his junior high art classroom, were used to store what turned out to be blueprints.

Johanna had shrugged and explained, "He would fold them, but he hated rolling the blueprints. He hated having to pin them down."

Eleri nodded, and Donovan had to say he understood. It made logical sense. What he was learning of Marat Rychenkov was that the man had been nothing if not logical. Just like his wife.

Sitting up on the shelf were three rows of drones, each level was home to a different variety. Two were obviously for flying. The third, Donovan guessed, might walk, or roll? "These?" he inquired, pointing to them.

"Something else he's working on. He liked playing with the drones."

To his left, Donovan saw a row of humanoid-type robots. This time, each one was unique. Most came up to right around his knee.

Three of the designs involved curved legs, one with a spider-type design, and another that looked like a stick-figure dog.

"Things he was building," Johanna explained again, having followed Donovan's interest. "Two of them, he bought and rewired, and the final three, as you can see, are *frankenbots*. At least, that's what *I* called them. He didn't like that term, but I didn't know what else they might be."

"Does he have patents on any of this work?" Eleri asked.

"I don't think so, not on this work," his wife said. "Just things he was messing around with. You know, he would come out here and solder a motherboard, or plug two of them together in some way, put up the oscilloscope. He'd use the voltmeters and test them to be sure everything worked. He has a box of batteries, but some of those are strange batteries that even I don't know what they go to."

Donovan had leaned over and peeked into the box, almost bonking heads with Eleri. The container was several feet wide and several more deep, and while it was mostly filled with nine volts and triple- and double-As, also in it were a variety that Donovan had to admit he did not have a ready letter for.

Now, back at home with Eleri and speaking freely, Donovan was forced to admit several things. "Though it seems clear that he was murdered for something in that house, I don't know how we'll find it. I don't think the killer has found it either, though. So our job should be to find it first. But *how?*"

Eleri turned and looked at him. "I'm just grateful that he was organized. At least if we do get a tip in any general direction, we'll have a better idea where to start looking. But my God, he must've been working on forty different projects at once. If any one of them was a thing that got him killed—well, I agree—I don't know how we'd ever figure it out."

The one thing Donovan was glad they had cleared up was that they did not think Marat Rychenkov had a lover on the side. In his normal life, Donovan would've looked at Marat and thought, "This was a man who was too nerdy, not attractive enough, and far too involved in his work to be having an affair on the side." But as a medical examiner, and later as an FBI agent, it had been drummed into him that there was no way to determine those things from looks alone. He'd seen actors and Hollywood elite, faithful as the day is long, and others, the ones you would never suspect, managing to carry on multiple affairs, even behind the back of a spouse who suspected it.

However, Johanna Schmitt was quite certain her husband was not having an affair. Normally, Donovan and Eleri would've needed more evidence, but the widow had quickly provided it before they even asked.

"If he was having an affair, it would have to have been with a ghost," Johanna made her case. "He was here *all the time*. When he wasn't here, he told me where he was going. And he came home on time and he never smelled like anyone else's perfume. I could always track his phone, and I can't tell you the number of times he butt-dialed me and I heard his whole conversation and he didn't know it."

Though a spouse convinced their partner was faithful was a useless piece of evidence, Johanna made a compelling case. She told them to look into her husband's case, to check everything. If they found he was having an affair, she would accept the results. But she didn't think they would find a secret lover.

Donovan was ready to agree with her. He wasn't about to declare it so, but his firm belief was that Marat Rychenkov had not been killed over love gone wrong. It had to have been over his work. But which part?

It was Eleri's last question to Johanna Schmitt that still gave Donovan pause.

"Did your husband have any idea that he'd been targeted? That someone might want to murder him?"

Johanna had gone still, her eyes widening with grief again. "No. He didn't say anything to me, and he wasn't acting differently. I don't think he had any clue he was about to be killed."

14

Eleri headed into the *Up N Atom* again the next morning, once again with her laptop tucked under her arm. Once again, her plan was to pretend she was looking for work while actually doing what she needed to be doing to solve a case that now more than just the mayor and his staff knew about.

The idea was for her to get out and about, to be visible, and to talk to as many people as she could. Assess everything she could see. ID as many people that passed by as possible. So, no big deal, just sit and sip her drink and do all the work of a local encyclopedia with a built-in facial-recognition program. She was going to need the extra shot of Climate Change for this.

A second option—the one Eleri personally liked better—was that she might see and greet people and get an opportunity for conversation. Because yet another job she had was to sort through the full set of video recordings that were coming in from the Rychenkov-Schmitt home.

Within several hours of her and Donovan leaving Johanna Schmitt's house, the night before, Wade had turned up on her doorstep. First, he showed up as himself. In his pocket, he carried a hard copy of a program that he'd had designed and sent to him from the Omaha FBI branch office. His first job was to upload it to Mrs. Schmitt's phone and the main smart-system in the house.

The most important thing about the program was that it piggybacked an existing alarm that triggered her phone from the house. While it wouldn't change her codes or anything visible or functional, it would report immediately when anyone entered the home—whether through a door or window or air vent, with or without a code.

Johanna would now need to enter a second, additional code into her phone either before or just after she entered and exited her own home. This would let the upgraded home system know that the visitor was the owner and not to ping her. Now, no matter where she was, she would know immediately if someone was coming in. And so would the FBI.

Johanna had already changed her access code once earlier in the week, hoping that would thwart her intruders. But she found they could still get in without breaking anything. This, in turn, led her to doubt the intruders even existed. She began doing basic testing for mental faculty loss, figuring she must be going crazy. She'd finally broken down and told Maggie her suspicions. That was why having the FBI confirm her thoughts had been such a huge relief, Eleri knew. That's why Mrs. Schmitt was willing to play along with all their requests.

The person who'd been entering her home appeared to have used the appropriate code. While that should have provided a huge break in the case, it turned out to give them virtually zero forward momentum, much to Eleri's frustration. Johanna had not been able to list a single name of anyone who might have gotten the code to her home. She believed only she and Marat had it, and said, no, they didn't share it. Ever. She'd even put her hand to her chest and said, "That would be stupid!"

Now that she was the only one living in the home, she believed she was the only one who knew the newest code—which led to her willingness to entertain the idea she'd been going crazy rather than believe she actually had an intruder. With Eleri and Donovan's evidence, it now looked like someone had managed to obtain the new, altered code to the home, *though she'd given it to no one*. Worse still, the list of people who had the skills to hack into the home system didn't exclude any suspects from the list of local residents—except maybe Eleri and Donovan. Eleri had not admitted her lack of skills in front of Johanna.

Johanna had scoffed. "Bennett brought in the best designers for the houses, and he brought in good quality construction workers, but . . . well, they were good, the house is solid, not like a lot of new construction. But they weren't that intelligent, as best I can tell. I mean, calling this a *Smart House*? I think the high-schoolers across the street could hack their way in. I'm honestly surprised we don't have more crime than we do!"

Eleri almost said maybe they *did* have more crime, but the crime was so well committed that no one had discovered the missing pieces yet. She bit her tongue, instead. She had enough on her plate without looking for more cases to solve in Curie.

Even so, now she had fourteen-plus hours of footage from several views around the Schmitt house. Wade had come back and installed the cameras last night, and now Eleri needed to scan it all to see if anyone had been around Johanna's house since the night before. Probably not, since Mrs. Schmitt had been home overnight but if anyone was casing the yard or coming close to the front door, Eleri wanted to know who they were.

She hadn't mentioned that the cameras he installed *inside* the home would also tell them what Johanna did and everything she talked about there. Still, Johanna had probably figured that part out for herself.

Eleri headed into the line for coffee, laptop bag over her shoulder, and tried to keep an eye on the shop while she scanned the menu. The door opened behind her with a slight squeak and a loud ding, and a few more people got in line behind her. The next time it dinged, she turned to look over her shoulder, just as a course of habit, and she saw her friend from a couple of days ago.

"Oh hey, Eleri," Kaya Mazur waved and Eleri—understanding that Kaya was now part of a small loop leading back to Marat Rychenkov —hopped out of line and let the two other people between them step in front of her.

"How are you doing?" she asked.

"Good. Aside from losing Marat, life's been good. Are you now able to order your coffee on your own?" Kaya's eyes had dimmed at the name, and the fact that she mentioned the man's death meant he'd been a friend.

Eleri laughed at the comment about her ordering skills and replied, "Yes!"

"What are you getting today?"

Good, Eleri thought, she was in the right place. But she said, "I'm getting the Functional Adult." It referred to a blended drink with an extra shot of protein powder and extra caffeine.

"Oh, those actually work," Kaya said. "Just beware. You'll have energy for the next five hours. You won't be able to nap or change course!"

"I need to stay on course. Today, I'm also trying the extra shot of 'Dopamine'."

"Ah. The white chocolate. Sounds like a plan. Do you mind if I order the same?"

"Do it with me," Eleri offered grandly, trying to make a friend. "I'm buying."

As always, the pang hit her that she was being deceptive. She wondered: *If I ever see this woman sometime in the future, will Kaya Mazur hate me?* She'd always relied on her gut instinct and had even learned recently it was often more than just a hunch or an idea. But she had to trust it when it told her Kaya and the Mazurs were not her prime suspects in this murder.

Her instincts aside, she refused to discount good, old-fashioned leg work, as she was petrified that one day someone would break her system and her gut instinct would be *wrong*. She was petrified of failing in that way, because she'd had to defend information she got through intuition so many times in the past—and also because she didn't know how she even would defend her method, if she was called upon to do so. At least she knew Donovan and Westerfield had her back.

Eleri turned to her new friend and said, "I'm hanging out looking for jobs again, but you're welcome to join me if you want." She'd thrown the last offer out casually. It was a practiced line, trained in the FBI to be thrown out as though it were off-the-cuff, to catch a suspect and make them an unsuspecting friend. Adults in general were not good at making new friends, and the Bureau trained its agents well. Thus Eleri was here to make as many new "friends" as she could.

"Hm. Maybe for a little bit, if you don't mind."

The baristas kept the patrons moving through very quickly and, in a moment, they had placed their orders. It pleased her that Kaya simply said yes and let her buy the coffee as a thank-you for her previous help, but it was even better when Kaya replied, "I'll buy the next time I run into you."

"Sounds like a plan."

They set up in the corner. Kaya checked in on her phone while Eleri put her laptop out on the table as though she were truly going to do work. She couldn't check video footage with Kaya here, but she could at least open things up and pretend she was looking at emails. She logged into a dummy account under the name Eleri Miller. It was already subscribed to several different online programs, so ads for shoes, life insurance, and even erectile dysfunction pills popped up and filled her inbox as she opened the page.

When Kaya looked up from her phone, she made an odd face. "Joule said she saw you over at Johanna Schmitt's house the other day."

"Yes," Eleri said, grateful they had prepared Johanna for this. "Yeah, my friend and I were in the neighborhood, so we stopped in. I was with Maggie Wells earlier yesterday and she said Johanna was really concerned about her husband, and she hoped I could help. I'm not a doctor, but I am a Human Biologist, and anyway, I can read the autopsy and toxicology reports, and I just . . . I wanted to be helpful."

“She was frustrated with the way things were handled and how long it took to give her no answers,” Kaya reported, proving the earlier theory that the Mazurs were friends with Johanna Schmitt.

Eleri tried to hide the gears in her brain turning. Kaya was another insight into Johanna's thoughts on Marat's death. She waited, hoping Kaya would offer more, and was pleased when she got lucky. "They held his case for long enough, I got the feeling she was suspicious of something."

"I think she was," Eleri said, able to confirm that much. Johanna would continue to tell people how she felt, though at least she would now be able to say that she had spoken to Eleri and Eleri had helped to allay her fears. "I helped her look through the report and see that some of the things that were in there actually did make sense. I mean, not that it would make anyone happy, but it was why they had held his case for longer."

"Well that's good," Kaya said. "I hate the whole situation and I really hate seeing Johanna upset on top of it. Well, I made a casserole and I took it over, but I didn't really feel there was anything else I could do. At least you were able to give some real help," Kaya said.

"Casseroles are real help." She wanted to tell about her sister's funeral, and that her mother ate only when people brought food. Eleri thought maybe her mother only ate out of obligation, so friends bringing food had been beyond helpful—but she couldn't say that. She couldn't give out pieces of her real life, because she wasn't *really* a friend. Eleri knew the sadness from holding back showed on her face and could only hope that it would be read as concern for Marat Rychenkov.

The topic changed and Eleri let it, though she cataloged what she could about Joule and Cage and Kaya's husband Nate. She shared pre-selected details about Donovan and their friendship. But nothing else emerged about the murder. Kaya left about fifteen minutes later, saying she had to get into work, and Eleri got down to the business of watching the footage from in and around the Schmitt house.

As she filtered through hours of nothing happening from camera after camera through the night, Eleri told herself to be proud that she'd managed to stitch this small loop of friends a little closer. She'd covered for Johanna's change in feelings and maybe made another connection.

Clicking her way through the footage absently, Eleri forwarded through places that seemed pointless. Then she slowed and carefully watched the areas that seemed more important in only slightly faster than real time. Still, she turned up nothing.

Until the cameras read 8:15 that morning.

Johanna Schmitt had left her house, locking up and heading out the front door to the car, which was still sitting in the driveway. Not fifteen minutes later, a man in uniform headed around the side of the house and into the backyard to read the meter. Only he never read the meter. Instead, he headed to the back door and let himself in, getting the code right on the first try.

15

Three evenings later, Eleri sat at the dining table, frustrated enough to feel it in her skin. She sat with her irritation, hoping something would pop or an idea would come to her, or the phone would ring and things would change. Her frustration came from the abundance of information she had, none of which solved anything or even pointed her in a direction to start. It seemed the more she learned, the more complicated the case became—not less. She let herself seethe and boil as she waited for Donovan to walk through the door.

He came in by way of the garage and took one look at her as he turned the corner from the kitchen. "You look upset. And here I was thinking we should get pizza."

"Jesus," she groaned, putting her head into her hands. He hadn't been gone that long and pizza was probably a good idea. "You're right, we should go out for dinner. In fact, we should probably do it as often as possible. It lets us both eat and be seen. Hopefully, we'll see some people we know and get somewhere. *Anywhere*!"

"What's going on?"

He'd been at the CDC again. Donovan had gotten the dreaded call the day before to be a backup physician with the local walk-in clinic, and though he believed he'd relatively passed muster, he was pretty sure he hadn't impressed anyone—or so he said. Unfortunately, that was a balancing act between getting him out and about in town and him exhibiting an anxiety level Eleri had not witnessed in him before. But they needed him in that job. Being a walk-in clinic doctor gave him access to a lot of information about people that the agents would not otherwise get.

Still, he'd been stressed enough that he'd gone off to the CDC this morning to avoid getting called back in. He said he would re-check the clothing being held in evidence from Marat Rychenkov and also see if he could come up with anything they had missed.

When she asked him if the clinic was really that bad for him, he'd replied, "The day may have stressed me out more than it possibly helped any patients."

Frowning, she'd asked, "You don't think you missed anything or caused any problems, do you?"

Though he looked defeated, he'd at least shaken his head in the negative. "No. I can correctly identify and test for strep when necessary. It just freaks me out. I'm always afraid I've treated them for strep and missed something big. I'm not actually a *live person* physician." He'd said it through clenched teeth, despite the fact that his current MD licensure claimed otherwise.

Eleri had brushed it off the evening before. "Well, you all survived, and people got their antibiotics."

"And I re-set a dislocated shoulder, but not the broken bone. That one I handed off. No one wants to see my casting technique."

She'd laughed. "We cast foot prints better than we cast broken bones."

That had earned a small grin and an, "Amen."

At least today had been good for Donovan—but now it was Eleri talking through clenched teeth. "I've watched all this footage. Our intruder is coming almost every day. Which—if Johanna's records are correct—shows an increase in visits. But it hasn't been enough days to statistically establish that pattern yet."

"Did Johanna tell you that?"

Eleri glared up at him until he tried a different tack.

"Did you figure out who it is, or at least find any leads?" He'd seen the videos she was pulling up each evening, though she'd also gone through hours and hours of footage with no movement from multiple cameras. She'd marked the time where their visitor showed up.

"I don't know," she said. "You can't see much. Though I can see the person going in and out of the house and moving things around, I can't get much information on them. And today's episode of *Visiting Johanna Schmitt's House While She's Out* did not yield anything new. In fact, I'm not even convinced it's always the same person."

"Are you serious?" Donovan's expression seemed to snap to a more grave look at that news.

"I'm serious." She pointed at her screen as though it might explain. "Look. The perp appears to be two different sizes on different visits." She pointed to the video she'd opened of the first visit they'd caught on film.

Though the intruder was thoroughly covered, he was wearing worker apparel from the local gas company. He'd gone around the back of the house with his meter reader in one hand and his work bag in the other. However—as was clear from the video and guarded from street view by the fence—he went right past the gas pipes and headed for the back door. That was something a meter reader would likely never do.

From the hidden camera Wade had installed there, Eleri was able to see the intruder punch in the door code, correctly, on the first try. The door opened—exactly as they planned for it to happen—and he'd gone in. It appeared he had no idea he was being watched this time. He'd checked Marat Rychenkov's office again, then the kitchen, carefully putting each thing he touched back in its place before leaving.

She told Johanna about the intrusions when they happened, and Mrs. Schmitt would avoid those areas until Eleri or Donovan or Wade could go dust for fingerprints. But the video showed flashes of blue each time the perp reached his hands out from under the cover of the long jacket sleeves. The color told Eleri his hands were covered in common, latex-free gloves, which was probably why he'd covered them so efficiently with the jacket while heading inside. The flash of blue on his hands would've given it away to anyone who saw him.

Eleri flipped ahead to her marked footage from the next day. This time, their perp came to the front door and stood blocking the street view as he entered the code. Then he acted as though he was speaking to someone inside and being allowed in. This strategy would only raise flags if someone already knew that Johanna Schmitt was not home, and since she'd been keeping such odd hours, the timing alone wouldn't alert a neighbor.

Cuing up video from the third visit, Eleri pointed again and said, "This is where I become uncertain that it's all the same person."

On the third day, a person had come in from over the fence in the backyard. This meant a car didn't even pull up in front of Johanna Schmitt's home or even on her street. The car—if there was one—was likely on the street that ran parallel behind her home. Again, the perp was dressed just like a meter reader.

"Here. And here." She pointed to the house that shared a backyard fence with the Rychenkov-Schmitt home. "So I think they parked at this house and went into the back yard as though to read the meter. But instead, they hop the fence into Johanna's place and go right to the back door. This requires both houses to have no one at home, but that's more than plausible, since it was mid-day."

"Do you have evidence of him coming over the fence? Can you see it?" Donovan motioned her to rewind.

She shook her head. "But he appears in the middle of the far back of the space—as far back as the cameras reach, because we were certain no one would come over the fence." She sighed. "And we do have cameras telling us he didn't come in the front or around the sides. So unless he dropped onto the roof and then jumped there—facing toward the house, mind you—he came from the direction of the back fence."

They had an excellent array of cameras at the house—or so Eleri had thought. The first night, they'd had Johanna turn off her circuit breaker and Wade had come to the home again—though this time he was dressed as a Curie Power employee. Taking a ladder, he installed very small cameras under the eaves, covering almost every corner of the home and getting clear views of both porches, under the guise of checking every power line at the house.

After he'd installed all the cameras, they flipped the circuits back on, making it appear as though Curie Power had showed up and fixed the problem. Eleri was then able to see in and around the house in live feeds and recordings.

The first thing these recordings told them was that Johanna Schmitt was right. Someone *was* repeatedly entering her home and searching for something. The second thing it told them was that the intruder didn't seem dangerous. Despite Marat's murder, this perpetrator was carefully avoiding Johanna and not even causing damage.

Eleri was holding out hope that they might find what he took and use that to help find out why Marat was killed.

Eleri pointed to the images going by on her screen, hoping to show Donovan why she now thought there were two people involved. "Look. Look how tall he is next to the back door. He's shorter than the first day. And smaller."

"Probably." They both knew not to trust first appearances on camera images. Eleri hated pictures. Donovan leaned over, motioning for her to flip back and forth between the two pieces of footage. They watched both snippets several times. "He does look shorter. He doesn't come up to the same brick."

"No," Eleri said. "So now we have at least two people involved in breaking into Rychenkov's home."

"*Shit,*" Donovan muttered from over her shoulder.

"Exactly," she said, though she felt her teeth clenching again as she said it, her frustration mounting. She'd held out hope that Donovan would look at the images and tell her she was wrong, that it was possibly—or even clearly—the same person and she'd just misinterpreted things. But he hadn't. That meant two people, and two would be harder to find.

It was more than possible any resident of Curie had already figured that out. One person could be known missing at the times the crimes were committed, but two people could tag each other out, alibi-ing themselves for at least a portion of the crimes and making the investigators' job about ten times harder.

"Okay, we're screwed with that. Let's see what we can find out." Donovan rested a hand on her shoulder, and she was grateful for a direction that might yield something.

The second day, the perp had gone into the garage. He'd stood for some time, carefully looking at all the pieces Marat Rychenkov had arranged on his shelves. Though Johanna had told them she would not have been able to tell if anything in the garage had been moved, at least now they knew the perp had gone in there.

He or she eventually chose a few items and picked them up. He booted up an old laptop, carefully touching only the edges in an attempt to not disturb the dust that was settling on it. After a few moments, his fingers tapped on the keys and Eleri cursed.

"Dammit! We should have turned on the cameras in all the monitors in the house!" She was mad she hadn't thought of it before. If they'd enabled the laptop to snap a shot of anyone opening it, they would have the invader's mugshot. "We could have seen his or her face! Right there!" She was jabbing her finger at the screen and trying not to break either.

Donovan patted her on the shoulder again. "We'll do that tonight."

They watched the perp tap the keys for a while, then leave. Eleri sighed. "We'll have to check that. See if he emailed himself something . . . because he didn't download anything physical, it seems."

They gave up and watched the third visit. It had occurred that very afternoon. Now, Eleri watched the video of the smaller person getting into the house. "This was just a few hours ago, while Johanna was still out,"she murmured. This time the intruder rifled through boxes in closets, examining what Eleri assumed were important papers.

When the perp again failed to look up directly at a camera, or even hold a paper up for them to see what he was looking at, Eleri's frustration rose again.

"Let's get that pizza now," Donovan suggested. "I'm hungry, and pizza makes everything better." He was standing before he finished the sentence. "Besides, maybe we'll see something that cracks this whole case wide open."

Eleri felt better as soon as they left the angular house. And the pizza joint smelled good enough to make her hunger override her frustration. When the pizza arrived at the table, she had her plate ready and was reaching for a slice even as the server was asking if it looked okay. When Donovan held a hand out to stop her, she assumed it was to keep her from burning herself. She didn't care.

But he'd looked up at the server in stunned surprised and asked, "Do you use a template? Are all the pizzas cut so precisely?"

She noticed then, the perfect sixths on the circle. As their second pizza showed up on the heels of the first, she looked and saw that it, too, was immaculately sliced. Eleri took her piece anyway and was already biting in as the server responded.

"Yes, we started using a template when several of our cutters got sloppy and the guests complained . . ." There was a pause, then, "The residents around here can be . . . *precise*."

Eleri thought the young man probably had wanted to say "uptight," but had politely held back.

She'd eaten five slices, all the while waving at the few people she knew, but not managing to strike up any conversations or get anything meaningful done. In the end, though she was full, she was still frustrated. She couldn't recall the last time she'd eaten pizza while she was in such a foul mood. Despite the smile she pasted on her face, her thoughts churned while she was eating, and Eleri didn't like where they were headed.

When they arrived home, though, she was able to unleash. "We've got to get Johanna Schmitt out of that house!"

Donovan nodded in agreement, but she wasn't done letting her irritation roll off her tongue. "I know she wanted to stay and we needed that cover. But this murderer keeps looking for something in particular that they aren't finding. I can only imagine how long it will take them before they get frustrated enough to try to get the information directly out of her. And she doesn't know what it is."

"Agreed," Donovan said, "but we need to *catch* these people. If we take her out of the house, then we save her but we may lose our opportunity to catch our perps. Is it possible the intruder and the murderer are separate issues?"

Eleri understood what he was asking. "It's possible, but not probable, and I think her safety is at stake now."

Donovan agreed and they began working out a plan. "Can we do this without alerting them that we were watching?"

"I don't know," Eleri said, now sad and worn out. Her brain was no longer running at full steam and her new level of worry wasn't helping. "Maybe . . . maybe we get them to believe she's on vacation. That might encourage them to go into the home more carelessly."

"We also need to up our camera game. We put them all up high, not thinking our perp would be smart enough to keep covered even inside the house, but . . ."

"But," Eleri filled in, "this is Curie, Nebraska. Everyone is above average IQ and honestly, if I was casing that house, I wouldn't have taken my hood off, either—cameras or not. Keeping my face in the shadows only works to my benefit."

She had been frustrated by the gloves, too. They hadn't been able to get a lead on something as minor as the perp's skin color or any possibility of tattoos. They'd vacuumed for stray hairs but found nothing.

With the decision made, Eleri called Johanna Schmitt's phone and let her know they had a new plan. But the woman didn't answer and she wound up leaving a message.

"What?" Donovan asked, looking up from something on the table. "You look worried."

"It's eight p.m. and Johanna Schmitt didn't answer her phone for me . . ."

16

"Shit." Donovan muttered it, though he would like to have yelled it at the top of his lungs. He couldn't, though. It might alert others in the vicinity to what he was seeing.

He and Eleri had begun an active search for Johanna Schmitt barely thirty minutes after Eleri's first phone call didn't go through. His partner had set a timer just after leaving the first voicemail, then dove back into viewing the footage from the Rychenkov-Schmitt house.

They'd learned early on that you couldn't just remember to do something later—not when a case was at stake. Unfortunately, they hadn't realized far greater than the case was at stake tonight.

When the timer had gone off, they had been fully absorbed back into the work and were both startled that the thirty minutes had already passed.

Eleri checked her phone before looking up at him. "Mrs. Schmitt hasn't called me back. Your turn."

So Donovan had placed a call very similar to the first one Eleri had made. He'd tried the landline at the house, though they had cameras there and could see she wasn't home. He wondered what the likelihood was that she was in fact home, but out of camera range, but he came to the conclusion that it was incredibly low, given that her car wasn't in the driveway.

He hoped she'd forwarded her home phone line to somewhere

else; people around here might do that. Still, it yielded no answer. When he got her voicemail, just as Eleri had earlier, he left a second message with greater urgency and called her cell phone, once again getting no answer other than her recorded message.

Deciding action beyond dialing was now necessary, they'd tried her local haunts, trying to remember where it was she had gone that afternoon. Though Johanna Schmitt had very readily handed over as much information as she could about herself and her husband each time they asked, she'd not been good about remembering to make frequent and regular updates. She was inconsistent at best about letting them know where she was going each time she left the house. Her phone and GPS had always confirmed what she told them after the fact.

She had a class to substitute teach tonight on the high school campus—they knew that much. If she had arrived safely there, then their worries should be lower. It was the trouble she might have run into before that which concerned Donovan. No one would have reported to them if Mrs. Schmitt hadn't shown up to teach or likely even have called the police.

He'd wanted to knock on the door of the Mazur family across the street to see if they knew anything. If it came to that, he might just do it—but right now, he didn't even know the woman formally, only what he'd investigated of her. Even Eleri's position as new friend to Kaya was not a strong enough bond to simply knock on the neighbors' doors and ask if they knew what had happened to Johanna.

"Is she possibly in the house?" Donovan asked, wanting to be sure they hadn't overlooked the obvious.

"Unless she's in the bathroom or on her bed, and got there via teleportation, no. I've double-checked all the footage. We saw her leave and we don't see her come back."

"She could have drilled a hole into the upstairs bathroom via the roof," he offered. "We don't have cameras there." While it might have sounded snarky, he had to remember that they thought they had a thorough sweep of cameras, and yet someone had managed to come in, probably over the back fence. And they couldn't prove it, because their visual sweep was not as thorough as they had originally thought. It was normal for a thief, or a perpetrator, to thwart the best-laid plans—and he suspected that in Curie, Nebraska, that was an everyday circumstance.

After a short discussion, they opted not to check the house—not because they didn't believe Johanna Schmitt could have dropped in through the ceiling, but because they believed the likelihood of that was lower than of her being somewhere else. It had taken thirty minutes to work up a plan. They had to have ready answers and be in agreement if asked about why they were out and who they were visiting at each location. Their answers had to make their visits seem absolutely normal. But they'd taken the time to do it right, as they fully expected to find everything was okay.

So they had walked down the halls of the high school, with Eleri making casual comments the whole way. "I'm thinking about applying for work here. I saw that the school offered Anatomy and Physiology last year, but not this year. Perhaps they are missing a teacher."

Donovan answered her, encouraging the fictional Eleri Miller to apply to teach, even though she didn't have a teaching certificate. They kept the faked conversation going until they got to Room 342.

"Donovan, I don't even know what to say. This is one of the most beautifully designed high schools I've ever seen." That part of her conversation was probably quite real. Donovan hadn't yet brought her on an official tour here, though he'd come through with Marshall Bennett showing him the way earlier. He suspected the high school was Bennett's crown jewel for prospective residents that the Mayor liked. The tour had been far too smooth for it to be Marshall Bennett's first time showing the place off. Now Donovan repeated some of the information to Eleri as they walked the halls.

The place sparkled, the floors mopped to a high gloss, the hallways sporting lockers, but above them papers, artwork, all of exceptionally high caliber for a high school. One set of lockers featured what appeared to be a small, hand-built rollercoaster, with a marble rolling across it. Underneath it was a small plaque that read, "Perpetual motion experiment. If you see the marble has stopped, please note the time and place the marble back at the designated starting point." Donovan watched as the marble rolled on and on, around and around the long track, even though no one else appeared to be here at this hour.

He pointed to a plaque on the wall. "National Merit Scholars."

"That's an impressive number, for how long? The school is twelve years old?"

"That's just this last year. Previous winners are in other halls." He watched as her mouth fell open. The school had approximately twenty times the national average of scholarship recipients through the nation's most famous program.

"I'm glad the building is still open," she commented, probably to keep the conversation going.

"They run classes in the evening, allowing curious minds to come and learn from other local experts." He waved a hand toward one of the rooms. "It's like the same way someone would take an MIT online course, but in person, with the ability to sit at a desk, raise your hand, and ask a question of a teacher at the front of the room." The teacher could, of course, answer with the smart board, as every single room had one.

He noted that the Biology wing had live animals in most of the classrooms and fish tanks embedded in one of the walls. His high school classroom had been lucky not to have mold. Though he'd attended six different high schools, none had enough books, nor chairs, nor teachers, and certainly no one had worried about tablets for the individual students or National Merit Scholarships.

They hit Room 342 and found the door, though closed, led to a well-lit classroom. Turning the knob, Donovan looked up and down the hallway, and noted Eleri surreptitiously doing the same. No one was up here. The class Johanna was filling in for should have been well done by now. So perhaps, not being the regular teacher, she'd not closed up the room, or had mistakenly left the lights on, something like that. Still, they ducked inside to check.

A teacher's office was attached to the far side of the room, the door only partly closed. He and Eleri barely glanced around the empty classroom before they dashed for the office.

Donovan peered through the small window and pushed at the door. His glance into the room had not revealed anything other than shelves of books on two sides and a small window to the outside on the third. The door only swung about a foot and a half open before it bumped into something, not going any further.

His heart sank then, the bad feeling settling into his bones. It had only gotten worse when he stuck his head in and looked down. The thing stopping the door was a foot.

"*Fuck, fuck, fuck, fuck,*" he'd whispered, and Eleri had known then.

As the two of them had grown to trust each other over the past almost two years, she let him look and did not rush him for space in the doorway. Instead, she stepped back, allowing him to pull the door slightly closed, then slide through the opening and step to the other side. Once he was in, Eleri poked her head in, but they both understood the importance of not bothering the body first.

Johanna Schmitt hadn't moved in the slightest, and though he already knew the answer, Donovan knelt down and tested for a pulse. "Shit, El. She's getting cold."

He launched into investigation mode, not sure how long they would have before someone found them with the body. He watched as his partner started calculating time since death, even as they both pulled out their phones and began snapping pictures.

Eleri started, her voice soft. "If the class ended at seven and it's eight-thirty now, then she can't have been dead for more than an hour probably. We need to find out if she taught this class or not. Maybe the body was in here the whole time class was going on."

"I don't think so," Donovan said, reaching into his back pocket and pulling out the pair of blue latex gloves that he constantly kept on him. At least his cover as a physician made that seem somewhat normal. Though he'd never carried gloves along as an ME, as an FBI agent, he now also had a foldable CPR barrier, allowing him to give any mouth-to-mouth without full contact. But this time, unfortunately, he only needed the gloves. "She left the house at four. She would have had to have come here, and been killed, and then a class would have come in and not noticed, even though the door was only partly closed. Had any of the students come early, they would have known. It's possible, but not probable."

Once they had a satisfactory number of pictures, he asked Eleri and they agreed: it was time to move the foot, open the door fully, and let Eleri in. Closing the door behind her, they squatted down together, using phone flashlights to illuminate what they'd noticed before. What they'd seen in the pictures of the first body was now confirmed here.

Eleri looked at him. "Rope marks, wrists and ankles."

He pointed to the marks. "But she fought."

17

Donovan woke up late the next morning, and so had Eleri, he noticed. No one had gone outside, trying to make friends with LeDonRic next door, or his girlfriend Maggie, or to see if he had a gaggle of high school students following him along in full medieval armor. This had not been the morning for that.

This morning had been a struggle between his own feelings about losing someone directly on his watch—and also about still covering up the facts about what they really were and why they were here. He had yet to resolve it in his own mind, and for a moment, he wished he was back in the ME's office in South Carolina. The dead bodies there were not his fault and he rarely had to interact with the people their deaths impacted. He solved his puzzles and went home.

Now, he was rarely home. But in more ways, he always was home, he thought, as he watched his partner come down the stairs. He had Eleri, Wade, Lucy, and even GJ. Eleri schlepped down the steps looking as though her night had been as sleepless as his. They had been up until the wee hours.

Though they'd taken their own pictures and checked the body with their gloves on, they realized quickly that they were each playing the role of "random citizen." The thing that Random Citizen would do was to call the Curie Police Department. Donovan had already touched Johanna Schmitt to check her pulse in her neck, though it had yielded nothing beyond her already dropping temperature. They had also moved the body, ever so slightly, but since they'd had to do it to open the door in the first place, the PD would likely let that slide.

When the police arrived, they had made a justified argument for why they had done it, and no one seemed to be suspecting them or bringing up any charges. In fact, if they *hadn't* done those things, the PD would likely question them later, though Donovan thought he might just claim his Curie-level brilliance meant that he knew better than to touch or move a dead body.

They'd been questioned separately, and he had been forced to speak as Dr. Donovan Naman, primary care physician and erstwhile CDC adjunct. He'd had to account for every moment of his time yesterday, just to help them rule him out as the killer. Not used to being the suspect on the receiving end of the interrogation, Donovan struggled to make it work. His acting was subpar, but he hoped the police read that as him struggling with having found a dead body rather than as struggling to maintain an FBI cover story. But holding up his cover demanded that he do the full interrogation as though he were an average citizen, and the FBI demanded that he hold his cover until he was explicitly given permission to break it.

The upside was that he and Eleri had not even been in Curie when Marat Rychenkov had been murdered—and that much of the PD had no idea that Marat Rychenkov had been murdered in the first place.

Eleri looked at him now as she plopped into the chair opposite him. "Everything is going out the window," she said by way of greeting.

He could only agree. "I had a bowl of cereal. You want one?" He shook the box at her, as though that would be in any way enticing despite the dismal situation of the day.

She shook her head. "No. You and I both need to go to the *Up N Atom* and eat pastries and drink strong coffee and be sad and shaken."

He nodded. It was a good plan. They'd called Westerfield at four a.m., explaining everything they'd found and how they'd been interrogated. When they asked about continuing their cover Westerfield had insisted they maintain it.

"The problem now," Donovan told Eleri, "is everybody's going to know that Johanna was murdered. Two people don't just die the same way—*in that way*—coincidentally. The general population of Curie will know that Johanna was murdered, and they'll put it together and know that Marat was, too."

"I suspect the information about the ligature marks is going to get out," Eleri sighed. "Our jobs just got infinitely harder."

They both knew the police had managed to keep the majority of details clamped down regarding Marat's death—not because they thought they were releasing details of a murder, but because they felt one of their citizens likely had a kinky sex life, and they didn't feel the details were important to the public. But now, given the CPD staff of around fifty, something was likely to get out. "Do you think they'll be able to hold back the information about the ropes better because they're smarter?" Donovan asked Eleri.

"These people *are* smart," she replied, still not looking at him, "but I don't think that makes them any less human. Does it make them any less likely to feel that driving urge to share a secret with *just one person?* It might make them think twice about the content of what they share and hopefully about the consequences, but I don't think it will significantly slow the spread of information." Even her tone sounded depressed about that.

Donovan and Eleri tried briefly to figure out how long it would take for the ligature marks to make their way into public knowledge, though first the gossip would likely be that Johanna Schmitt had died barely two weeks after her husband. These people were far too smart for that not to look hell-and-high-water suspicious to everyone. This death was definitely going to be a murder investigation from the start.

Rubbing one hand down her face, Eleri leaned ungracefully back into the hard wood chair as Donovan got up to take his bowl to the sink and think about the two of them getting ready and heading out. "The upside," he said, "is that we actually *are* sad and scared and frustrated now. Our acting abilities don't have to be up to any level of showmanship today."

"No, but our filters will have to be top notch. We're really going to have to watch what we say. Also," she added, "everyone's going to be after us because we know details about the body, and they're going to want to know, too. So what do we tell and what do we not tell?"

They spent a few minutes deciding what kind of citizens they were going to be today—the good kind who said nothing or the ones who shared a single, juicy tidbit. All the while, the thought played at the back of Donovan's mind that he could not determine how Johanna Schmitt had died. Once again, there was no evidence of any foul play, other than the obvious. He'd even tried the less-than-obvious. He'd leaned over the body and sniffed it before the police arrived. Though it wasn't the same as having a Y incision on the thorax and the organs actually held in his hands, he got a good whiff. But he didn't smell anything that made him curious.

Eleri sighed heavily. "I vote to be slightly bad citizens. We share one detail. Make people hope to get more information out of us. Hopefully, one of those people will be the killer, trying to figure out what we figured out."

Donovan nodded, thinking about what kind of detail to share. Once they'd called the police, the investigation had been out of their hands, and though they'd both looked around and seen and taken in details, they hadn't been able to have a discussion yet. They'd been on the phone with Westerfield late last night. Then, almost as soon as they had hung up with him and thought about discussing the case, Bennett had called.

Donovan's phone had rung simultaneously to Eleri's, which almost always meant Westerfield, but given that they'd just hung up with the man and that the number was Bennett's, they both raised an eyebrow. That had been five a.m.

The founder had demanded a more thorough investigation from them. "How could this have happened on your watch?" he wanted to know. But there had been no answer for that. Not yet.

In the end, Marshall Bennett managed to tone his ire down a bit, and even apologized for yelling. He understood that he was just angry, and it really wasn't their fault, something Donovan wasn't sure he'd wrapped his own head around just yet.

That was when Bennett told them, "I'm giving you access to all the police reports. As soon as they're done, they come to me. As soon as I have them, Kate will forward them to you. Expect full cooperation in this."

"Of course," Donovan had replied, though he wondered what else Marshall Bennett might have thought he would get from the two FBI agents he had explicitly brought in for this case. Had he thought they might have seen the body and run screaming? Donovan told himself the old man was flustered and maybe even scared. His seemingly peaceful town was under attack by a killer. His dream was threatened.

As Donovan thought back, it meshed with what Eleri had said. *Smart* didn't mean *not human*. And as smart as Marshall Bennett was, he'd not been prepared for this.

Somehow, the town founder seemed to believe that intelligent people were better people. Donovan was realizing that that was not the case. Smart people were, in most ways, just like everyone else.

Johanna Schmitt had believed her husband's murder was a contained case. Though she had slept with a weapon under her pillow, she'd not truly been worried about her own life. She was more worried that she would disturb the intruder looking for Marat's things and that was what would put her in danger. Not any threat directly to herself, or at least not anything she couldn't protect herself from.

Of course, she'd been wrong.

They'd assessed the case, and yet Donovan and Eleri and Wade had all somehow missed the threat to Johanna Schmitt, and it had cost her life. They'd been too slow to see the real threat was to the woman still living in the house.

Now he let it all out, all his frustration and self-anger. He and Eleri were finally able to have some of the conversation they'd been unable to have the night before. Once he'd spent a minute being a pain in the butt, he got down to the work of assessing their information.

"What was she tied to?" he asked first. "She had ligature marks on her wrists. She was tied down. No one just puts ropes around someone's wrists for no reason."

"Well, don't put that past anyone here. Now that you mention it, that would be a great way to throw the police off track."

He muttered to himself that he'd been joking, but she had a point. Eleri continued, "Though her arms hadn't been splayed out, it appeared they'd been moved back by her sides after she died. Though the evidence on that isn't solid yet. It's something we want to look at harder when we see the body. I think she was tied to the bases of the bookshelves. They were relatively heavy. Maybe a leg of the desk."

"Is that just because you saw them and that's what you would have used?"

"Partially," his partner replied, her head now laid back across the rungs of the chair and aimed up to the ceiling, her hair needing to be washed, and her face needing a new expression. "But also, if you noticed the bookshelf on the right where I was standing, many of the books were tilted. They looked like they'd been jostled. Thus, maybe she disturbed them if she fought back and she was anchored to the bookshelf."

"It's a good thing it didn't fall over on them," he said.

"I know, but also I get the feeling that she wasn't able to fight too hard."

Donovan thought about that, and then he understood why Eleri said that. "She had ligature marks, but not really burns, no scrapes."

"Right. If I was tied down and I knew the person was trying to murder me, I would have pulled on those ropes hard enough to draw blood. The data says most people would. And Johanna Schmitt was already angry enough about her husband's murder to have fought hard."

"So," Donovan added to the train of thought between them, "did all her bruising come from getting her *into* the ligatures, not after?"

"I think so," Eleri replied.

But that only made the case stranger and stranger.

18

Eleri was heartbroken. They had recognized the danger to Johanna Schmitt, but probably thirty minutes to an hour too late. On the drive to the *Up N Atom,* Marshall Bennett had called their phones again, demanding that they come into his office. Donovan turned the car around as Eleri mentally postponed the pastry and the coffee, both of which she really needed, for later in the morning.

She'd wondered what Bennett was going to say, and was not surprised when he opened the office door to them, his face already red. His tension appeared like visible blood pressure, as though he had possibly already paced the carpet bare in several spots. She hadn't known what to say. Neither had Donovan, but he'd at least attempted it.

"Morning, sir." Eleri noticed her partner dropped the *good.* It wasn't.

Bennett closed the door behind them as politely as he seemed to be able to, given whatever was zinging through his system—anger, frustration, fear, maybe all of it. She was having difficulty sorting it out and wondered if Donovan could smell a distinction on the older man.

She didn't get to wonder for long, though, because Bennett moved behind his desk—probably a position he felt powerful and comfortable in—and suddenly smacked both his hands down, hard. She would have been startled if she hadn't been well enough trained to see it coming.

"I have a fucking *serial killer* in my town," he issued the statement like a demand.

Though Donovan started to answer, Eleri gave a small motion to him. This was actually her area, and she wanted to talk Bennett down. "No, sir, you don't."

"I have two murders with *weird signatures*," he said, throwing out a word he likely had heard on TV. As a businessman, he probably wasn't well-versed in his DSM psychological manual and diagnoses. "Isn't that what they call it? Because we have it!"

"Actually, sir, if you call this person a 'serial killer,' even just to your own staff, you're going to create far more problems than you solve."

Bennett left his hands planted on his desk and looked up at her, his eyes narrowing. "Is he—or is he not—killing serially?"

Though Eleri agreed with the linguistics, she had to explain. "There is a lot of overlap between the terms, sir, and—"

He interrupted. "I don't care about the terms—"

She interrupted back. "Yes, you do, because the terminology will help us determine how we go forward with this case. And the terminology you use will inform the public of how afraid they need to be."

That, at least, seemed to calm him down, and she launched into a pedantic discussion of the various types of killers. She hoped that, as smart as he was, and as much as he had loved the high end of intelligence enough to build a whole town for it, that speaking to him in this way would at least soothe him.

"Sir, there are *mass* killers—those who kill people all in one location, all at one time. The Vegas shooting spree was a mass killing. There are *spree* killers—these are people who walk down the street and kill many or all of the people they encounter. Some sprees are minutes, some are months, but they follow a path. Bonnie and Clyde are probably the prime example of spree killers. Both mass and spree killers generally have no connection to their victims. And then you have a *serial* killer—which is probably the closest term for what we have here, but it still isn't really psychologically the proper terminology."

"Go on." At least he was looking at her, listening carefully now, and she had his attention.

"Most serial killers kill for the thrill of the kill, or the torture. In many cases, they have some ritual they have to go through. They select a victim for reasons that please the killer or the ritual. They perform all the steps, usually in the same order and, in some cases, the kill isn't even part of the urge. They just have to kill the victim at the end because of the information the victim would have if set free, or because the damage from their ritual is too great. But serial killers, in general, kill because of an *urge*.

"You have to remember, though, if you ask ten psychologists or psychiatrists the definition of these things, you will get ten different answers. Our killer is in a grey area. I do not believe our killer is killing for any kind of thrill, and that's the big difference. I believe our killer kills out of some need—either to gain information or to suppress it."

"What does that mean?"

Donovan hopped in then, and she was grateful. "Our killer doesn't love killing. He may even hate it. He feels he has to kill to get what he wants."

"Then why the ritual?" Bennett pushed, though now he looked as heartbroken as Eleri felt rather than wearing the angry expression he had before.

"Maybe to throw us off the track. Maybe it's a way he knows that works . . ."

Eleri watched as Donovan trailed off. She could almost see the idea forming in his mind. She started talking before Bennett saw it, too. "What this means is that profiling the victims by their location—or their looks, or ages, or professions—isn't going to help us here, not at all. If you announce to all of Curie that there's a serial killer in their midst, the people of this town are going to look up that definition and they're going to draw some conclusions . . . and some of them will be very erroneous conclusions. Then they're going to change their lives and their children's lives accordingly. And if they draw the wrong conclusions," she was practically leaning over from the front side of the desk now, almost nose-to-nose with Marshall, "they will not only *fail* to protect themselves, they may put themselves further in harm's way. So how you distribute this information to the town is of the utmost importance."

Eleri took a deep, badly needed breath before continuing. "For example, you called my partner and I in here this morning. You failed to give us an alternate route into the building. We found one anyway, so that people did not see two newcomers to town—strangers—heading into the office of the mayor and founder. That would have likely blown our cover. You're going to have to be as careful about this as we are, sir, and any help you can provide us would be greatly appreciated." She changed her tone at the end of that, hoping to enlist him as a helper rather than smack him down as a fool.

Then she upped her tone even a little more, hoping to calm Bennett and put him squarely in their court. "My conclusion is that Marat Rychenkov had something—either an object or knowledge—that the killer wanted. We've concluded that the killer had access to the home information. We told you, remember? He used the door codes, and he used the door codes correctly, without fail, even after Johanna Schmitt changed them. That indicates a system hack. That person repeatedly came into the home and continued looking for something. So my partner and I think they killed Marat Rychenkov without the information or the object already in hand."

"They must have believed it would be easier to find after he was dead." Bennett was getting into the game now, and Eleri was glad to have him on their side rather than yelling at them across the desk. "So if we can figure out what that thing is, we may be able to figure out who the killer might go after next."

"If anyone at all," Eleri said. "It's plausible the killer got what they needed out of Mrs. Schmitt. To be fair, she told us firmly that she had no idea what it was. If she was holding out on us, the killer might have gotten her to tell whatever information she had."

Donovan entered the conversation again then. He'd been watching them go back and forth almost as though he were at a tennis game, but Eleri could tell his mind had been churning with something else the whole time. "Get the police and the medical examiner, when they run the tox screen, to check for Sodium Pentothal," he said now. "It'll be a few days before we get that result back."

Bennett frowned at him. "Truth serum?"

Of course. *Of course* the mayor of the town knew it by its chemical name, Eleri thought.

"Yes. If they wanted information out of Johanna Schmitt, that's the most likely way to have done it," Donovan told them.

Bennett absorbed that information the way he absorbed everything: casually. But Eleri knew he would not forget. He seemed to have come to terms with his role in moving the investigation forward, even as he changed the topic. "The police reports are here."

"Did you email them?" Donovan asked and was relieved when Bennett shook his head and said, "Not yet."

"Give us hard copies, please."

Eleri quickly explained how they had to keep the records out of any computer program that could be hacked, but they had to do so without alerting the killer they were on to the hack. *Let Bennett chew on that one for the next day,* Eleri thought. *It might keep him out of their hair.*

After leaving, they snuck back out to Donovan's car and finally made it to the *Up N Atom*. Eleri had copies of the police reports on her, and they weighed heavy in her bag.

19

Eleri and Donovan had been at the coffee shop for a good thirty minutes when they decided to call it a loss. *At least they'd gotten coffee and pastries,* she thought. The hit of sugar and caffeine had done her good.

They'd purposefully taken seats at the long, group table right in the center of the place. As Eleri had nothing on her screen that she needed to shield from anyone this time, they were trying to be as visible as possible. She turned to Donovan to declare the morning a bust and was reaching for her foil pastry wrapper to toss it, when Kaya Mazur came in with her husband Nate and the two kids, all of them looking forlorn.

"Kaya!" Eleri called out at the same time Kaya called her name back. The woman rushed over and grabbed Eleri's hands.

"I heard you were the one who found her," Kaya said, her expression worried for her new friend. Eleri nodded in a tight movement, letting the tears well in her eyes at last, grateful she didn't have to cover her true feelings about the situation. She let the explanation fall out of her mouth—even though the words were slightly false—just the way someone would if they had been through a traumatic situation that they were not prepared for.

Eleri and Donovan were overly prepared, but now she let the story roll off her tongue. "We were at the high school. We heard they did classes and I was thinking maybe I could teach some . . . While

Donovan and I were walking down the hall, one of the rooms had the light on, and we went in to check it out and . . ." She took a breath and continued her purposeful babbling. "The office door was open, so we knocked and then . . ."

She let the last words trail off. Everyone knew what had happened after that—or at least they believed they did. She hoped no one knew that Donovan and Eleri had done a cursory FBI investigation first.

"I'm so sorry you had to deal with that." Kaya squeezed her hands while Nate looked over her shoulder. The two kids stood behind them, clearly watching their mother, though not fully engaged. Kaya turned with a start, realizing she'd missed a step in etiquette. "Oh, I'm so sorry. This is my husband, Nathan. Nate. I believe you've met Cage and Joule?"

The two kids barely nodded, as did Eleri. She looked to them. FBI training urged agents to speak directly to kids whenever possible once the kids were above the age of three or four. She found that worked in everyday life, too.

"You're not in school today?" she asked, though she didn't use a tone in that was derogatory or judgmental.

It was Cage who shook his head. "No. I couldn't."

Kaya filled in. "The kids were over there all the time. I mean, it was hard enough losing Marat, but now this."

It was then Joule's eyes welled up. She'd been holding it back, but the tears spilled freely now, and Kaya turned and hugged her daughter, though Eleri had been about to jump up and do it herself. The poor kid.

But Eleri was filing away the information that the children had been at the Rychenkov-Schmitt house repeatedly. They'd worked with Marat Rychenkov as his students and maybe his young friends. He'd taught the occasional high school class, but they also had been in the home.

Shit, Eleri thought. How are they going to interview these kids without blowing cover or angering their parents? But it was definitely something that needed to be done.

That was when Eleri noticed it. Though Joule was crying at her loss, Cage looked wary. He was glancing around the coffee shop as though he was trying to suss out which person was the killer. She hoped he knew that she had not lived here when Marat died, and that she could not be responsible. She needed him to understand that she was on his side.

She'd already established herself as a human biologist. Re-establishing herself now as a forensic expert or doling out forensic advice of any kind would come across as weird, and she couldn't afford the slightest misstep of weird in this town. These people would figure it out.

"Do you want to join us?" Eleri asked, motioning to the table where Donovan still sat. They'd picked the community table for exactly that purpose. She wanted to offer to buy the family their coffees and pastries, but felt it would be going a little too far. Technically, she was in no more shape to console the family than they were to console her. She was the one supposedly traumatized by finding the body and being up all night with the police.

She had thought that had been the hardest thing—not blowing her cover to those who were professionals, law enforcement officers like herself. But now, as she looked at Cage and Joule, she saw Joule catching on to Cage's demeanor and pulling her tears back to start looking around the *Up N Atom* with a suspicious eye. The girl seemed to be trying to glean information, and Eleri wondered if she had a future investigator on her hands. An event like this could make that happen, as Eleri well knew. The problem was, right now, they were part of *her* investigation, and she thought these two might be the toughest nuts to crack.

"Oh," Kaya said. "I think we're just going to grab our own space and sit and be a family for the day."

"I am so sorry." Eleri put her hand on the woman's shoulder in a half hug before reaching out and shaking Nate Mazur's hand. "It's really nice to meet you. Kaya talks about you all the time, and I'm sorry that I'm finally meeting you but it's under these circumstances."

"The same to you." His tone was flat, though it was hard to read the why of it from his expression. "I'm sure it must have been a shock."

Though Eleri nodded, as if it had been, she saw in his eyes that he, too, was questioning everything. Whether that was because his friend was murdered, or because she and Donovan had slipped up in some way, she couldn't tell.

This time, they'd actually succeeded in folding up the foil paper their pastries had come in and putting their cups into the dish rack.

Donovan pointed to a spot in the trash center for foil and Eleri answered the question before he asked. "They recycle it. A local kid melts it down and forges them new foil out of it."

"Of course they do." Luckily, he whispered the words.

Eleri hid the smile that wanted to pull at her mouth. Now was not the time. They made it out the door without running into anyone else and headed back to the Frank Lloyd Wright house. The large stone sign for Pythagoras Point mocked her. With its curves, it seemed wrong. *The only thing that has a curve in the whole neighborhood just has to be the welcoming sign bearing the name Pythagoras,* Eleri thought.

When they arrived at the house, Eleri plopped down in the recliner in the living area, glad to be out of the hard chair of the dining table where she seemed to have set up personal and emotional camp. She stared out the back window, at the bushes that bordered the tall wooden fence, each angle precisely cut. It was Pythagoras Point. She saw right triangles and hypotenuses everywhere she looked. *Hypotenii?* She didn't know, but surely even the kids at the high school did.

With a bone-deep sigh, Donovan stretched out across the couch, though his head was up on the arm and his feet were hanging over the other end. His sound mimicked the feelings pushing at her ribs.

"Donovan, we have to interview those kids. I think we have to interview the entire Mazur family."

"Yeah," he said. "But who else? We blew our cover to Johanna Schmitt, and she's dead."

"Well," Eleri said. "Ignoring all feelings of our fuck-up regarding her death, revealing ourselves to her was the right decision. Clearly, we picked the right person. We just didn't protect her well enough."

It was Donovan this time who tried to allay her anger at herself. "Eleri, we had no idea we needed to protect her. They were after Marat's stuff. Not *her*. A point Johanna herself argued vehemently. We did offer her more protection. She didn't take it."

Eleri tried to absorb his absolution while simultaneously ignoring it. "Who else do we need to go to now?"

"Shit," he said, and then hauled himself off the couch and went back to his paperwork. He wasn't ignoring her, though. She knew he was diving into the information to find an answer for her question.

Though they had tablets and computers, though they'd been watching the footage, Eleri had become more and more concerned this morning. "Donovan," she said, "we need to move to paper tracking."

"We can't move video to paper," he protested with a shrug.

"I know, but pretty much everything else we can. I think we need to take our video and travel it on USBs rather than internet. Somebody hacked the Schmitt-Rychenkov home. They had the code. They had it as soon as she changed it, and we've been emailing videos. Maybe that's why they kept the hoodie on and their hands covered. Maybe they knew that we were watching—even inside the house. Or, at least, they suspected it. If there was something Marat Rychenkov had that was worth stealing and killing over, then it would be reasonable that *he* would have had some kind of surveillance on it, too."

Donovan picked up on what she was saying. "He would have had some kind of security, especially if he knew he had something that valuable."

"Did he? That's a good question," Eleri said, not leaving her position sitting sideways in the recliner. Her body almost couldn't move because her brain was eating all her energy. "We should have asked Johanna Schmitt *that* question."

And now we can't, she thought.

Donovan either didn't see her slip into self-blame or he ignored it. "—and the cursory look at this house says there's no security. Marat kept all the robotics in the garage, where a person could simply pry open the door and get to it. Sure, he or Johanna would likely have heard that happening if they were home, and anyone on the street would have seen it. But the security level is very low. At least to the naked eye."

Eleri was forced to agree.

"Let me find my notes." He rifled through his work, even though she still felt almost paralyzed by her thoughts. They would have to go back to the Rychenkov-Schmitt house. Who had Marat Rychenkov spoken to the most? Who had Johanna Schmitt spoken to the most? And had she been killed merely because of her relationship to Marat, or was there something more between her and the killer?

Donovan, now standing at the table, listed names. "The people Marat spoke to most were Jivika Das, Greg Whitlow, and Kaya Mazur."

Finally finding her ability to move, Eleri stood up. "They just became our prime suspects."

20

Twenty-four hours later, Donovan stood in Marshall Bennett's office once more. This time he, Eleri, and the mayor were watching live video of the police interviewing their prime suspects.

Yesterday, they had quickly realized the futility of their position. They needed to interview three chief suspects—Jivika Das, Greg Whitlow, and Kaya Mazur—but that was going to be an impossibility, giver their cover stories. The only real access they had was to Kaya, and she was as Eleri's new friend. They weren't even close enough friends for Eleri to ask any hard questions. So they were going to have to deal with being a full step out of the loop.

The interviews would have to be left up to the police. Eleri and Donovan, as the acting FBI agents, created a list of questions they had Bennett forward to the Curie PD to use in the interrogations. Not that the PD probably appreciated that.

As far as the PD knew, Bennett was the source of the questions. Donovan decided to wait and see how far that took them. If he and Eleri had done their jobs, the PD believed they were the only ones investigating what was now a pair of murders.

Since they couldn't do the interviews themselves, they'd asked Bennett for a hack into the system at the police department. He'd managed to provide that quickly, which Donovan appreciated. The interviews were always recorded for the sake of both the interviewees and the officers, so all he had to do was find someone who could loop the live feed to his office. If anyone knew that loop was occurring, at least it was going to the mayor's office and not to the town newcomers. It was the best they could do.

The three of them sat in Bennett's office with him occupying his main seat. Eleri and Donovan had pulled up chairs to his left. They'd once again snuck in through the back way. Donovan didn't like it, and he'd made that clear to Bennett before they'd even sat down.

"Sooner or later, we're going to get caught. Someone will realize that these two random people just keep showing up at the mayor's office for no reason. Our only saving grace is that Kate knows who we are and can stall for us."

Bennett had apparently not considered this before. Donovan entertained a brief, smug thought that while Marshall Bennett might be a fantastic founder and mayor, he'd be a crappy FBI agent. Still, Bennett had been able to get the interview in the PD looped onto his office computer, which at least made a reasonable amount of sense if anyone hacked it. Bennett was up in arms over two murders in his sleepy, intelligent little community, so of course he would want to watch the suspects get interrogated. They were just counting on no one knowing that he had two feds stationed in town.

Bennett nodded to acknowledge Donovan's problem and then queued up the feed of the interview room as an officer led Greg Whitlow inside. Turning to Donovan he asked, "Do you want a loop back to the officers, so you can feed them questions you want the officers to ask?"

Donovan almost threw his head back and laughed. He barely managed to quell the reaction. "I would love to be able to do that, but it's not the technology that's an issue. If I had a dollar for every time a police officer offered some love to the FBI, I would be in debt."

Bennett had appeared righteously appalled. "My officers are not like that! This is an investigation and the point is solving the crime, not pissing on territory."

From the way he threw the words forward, Donovan at least believed that Bennett believed it. However, though Curie was made up of only the best and brightest, Donovan was confident that the police officers—just like everybody else in Curie—were most likely human.

One of the problems of the best and brightest—as Donovan had learned long, long ago—was that they all believed they were the best and brightest. They didn't want anyone else telling them how to do things, particularly their jobs. So, he shook his head at Bennett and simply said, "That's not necessary. I'm sure your officers will do a fine job. We'll figure out another way to ask questions we think of on the fly, if we have to."

Bennett shrugged, seeming to both wonder if Donovan was just giving up, and also trying to assess whether he should just take the win that his officers were excellent, and leave it at that.

They grew silent as they watched Greg Whitlow's interview get started. Whitlow was a physicist with a specialty in kinematics. The officer asked him to state his name, his employment, and his relationship to Marat Rychenkov. Donovan wondered if any of the interviewees would notice that they were not yet getting asked about their relationship to Johanna Schmitt.

Whitlow told them, "Marat and I talked. I think I answered a handful of questions for him. Look, if you toss a ball in the air and you want to know how high it goes, I'm your guy. I can calculate your air resistance, the speed at which it will hit the earth, and the amount of deformation it will experience upon impact—that kind of thing. Whether you can expect your car crash to fling your passengers three hundred feet or not at all."

"So, what kind of questions did you answer for Rychenkov?" The officer asked him. Though the interview was not actually an interrogation, and the officer was not confrontational at all, they could tell Whitlow was a bit nervous. As smart as he was—and especially if he was innocent—he would know that there wasn't anything they could or would get from him in this interview. Still, he seemed twitchy.

Bennett pointed that out. "Do you think it means he's guilty?"

Eleri was the one who shook her head. "Lots of people simply get nervous when interviewed. If you read his level of anxiety, you can see it doesn't really change. He's reacting pretty much the same the whole time, so the questions themselves don't appear to be triggering his upset. I'm guessing he'd look just as twitchy if they asked him what kind of salad he liked best."

"Ah," Bennett said, shaking his head and taking her word. They watched as Whitlow explained more about his interactions with Rychenkov.

"Marat and I even went out one day with a handful of drones. With the drone off, we threw it as high as we could into the air and let it smash into the earth at top speed." He almost smiled at the memory. "I asked him if the drone was fully-loaded, wanting to calculate for the right weight and all. But Marat brought a launcher with him, so we launched these things higher and higher, to see how much damage they sustained upon hitting the ground. They held up pretty well, but there was a definite maximum velocity of impact they could withstand." Whitlow was in his element now, and this was the least twitchy he'd looked the whole time. "We discussed the necessary changes to keep a drone from breaking, should it fall out of the sky."

They'd done this experiment in a local field, he told the investigators. As it turned out, Whitlow had never even been in the Rychenkov-Schmitt home. The officer then followed up, asking, as Donovan had hoped, what kind of relationship he had with Johanna Schmitt. That turned out to be almost nothing. Whitlow's answers were once again anxiety-ridden and so short that the interview concluded almost immediately.

Donovan looked to Eleri, and he could see in her eyes that she, too, believed Whitlow to be a dead end.

The next suspect they led into the room was Kaya Mazur. She did not have Whitlow's natural nervousness. In fact, she tried to interview the police officers, clearly curious about what was going on.

"I'm a nuclear physicist," she said. "I mean, sure, he asked me about atomic numbers and he was looking at some alloys. But, honestly, he was just always asking questions about the work I was doing. There's a huge push to move computing into subatomic particle devices, and he seemed to think that would be the future of robotics, too. He wanted to make his 'bots so they could have their systems easily swapped out as the programming and even the hardware for that changed. While I'm more on the reactor side, I've got a great interest in subatomic computing, and he was smart to be thinking ahead."

It was clear that her area of expertise did not overlap that of the police officers, and it appeared they weren't even sure what questions to ask next. Eleri glanced at Donovan, and he almost laughed as both of them shrugged simultaneously as well, understanding no more than the basics of what she was talking about.

Donovan wished they had gotten Wade in to watch this, but it was mid-morning and Wade was in the middle of teaching his class. Donovan pushed a note across to Eleri. They decided to write them to keep a record of what they'd said, and also in case Bennett's office was bugged, or if their own hack line into the interview was also hacked.

He scrawled, *We need to put Wade on Kaya. They need to be friends.*

Eleri nodded, clearly thinking the same thing, and merely wrote a check mark next to his note.

Just then, Kaya jolted forward. "Do you think he was killed because he was trying to make his drones sub-atomic computing compatible?"

The officers remained steady, answering, "No, ma'am, we don't suspect that."

But now we do, Donovan thought and jotted it down on the page while Eleri nodded.

The officer then steered the conversation to Kaya's relationship with Johanna Schmitt. Kaya Mazur went on about it for almost an hour. The two had been good friends from the time Johanna had moved to town. They'd been in each other's homes. Her children had gone over and had been given coding lessons and cookies.

"Johanna Schmitt made cookies for your children?" the officer asked, making a note even as she asked.

"Marat did." Kaya was not able to hide the hitch in her voice. "He taught my children how to fly drones and how to make the perfect, crackled-top gingersnap. We exchanged holiday presents with them every year."

As Donovan watched, Kaya's voice broke, and he understood why it wasn't long before the officers let Kaya Mazur go as well.

Donovan again glanced to Eleri and they shook their heads simultaneously. Kaya Mazur did not play as their killer. Eleri looked relieved. Donovan had tried not to let his partner's friendship interfere with his assessment, but Kaya's grief felt authentic.

Jivika Das was the last one in. A biological mimicry specialist, she ranked the lowest on Donovan's radar. She studied spider's webs and human knees. Her resume said she'd helped a small town in the Gulf of Mexico replace their oyster population with two non-bivalve species that would accomplish the same ends and anchor the brackish water ecosystem that was failing. He had yet to connect her to anything anyone might have killed Marat Rychenkov for.

Besides, Kaya Mazur had asked about alloys, which tied into Greg Whitlow's ideas. There was at least now a clear path to follow toward what Rychenkov might have been killed for. So Donovan sat back and much more casually watched as Jivika Das was asked similar questions to the first two. She produced similar answers until she was asked what Marat Rychenkov had been discussing with her.

"Bees," she said. "We talked about bees. He had an army of drones that he was making."

Donovan frowned and leaned forward. There was something in her tone, and he looked to Eleri. *Lying?* He scratched on the paper, wishing he was there and he could smell the suspect.

No . . . she wrote back. But the ellipses following the word were telling, and he knew she had the same questions he did.

"Why would he ask you about bees?" the officer inquired, tapping his pen on the tablet in front of him as though it were an absent-minded gesture. It wasn't. It was the officer's tell. Donovan had picked up on it and he wondered if Jivika Das had, too.

"They function as a hive. Marat was trying to get his robots to function similarly to the bees." She smiled, but the smile seemed crooked. "He also asked me about spiders. He was trying to get one of his robots to walk with an eight-legged, tripodal gait. Then he asked about my work with bivalves."

The interview continued on as the other two had. Though he couldn't tell if the officers noticed, Donovan did. Jivika Das was lying.

That's our suspect, he wrote on the pad of paper beside him.

Eleri didn't take her eyes off the monitor but for a second. Still, she nodded.

21

It was that same afternoon that Donovan tried one of his most underhanded tricks. LeDonRic next door often was home early in the afternoons and appeared to watch his nieces, though Donovan had yet to figure out what the brother, Marshawn, was doing that kept him out later in the day.

According to Bennett's files, Marshawn was an inventor, while his older brother LeDonRic worked in one of the local think tanks. If he had to guess, Donovan would have thought it would be the other way around, with Marshawn more likely to be home in the afternoons. But LeDonRic seemed to enjoy having his nieces around, and often the Mazur kids followed along.

While Donovan felt that Kaya Mazur had directed them to tug at some interesting threads during her interview, he did not think she was a major risk. No one had yet interviewed Nate Mazur, and Donovan wasn't sure if he and Eleri would be around to watch that interview, if it happened.

Also, Donovan desperately wanted to interview the kids. While he didn't know about Emersyn and Madisyn James, he knew the Mazur twins had repeatedly been inside the Rychenkov-Schmitt home. Donovan was hoping, whether or not any of the family was at fault in any way, that they might be able to help him solve something —*anything.*

If Cage and Joule had gotten lessons in robotics and how to bake a cookie to perfection, then they might know what else he'd been working on. They might just know better than any adults would. While Marat might have hidden his secret from the adults around him, it was possible he'd flat-out told the kids. Or, more likely, maybe he just didn't guard himself as well and let something slip. The kids might not even know that they knew something.

It was a tricky game, Donovan knew, to get something out of them without flashing his badge. He had to be incredibly subtle—and that was not his strong point. Ever.

Donovan had already pulled school records. All four children were exceptionally bright, even by Curie standards, and that stunned him. Because both the Mazurs and both James brothers had tested in at the high bracket, the children weren't required to meet their own IQ bracket. Still, the school tested all the incoming children to make sure they were putting them into the proper classes.

The top-of-the-curve scores in that group were probably the reason they were all friends in the first place. In the high-quality mix that was Curie High School, these kids were the cream of the crop. But that meant Donovan had to tread even more carefully. If he fucked it up at all, they would likely catch him—even before their parents did. Kids were less likely to have preconceived notions he could play to. *At least they're high schoolers and not pre-schoolers,* he thought.

When the teens came home, he was still out at the mailbox, having lingered just a little to make the walk take longer and hopefully run into them. He waved as they all headed up the walk behind LeDonRic.

"How are you doing?" Joule hollered out, and Donovan leapt at the opportunity.

"Not so good. I mean, the whole thing sucks, and on top of that, Eleri likes to bake when she's sad. So she's making sugar cookies and she's not baking them right."

Joule frowned, "So?"

"So now I'm sad *and* I'm eating bad cookies," he said, "Just to be nice."

It was Cage who leapt into the conversation then. "You need to hit them with high heat and then turn it down a little bit. It helps the tops get crispy and then crack, while the insides stay soft."

"Thank you," Donovan said, and he looked down at the ground

and then looked up, hopefully with a question on his face. "How would you know if your oven was miscalibrated? I think part of the problem is that the oven is off a bit."

It worked. Curie was likely the only place that scheme would work, but it did.

LeDonRic and the children took pity on him, and they headed across the lawn and in through the front door he held open for them.

"Let us take a look at it," LeDonRic told him.

The oven *was* miscalibrated. Donovan knew this because he had turned the knob and then rotated the print dial on the knob ever so slightly so that it would misalign. It had taken some work to create the problem and not make it look like an idiot had messed with it. He'd made sure that when the dial said the temperature was 300 degrees, it was actually closer to 325—enough of a difference to overcook something but not really burn it.

Inside of five minutes, he had another batch of "Eleri's" already prepped, raw cookies on the tray and baking. Four kids crowded their faces around the window to his oven, watching as the cookies softly rose.

"It does look like it's running a little high," Joule was saying, and she reached up, absently turning the knob, ever-so-slightly adjusting the heat for him.

While they watched and tinkered with the heat settings, Donovan turned to LeDonRic. "So, I noticed our house has a gas stove top *and* an electric oven. It was built that way, right? Seems like an odd combination."

LeDonRic didn't appear to think so. "The first residents voted for that combination. *I* voted for it. I guess it is unusual to find both in the same house, but it's the best for each application. Whether you're making cake or a science experiment, that's the best way to be able to control the settings."

"Huh," Donovan said, revealing that he baked neither cakes nor science experiments, at least not with any precision. But since that lack of skill went along with what he'd already demonstrated, it didn't matter.

He paused as he turned and saw that Joule's shoulders had dropped. Even Cage beside her didn't look any too happy about the cookies, though Donovan had eaten a few from the first "failed batch" and could say he and Eleri had managed to make a reasonable recipe.

"What's wrong?" Emersyn asked her friend.

"Marat taught us this."

As Donovan watched, fat tears fell from Joule's eyes, and he felt like a complete shit for doing this to kids. He reminded himself that the kids would want Marat and Johanna's killer—or killers—found.

It was Madisyn who reached over and put her arm around the girl. "He's living on in you. See? It's only been a few days, and already you're spreading one of his secrets. You just have to keep doing that and keep letting people know so that he keeps going."

It was a nice sentiment, Donovan thought, but the man had been murdered, and it was up to the FBI to solve it. He tried to steel himself against the young woman's tears and get down to business. "*He* taught you this?"

Joule nodded, "He taught us how to make the perfect top on cookies. He probably would have voted for the electric ovens and gas stove tops if he'd been here when the town started."

"Madisyn is right. You can carry on his legacy by sharing him with other people," Donovan said softly. "What else did he teach you?"

In that moment, he prayed they would answer—and luckily, they did.

It was Cage who spoke up next. "He taught me how an accelerometer works. We learned in school, too, but he taught me the year before, so by the time we got to class, I already knew."

Donovan smiled and waited for more.

"Johanna taught me how to write code in two languages," Joule piped up, "And how to knit." Her eyes looked downward for a minute, and then up. "We knitted a sweater in binary that had the best pages of Winnie the Pooh on it."

Donovan tried to keep his mouth from falling open. He had to remind himself he was learning things. For example, the kid spoke binary. The kid knit Winnie the Pooh in binary into a sweater. He should not have been surprised. But it also meant that Johanna knew binary. He wanted to jump on them and say, "What else? What else!" but he kept his expression sad and waited.

"You should wear it tomorrow," Emersyn said.

"He tried to teach me how the human heart beats," Cage added, "Though he had only just learned that himself, so I don't know if he really did a good job. He did teach me how to make a robot that rolls and knows when to stop and when to push."

"Now," Joule said, and Donovan had no idea what she was referring to, until she reached up and turned the knob on the oven down another twenty-five degrees. All four heads peered into the window on the oven again, watching the cookies as per Joule's instruction.

"I don't know who would have miscalibrated this oven," Cage said, "But it looks like it's just off. Like the knob is off." He pulled it from its pin and began fiddling with it. Within a moment, he'd found the altered dial face, peeled it, and asked if Donovan had super glue.

"I don't. I just moved in." At least that much was true.

"Well, it should stick when I put it back on–but clearly it can be bumped out of alignment." Cage then went on to explain how to put the knob back on and line up the numbers.

Ten minutes later, the kids had continued reminiscing about Marat and Johanna, about them coming for dinners. About Marat giving them small motherboards one holiday season and then robot housings to put them in the next.

Then, finally they pulled the cookies out of the oven and set them up on top of the stove top with perfectly crackled tops. Donovan handed over most of the cookies to the group as they seemed anxious to get back to LeDonRic's next door and he didn't want to hold them any longer. The art of finding out what they knew was about not letting them know that he was finding it out, and he was afraid he'd already pushed several boundaries in that regard.

They thanked him and promised to return the plate he'd sent, given that he and Eleri had very few dishes. Donovan watched as they headed back across the lawn before he went upstairs into his office and returned with the things he'd removed from the table earlier, so they wouldn't see. He sat down and began taking notes on everything the kids had told him.

22

Eleri had spent the afternoon out, leaving the house in hopes that Donovan could carry out what he'd dubbed "the cookie plan."

She'd considered going back to the *Up N Atom* but thought she might have run the course there. Only so many different people came through the place, and she was concerned about being too obvious. So, while it was only next door to the coffee shop, she'd gone to *The Atomic Diner* this time. She figured that, since it was later in the day, the restaurant might be more heavily populated than the coffee shop now.

She perused the menu until she knew what she was going to order. Still, she had to ask the server, "Why are the burgers filed under 'Theory of Gravity'?"

The redhead with a tag that said *Wendy* smiled at her. "That's because they are so good you can't resist the pull. Also, I think, because if you eat enough of them, you'll experience gravity more fully. Now what I haven't figured out is why the alternate burgers are under 'Electric Universe'."

Eleri found that the names of the burgers now made more sense. The basic burger was an *Aristotle,* and the chain of physicists worked their way up to a *Hawking*—which was fully loaded. She ordered a *Newton* with a milkshake, thinking that eating her feelings was more than plausible, and perfectly acceptable, given the circumstances. No one would question her here.

She handed the menu back without explaining that the turkey, portobello and meat substitute burgers were under "Electric Universe" because only about ten percent of people believed in the alternate theory to gravity. She was proud of herself for knowing that one. She would have to bring Donovan back here.

Just like her first time at the *Up N Atom*, she chose a table in the corner and tried to position her back and her laptop to where no one would be able to see what she was viewing. It wasn't quite as easy to put herself against the wall in the diner, as the booths tended to sit orthogonal to the walls. But the backs of the cushioned seats were high and she did a decent job of blocking the sides of her laptop screen.

While she set up, she tried to watch the comings and goings from the diner. Greg Whitlow came in and sat at a table facing the front door. In just a few moments he was joined by another man, one with a face Eleri didn't recognize.

Quickly, she tapped on her laptop keys and traded the video she was pulling up for the information Bennett had originally sent to them. She had backgrounds on almost every citizen, if she could just face-match them. She also had locations for their work and homes, and Bennett had set it up to link people and show her their DMV pictures so she could more easily place who she was following, chatting with, or in this case, surreptitiously watching across a diner.

In addition to the full dossier on everyone, they'd had Bennett sorting through all the citizens in town—all thirty-plus-thousand of them. His goal was to try to remember whom he had specifically let in and which ones he didn't remember why he'd granted permission to live in his town. Marshall Bennett had already given them several infusions of files, each containing all his information on the people he did not specifically remember letting into his town. Eleri and Donovan had spent time vetting each of them, but had come up cold so far.

It took Eleri a moment to recognize that the man with Greg Whitlow was Keyoor Vergheese, another physicist in town, as the think tank was full of them. Vergheese held a double PhD in physics and theoretical mathematics, and Eleri, even as nerdy as she'd always thought she was, felt her brain twist.

Though she was unable to hear what the two were discussing from this side of the restaurant, the conversation appeared both animated and cordial. Vergheese was not on the list of names that Bennett didn't recognize—at least, not yet. Bennett had been clear he wasn't done going through all of them. So she had nos and yeses, and still a good chunk of 'unknown's. However, Keyoor Vergheese had made Bennett's top cut: He was one of the people Bennet specifically remembered bringing into Curie.

The work of sorting the files was time-consuming, both for the mayor and for them, but Bennett had been writing the occasional note and he remembered Vergheese's resume and that he had wanted him in the local think tank.

What Eleri, and even Donovan, had not been able to decide yet was how far Bennett's memory went toward clearing the person as a suspect. Her concern—which she'd expressed to Donovan—was that people might be sneaking into town, undercutting Bennett's full vetting system. The place was big enough now that Bennett didn't recognize every face, as he had in the early days. So, while she suspected that people had, in fact, either hacked the system or worked their way around it, or possibly even bribed someone for their entry—whether or not it pertained to the murders of Marat Rychenkov and Johanna Schmitt—she was not yet sure.

Keeping an eye on the two men, but also looking around the diner as best she could, Eleri placed as many faces as possible. She was unable to vet the vast majority of staff. Ultimately, she came to the conclusion that they were likely not residents, but "day-trippers," as Bennett often referred to them. They did not have files, and that presented a major problem.

They might live in Lincoln and drive in daily for the job. Or they might be from south of Curie, where there was a small town called Beatrice. It was spelled like Beatrice, but the accent came on the second syllable, making it "Bea-AH-trice," which Eleri found to be wonderfully Nebraskan.

The day-trippers would commute in for the day, work their jobs, and turn around and leave. It tended to be about a thirty-minute drive either way, though there were several other smaller townships and even some of the kids from local farming families working in Curie.

Though Bennett allowed them in to work in his perfect little community, he did not seem to hold them in high regard, something

Eleri wondered about. Bennett had even said many were U Nebraska graduates coming in to "pump gas and maintain the facilities." He'd scoffed as he said the words. When Donovan pushed him about the fact that these were college graduates, Bennett quickly snarked, "The N is for knowledge."

Eleri had both laughed and been appalled, and she again found herself wondering. Here was a whole group of people who had reason to possibly hold a grudge. Were any of the day-trippers at fault in the murders? Had they decided Bennett's rules were elitist and discriminatory? Had they decided to get in on some of the action in Curie? She didn't know.

She did know she and Donovan had checked out all the workers who had come to the Rychenkov-Schmitt home in the past month. Johanna had listed what she knew and had quickly pulled out a house log that she kept so they could keep track of repairs, upgrades, and what they had paid for each. Eleri would have been in complete awe of the woman if she had not seen the jumble of shoes she kept under her bed.

With her list in place, Eleri now covered it with another page. She didn't need anyone passing by or asking if she needed a refill on her Atomic Tea to see that she was listing the names of the patrons, their professions, and whether or not they had Marshall Bennett's seal of approval. When Whitlow and Vergheese left, she went back to watching the video footage from the Schmitt home.

Even watching four different camera feeds simultaneously wasn't getting her through the hours quickly enough. She watched much of it on super-fast forward and found herself tripping over movements that went by too quickly. She would then have to back up the footage only to see that a few random creatures had strayed into the backyard. Once she was caught when a dog had come up to the front porch in the middle of the night, sniffing for something.

Eleri paused at each hint of intrusion and watched carefully. She wondered if the dog belonged to someone who had stopped in front of the house and was maybe eyeing it a little too carefully. She watched it again, but in the end, she couldn't conclude there was anything other than a dog having been let out to wander the neighborhood on his own. For a moment, she wondered if the dogs here were not also intellectually exceptional.

She watched the video from all through the night, four camera feeds at a time, and found no one had broken into the Rychenkov-Schmitt home. It was not until she was watching the daytime feeds that she caught it. In fact, as she rewound the video, she realized it came up right as the footage butted up to the live feed.

Someone was at Johanna Schmitt's home *now.*

The time stamp showed Eleri he'd been at the back door all of five minutes earlier. She watched as he entered the code and walked right into the home.

Shit! She wanted to scream it loud and long. Someone was actively committing a crime and she was stuck at the diner, with half her burger left. She raised her hand for the check and began closing her laptop and gathering materials.

She didn't want to call Donovan—and per their own paranoid protocol, she couldn't. They were worried about their communications being hacked. Even texting him would be too risky. She'd screwed up by not developing a signal phrase, like texting him to ask him if the cookies tasted good, but she'd not expected to catch a break-in right in the act.

The server, though one Eleri would have called fast and prompt earlier, now seemed to take forever to bring the check and to-go box to her, though Eleri was sure that was her own impatience speaking. As soon as she was packed up, she left cash on the table rather than paying by credit card and headed right out the door.

Her main problem was trying to appear calm. People anywhere might wonder about someone jumping up and dashing out of the diner. The last thing she needed was to be remembered when she was out and about. Once in her car though, she blazed through town, debating whether to get Donovan or to head directly to the Rychenkov-Schmitt home.

Given that the break-in was already in progress, and though there was nothing she could do, or probably would do, she headed toward C'thulhu Heights. Maybe she could see someone driving away from the home, or just pass by as they were leaving. Maybe—even if she couldn't ID the person—she could find some characteristic about them that would help narrow down their hunt.

Instead, when she pulled up, the house was dark and quiet. Turning the corner, she opened the laptop and logged into the feed again. If she was hacked, she'd give something away, but the chance to catch their killer in action was too tempting, and she had taken it.

The footage booted up and revealed the house and yard were both empty.

She'd missed her chance.

23

Though Eleri was frustrated and exhausted, there was nothing she could do now. She'd missed the intruder, and as her case was not going to magically be solved tonight, she had to maintain her cover.

On top of that, despite the darkness creeping into the sky, she wasn't done for the day. She and Donovan quickly changed clothes and headed out into the evening.

As they headed into the city of Lincoln, she recounted what she'd seen. "I did see several cars leaving the C'thulhu Heights neighborhood on my way in. At the time, I had no idea if any of them was my perp or if the perp was still in the home."

"Makes sense," Donovan replied as they wound through Copernicus Circle. She took a moment to look at the dynamic sculpture of the solar system. At least the planets were pretty. The lights at night made them glow, something she'd not seen before. Still, she pulled her focus away from the shiny, nerdy things and worked to get her information to her partner. It was one of the most important things she could do in the case.

"I'm pretty sure none of the drivers I saw were the person breaking into the Rychenkov-Schmitt house." The intruder seemed to be long gone by the time she arrived and was likely driving carefully around the neighborhood as though he was just out for a stroll, a cruise, or whatever. "The murderer has made it clear that he—or she, or both of them—can get in and out of the house with relative ease. No one has reported any suspicious activity. And I would think the past three days, with Johanna now murdered, too, would make people actually pick up the phone and call if they saw something sketchy."

"I want to believe you're right." The car left the city limits and she found herself out of the lights and buffeted by cornfields on either side. They drove casually into Lincoln and she thought of her own frantic exodus from C'thulhu Heights, and how she'd been trying to case the whole neighborhood and catch an intruder as he left. But she'd come up spectacularly empty-handed.

The problem was, she wasn't even sure their perp was a male. From the footage, they could see the body was an average size, the shoulders not terribly broad, the outfits never revealing enough to determine a shape that would indicate a gender. She didn't have the normal things to help her rule out suspects either, like skin tone, tattoos, hair color, anything. She'd been close to screaming and smacking her steering wheel in frustration, but she couldn't even do that, because what if somebody saw her?

Instead, she'd pasted on a smile and waved as she passed other drivers or the occasional person walking on the street. Whether or not she knew them, she lifted her hand in a friendly gesture. Just being a friendly neighborhood newbie on the outside, while on the inside, she grew ever more frustrated with missing her suspect.

Once she'd gotten back to the Frank Lloyd Wright house, she'd sat down, almost thumping her laptop too hard onto the table as she popped it open for Donovan. Pulling up the appropriate footage, she pointed.

"Oh, wow! They were just there!" He'd leaned in close.

"Yes," she said, "and I missed them. I raced over, but they were gone before I got there."

He sighed and tried to console her. "We have to head out to do the autopsy in Lincoln. I was hoping you'd be back sooner."

She'd shaken her head. "This was why I wasn't."

"It was a good call. They just don't all pan out."

His consolation hadn't fully sunken in, and Eleri wasn't sure it would. Still, she'd changed and hopped into the car within just a few minutes. Too irritated to take care with her cover, she figured it was good they were getting out of town while she cooled down. She continued trying to tell him who she saw on her botched mission.

"One of the drivers I saw was Wade. One was a mother in a minivan. Though the windows were a bit tinted, I think I saw three young children inside. I have a really hard time believing that she put on coveralls and broke into this house while leaving three small kids in her car."

"That is hard to swallow," Donovan said. "I don't put anything past the residents of Curie, though."

"The third was a teenage girl, about Emersyn and Madisyn's age, somewhere in there, so I don't think she was our break-in either. It wasn't Joule though. Also, she was driving a very flashy sports car, not the kind of thing you would drive around to break into a home."

"Or *exactly* the kind of thing you would drive around to break into a home," Donovan countered. "I mean, it's Curie. If someone's smart, they'll do the exact opposite of what we would expect."

"Like leave their fingerprints all over the place," Eleri thought, getting into the game, "Or they might leave hair and DNA, and then say, 'But that couldn't possibly be me. I'm too smart to have done that.'"

Donovan nodded.

"Shit," she said. "That means most of our rule-outs aren't even really rule-outs. We're so fucked." She said it with as much of a wry smile as she could muster, though inside, she just twisted up a little further.

But then, Donovan aimed her back toward what needed to be done. The body of Johanna Schmitt was now waiting at the CDC offices. Unlike her husband, there was no spouse to complain about the long wait time. Also unlike her husband, there was no hiding that this had been a murder.

"Let's go do an autopsy!" Donovan tried to throw a little glee into it, although he fell short. It was hardest when it was someone you'd known.

"You're doing it?" Eleri asked.

"I requested it. Initial tox screens are back and so are the DNA preliminaries. I wanted them first this time."

She was glad she'd put a bag of gummy animals into her purse and carried change for the vending machines. Autopsies could go on for hours, especially one like this, where she suspected that there were few clues. She also suspected those few-and-far-between clues would be necessary to solving the case. There was no room to cut corners.

After getting into disposable coveralls, Donovan set his recorder down and started dictating his initial findings. Eleri stood by with her notepad, both of them looking like paper monsters. Her intent was to take handwritten notes—all the things that didn't belong in the official report, and all the ideas and questions they needed to follow up on. Anything specific to a NightShade investigation that would never wind up in the official paperwork. Also, she would hold spare organs and act as his assistant when necessary.

She swallowed. It was hard seeing Johanna there on the table. It was harder thinking it was her fault the woman was dead. But Eleri shoved that idea aside. She couldn't change the past, and the best thing she could do for Johanna and Marat now was to solve their murders and at least get them some justice.

"Tox screens are negative," Donovan said, having looked at the results for probably the third time. He hadn't wanted it to be negative, and neither had Eleri, so he kept looking, she assumed, hoping he would find something new each time, some little quirk or anomaly that led him to something. But even after three times searching and comparing each number to the normal ranges, he'd found nothing.

"You got a hit on the Sodium Pentothal, though," she told him.

"Yes. I'm glad we checked." *He was the one smart enough to point out the need for that test,* she thought. "We'll be sure to find and note the injection site."

"So whoever it was wanted information from Johanna Schmitt," he said. She watched as he nodded, glad they could at least figure that part out. But that was all they could conclude from that one test. So Eleri did some of her own observations, starting at the beginning and walking around the body, looking for physical clues.

The body was still clothed, untouched, as they'd requested. Given that they had no reason to believe there was any kind of bio-agent or anything the CDC should be worried about, the CDC had allowed the unusual request.

Donovan hit the button, turning off the recorder for a moment as he leaned over the body. Slowly, he breathed in. He trailed from head to foot and back up. Then he looked up at Eleri. "I smell something."

She almost asked him, "What is it?" but knew that if he could identify it, he would have said so. Instead she asked, "Can you identify a chemical class that it belongs to?"

He shook his head and looked frustrated. It seemed to be their normal expression for this case. "It smells familiar, but I can't place it."

"So what does it smell like?" she prodded.

"Like dairy. It's like butter," he said, "but a bit chemical-y."

She wrote his comment down, having no clue what it was. At least there was some level of information. "How strong is it?" she asked.

"Faint, very faint."

She leaned over and sniffed the body. "I don't detect it." In human terms, she would have been said to have a “good nose.” She could occasionally smell when a dead body had been diabetic in life, or had an infection. But Donovan made her senses seem pointless in comparison, and she trusted what he said.

Though it was something, it was only a scent. Until they found the next connection to it, it was yet another puzzle piece that connected to nothing. Giving up on getting anything else from the smell, Donovan punched the recorder back on and began working.

They checked first for bruising, lifting arms and legs, rolling her over, looking for what was obvious. She had marks on her forearms. *Typical defensive wounds,* Eleri thought. When they turned the black light on, far more bruising was visible. Johanna Schmitt also had marks on her legs and shoulders.

Next, they removed the clothing, being as reverent as they could while still doing their job.

“Look!” Eleri pointed and Donovan immediately grabbed for the black light.

What had been a red mark on her shoulder turned into a fairly reasonable facsimile of a handprint-shaped bruise under the special light.

“It’s not enough to make a determination,” Eleri lamented. “Her shirt and sweater must have protected her.” *But not enough to save her,* she thought. In the end, all the clothing had done was damage the evidence.

“She fought harder than it originally appeared.” Donovan was still looking down at the bumps and bruises that showed under the light. “Not enough to break the skin.”

“Why not? That’s what’s bothering me.” Eleri talked freely as soon as Donovan turned off the recorder again. “She knew her husband was murdered. She even had her hands and feet tied while she was alive, yet she didn't fight enough to even break the skin. Though she *did* fight back some."

When they gave up on this path, declaring it yet another unconnected puzzle piece, Donovan turned the black light off and cut the initial Y-shaped incision. According to autopsy format, he pulled out each organ and weighed it. Not according to autopsy format, he lifted it in his hands to his nose. He opened Johanna's stomach and reported, to both the recorder and Eleri, the contents of her stomach. "Pasta, red sauce, about three hours before death."

"String theory, red quark," Eleri muttered, and he looked up. She explained. "She ate at *The Atomic Diner* before her class. We have that in the report." She tapped the end of her pen on the notepad as though to show it to him. "She must have had the string theory pasta with red quark sauce."

Donovan looked at her, and she shrugged. They continued on, slowly, through the paces of the autopsy, stopping periodically. They would turn off the recorder and add in extra steps that made sense to two FBI agents from NightShade. Most yielded nothing of value. When at last Donovan closed the incision, they moved the body aside, but they still weren't done.

They took the clothing and carefully checked it for blood, fibers, and anything else that might identify Johanna Schmitt's killer.

"I don't see *anything*." Eleri sighed, though she knew the CDC techs would check it under every light filter and vacuum it for fibers in the morning, now that she and Donovan had concluded their autopsy.

Donovan, still in his gloves and full gown, pulled his mask down under his nose and carefully lifted the clothing to his nose. "It has the same odor as found on the body," Donovan told her.

"Is it the same as what we found on Marat?"

"Maybe."

When they had the clothing bagged and ready for the techs, they turned to the piece they had saved for last. Neither of them had wanted the autopsy contaminated by any prior knowledge of the killer. But the CDC had swabbed the body in several obvious places when she'd been brought in. They'd not been lucky enough to have a bite mark to swab, but her defensive wounds had yielded something. The lab had already run allele matches and Donovan laid the electropherogram maps out on the counter.

The DNA samples from each of the swabs matched to Johanna and faint trace amounts all matched to the same unknown assailant.

"Damn," Eleri muttered softly, feeling the late hour press in on her. She was going to need those stupid gummy fruits as soon as she was out of the lab. "Not enough clarity to get a match in any known database."

"No, but we do know it's a male. And while there's a lot of dropout here, we can start collecting DNA from anyone we suspect. We can't match, but we should be able to rule out at least some people."

"At least this time," she said, "we don't have jack shit."

24

Donovan had expected to come down the stairs this morning with a renewed vigor for the case, but it hadn't happened.

He'd slept in again, thinking that would help. He'd wandered down here, careful not to wake Eleri. He puttered around the kitchen for a little bit, making himself first one bowl of cereal then another—different—one, as though that would make everything okay. It didn't. He could not find any motivation to do anything.

He sat on the couch to eat his frosted flakes and looked out at the backyard, contemplating the small section of grass corralled by the tall fence. He could see the roof of the house that sat directly behind his. Given the single slope of the designs—rather than a normal, pitched roof—he couldn't see in or even see any windows. He could see a little bit of the sides of the houses caddy-corner to his backyard, but there was foliage in the way.

He liked that the neighborhood here had preserved the trees as much as possible during the building. Not that he would have chosen this chunky-looking, abstract looking design for himself. He didn't dislike it, but he would have chosen something more organic. Even the way the houses were set on the lots was in perfect orthogonal layouts. From where he sat, he could not see LeDonRic's house next door at all.

Attempting to call eating his cereal "doing work," he did have to feed himself, after all—he tried to think of ways that he and Eleri might collect DNA samples from Curie residents to test against the DNA they had recovered.

The first problem was that the sample from Johanna's attacker was scrappy at best. A good electropherogram showed sharp bumps where a person had certain alleles in their DNA, but this one, like many bad ones, had places where instead of a nice peak, there was only a little mound. Whether that meant it was there but there wasn't enough to detect, or it meant the duplication system for small samples had randomly dropped it out, or if it meant it wasn't there at all was entirely unclear.

So there were numerous spots on this DNA graph where one would have to look at the allele position and simply mark it unknown. Otherwise, it would be easy to rule out too many people and possibly rule out the killer, or rule *in* too many. He wondered if it was worth it to run tests on everyone they could possibly gather samples from, and whether Westerfield would fund such an endeavor or not.

Donovan ate his last bite of cereal and, still holding onto the bowl, rested it on his leg as he thought. That was the second problem: it probably *wasn't* worth it. Testing that many people that fast would be expensive and time-consuming. In order to have any usefulness at all, they would have to rush the results. They'd rushed the screening on Johanna Schmitt, because any DNA they found on her would most likely belong to her killer and would have hopefully pointed directly to someone and given them an arrest.

What Donovan was pondering now was merely collecting samples from everyone he could. That would be a crapshoot at best. It wouldn't be one test, it would be twenty, or fifty, depending on how good he was at collecting the samples surreptitiously. They would be small samples, much like the kind run from Johanna Schmitt, not the kind people sent in to the hobby DNA places where they were asked to fill a vial with spit. No, this would require a primary step of duplication of the DNA that was found. The PCR process to do that would take time and often created dropouts and errors. It wasn't a huge risk, but it was a big enough one that the expenditure of testing everyone he could gather DNA from was less and less feasible.

Westerfield would certainly rush order a test if Donovan and Eleri had a reasonable suspicion on someone. As of yet, they had no one.

Westerfield had called the day before, and would surely call today as well, given that they'd just performed the autopsy, to keep up with where they were in the case. Donovan was not looking forward to saying, once again, that they had done a lot but made little progress. As of right now, they had two dead bodies and zero real suspects.

So he sat there on the couch, looking out the window, until Eleri came downstairs. Though he wasn't sure how long it was, it was probably at least half an hour. She plopped down next to him on the couch, once again looking a little worse for wear.

He'd seen her dressed up for the parties her parents threw. He'd seen her all put together to go out for an interview, but he'd also seen her like this. He probably didn't look any better. The case was wearing them low.

The words out of her mouth were not the ones he expected. "You should call Walter," she said.

"What?"

"You know, *your girlfriend*. Please tell me she's still your girlfriend." Eleri closed her eyes and squinched her face, as though she would be unable to withstand a negative answer.

Donovan laughed. "Yes, she's still my girlfriend."

"Then you should call her."

"Why?"

"Because you haven't called her in several days, right?"

"We don't talk like that. We're not like you." He was leaning back against the couch too, now.

"No, I get that. But she's your girlfriend. You feel like shit. Well, you look like you feel like shit, anyway."

He laughed, since he'd just been thinking the same thing about her. "And you feel better after you talk to her. I know you don't want to burden her. I do understand that, but what you need to learn about friends and girlfriends, is that that's our job. Like right now, Avery's not available. He's already out at the rink practicing or in some gym somewhere doing thirty thousand squats or whatever that coach makes them do. I don't know. I could call him, but the coach would get mad, so I'm going to lay this on you: I am so fucking frustrated."

"Yeah, me too," he said, wondering if he should get a third bowl of cereal, even knowing that he didn't have a third type in the house. Sadly, that was the extent of his decision-making ability this morning.

"We should have something more by now," she said.

"We should," he agreed.

"We let Johanna Schmitt die."

"Not so much." For the first time in her little rant, he disagreed with her. "We had no reason to believe she was in danger. They were looking for something of Marat's. Marat seemed to be the problem. The killer had already removed him. *She* didn't think she was in danger. As soon as we had any idea that there was a danger, we made immediate efforts to remove her from the situation."

"I know," Eleri interrupted, "but I think part of the reason she didn't think she was in danger was because first she'd thought she was hallucinating all of it, and second, when we told her *we* didn't think she was in danger, she bought into it."

"El, that's plausible," he replied, "but even so, I don't know how we could have assessed it differently." *Unless we were psychic.* But he didn't say that out loud, because he knew she probably *was* psychic on some level. It didn't matter anyway; she picked up on his thoughts.

"Not without being psychic?" Eleri declared as she sat upright and looked at him, her snarky tone indicating what she thought of that. "Then what good am I?"

"El, you can't blame yourself for not seeing everything. You get whatever information you get, and you didn't get this. When you didn't get the impulse that Johanna Schmitt was in danger, we didn't know to go looking for it. That's not on you. You did get that impulse later and we acted on it."

She leaned her head back against the edge of the couch again as her stomach grumbled. Having slept in late, and now walking down here and talking to him without eating, he could almost smell the hunger on her.

Still, she'd rather complain, and he understood. He would, too.

"When I thought these things were just hunches that I had, I took them. I ran with them. I did a lot of good, but I didn't blame myself when I missed something, because the hunches were out of my control. I thought of them as things that came *to me*. Now, I know better. I know that I have some control over it, *or I should,* and I'm wondering if I shouldn't leave the FBI for three months, go to a retreat somewhere, and try to hone my skills. Because I missed this. Big time."

Donovan thought about that for a moment. What she said made

sense, "But," he replied, "by the same token, so should I. I smelled something buttery or dairy-smelling on the body last night. Should I go somewhere for three months and do sniff tests so that I'm better able to classify all the chemicals I might smell? I could have saved her life if I'd identified what was on Marat. I could still save the next life if I knew what this was."

"Maybe," Eleri replied. "But the problem is, just because you know the chemical compound doesn't mean you could actually save the person."

He paused for a moment, letting that sink in. "*Exactly,* Eleri," he said. "Even if you had known that Johanna Schmitt was in danger earlier, it wouldn't have necessarily saved her life. These people wanted her. They've been able to get in and out of the house—"

"We could have taken her out of the house!" Eleri protested.

"We could have, but they've been able to get in and out of her house even with a code change, with no problem at all. What makes you think they wouldn't have found her in another house? They found her *at work*! Should we have taken her completely out of the state, at which point we would have lost all her information about finding these people? We wouldn't have been able to do anything of value. And we didn't think this would happen."

She sighed heavily, and Donovan at last found the motivation he'd been looking for. "So let's do something now. Let's look up the chemicals, to narrow it down."

Finally pulling his ass off the couch, he extended a hand to Eleri. He sat at his computer while she opened her own and fixed herself a bowl of cereal.

Five minutes later, he got his first hit. "2-acetyl-1-pyrroline. It gives off a *buttered popcorn* scent. Probably not the right thing, but it should go on the list."

"Streptococcus milleri," Eleri said a few moments later. "Smells like butter. I have my fingers crossed that this is not going to be a long list," then she added, "Butane-2,3-diol."

"Diacetyl," he said, but it was almost ten minutes after the last addition to their collection. Fifteen minutes later, they called off the search. "Okay, he said, we know a short list of what it might be. How do we narrow *this* down?"

25

The problem, Eleri decided, was that Donovan had smelled butter on the victim. "Victim" was how she tried to think of Johanna Schmitt now, rather than as someone who was becoming a friend. So Donovan smelled butter, and they had narrowed it down to three different chemicals. One option had been *streptococcus milleri,* the bacteria responsible for strep infection, but Donovan had asked the CDC to run a quick test, and the microscope had revealed no strep microbes. They promised to run a culture, but Eleri was calling it a negative.

"So, if you didn't smell a random and unrelated infection—"

"Which is unlikely, because I also smelled it on Marat."

"No, it's plausible they had the same infection. They lived in the same home." She shot down his caveat. "If they were unrelated, yes, but that's not this case. Still, I think that's not it. Likely, something on our list of chemicals is in a compound that was given to her. Unless, she's smelled like butter before? When she was alive?"

Donovan shook his head no, and Eleri continued. "Then it's likely something we haven't tested for. Some medication or street drug that made it less likely for her to fight back."

"Excellent," Donovan said. "I'm not a chemist. I don't know which of those chemicals would cause that kind of response, or which drug would create that kind of chemical when it broke down. I mean, I looked them up, and none of these chemicals is actually a drug that does that or is a breakdown product of a drug that does that."

"I know," Eleri said, "and the shitty thing is, the easiest way to find out would be go into town and find a chemist and ask them. But we can't do that."

"Maybe we can," Donovan mused, his brain churning as he looked off into the middle distance. "Maybe we can get Bennett to get the PD to ask. We could give them the information, tell them what to ask the chemists, but don't tell them what the situation is."

"They'll figure it out," Eleri said. "If we give them enough information—what you smelled, what the possible chemicals are, and that it might have been used to subdue someone, and the PD is asking the questions—they might very well figure out that it pertains to Johanna Schmitt's murder."

The two of them debated for a while whether the question might sound better coming from Bennett, but decided that it ultimately would not, and maybe it didn't matter if the chemists understood that Johanna Schmitt had been drugged. At least, Eleri and Donovan thought it might not.

"What's the worst case scenario?" she said. "Somebody spreads the information around? The killer learns? Maybe people start watching their drinks."

"I don't know."

"There's some negative to this getting spread around, too. The killer would know that we are onto at least part of what he did."

"Well, the part that the PD knows," Donovan interjected.

"Yes, but the less they know that we know, the more we can do our job."

"I'm not sure. My hands feel so tied right now," he said. "I really want to interview those kids, too, but we can't do it."

"You got some decent information out of them the other day," Eleri reminded him.

"Yes, but for the amount of time and effort it took to get that little information, an interrogation would be far, far more useful."

"*Interview*," she said, laughing. "We don't interrogate kids, remember?"

"I don't know," he said. "I'm about to interrogate these kids. We've got two dead bodies."

They'd eventually come to the decision to have the police question a local chemist or two, and they passed that information along to Marshall Bennett. But that task wasn't their only work for the day. They'd ended up getting up, and getting dressed, and deciding that the thing to do was to get into the Schmitt-Rychenkov house themselves. Johanna had showed them around when they visited, but it had been a brief tour, as they'd spent the bulk of their time interviewing her.

"We haven't done a good, full search of the house," Eleri pointed out. "We've been letting the killer do it, and we haven't wanted to bother anything, so that the killer wouldn't notice, as Johanna did, that someone else had been in."

"But you think it's time to risk it?"

"I do."

So though they'd already called Bennett with one assignment that morning, they enlisted him for a second. Dressed in disguise so hopefully no one would see them going into the house, or at least not recognize them, they headed out and had the mayor let them in the front door.

It was a Saturday morning, and people would be out and about. In fact, they passed a family with a young girl on a pink tricycle heading down the sidewalk on their way in, and several more as they turned the corners to get to the Rychenkov-Schmitt home.

The stone front looked daunting this morning, Eleri thought. On the other hand, she only looked *interesting,* with her hair tucked up under a dark brown wig that fully changed the shape of her face. But it wouldn't change her voice, or her size, and if somebody found them, it wouldn't stop them from recognizing her.

Bennett, along with his assistant Kate, met them at the door and followed them into the house. This time, she and Donovan wore shirts that said they worked for Curie Gas. Hopefully, that was something no one would question. With two deceased homeowners and no one watching the place, the gas had to be checked out.

Once inside, Bennett and Kate sat on the couch and worked on their tablets while waiting. Eleri and Donovan began searching.

Eleri took the offices upstairs, while Donovan headed for the garage. She searched the drawers and, when that yielded nothing, she searched for panels at the backs of the drawers. She pulled the files out completely, lifting the heavy masses in pieces and knocking on the bottoms. She was looking for false hideaways, fake fronts, and unused space.

The desk yielded nothing aside from a very cute, flip-down front panel, which was part of the design. However, the only thing Marat Rychenkov kept there was a massive pen collection. Eleri even unscrewed a couple of them and rattled the others, looking for information that might have been hidden inside.

The question was, how much effort would Marat Rychenkov have gone to to hide his work? He hadn't seemed to even know he was in danger. However, the answer had to be that he'd hidden it pretty well, because the killer had come back several times, maybe even once with a friend, and still not found it. Eleri renewed her search.

Marat's office turned out to be a bust, and though she had tried to put everything back exactly as it was before, it was clear she had rattled the interior.

She headed next into Johanna Schmitt's office, and here, she got lucky. Three drawers in, she found a rack with hanging file folders, but the drawer wasn't very full. However, as she pulled it out, she noticed it weighed ever-so-slightly more than she'd expected. At first, she thought she was wrong, but when she tapped on the underside of the drawer, a false bottom slightly shifted. After three tries, Eleri managed to pull it up.

Three lab notebooks waited inside for her.

Johanna's? she thought, lifting them out. Johanna had no idea her husband had anything worth killing for . . . *Unless she'd been lying*.

Eleri flipped over the lab notebooks, checking them for marks or titles. They were unlabeled on the front, just like Johanna's. However, once she looked inside, these pages were clearly not in Johanna Schmitt's handwriting. Deciding not to search further until she had more information, she picked up the notebooks and headed downstairs to Donovan.

"I found three lab notebooks," she told him, "in Johanna's office."

"Johanna hid them?"

"Maybe. But they are in Marat's handwriting."

"What do they say?"

"That's just it. They're coded," she said. Her irritation, mixed with admiration, showed in the depth of her voice. She handed the notebooks to him and watched as he flipped through.

"Hmm," he said. "The code doesn't look unbreakable, but I can't read it."

"Same here. Did you get anything in the garage?"

"No," he said. "I have the feeling that I'm looking directly at it and I can't see it."

"So, let's do two sets of eyes. Come up to Johanna's office with me and help me check, and then we'll both come back down here."

While Marshall Bennett and Kate looked up each time Eleri passed by, she just shook her head and they went back to reading. Having them sitting there was a good reminder that this wasn't a full FBI home search. They only had as much time as the gas company would use, and that probably wasn't much longer.

Together, she and Donovan searched the rest of Johanna's office. They checked the back of the closet, the high places and the low, and found nothing more than the notebooks Eleri had already discovered. When they declared the rest of it a bust, they headed back down into the garage and began a similar search.

"He's already used a false bottom drawer once," Eleri said, so they put extra effort into checking the drawers.

"I already looked at the circuit panel, but it's legit," Donovan told her. She nodded and checked behind the punchboard Marat had used to hang his tools.

"Shit! El. I got something." Donovan held a piece of wood in his hand. There were only four drawers in the built-in workstation in the garage, but the bottom one had also had a false panel.

Given the pile of papers and old motherboards on the floor, Eleri guessed it had been buried deep. "What was in it?"

Donovan held his hand out displaying a small drive.

26

Donovan found himself once again sitting at the main table in the Frank Lloyd Write house, thinking maybe this wasn't the best idea. He had set up offices for both himself and Eleri *upstairs*. The offices were upstairs on purpose. However, in the issue of working together, they'd wound up almost exclusively working at what should have served as a dinner table.

He'd put the offices out of the way on purpose, to keep their work away from anyone stopping by. With the open floor plan down here, anyone who made it to the front door would see they worked at the table. And if a visitor saw *what* that work was, their cover would be blown.

Still, the table down here gave them the space they needed to spread out. Here, they could work face to face, tossing their problems back and forth. They would run into each other working here and catch an idea, so it seemed worthwhile, although both knew that if someone came over to the house, he and Eleri were running a huge risk.

Interestingly enough, a knock came at the door right then. Eleri was upstairs in the shower, and so Donovan popped up even as he rotated his laptop to keep the screen away, hitting several buttons to blank out the screen. He also had to make sure that Rychenkov's notebooks were well hidden, so he pushed them deep into the bag he kept beside his seat for just this purpose. God forbid somebody recognized *those*.

When he finally got the door open, Maggie Wells stood on his small front patio. As Donovan said hello, Maggie's visit made him proud, and he chalked it up to his and Eleri's ability to go out and make friends in this community as quickly as they had.

LeDonRic stood on the step just behind her, but even so, managed to tower over his girlfriend. Still, it was Maggie who spoke. "Hey, I'm sorry, this is late notice, but we wanted to invite you to dinner tonight."

"Oh?" Donovan asked, letting the question hang, as it sounded as if Maggie had more to say.

She did. "Apparently, the kids were talking about Marat and Johanna when they were over here helping with the cookies yesterday. The kids said they wanted to thank you, that you had gotten them thinking about what their friends had contributed that would live on."

"We mostly talked about cookies," Donovan mumbled.

"You helped them more than you know. So, anyway, we all decided we wanted to do a dinner tonight and just tell our good stories to remember Marat and Johanna. I know that you never met Marat and that you only knew Johanna a little bit, but I got the impression she and Eleri really hit it off. I know—I'm the one who pushed them together."

Donovan only nodded.

"So anyway," Maggie continued, "it's up to you, but we thought you guys might like to come. We just wanted to share our memories. We think it's going to be a while before we have Johanna's funeral because of the . . . situation."

Ignoring the phrasing about the "situation," Donovan quickly thanked her for the invite and readily accepted for both him and Eleri. He'd been looking forward to sitting down and reviewing whatever was on Rychenkov's USB. His hope was that there was a key for the code or a clue to help them break it.

He hadn't found one while searching through the notebooks, though it made sense that he wouldn't. Anyone as smart as Marat would not take the time to code his notes and then leave the key right there with the notebooks. But now, instead of going through the USB and looking for files, he was heading to the grocery store looking for a side dish.

He knocked on the bathroom door upstairs and informed Eleri about the new plans for the evening. She sounded excited, though he couldn't quite tell if she wanted a dinner with friends or a mining expedition for information. Likely, it would be both. So the two of them headed out to put together their part of the meal.

Donovan figured they had just enough time to buy their food and show up to the dinner. He'd volunteered them for a salad and was proud that he'd remembered to ask what other foods the guests might be bringing and how many people would be attending.

Eleri was walking him through the necessary vegetables for two different salads. He wasn't really following, but he understood where she was aiming. Then she made them buy two big bowls to serve it in. "We don't have these."

"Yes, we do." He could have sworn he'd seen something.

They made it home and, though he'd argued against it, it turned out that Eleri was right. They had no serving-size salad bowls. Only cookware. *Undercover life was going to be the death of him.*

"I knew it!" Eleri said with the kind of limited glee one got from winning something almost useless. They had two pans, three pots, and only the most rudimentary of kitchen supplies. "I wonder if our lack of kitchenware and our lack of buying any new kitchenware makes it look like we're not planning on staying?"

For a moment, Donovan almost wished he *could* stay here. Curie was a big, bubbling pot of crazy, but he liked it. He shook his head. "I don't think that's the case. I showed up with a moving van and I don't think people saw that it was mostly empty. Also everyone seems to understand we don't cook very well, so I don't think our lack of kitchen supplies is a red flag."

They put the fixings into the bowls, gathered their bottles of dressing into a spare bag, and headed next door. Eleri could not have been more excited, and truth be told, neither could he. All four of the kids would be there, as would both the Mazur parents, LeDonRic and Maggie, as well as Marshawn James, LeDonRic's brother, and the girls' father.

LeDonRic had a table much larger than Donovan would have expected for a single man. Then again, it was a big house, and when

Donovan looked at Maggie, he wondered if maybe his neighbor didn't plan on being single for much longer.

Marshawn and his two daughters arrived last as Maggie was setting everything out with Joule and Cage's help. Once they were all seated, Maggie decided a little reverence was necessary. Though it wasn't religious, they all joined hands and Maggie gave them a short time to offer a prayer in whichever way they thought best, or a moment of silence for the two stunning losses the group had suffered.

When the moment ended and Maggie lifted her head, everyone dug in, chattering about the food. The melancholy left briefly, but it was Maggie who brought the meal back onto point. "Okay, let's do this. We're going to eat, and we're going to try and keep it happy, but let's share our best stories."

Cage started, but first he looked to his mom. "Do you remember the time Johanna's crock pot cracked?"

"Oh, my God." Kaya put her face in her hands, and she laughed though she had tears in her eyes. She motioned to Cage to tell the story.

"So the crock pot was very old and the ceramic bowl was built into the housing with the heating mechanism. So, when it cracked, all the food went into the heating unit. The chili she'd been making fried on the coils. I would think you couldn't set chili on fire, but somehow she managed to do it."

"It was on fire?" Eleri said. "Did she burn down the house?"

"No, it was a small fire. It was relatively contained, and she actually laughed at it—"

"She loved that chili though. She had to have been mad to lose a batch."

Cage nodded, "But she had Fritos sitting out for when she served it. So she took one and held it into the fire and we lit Fritos off of the flames and she explained to me about the coils and how they worked." He offered a sad smile.

"Please tell me you eventually put out the fire?" Donovan entered the story for the first time.

"Of course! She had these little fire extinguishers, four of them. Even though only two people lived in the house, she said she knew things like this tended to happen, especially around her. So she had a little fire extinguisher for every person. We each grabbed one and we put it out. It was a horrible mess, though."

Joule chimed in next. "Marat left her with the cookies one time, remember? And she put some special kind of sugar on them, and she caught that on fire, too."

"Oh, that's right. She wanted to use the baking glitter on it, and she didn't know that cake glitter was for decorating and not baking. Because it's *flammable*," Kaya filled in the rest of it.

Eleri smiled, and Donovan did, too, although he wondered about the Mazurs leaving their kids for science lessons with a neighbor who seemed to repeatedly create open flames in her home. "Did she have a history of setting things on fire?" Donovan asked, hoping for information and trying again to be part of the conversation.

"Only in her kitchen," Kaya replied with a smile. "In her lab, things sparked and arced, but those conflagrations were always on purpose."

"She had a lab?" Eleri asked, and it was Emersyn who began to fill in that information. "She had a job for a few years when she got here. That's where her lab was, right?" She looked to the adults for confirmation before continuing. "And I know the garage looks like it's Mr. Rychenkov's, but if you've been in there . . ."

Donovan and Eleri both nodded to fill in the space. "She showed us," Eleri offered.

"Well, there's a corner table that was hers. She liked to tinker."

"Oh!" Donovan said,. "That was the corner where the fire extinguisher sat?"

"Yes," Kaya grinned. Madisyn and Emersyn chimed in then, discussing how Johanna had given them all knitting lessons, but Emersyn complained that she was the worst at it. It was Cage who admitted to being the second worst, and they all said that Joule was the best.

Donovan sat back for a moment and watched the table. He knew Eleri had been looking for hints and clues, but she had signaled nothing to him. They were sitting next to each other and had agreed that a tap and under-the-table point would direct them. But now, as he almost physically pulled back from the conversation to watch and listen, he saw that Marshawn had done the same thing. He and Nate Mazur weren't very participatory tonight and Donovan—though he didn't signal Eleri—decided to keep an extra eye on them throughout the meal. Though if either man was capable of murdering someone his children so loved, that would put him in a different realm than what Donovan was expecting of this killer.

"Do you remember when we took all the drones out?" Madisyn chimed in. "When he took us to the park to fly them?"

"I didn't get to go," Emersyn, the youngest, almost pouted, and Donovan was surprised to see that behavior from such intellectually mature kids. But as Eleri reminded him, it didn't matter how smart someone was, they were still human.

So their killer might be smarter than all the rest of them put together, but his human instincts would likely get him caught. Donovan looked at each adult around the table. Marshawn, LeDonRic and Maggie, the Mazurs . . . and then he looked at the kids and wondered if one of them might have killed their friends . . .

27

Donovan and Eleri met up for lunch the next day. They still hadn't managed to carve out time to look at what was on Marat Rychenkov's hidden USB or even try to crack the code in the notebooks. Eleri had sent pictures of the pages to Wade and to GJ Janson—another agent who'd cracked a code for them before—but that was all they had managed. There had been more pressing work last night, and now there was work that had to be done during the daytime hours. Maybe tonight they would get to it.

Today, he was following Greg Whitlow, and Eleri was following Jivika Das. The job of trailing someone unnoticed was always difficult. It was even harder when everyone in town supposedly could recognize you, so there was no space for a stakeout or anything like that.

He followed the man to work, taking a sharp right in the other direction as Whitlow pulled into his office building. Though he couldn't prove the physicist had gone to his office or even to his building, it was the best Donovan could do and still maintain his cover.

He'd seen patients at the clinic. All but one had been local residents. Though he'd tried to memorize names and faces, it-wasn't his strong suit. Thus, there was a greater chance of someone recognizing Dr. Naman than there was of him recognizing them. So he took the turn and watched as well as he could.

They needed to put tracking devices on the three cars, but hadn't been able to get to them this morning. He had two in his pocket, just in case the opportunity arose. Two hours later, it had not—but he did see Whitlow leave. Donovan pulled into traffic several cars behind him. He watched as Whitlow met up with a friend and went into *Michelangelo's*, an Italian restaurant.

It was a dead end for Donovan, since following the man into the restaurant would be too much. So he turned the car around and met up with Eleri at the *Atomic Diner*. Donovan ordered the Hawking burger, the fully loaded one, while Eleri went for the LHC Rap.

"Oh, didn't see this last time. I have to order it because the name is so funny." She grinned down at the menu.

"Why is the Large Hadron Collider Wrap funny?" He didn't get it, but that was a normal feeling in Curie.

"Google it, but R-A-P rap. Not like a sandwich." Eleri watched while he pulled up his phone and watched some very funny but not musically talented scientists sing about what the LHC experiments did.

"Got it." He looked up and lowered his voice. "Whitlow went to work this morning. He then went to lunch with Keyoor Vergheese.""

"Like yesterday," Eleri said. "I mean, it could just mean that they're friends."

"Yeah. I walked close by him yesterday, El," and he waited for his tone to catch her attention. "Vergheese's like me," he said, and watched as her face transformed, her eyes opening and her mouth becoming a small O.

"You mean—like Wade?" She didn't want to say the word there in the diner. It didn't appear anyone was listening in, but God forbid they were. Donovan nodded.

"He's a . . . *physicist?*" Eleri asked with an extra push on the last word.

Donovan, catching her snarky code, smiled. "Yes."

"Are there more here? Of that kind of *physicist?*"

"I haven't encountered anyone. I mean, I can tell more by looking than I used to."

"So can I," she mused. "I just thought he had . . ."

She trailed off, but Donovan knew what she meant. There was a bone structure to the face, to the shoulders . . . once the signs were understood, it might be possible to tell just from looking at a person.

Donovan had known enough to get closer and breathe in slightly as he passed the man on the street. He suspected GJ Janson was better at the visual identification than either of the two of them, but Donovan had never had to rely on that. He could *smell* the wolves, and Vergheese smelled like one of them.

She sighed and leaned back. "Damn. I had hoped this would just be . . . normal." There was a brief hitch, as she had probably intended to say "a normal case" and caught herself.

"I don't think it means anything, at least not yet," Donovan said, but he was in agreement. This had seemed more like their first case, more like where things were just people gone astray and not the craziness they'd been encountering in their recent investigations. Not the craziness Nightshade was known for. "Then again," he said, putting his hands out on the table, "is there anything about this town that *is* normal?"

Eleri had the decency to shake her head. He'd certainly shifted his definition of *normal* a long time ago, and he'd shifted it again when he joined Nightshade. Now his working definition was "things he could state honestly in a court of law."

They'd met up for lunch in an attempt to not appear as though they were following the respective people they were. "Jivika went to work this morning," Eleri said softly. "She's been there all day. She's in the think tank, too. The one Marat used to be in."

"Did you get a list of her projects?"

Eleri nodded. "Well, Bennett has them. We need to go by and pick them up."

Donovan shook his head. "I think we should have Kate deliver them. We can't keep going to his office, and we're going to have to go there for certain things. We need them to deliver to us as much as possible."

He quit talking abruptly as the server came back with the drinks, interrupting himself to thank her and hoping it didn't look like he was hiding what he was saying. He waited until she had left to talk again. Surely, some people around here had national security clearance, so their conversation wasn't that odd.

"I got the results from the CDC and Bennett has the information from Curie PD," he said, "from their interviews with three chemists in town."

"Did he email it?" Eleri asked suspiciously. He'd felt the same way.

"When Bennett asked how I wanted them, I told him again that we needed paper." Even that call was sketchy, but he figured that listening in on a phone call would be much more difficult than hacking an email. At least temporally, the phone call disappeared once it was done.

"And what do we have so far?" Eleri asked as she leaned across the table, her voice still low. She now had a fake smile on her face, as though they were discussing something silly and casual.

"First, the CDC checked if there was anything other than our short list of chemicals that smelled like butter or dairy products, and there wasn't. Bennett verbally confirmed that the chemists agreed with that. Next, given that the CDC did rule out *streptococci milleri*, I had them test for the three chemicals we figured out. Luckily, it was a task the CDC could do quickly. The smell on Johanna Schmitt was confirmed as butane-2,3-diol," he said.

"Does that tell us something?"

"Not yet that I'm aware of. But it gives us something to work with and find specifics."

"Well, let's see if we can get Kate over here to join us for lunch," Eleri said. "Is it okay to be seen with Kate?"

"I don't know, but we can say she's helping you look for work. I think we need to add to our cover story that you're an old friend of Bennett's or the daughter of a friend. It will explain things if anyone notices we see him a lot."

"Good idea. We can say we just didn't want to tell people we were friends with the Mayor or look like we were getting special treatment. But if anyone asks, that's what all of us will say."

Thirty minutes later, as they were finishing up their meals, Kate walked into the diner. Like a good agent, she sat at the counter for a moment, then swiveled around and acted as though she was just seeing them. *She has skills,* Donovan thought, *possibly better than either mine or Eleri's.* For a moment, he wondered if that should worry him —or if he should recommend her for a position with the Bureau.

"Hey, y'all." She sat down next to Eleri as Eleri scooted over and made space for her. Then she leaned in, a smile on her face, her hand waving as though she were brushing off some comment. *Yes,* he thought, *she has mad skills.*

"I have some paper results, and I can give them to you. In fact, what I'm going to do, Eleri, is just slip them into your purse."

"Can you tell us?"

"Mm-hmm." Kate smiled, waved a hand again, and shook her head. Then she delivered confidential information from a police investigation as though she were telling a joke. "They think—that is the PD thinks—from their talks with the chemists that there's one likely chemical that would create that smell. The chemist told them he would suspect the butane one. Butane-di . . . There's some numbers. Shit, I don't remember," she said.

Donovan waved her away. It was okay, he and Eleri did remember, and interestingly enough, the chemists had come up with the same chemical that Johanna Schmitt had tested positive for. He was listening much more closely now.

"The other two chemicals on the list are related to cleaners or solvents, and while they would likely kill a person in high enough quantity, they wouldn't subdue them. Those chemicals would probably cause seizures, something like that."

"And they would have shown a cause of death," Eleri added with a smile as though Kate's story was funny.

The assistant nodded and continued. "This one, the butane number thing, is not a chemical that anyone knows, but the chemist did point out that it's related to GHB."

"Oh shit," Eleri said. "Is it one of the breakdown products?"

Kate shook her head. "No, I do remember that part. It's not, but the notes mentioned one chemist suggesting you might get it if someone was making their own GHB and fucked it up . . ."

"Or they were making an alternate variety?" Donovan wondered aloud, not putting any of those possibilities past the residents of Curie. They could easily be cooking up their own drugs. "If they made a similar drug, they could get different breakdown products."

"That might explain the lack of any defense from Marat and limited defense from Johanna," Eleri said.

The server interrupted them then, asking if Kate wanted anything, and she opted for a milkshake. "They have the best ones here," she said, at a slightly higher decibel level than the things she'd previously stated. Luckily, they were in the last booth, and no one was in the booth behind them or the table beside them. The servers coming in and out of the kitchen were their only worries, but they seemed legitimately busy.

Donovan was sitting back, his thoughts churning. The GHB made sense. It was a common street drug and date-rape drug. It made the victim compliant, which made everything click into place: that might be why Marat Rychenkov had no defensive wounds at all, even from the bindings. It explained how he'd been easily tied up, when Johanna Schmitt insisted it was not a bedroom game they had ever played. A man had to be feeling a little off to let someone else tie him down while he was still alive—unless he thought there was fun involved.

Johanna, too, had been tied up, and as Eleri pointed out, while the blacklight revealed that she fought back harder than was visible to the naked eye, she had not fought as if her life was at stake. She'd left no scrapes, blood, or open wounds, as anyone normally would have, particularly if she had been able to tell that this was the way her husband had died.

GHB would explain why she fought back somewhat, but not as hard as she should have. GHB explained that she was awake—not unconscious, which had been an option—but malleable. Not a dead weight for the killer to have to haul around.

In fact, the GHB derivative explained all of it. Now the new question became: Who could either obtain or synthesize off-brand GHB?

28

Donovan sat at his computer, watching as Eleri practically paced a track into the floor.

"Well," she said, "Now, at least we know how they did it. Our killer drugged them using some kind of GHB or GHB-alternative, which explains why they didn't fight back. And then he tied them down and . . . *Shit.*"

Donovan almost smiled.

Eleri rescinded her original statement, frustration coming through her tone. "Okay, so we *don't* know how. At least we know the first part of how. We know why they didn't fight back," she said. "We're still stuck on the actual *how*. And we still need to figure out *why*."

Donovan tapped at his keyboard a couple of times. "Come sit down. Let's watch this and hope the *why* is in here." He pointed to his computer screen.

They'd finally reached a spot of time where he could open up the information they had found in Marat Rychenkov's garage.

He and Eleri had gone their separate ways earlier in the day after meeting up for lunch. For the afternoon, Eleri had followed Greg Whitlow and Donovan went after Jivika Das.

She was boring to follow. If she ate with a friend, he didn't know, because she stayed in the building all day. She left promptly at five p.m. and headed straight home, where she lived alone. Donovan had tried to watch for a while, driving by as many times as he could before it became creepy. As best he could tell, Jivika watched the evening news and walked around her house a little bit.

On the route home, he'd sat at the light, waiting to get a right-hand turn into Copernicus Circle to take the cross road to come back to Pythagoras Point. He thought how desperately he wanted to be a regular *agent* again.

When they'd been in New Orleans, he hadn't been an acting agent, though he'd had the badge on him at all times. Eventually, he and Eleri had almost declared themselves back on the job—not that they had that kind of power. He'd not been in a capacity to act with the full force of the FBI behind him. Now, here he was again, only this time with the opposite problem. He was acting at the direction of the Bureau. He *did* have the full force of the FBI behind him. But that same FBI was demanding that he operate under cover.

All he wanted to do was storm Jivika Das's door, flip open his badge, and ask her what she knew about Marat Rychenkov's death. But it wasn't going to happen, at least not anytime soon. Westerfield didn't seem to want to budge on the issue of the three of them maintaining their cover.

Wade had been a big help. He'd been interviewing parents surreptitiously while supposedly discussing their children's high school physics projects with them. But for everything Wade turned up, they all still felt as though they had five hundred puzzle pieces that belonged to somewhere between three and five hundred different puzzles. Some of the pieces had looked interesting but couldn't be connected to anything else. And, though in his off time he'd been working on it, Donovan had not yet been able to crack Marat Rychenkov's code. Neither had Wade or Eleri.

"Let's open the files," Donovan said. He watched as Eleri managed to reign in some of her nervous energy and come plop into the chair next to him. For a moment, he wondered if somebody could have quietly hopped the backyard fence and snuck up to the window and could now be watching them. Could they see the computer screen through the window? Donovan hoped he would've heard them approaching, but with ordinary, human ears—*without his ears changing*—his hearing wasn't as sensitive as he would've liked. There was also the possibility that someone was watching in a less physical way—that they had somehow hacked his system.

Given that he was on his FBI laptop—not the show one he'd been given—and that the FBI had been through it several times, he wanted to have faith that hacking couldn't happen. The Bureau tech team was supposed to have made it un-hackable. No one should be able to get into his system without triggering the FBI alert. That meant that if a hacker somehow were able to hack it, even read keystrokes or feed themselves video from his system, Donovan and Eleri would have been warned that a hack had occurred.

That had been something Donovan had trusted implicitly until he arrived in Curie and got to know these people. If anyone could hack around an FBI alarm, that person could easily live here.

Trying to ignore his concerns, he clicked a button, expecting this material to be encrypted as well. To his surprise, and apparently Eleri's as well, it wasn't. Though he was desperate for a file labeled "Why Someone Might Want to Murder Me," nothing of the kind existed.

He was noticing the same thing as Eleri frowned and leaned forward closer to the screen. "It's all videos."

"Then I guess we watch." Once again, he expected to be thwarted, but he wasn't. He hit the play button and the video opened right up.

They watched as Marat, fully alive and almost as gleeful as a kid, looked toward the camera. "Johanna, is it on?"

"It's on." They recognized Johanna's voice, and Donovan felt his heart stutter. Despite his constant reassurances to Eleri, Johanna Schmitt's death *had been* a failure.

Interestingly enough, he could watch Marat and not feel the same thing. He'd not been in town when Marat died, he'd never met the man, and none of that was in any way his fault. But *Johanna* . . . thinking of Johanna made him wince, made his breathing stop sometimes and his eyes begin to feel the pressure from behind.

Her voice came from the speakers again. "Go, Marat. Do it."

He and Eleri watched as Marat Rychenkov gleefully walked away from the camera. He held a system in his hands that looked almost like a video game. It looked like a hand controller but a little bit larger. Still, Eleri was pointing that out as Donovan saw it. "So it looks like he stole that from a gaming system, but not one that I know. What's he going to control?"

They watched, then, just as Eleri uttered the words, the camera—clearly controlled by Johanna Schmitt, panned downward. On the ground was an array of dots. Or at least that's what Donovan thought they were, until they began to buzz. After a moment of this, they lifted into the air and flew away.

"His drones," Eleri murmured.

It took Donovan a moment to realize he was looking at the ones from the bottom shelf in the garage. He had seen three sets and this was the contingent of tiny, black, round drones. Those had been greatest in number and smallest in size. He watched as they lifted off of the ground, remaining in the formation that they'd been parked in.

They buzzed and then—while he watched and Johanna commented from somewhere off screen—they flew right over her head. Marat controlled them from the small console. Donovan saw this as the camera panned back toward her husband. Johanna's laughter came through loud and clear. "You did it, Marat! They're off."

"Yes. Let's see what happens." Her husband's tone was now less celebratory and more experimental.

But Donovan watched carefully as the drones flew in formation. Johanna turned, wheeling the camera, trying to follow their flight. The background showed that they were at a park, and Donovan and Eleri watched as the grouping buzzed past the seesaws.

Marat flew the drones directly toward the swing set, and Donovan watched, fascinated, as they parted like a flock of birds, avoiding chains and slipping under arches. After that, they buzzed their way cleanly through the monkey bars.

"So far, so good," Johanna commented, but a moment too soon. Just then, the camera watched as Marat flew the grouping into a tree. Though the drones managed to miss the trunk, several got caught up in the leaves.

Donovan paused the video. "Do you think the drones couldn't see the leaves, or maybe the leaves moved at the last moment?"

"Maybe there was wind," Eleri said. "I don't know."

So he hit the play button again and watched. The camera then almost immediately panned downward, as though she were done but forgot to turn off the recording. Marat's voice came through. "No, no, Johanna. Keep filming."

Several of the drones had dropped to the ground. Several others remained up in the tree. But for the most part, the batch went on. They flew around the park two or three more times, with Marat purposefully running them into treetops. A few were lost each time.

That was it. The video ended. Donovan frowned.

"What did we watch?" Eleri asked.

"I don't know. Maybe it'll become clear in the next one." So they watched another video.

This time, there were fewer drones. Donovan recognized a different batch from the shelves in the garage. Whereas they appeared to have been ready to go before the filming started in the first video, this time, they started from off. He and Eleri watched as tiny lights blinked on, first in the center drone and then in the remaining twelve drones around him. One at a time, each one blinked a small red light, until finally all were lit. Donovan had no idea what he was watching.

“Oh, that looks good," Marat commented, though he was facing away from the camera.

Once again, Johanna filmed the whole endeavor. Once again, the drones flew around the park. They flew around obstacles and they flew into trees. This time, Marat only lost two.

"But he started with a smaller number," Eleri pointed out. Again, they couldn't solve anything. Donovan still had no idea why this might be important.

They watched another video that looked much like the first. Then, in the last two videos, Johanna wasn’t present. This time, the exercise seemed to take place in a closed room. It had chairs and a lectern, as though he were in a classroom in a church or community center or something like that.

Donovan and Eleri watched again as Marat started the camera and propped it into the corner, his kind face filling the screen. Whatever skills the man had with robotics did not carry over to his camera work.

The fourth video looked much the same, though this one occurred in the same room, with the same set of drones, and apparently the same task. Several of the drones dropped out of the chaos along the way.

But in the last video, Marat only hit a button and set the controller down, almost as though to show the watcher he didn’t need it. Donovan saw the drones take flight and zoom around the room in various directions. This time, their flight looked like chaos. Four minutes of wild activity later, they returned. Each drone settled down into its original starting place as though nothing had happened.

Marat turned to the camera and smiled.

29

"I don't get it," Eleri sighed, more frustrated now than before they'd opened the file and seen what was on it. "What did we just watch?"

"We watched Marat Rychenkov playing with drones," Donovan answered, though by the tone of his voice, she could tell he also hadn't figured out anything beyond that.

They watched all the videos. When they'd gotten through them all once, they immediately viewed them each a second time. This time, they listened carefully to the words between Marat and Johanna, checking for any obvious signs of code passing between them.

Eleri shook her head as they entered the last video in which Johanna was present. "I don't hear anything. The conversation isn't stilted. There aren't any strange wordings. It doesn't sound like they're speaking memorized lines or anything that could indicate a code. If they are doing it, they're damn good."

Donovan also shook his head, but he was agreeing there was nothing there—at least not that he could detect. "If they were passing some kind of sign language or signals, we would at least see Marat's side of it. If we only saw Marat's side of it, then it wouldn't be the thing that was important to have on the video, right?"

"I would guess," Eleri said, and as they spoke, Donovan went back to the first video and they watched it all a third time.

"What are we looking for this time?" she asked.

"The drones. Let's see if they spell out any words or numbers or tell us anything that will help break the code. Or maybe they *are* the code."

Eleri agreed, and the two of them leaned in close to the screen again. This time, they ignored the conversation between the husband and wife and watched as the batch of many small drones lifted off the ground, their little wings in flight, buzzing like hummingbirds and bees.

The machines stayed in formation until they got to the swing set, at which point they moved around the items in their way. They flowed almost like water, moving slightly to one side or another, not bumping, and then reassuming the original formation once they were clear of the obstacle. The swings themselves, the chains, even the monkey bars, posed no problems. But at last, they came up against the trees.

Already knowing what would happen, they paused the video here again.

"How many did he lose?" she asked.

"Three or four."

"Is that a code? . . . I can't imagine it would be, though," she answered her own question.

Donovan answered her anyway. "It's got to be too random. I mean, the only other option is that he flew the drone set into the tree, knowing that he would control dropping a certain number of them out. That would mean they *could* fly through the trees safely, which it really appeared they couldn't. Thus, he didn't drop them on purpose."

Eleri was nodding her agreement, though her eyes were going unfocused. Donovan kept talking. "And he was swearing when the drones dropped out, which is probably why Johanna turned the camera toward the ground."

Though they analyzed all the drone movement, the machines didn't spell out any words. They didn't light up in any particular way that could be followed.

"It's not Morse," Eleri said. "Nor binary."

"No, I don't see any alphabets either."

They watched through the whole thing again, coming to the end of the first video with no better idea what it might mean than they'd had the first time.

"Maybe it's a dummy. Maybe the code's in the next video." But they watched it, too, and found nothing they could crack. There was nothing of use to solving the murders, other than the drones flying around the park.

"Does it matter the order that they're in? Do the first letters of the video names spell out a five-letter word?"

As they looked, they realized the videos weren't even named. They just bore what looked like a random naming system given by the camera.

"The video systems are different," Donovan pointed out as they looked at the pulled-up display.

"Yes, it appears these three are from Johanna's phone." Eleri pointed to the screen. "I'm assuming that because she was clearly the one filming. And the other two are from a different phone entirely. I guess it could be the same, but the setup is different."

"Johanna was there—we saw her in the first three—and in the last two, it looks as though Marat is filming it himself without anyone else present."

Donovan hit the button and they watched *again*. This time, Donovan made an observation. "In the fourth video, some of the little drones fly into things in the room. One of them flew into a chair and it dropped out. One of them flew into something else. But in the second one, they don't. All the drones make it back."

"Right," Eleri nodded. "And in the fourth and fifth videos, Marat's wearing the same clothing. So we need to get some geo-tagging on this, and some timestamps, and see if these two were filmed one right after the other. It looks highly plausible, given the scenario."

"But the first three," Donovan said, "appear very much to have been filmed on different days. They're both wearing different clothing. Johanna's voice sounds a little different. The cloud cover's different. It looks like they're even at different *times* of day."

"Okay, so we need to get the FBI analysts to look at this. I think we need to take it in." Eleri finally came to the conclusion that they wouldn't be able to get everything they needed without doing so.

Donovan agreed with her, and he added, "We need to get together with Wade. We need to have a real brainstorming session about everything we've learned in town, and I want to call, but we can't, and I want to go over, but we *can't*."

Eleri agreed. "So we call the Bureau field office in Omaha, and have them call Wade on a secure line. They can set up our meet up there at the branch office tomorrow."

Donovan agreed. They set up the call, knowing they would only get a return call if something was wrong and Wade wouldn't be able to make it.

Then they watched the videos on repeat into the night. When it was dark outside, Eleri finally called off the dogs. "It's time. We need to go change. It's dark enough, but any later, and we will look weird."

They'd agreed that they would put a tracker on Jivika Das's car this evening. They would hit Greg Whitlow's tomorrow while he was at work. They were trying to make the two missions to attach the equipment—times and methods—as different as possible in hopes that no one would recognize that the same thing had happened to both cars.

After closing out the computer and tucking the small drive into a safe space, they headed off to their rooms. Eleri dressed in dark colors, but nothing that would look like they were about to commit a cat burglary. Just enough so they didn't draw attention.

As they drove toward Das's neighborhood, Eleri told Donovan, "The good news is, it's plausible I could be buying a house in the neighborhood, and there's a home for sale several doors down from Jivika."

The first problem they noticed as they turned into the subdivision was that Jivika lived in a neighborhood they'd only driven through before. Kangaroo Court was a development where Bennett encouraged the residents among them who had strange pets to live all together. He even had an enclosure in the middle as a dog/other creature park.

The central space was several acres large and featured obstacle courses, horse jumps, and smaller, gated areas that were designated for trick rabbits or ferrets or something Eleri had yet to figure out. The "Court," as it was called, was the center around which all the houses were built. Other separate areas included spaces for deer to exist happily in the neighborhood. Eleri had even seen them wandering in and out between the homes. It seemed more than one resident had planted deer-friendly gardens, and she'd seen signs suggesting rabbits were welcome, though Eleri had not figured out if that meant wild ones or the neighbor's pet or both . . .

Bennett had worked to create Kangaroo Court with a team including a developer, an architect, and a biologist in an effort to establish a safe haven for both animals and animal lovers.

“Is that a ferret?” Donovan pointed out the window, his question more of a shocked statement than something requiring an answer.

Eleri shrugged. She’d seen a small streak go by but hadn’t caught it well enough to identify the species. The kicker was that there was no person out with it. It must be wild, whatever it was.

The problem, she realized as they began driving around, looking at the houses even though many were not for sale, was that people with strange pets apparently walked their animals at strange hours. There were more people and animals out on the sidewalks than she would have expected.

"Is that a llama?" Donovan asked, "or an alpaca?"

"I think it’s an alpaca, but I'm a human physiologist. I can't promise you I can tell the difference." This time, Eleri did see the animal in question. A young woman was walking down the street in a hooded jacket, her hands in her pockets against the chill that increased as the night got older. And the alpaca, or llama as it were, followed along, docile on his leash.

Eleri parked her car in front of the house that was for sale. As they got out of the car, they looked the house up and down as though Eleri were a prospective buyer. Once they had sufficiently checked out the empty home, they walked down the street toward Jivika Das's.

Eleri had noticed in the morning—and Donovan had confirmed from following her in the evening—that Jivika, like Johanna Schmitt, parked in her driveway, not inside the garage. At least it made their job easier. She and Donovan chatted about the neighborhood, about the lights, about the animal noises, and for a moment, Eleri wondered if Donovan's sensitive ears and senses were going crazy. They had to be, with this much strange wildlife so close.

But she didn't want to say anything. It wasn't necessary, and the rule was you never said anything that might blow your cover unless it was absolutely necessary. Eleri's phone pinged, and she stopped to check the message that had popped up.

"It's from Maggie," she said, holding up the phone to Donovan. Maggie wanted to know if she would go to coffee the next morning. Her new friend had said she usually went with Johanna once a week.

She read the message out loud. "I can't not go. And I can't bring myself to go alone. Can I pester you to be my new coffee buddy?"

Eleri texted back that she would definitely be there, before sliding the phone back into her pocket and using the motion to palm the tracking device. Her heart kicked up a little, though she'd learned not to let it show.

She'd been standing near Jivika's car, the text a perfect excuse to turn and act as though she was turning away from the streetlight to see her phone better. She faced the car now.

Eleri had worn heeled boots for just this purpose, and as she turned to follow Donovan, she let her ankle look as though it was twisting. With a small cry, she fell down right next to Jivika's car.

As Donovan looked startled—a good job on his part, because he'd known exactly how this would go—he reached down to help her up. Eleri reached one hand for his and the other for the tire well. She sure hoped she looked like she was bracing herself instead of surreptitiously placing the tracker just under the lip of metal around the back tire.

She was finally standing up and brushing herself off when she heard the voice. "Are you okay?"

"Oh, I'm good now." She smiled and offered a nod as though it was okay.

"I saw you go down."

"Thank you for checking on me." It was only then that Eleri noticed the cat on a leash.

The woman startled her with the way she frowned at Donovan, then looked to Eleri with a suspicious hint in her eye. "Are you a neighbor?"

"Oh no. I mean, not yet! I'm checking the place out though, looking to buy the house," she pointed back down the street, toward the "for sale" sign. "I have a realtor friend back home who told me to check out the neighborhood in the evening. See if the streetlight comes in through the bedroom window or if everyone can see you eating dinner. What the nighttime traffic is like. Or in this case, if the alpacas cry at night or something."

The woman's face lit up with a laugh. "Oh no, he's a llama, and they are pretty quiet. But the whole thing about them spitting is true. Don't try to pet one."

Eleri was laughing, but just then the woman squinted her eyes at Donovan. "Are you the new doctor at the clinic?"

He had to say yes. And Eleri thought it went as well as it could, but the fact was, they had been made.

30

Though Eleri was confident they hadn't actually been caught planting the tracker on Jivika Das's car, it was clear they'd been seen and Donovan had even been recognized. Thus, they decided to hold off on placing a tracker on Greg Whitlow's car for another day.

Given the change of plans, Donovan headed into the clinic in the early hours, attempting to get in a reasonable shift before noon. Eleri didn't wake up to wave him goodbye; she had another job this morning.

Hopping into her car, she checked that she had everything she needed tucked under the seat beside her and ready in the trunk. She was grateful she had a garage in which to hide her prep work. Their cover didn't really allow her to leave her gun sitting out in the open, so it was now under the passenger seat, handy enough if she needed it, but out of sight in hopes that she wouldn't. On the seat, she placed her purse—like a normal driver. Starting the car, she headed south.

Eleri drove toward the small town of Be-Ah-trice, thinking the name through her head as she passed farm houses and corn fields. Most of the corn wasn't even edible, it was for livestock, but the sheer number of farms showed the American necessity for the crop. In fact, that was why Marshall Bennett had picked this area to put his town in: open space and low land value. He'd literally carved Curie out of cornfields.

As she hit town, she saw one-story brick buildings lining either side of the street. She passed banks and a small coffee stand. Some kind of pump marked the far end of the town. Taking the turn Kate had prescribed in her directions, Eleri swung left out the end of the small berg and was soon driving through other squares of cornfields.

Her directions had been clear, even if the road had not. After the next turn, she wound up on gravel, and five miles later she was at a crossroads, unmarked by signs and with no homes in sight. It was exactly what she wanted.

She slowed the car, letting it idle as she pulled over to the side of the road. Acting as though she were having car trouble—for the audience of zero people and a bird overhead—she looked at her tires and opened her hood and stood there, waiting for her "random" friendly patron to come along.

It wasn't five minutes later that Kate showed up and pulled in behind her, acting like a helpful stranger. *Nebraska Nice* came to Eleri's mind. It was a good sentiment, and she was just taking advantage of it.

The two women looked under the hood and then around the car. They reached in toward the engine, not doing anything, though Eleri knew the small actions made it look like Kate and she were checking the car out.

They exchanged a few words. Kate asked–if she'd had trouble finding the place, and Eleri had almost laughed, but they circled to the back of the car and this time popped the trunk.

Kate, like a true actress, looked around and eventually set her purse into the trunk, as though it was simply a convenient place to put it that didn't involve a dusty gravel road. While she postured, Eleri opened the lid of the book-sized box she'd brought to show Kate what was inside.

"I want to track every drone," she explained, "but that's not possible, so we're giving you three trackers here. There are three sets of different styles of drones in Marat Rychenkov's garage. Donovan and I could do this, but it's getting to be too much of a risk. Donovan got recognized as the new doctor in town last night. We did tag another car belonging to a town-member. But we can't do too many and we still have another one and maybe two to go."

Kate was nodding along, as though hearing what was wrong with the car, when Eleri got to her final question. “So, do you think you can pull off placing the trackers on the drones yourself?"

"Depends on what's involved," Kate said, "but I'm up for anything. I want these cases solved. They’re driving Marshall crazy."

Eleri noted that Kate called her boss by his first name and wondered if it meant anything. She didn't tell Kate, and she hadn't told Marshall Bennett why they were tagging the drones. In fact, Eleri had no idea why the drones themselves might be important, only that Marat had hidden the files. It didn't matter that they didn’t yet understand anything they’d seen. Marat had thought it was worth hiding—which made it worth tracking.

Turning back to Kate, Eleri said, "I believe the biggest problem is, unlike with a car, you can't simply stick a tracker onto the drone."

Kate had picked one of the devices up and turned it over in her hand. She checked it out while still acting as though they were looking in the trunk for something to help Eleri's car.

"Well," Eleri conceded, "you *could* actually stick it to the outside of the drone.”

“The problem is that it would be obvious," Kate said. "And the whole point is to have anyone checking them out not know they're being tracked. As soon as they know, it's useless."

"Excellent. FBI 101, A-plus," Eleri said and watched as Kate smiled. "So what Donovan and I decided—and given what we saw in the videos and what we saw when we were there—is that you're going to need to open a drone from each set and place the tracker inside."

“Which one do I pick?”

“We have no idea which one is the lead or the most important, so it doesn’t matter. Do whichever one is easiest.”

Kate nodded. “How do they come apart?"

"That's just it. It wasn't something we were looking at when we were there. On the videos, the large white ones appear to be made from two halves, screwed together in several places. It looks like you can just unscrew them, but honestly, it relies on Marat not having glued them shut. The whole plan also relies on there being extra space inside the drone. You may have to get creative. I don’t know."

"Well, most components have extra space. The motherboards are really very tiny compared to the size of the box."

"An excellent point," Eleri said. "And my hope is that at least the white ones have that. I don't know about the small black ones."

She hated that she had no better terms to describe the drones than just using the color and size of the individual bots. Clearly, she needed to learn more about drones: what they did, what they could do, and why Marat might've been killed for them.

Kate nodded again as Eleri put the tracker back into its nest and closed the box. Kate took it and easily slipped the whole thing inside the large bag she'd brought, exactly as Eleri had planned. Kate always carried the large bag, perhaps for exactly these kinds of assignments.

With the trackers now in Kate's possession, the two headed to the front of the car, where Kate looked under the hood and acted as though she was pushing a wire back into place. Eleri continued talking.

"What I'd like to have you do is visit the house every few days. So if you go now, people might think it's suspicious, but not so much. Everyone knows that there were two murders, that both occupants from that home were killed. And everyone knows that you and Bennett are very upset about everything that happened, so I think it's okay if you visit several times. I'm not sure how many more times Donovan and I can use the pretense of being city workers as cover, and we may have to do it again, so I'll be using you as much as possible," Eleri warned.

"Of course," Kate told her and reached out and shook her hand.

"So, go today, check through the house, and place the trackers into the drones as soon as you can. Check to see if anything has been moved, anything you can notice. A quick visual sweep is fine. And then, in three days, I'd like you to go back and put a For Sale sign out front. And, if we're still investigating, in three more days, go back and check on the house again."

"Will people be visiting? Like prospective buyers?" Kate asked. "Do we need to show it? Do I need to set it up with a realtor?"

"I would suggest that you do, though we'll try to hold off on actual showings for a while. I hate the idea of having people walk through the house, but it's the only way to keep things looking normal."

Kate moved to shake Eleri's hand, but Eleri leaned into the car and produced hand wipes from inside, as though they were something she always carried and not just for today when they were pretending they were getting under the hood. But once Kate had cleaned her hands, she then offered a hug. Eleri found the gesture slightly unusual until Kate whispered in her ear.

"Will we get to have a funeral for Johanna soon?"

"I think so," Eleri told her.

Then, as Kate turned around and drove off, Eleri headed into Omaha to the second half of her day. She wasn't sure if she was looking forward to it or not.

31

After Donovan finished his shift at the clinic, he climbed into his car and pointed it out of town. Luckily, the shift had only been five hours and not a full eight. Even so, he felt the need to stop at the *Up N Atom* for a drink on the way out, going with Eleri's suggestion of a Caffeinator with a shot of "DEA certified"—a rare bean that was from Columbia but not used to mask drug shipments. He'd walked inside hoping to see people he knew, maybe make some acquaintances into friends.

Donovan had been working, but Eleri had been networking. Perhaps Westerfield had been right in the way he assigned them their jobs, because it turned out no one spoke to the tall, partly Indian-looking physician. Though several people smiled at him as though they knew him, he didn't manage to start any conversations, and he developed a stronger appreciation for Eleri's skills. *At least,* he thought, *the coffee was good and he'd been out and about like a normal person.*

With his Vici-sized coffee—the tallest— in hand, he headed back to the car, then drove toward Omaha. It took more than an hour to get to the FBI branch. Though he'd hit some traffic, having been all over the U.S., what he'd encountered in Lincoln was not what he would refer to as "bad."

He wondered, as he turned into the lot for the FBI field office, whether anyone had followed him. Did his car have a tracker on it?

Had anyone in the town of Curie grown suspicious of them or of Wade? Had someone found the USB before he and Eleri had? Had they put a tracer on *it*? He contemplated the possibility of someone following them even as they investigated that person. Normally, he wouldn't have thought in such crazy circles, but Curie made him a little insane.

Once he'd parked behind the building, he passed through security and headed down a hallway and into the conference room he and Eleri and Wade had booked for just this purpose. As the two stood up to greet him, he almost stepped into Wade's arms and hugged him. He'd never been so glad to see a friend. Wade still looked like Wade—glasses, white t-shirt with an open plaid shirt over it, khaki pants—and that was comforting to Donovan, too.

But he didn't do it. Instead, he fished the small drive out of his pocket and placed it on the table. Eleri had brought Marat's notebooks, and Donovan pointed to the pile of Marat Rychenkov's belongings that sat in the middle of the table.

"We need to get these scanned."

"I've got a wand here," Wade said, and reached into the seat beside him, bringing out the device that would detect radio and satellite signals. He waved it carefully over each of the pieces. Donovan breathed easier when Wade got to the last one and the wand had made no weird hums, clicks, or buzzes.

Leaning on the table, not yet ready to take his seat, he told the other two, "We need to have the FBI techs scan our cars also."

"I know," Wade said. "Eleri and I already ordered it. If you want to go out and tell them where you parked, they'll get on it."

"*Of course you did*," Donovan said, and Eleri's face suddenly lit up.

Wade frowned at her, wondering until she explained, "That's what Donovan and I say about Curie residents. He must think we're awfully smart."

Donovan felt his mouth quirk but headed down the hall again to report his car to the analyst in Office Number 30. The clerk had been assigned to their little group, and Eleri and Wade had already taken advantage. Donovan was grateful not to have to set up the scans, and he was praying to God that nothing was found. If any of their cars were tracked, they'd have to leave the tech in place and merely change where they drove the car. That would suck, but more importantly, it would mean someone was onto them and already had an idea of where they went, depending on how long the tracker had been in place. He crossed his fingers.

This time, when he came back down the hall, he had a soda in hand and a bag of Fritos. He felt like he needed a pop of sugar, salt, and his daily dose of FD&C Red #40.

Eleri didn't even lift an eyebrow. Wade had the notebooks open and was rifling through them, but he closed them as Donovan came in.

"Checklist time," Eleri said, and Wade was the first who jumped in.

"Okay." He pulled a small notebook from the pocket in his shirt and began flipping through. Donovan noticed what was in it: notes Wade had been taking all along. That meant that if anyone attacked him and stole the notebook, or if it fell out of his pocket and someone read it, Wade would be "made." At the very least, they would think he was a PI. But it was Wade's job to protect his own notes, so Donovan didn't comment.

"I've been talking to the parents." Wade looked into his notebook. "I talked to Marshawn James again. He's an inventor but a chemist by education. Emersyn—his daughter who's in my class—is supernova bright. She's in with the older kids, even in Curie. And I also went back to Bob and Brenda Donatti. They are the foster parents to Jeren Waits, the kid in my class. Bob is a chemical engineer and Brenda is a theoretical mathematician." Wade paused, and then added, "I get the feeling Brenda tested into the top level and Bob made the along-for-the-ride grade."

Donovan raised his eyebrows at that and wondered if it made a difference. Should the focus be on her? But Wade thought only one of the students' parents, Abrahim Das, deserved Eleri and Donovan's attention.

"Das?" Eleri asked. "Like Jivika? They have a kid?"

"No, he's a stepfather to one of the kids."

"Okay." Donovan felt his breath let out at the same time Eleri's did.

Wade continued. "He is Jivika's *ex*-husband. Mechanical engineer. I pulled their divorce papers, and the split is only four years old. She cited him stealing her ideas when they were married and they didn't fight over any physical properties, but the divorce got bitter over the intellectual ones."

Curie, Donovan thought, and he watched as Eleri made her notes.

As they wrapped up Wade's information, Eleri told them she also had information from Bennett. Eleri must have arranged it with their assigned analyst from down the hall, because the young man arrived at the door with a stack of papers.

"I can't believe you guys wanted this old school tech," was all he said as he plopped the papers at the open seat at the end of the conference table.

Eleri grinned and shrugged, seemingly trying to lessen the sting of being sent to the printer. "Paper can't get hacked."

He plopped a second stack on the table and asked if they needed anything more. He seemed grateful when they said they didn't.

"What's this?" Donovan asked.

"Bank account information. Wade and I put in requests for a handful of people we were looking at."

They spent the next half an hour flipping through statements from a variety of banks, savings, and even a few offshore accounts. Though he'd read things like this before, he wished all the banks could create the same format of report.

An hour later, Donovan was leaning back, his soda gone and his chip bag empty and crumpled beside him as he finished the pile. "Well, the Mazurs make more money than I expected. Johanna Schmitt and Marat Rychenkov did too, but they're the ones who are dead, and no one seems to have taken their money, so that's not the motive."

He wondered for the first time where their money would go. They had no children, and he didn't know about next of kin. Nothing had popped up so far. No one had shown up to take over the funerals or make an offer on the home or even try to claim the cash from selling it. So, as of yet, the estates those two left behind weren't part of his and Eleri and Wade's problem. No one appeared to be related to them enough to create a stink . . . or to have killed them. "But LeDonRic James makes about as much as I suspected he would, which is a lot."

"He's comfortable, but not wealthy," Eleri reported from her pile just a moment later, reminding Donovan that her idea of "wealthy" was radically different from his. "Marshawn does not have as much money as I would have thought. I got the impression that he got rich selling that mop thing he invented."

"But he's doing okay?" Donovan asked.

"Yeah. He created the polymer compound used in a new type of sponge, then sold the rights to the composition of the sponge to some big company specifically for use in a mop. Then, it appears they didn't create or market the mop for three years, and the contract expired. The rights auto-reverted to him. That means he got a couple hundred grand from the original sale, and then later he got all the rights back to the mop. He spent some of the money over the years, and then spent most all of what was left creating an infomercial." She flipped through the pages in front of her as Donovan watched. "So most of it's been spent, but the mops are selling relatively well, at least from the looks of his bank statements."

"All right, that's not as cut-and-dried as I thought, but it doesn't look like motive," Donovan said, and the two of them turned to Wade.

Wade practically threw his hands up in the air. "Marshawn seems to have both made and lost a lot of money along the way. But he's good now. To be fair, everyone here is living on pretty decent salaries. I'm the poorest of any of us."

"Well, you're a teacher," Eleri said.

"Fuck that," Wade told her. "The teachers here are actually reasonably well-paid. These people value education, but I'm only teaching one hour per day . . . and I still have to attend faculty meetings," he lamented.

"At least they didn't ask you to do crosswalk duty or chaperone the cafeteria," Eleri pointed out.

Oh, Donovan thought, remembering his own student years. He'd seen teachers in his various schools performing lunchroom duties, though it wasn't something he'd thought about before. Wade merely waved a hand at Eleri as though none of that would have even made a difference, but then he pointed back to his stack of papers.

"Whitlow has some debt. A couple of credit cards run up to twenty grand each."

"How many?"

"Five."

"But he's in a think tank. Decent salary?"

"Yes. Honestly, he's been paying the cards down. Looks like he had some gambling debts originally—that's where the problems came from—but he hasn't done anything fiscally stupid in a few years. If he keeps going the way he's doing now, he'll be out in about four or five years."

"Shit," Donovan said. "Why isn't anybody obviously upside down and in need of money?"

"That would be too easy," Wade told him.

They turned their attention from the useless bank statements to Rychenkov's notebooks then and began trying to crack the code.

Thirty minutes later, Eleri slammed her notebook shut.

32

Donovan closed the notebook he'd been looking at, frustrated. He'd thought today would be a good day, that he'd get to meet up with Wade again and solve something. He'd thought he and Eleri and Wade would sit around a table and make great strides in the case. But it hadn't happened that way.

They'd ruled a lot of things out, but Marat Rychenkov's notebooks weren't yielding anything. Not *anything*. He'd even asked Eleri again if she'd managed to get any images or sensations from touching them. She'd snapped at him, "No, I'm not getting anything!"

Understanding it was just frustration, Donovan let it slide. But he was as perplexed as she was irritated that she wasn't picking up any kind of supernatural vibe that might help them. Something that happened in New Orleans seemed to have shut her down. They were going to have to do this one with good old legwork.

It was important that they get together today and look at the text in person. Donovan knew that—while they had sent pictures to Wade and to GJ—it was plausible the code wasn't even in the numbering and lettering that was inside. Maybe it was in the way the "words" were written. Maybe it was in the numbers of letters in the code breaks. Maybe it was indentations in the paper, or something written and erased, and written over, so it was necessary to have the physical notebooks in front of them to find it. But he'd found jack shit, and from the looks on Eleri's and Wade's faces, they'd found the same.

His page looked like a purely random scramble of letters and numbers, and he wasn't able to untangle it in any way. Normally, he was decent at code-cracking. He'd passed the FBI course. Not with flying colors, but well enough. Eleri had done fantastic at it when she was at Quantico, but even she didn't see what was going on in the damn notebooks. Though Wade didn't seem to get as frustrated as they did, when Donovan and Eleri slammed their notebooks shut, Wade seemed to catch on, and closed his more gently.

"Anything?" Donovan asked.

But Wade shook his head, making the whole thing a bust. They consoled themselves by ordering a pizza, not wanting to leave and waste time eating. There were only so many hours the three of them could get their heads together, and if they were out at a restaurant where they couldn't speak freely, they wouldn't make the best use of it. Even though they were in Omaha, it still wasn't safe to talk about the case or bring out the papers associated with it in public.

With the pizza ordered, they used their wait time to hit their next task: checking through the documents that Bennett had sent. He'd finished double-checking all the applications of the current Curie residents. Though he had been sending batches as he had them sorted, the mayor had finally finished the whole task. It was a huge job, and Bennett said he did the best he could.

There were just over thirty thousand people in Curie, Nebraska, and by the time Bennett was done, there were six thousand in his pile.

"So, one fifth of the town," Donovan said.

"Actually," Eleri said, "I think it's a slightly larger fraction of the applicants." She flipped through them and said, "Remember, there were no children who were the primaries on the applications. They were never considered 'applicants' the way the adults were."

"Didn't the children have to go through all the paperwork and testing?" Donovan said.

"No, not really. They were secondary to the parents, so when Marshall Bennett admitted—or didn't admit—someone, that decision was based on the parents themselves. So the children weren't included in any of his searches or any of these original files that he remembers or doesn't."

"You're saying he didn't search the whole thirty thousand?"

"No. Only the adults," Eleri told them.

"How many did he search?"

Eleri told him, "Only twenty-two thousand."

Donovan stopped and thought about it. It fit with what he knew of population dynamics. Children made up anywhere from twenty to thirty percent of a normal, healthy township. The eight-thousand Bennett hadn't looked at fit right in that gap, and Donovan wondered if he'd favored families with kids as a way of keeping the town going in future generations. Emersyn and Madisyn James and the Mazur twins certainly seemed like a bold step in that direction.

Then Donovan frowned at Eleri. "You know what I don't see too much of here? Older people."

Eleri nodded. "But that makes sense. To be in hospice care or even solidly into retirement, they would have had to move here and work and then retire. Who would apply to this town and then move everything for end-of-life care? The vast majority stay close to home." She looked to both of them, and neither he nor Wade found a flaw in her logic. "There are also virtually no family chains, either. Most small towns will have families representing cousins, siblings, or children who stay in town and raise their own children there. Grandparents are common in small towns, sometimes even four generations and two or three cousins over. When I was in college, taking genetics classes, we discussed that dynamic when we talked about alleles being identical by descent."

Donovan had nodded, understanding the term meant a person had a bit of genetic code in which both the maternal and paternal pieces were identical. In "identical by descent" cases, it came through both parents from a common ancestor they shared and was associated with inbreeding.

"Well, our genetics teacher asked," Eleri continued, "if any of us came from small towns, and if any of our families have been in those small towns for four or more generations. There were actually a reasonable number of students who had. The teacher then told them that they probably had some alleles that were identical by decent."

Donovan felt his lip curl. He did not remember learning that in medical school, despite numerous genetics courses.

"There are a couple of situations in Curie," Eleri said, "where one person came in, and a sibling, or a parent, or a child followed."

"Like the James brothers," Donovan said.

"Exactly. And Marshawn James brought his children."

"But that makes sense," Wade said. "Intelligence tends to run in families. There's a huge genetic component to IQ."

"Absolutely," Eleri agreed. "Still, there aren't many family chains, not yet, because the town is so new." She pointed, "This is our stack of unknowns, and it's limited to adults."

They each pulled out their own notes and searched the pile for anyone who had come in contact with Marat or Johanna, or whose name the FBI had found among those Marat and Johanna had dialed. Those were the first ones to tackle—the most likely to yield something of value in this crazy hunt.

Donovan looked down at the papers in front of him as another key piece of information came to him, and he began swearing. As Eleri and Wade looked up at him, the analyst arrived with their pizzas and interrupted. Whoever this delivery person was, he was a younger man who had graduated college, gone through FBI training, and come in as an analyst—although he must not have been very high on the Bureau totem pole, as he was fetching their pizza.

They still needed to buy their own drinks, and though the aroma was turning Donovan's stomach inside out, the three of them headed down the hall. Luckily, inside the Bureau walls, they could speak freely. Donovan explained his swearing.

"We actually need as much information as we can get about *workers* in Curie, too., he said. "We've been going after this as though our killer is an inside person, someone who passed all of Bennett's initial tests. But what if it isn't?"

"But the workers aren't as intelligent," Eleri complained. "Do you think they could pull this off? I mean, we still don't even know what the murder method is."

"But that's the problem," Donovan replied. "We're looking at it and assuming it's a highly complex method. What if it's not? What if it just isn't obvious? And, just because they're workers, just because they didn't get into Curie, that doesn't mean they aren't highly intelligent. Bennett turned away a handful of people with very high IQs that he simply didn't like, for whatever reason. And he picked that intelligence test. We can see that it works in the basic sense, but we don't know how accurate it is. The whole method is really dictatorial, when you think about it," Donovan said. "And you know what happens to dictators?"

"Coups!" Eleri and Wade said in unison as Wade plopped quarters into the machine.

Though the machine had a card reader, Donovan enjoyed the old fashioned clink of quarters, his sensitive ears detecting a variety of tones and even following the location of each quarter as it tumbled through the machine. Though he was frustrated with the case, he would enjoy the little things as he purchased his own drink.

"What you're saying," Eleri picked up, "is that it's possible someone who is highly intelligent is running these murders, and they're in town during the day, but not a resident. Well, that's a bitch," she said.

Obviously, it made sense or it wouldn't have been *a bitch.* Donovan filled in the obvious. "So we need to look at a lot more people."

"The day-trippers live nearby," Wade said. "So we need to see who Bennett tested and rejected."

"Absolutely," Eleri said, "but we also need huge numbers of people who didn't test. What if they're really intelligent and they just don't like Bennett's methods?"

"What if they're really intelligent," Donovan offered, "and they just don't test well, so they didn't even try?"

They were walking back down the hall with their drinks in their hands, and while it was interesting bouncing ideas off each other, every idea widened the scope of their search, and Donovan didn't like that at all.

After settling in to eat the pizza, they didn't take an actual break, but worked through the meal. With a slice in his hand, Donovan flipped through the paper files, trying not to get red sauce stains on his work.

For the first round, all they did was throw files into the middle of the table, pulling out papers for the people who'd been associated with Rychenkov and Schmitt. That pile at least was small, and it included Keyoor Vergheese, Jivika Das, and Marshawn James.

When they were done, there were more than a hundred names in their pile. Donovan was certain that they'd not only failed to crack the case, but they'd just made it worse.

33

Eleri's head hurt. It wasn't a headache she could treat with medication or caffeine, but the kind of ache when she had too many pieces of a puzzle bouncing around inside her skull. The pressure of the case made it feel as though rocks were tumbling in her head, and she could only hope that they were getting smooth and shiny, and would look great when they came out. But right now, she needed something to fight the feeling.

She and Donovan and Wade had all stayed at the branch office late into the night. Eventually, they'd given up and headed home, though they had to leave in shifts.

Eleri had stayed the latest, as Donovan was going to go in and work a full morning again at the clinic. They'd agreed Wade would be responsible for getting a tracker on Greg Whitlow's car. Though Eleri hated waiting, and could have done it faster herself, the fact that they'd been putting trackers on things in short order could've raised a flag if anyone was watching what they were doing. Besides, what if someone realized she was spotted beside two cars? The problem was the people around here would put two and two together and get "murder investigation."

Though Eleri had spent plenty of her life and her career paranoid about things she couldn't control, she didn't remember it ever being quite as bad as this. She was a firm believer in the phrasing, "It wasn't paranoia if they were really watching you." The problem now was—

while she didn't know that anybody *was* following her—she couldn't prove that anybody *wasn't*. Though she'd been in fishbowls before, this was the first time all the other fish were more than capable of figuring her out.

She no longer felt like one of the sharpest tools in her shed. In fact, she was pretty certain she was old and rusty, if she even qualified to be in the same shed with these people. She was also forced to protect the second biggest secret in town. The only person here with a bigger secret than the one she, Donovan, and Wade carried was the killer himself—or herself. Eleri was forced to admit that they had male DNA on Johanna Schmitt, but they also had two people responsible for the break-ins at the empty house. No one in town could be ruled out for being incapable of committing the murders.

Hell, even the high school kids had easily fixed Donovan's oven "problem" and knitted sweaters with Winnie The Pooh coded in binary. According to Wade, Madisyn James was building an interactive robot complete with AI and asking him questions about the physics of it, what kind of weight it needed, and how much joint strength it would require to walk or eventually run.

As a child, Eleri had defined herself by her family and her sister, until her sister had gone missing at age eight. Eleri had only been ten, but they'd been ten good, solid, formative years. Then everything changed. After Emmaline's disappearance, Eleri wanted to become an FBI agent. She wanted to find her sister, and she defined herself as being smart and hard-working.

But here in Curie, Nebraska? This was the first place where she'd felt downright stupid sometimes. She felt as though she had missed key pieces of this puzzle. If she could ask any of the townspeople, she believed, they would solve the murders in a flash.

But she and Donovan and Wade had to maintain their cover. The three agreed to wait to put the tracker on Greg Whitlow's car. To make it easier, and less obvious, Wade and Greg would have a parent meeting.

Wade had assured the two of them the night before that he could easily get under the car and place the tracker without Whitlow noticing. "Don't worry. I'll drop my coffee cup and roll it under the car. I'll get the tracker in there good." Though Eleri didn't doubt his ability, she still hadn't seen the requisite message on her secure system, letting them know it was done. She wouldn't see it until Wade was back at home on his FBI protected computer.

While Donovan had gotten up early, she'd managed to sleep in a little. It left her in the house alone. She was sick of cereal, though Donovan never seemed to tire of it, and she also needed to watch footage from the Rychenkov-Schmitt home—again. The cameras had been producing for over twenty-four hours. And though the agents were spot checking them regularly and hadn't caught any crimes in the act, all the hours in between also needed to be monitored.

She showered, dressed, and packed up to head out to the *Up N Atom*. She'd gone with Maggie the morning before, but it hadn't been a great friend-fest. Maggie had been sad, bordering on depressed, though it was fully understandable. It was hard to lose a friend suddenly, harder when murder was involved. Eleri had done her best to comfort the other woman, and they'd eaten and drunk coffee. Sitting in the corner, Maggie had talked about Johanna.

Though it was good hearing stories, Eleri didn't hear much that she thought she could use for the case. Maggie told her about Johanna's commentary on growing up as she had. That she'd been expected to become a wife and mother and had wound up doing most of what had been planned for her. Her first degree was in Home Economics, and she'd married as soon as she graduated. Apparently, she and her first husband had divorced relatively quickly, because he wanted children and she wanted another degree in something interesting.

She'd met Marat a little later in life, and the two had hit it off, but children had not been part of their equation. Maggie lamented that now there was nobody left to carry on the wonderfulness of who Marat and Johanna were.

It was Eleri who said, "But there are plenty of you carrying on after them. You do, and I've met the kids: Emersyn, Madisyn, Cage, Joule. They've all got a little bit of those two inside, so it's not as though their work and their . . . legacy won't go forward."

It must've been the wrong thing to say. Maggie had nodded, cried harder, apologized, hugged Eleri, and then headed out the door.

With Maggie as upset as she was, Eleri hadn't had much chance to steer the conversation toward the things she wanted and needed to know. At least she'd gotten coffee, and made more of a friend out of Maggie—she hoped. But that was yesterday, and today she was looking for a more positive outcome. At least she had control of the video and could check that box off their to-do list, even if she didn't see anyone else.

Finally, in the shop and glad she'd decided to come, Eleri stood in line without recognizing anyone except for the quirky barista—the one who still insisted on saying Vini, Vidi, and Vici with a hard V. This time, being adventurous, Eleri ordered the E=MCsquared, an *Up N Atom* special. She didn't doctor the drink at all, waiting to see what this concoction might be in its originally intended form. She added an egg pastry to her order, given that she'd skipped the cereal this morning.

Setting up shop in the corner as usual, Eleri cataloged the patrons' coming and going as she watched the video feed on her laptop screen. The Rychenkov-Schmitt home was her new binge. As usual, she watched it on a four-way split screen in fast forward, and was beginning to think she must have missed something.

No one had come into the home, not since she and Donovan had found Marat's USB. Eleri frowned at her screen, rewound, pulled footage from other cameras, and watched it all again.

Yesterday's footage, overnight footage, this morning—it all yielded nothing. It had been several days since the house last had a visitor. Their perp had been searching the home relatively regularly and—

"That's quite the frown you have."

Eleri jerked her gaze up and first noticed the paper cup that plunked on the other side of the table. Following the short, trim cut nails up an arm, she spotted Kaya Mazur at the end of that steaming coffee.

Good, Eleri thought. The timing was right, and Kaya often stopped in about now. "Hey." She put on a genuine smile, glad to see the woman. "How are you doing?"

"Apparently I'm doing better than you," Kaya said. "You look like you're about ready to kill that computer."

"Job hunting," Eleri said. "It's probably a good thing you interrupted me, or I might have strangled my laptop, and it's just the messenger. Now that you're here, I'm going to get rid of it." She hit a button, quickly pulling the security footage from the screen and shutting the laptop. "Are you staying?"

"I can. A little bit," Kaya said, and Eleri patted the seat beside her, motioning Kaya to come around to the side she was on so they could chat.

"So the job hunt is not going well?" Kaya asked.

"Less than stellar. I interviewed with several of the think tanks, but they don't seem to *think* they necessarily need a person with human physiology degrees."

"That was one of the perks of moving in early," Kaya told her, taking a sip from her coffee. "We had jobs waiting. The town was empty, and we were filling it in. It got busy quickly enough, but Bennett made sure that all of us who were in the first round had secure job positions. Now, it's a little more like a real town. What are you drinking?"

Eleri explained her order and they traded cups for sips.

"Oh, that's good," Eleri said, as peppermint and a dash of vanilla hit her tongue, before taking her own coffee cup back.

"I haven't had that before," Kaya said. "Could you maybe find a job in Lincoln in the meantime?" She changed subjects mid-statement and seemed to think Eleri would keep up.

Eleri talked her way through options in Lincoln for a few moments, and Kaya eventually grinned and said, "Look, I was debating whether to tell you this or not, but I think it's funny. I know you see my kids sometimes, so you can't tell them I told you. Please don't, or Joule would kill me."

"Oh," Eleri asked, feeling a bit of juicy gossip coming on, and wondering whether it would be pertinent to the case. "I can keep a secret." It was true in ways that Kaya Mazur had yet to guess.

"It's the funniest thing. Joule is convinced that you're an FBI agent."

If Eleri had been taking a drink, she would've choked on it or spit it across the table. Instead, she hoped the shock on her face looked like an actual reaction to being accused of being an undercover FBI agent.

"Really?" she said. "Okay. This I've got to hear. Why would she think that?" In fact, Eleri was actually very, very curious why a high-schooler might have pegged her.

"Actually, it's more than that. She thinks you and your friend are *both* FBI agents, and that you're here because we had a murder."

"Really?" *Holy. Fuck.* They'd been made by a high school girl.

Kaya continued, and as Eleri watched, she saw the mother really did find the whole idea humorous. *Thank God.*

"Yeah. I mean, you know we live catty corner to Johanna's house and Marat's? Last week, Joule saw workers going into the house. One was tall and one was short, and she decided that they were *you two*. She insists they had the same walks as the two of you do. And she thinks your time of arrival in town is suspicious." Kaya grinned at her own silliness and took another drink from her coffee.

Eleri was only glad that Kaya thought it was all a joke. "Well that's funny," she said out loud, adding, "I wonder what an FBI salary is. Maybe they're hiring!"

34

After Kaya Mazur left Eleri reeling at the table in the *Up N Atom,* Eleri tried to regain her focus. She had the rest of the footage from the Rychenkov-Schmitt home to go through, but her brain was agog.

Joule Mazur had *made* them. The teenager had seen them going into the neighbor's house and scoping it out for themselves dressed as workers. She'd recognized their gaits and put it all together. She even accounted for their coincidental times of arrival in Curie. At least her mother thought her child was being silly, but Eleri wondered how much longer she and Donovan could hold out. Eleri wondered if Joule had managed to keep her suspicions a secret from her twin brother, Cage.

The two kids seemed fairly close, maybe because they were so nerdy, or maybe because they were twins. But while they bantered a lot and teased each other, they didn't seem to truly bicker the way many siblings did. If Eleri counted that, then it meant Cage probably already knew Joule's suspicions, or he very shortly would. And if that were the case, then there was every possibility that Emersyn and Madisyn James would know in a few days, too. Again, if not already.

She was likely well and truly screwed.

Taking the worst-case scenario, Eleri had to account for the fact that there would now be four teenagers who were highly intelligent running around town who knew that Eleri and Donovan were FBI agents trying to solve a dual murder. At least Kaya Mazur hadn't mentioned the new science teacher at the high school . . .

Not cool, Eleri thought. She didn't think she'd ever had her cover blown quite so badly. She wanted to call Donovan, but the problem with that was the open phone line and the fact that she was still sitting in the *Up N Atom*. If she tried to drive right now, she was scrambled enough that she'd probably plow into a lamppost, and that wouldn't serve her purpose either.

So she flipped the laptop open again and tried her hardest to watch the footage. As she did, she found she had another major problem on her hands. She'd been right the first time. No one had gone into the Rychenkov-Schmitt home in quite some time—twice the average time span between previous visits, in fact. Though the visitor had searched the home repeatedly and on a regular basis, they either had given up or had found something else that they thought was adequate.

Maybe, in fact, the information that Eleri and Donovan were now pursuing—the notebooks and the drive—were either copies of the originals or had simply not been found. Maybe they'd been left behind by the visitor, because they were secondary to the real reason Marat had been murdered.

Eleri had to consider all these possibilities now. Unfortunately, her mind kept going to the fact that the people who seemed to have most often been in the Rychenkov-Schmitt home when Marat and Johanna were alive were Joule and Cage Mazur, the two who already seemed to figure out that Eleri and Donovan were FBI agents.

Eleri wanted to break cover badly, but there were so many protocols in place that would be blasted if she did it. She would have to first talk to Westerfield, to explain what they knew and that they'd been made. Thus, that breaking their cover wouldn't really be breaking it. And even if she did all that, Westerfield would still have to agree that this was the best solution. He very well might not. Eleri did not look forward to telling Westerfield that she'd not only been discovered but had been discovered by a high school student.

Secondly, she and Donovan couldn't just tell Joule and Cage that they were right. Legally, the twins were still under-aged—children, despite their obvious intelligence. Thus, the whole family would have to know, or at least one parent. Given that Kaya Mazur had already brushed the idea aside and found it silly, Eleri did not want to break that news to her. So she sat on it, as frustrated as it made her.

And third, Eleri added with a frown, this made Joule look more like a suspect. Eleri could admit her own bias in not wanting to investigate the teenager, but it would have to be done.

Eventually she'd watched all the video feeds and had seen nothing. Closing her laptop, she picked up her belongings and headed out, although it would still be a little while before Donovan ended his shift. So she took a turn to the right and made a few loops through the neighborhood of Kangaroo Court.

The name cracked her up. The Shire, C'thulhu Heights, even her own Pythagoras Point—each name had an air of seriousness to it, but Kangaroo Court had another meaning entirely.

Still, she saw several people out in the main fenced area playing with their dogs, Of course, she also spotted an actual kangaroo in with them, or maybe it was a wallaby, in the space she would have usually termed a "dog park." She turned the corner and saw a miniature donkey playing in one of the front yards, kicking up its heels as the sprinkler system came on. It wore a collar, and Eleri could only assume the small white flags around the border of the yard must have meant there was an underground fence and a shock system.

She passed Jivika Das's home and realized she didn't know what strange animal Das owned, if any. The backyards here were fenced with medium-height, wooden fences. Several had been built up taller, probably to contain whatever kinds of high-jumping animals the owners might have preferred.

Eleri hadn't heard a dog when they'd placed the tracker the other night, but this morning, she looked up and caught a cat in Das's second story window, so at least there was that. After seeing the house, she wound her way out of the neighborhood. Though she was pretending to want to buy the empty house several lots over, she couldn't be seen there too terribly much. She couldn't afford for Das to become suspicious of her, which the biomimickry specialist would not do unless for some reason Das became aware of someone scoping out her home. But if Das was the killer, then, well, she would be watching. She would catch on to Eleri relatively quickly.

Eleri brushed that thought aside. Hell, the high-schooler had already figured them out.

By the time she made it back to the Frank Lloyd Wright home, Donovan had arrived. "You're early," she offered by way of greeting.

"Ah, we got a lull. They sent me home."

"How are you doing with seeing live patients?" she asked, remembering how stressed he'd been the first day.

"It gets easier. They all have the same thing, so that helps."

She didn't comment that maybe they *didn't* all have the same thing, because surely Donovan knew what he was doing. He had attended and graduated medical school, after all. On top of that, he would never knowingly go into a clinic and perhaps under-treat or misdiagnose anyone. Then again, maybe he could *smell* strep or the flu.

She pointed to him and then pointed to the couch. "You need to come in here and sit down."

He offered up a wary look from the sides of his eyes. He'd been scrounging in the fridge, and his expression seemed to ask if it could wait until after he had food. But she shook her head; it couldn't. "Now."

Sitting him down and perching on the comfy chair across from him, she told him her two disturbing revelations of the morning. Both about Joule Mazur and about the fact that whoever was intruding into the Rychenkov-Schmitt home was no longer coming back to look for anything.

Donovan leaned back on the couch and sighed. "So you think they found what they were looking for?"

"I have no idea," Eleri sighed. They talked for a while about what to do about the high school kids and realized their job had just become infinitely harder. Donovan agreed that they didn't want to call Westerfield.

"We can't break cover anyway," he told her. "We can't trust high-schoolers to keep the secret."

Eleri agreed with all the points, even though she desperately wanted to be able to speak freely with even just *one* of the town's residents. Someone who might know something. Getting information out of people without them knowing was an art form. She was even relatively good at it; the patience was the part she lacked.

Eleri was just accepting her fate when her computer made a loud, buzzing noise. Within the same second, so did Donovan's. In one motion, both of them leapt toward the main table and flipped up screens and started clicking buttons.

"That's the home alarm alert." Eleri felt her heart still as she realized what it was.

"At Johanna Schmitt's," Donovan added the words without looking up from his screen. They'd set the alarm to call them every time it was activated—not just when it alerted the police or the fire department. It was another backup system that Eleri hadn't expected would ever get used.

Now, here it was.

She was starting to call up the video feed to see what was happening, when suddenly the alarm shut off.

35

"Shit!" Donovan practically shouted as he reached for the laptop Eleri had just aimed his direction. A minute ago, she'd offered to show him nothing, and now there was something.

Donovan watched as Eleri's fingers flew across the keyboard, clicking the trackpad buttons to bring up the images from the security cameras. She quickly dialed up the common, four-screen split view. And he watched as the image from the front door of the Rychenkov-Schmitt home loaded into the top left of the screen. Another appeared to be streaming an image of the back door. The third showed the inside of the garage, and the last one scanned inside the living area.

What became apparent was that someone had busted through the glass in the back door. It appeared, from the broken shards on the floor, that they must have broken the glass and reached in to open the door from the inside knob. The security feed was ever-so-slightly delayed, but the alarm was practically on point. Thus, it had activated but already turned off. Donovan frowned, not quite catching why that was important.

The alarm was set to signal the police or fire department, depending on what triggered it. But it alerted him and Eleri regardless of the cause. Now he could see the box, just inside the back door. Though no one was visible on the camera feed, the box was silent—

no lights, no sound—with the broken glass scattered on the floor beneath it.

Then his brain clicked as to why the alarm ending was an issue. The person who had entered had put the correct code into the alarm system, thus silencing it. If it was done quickly enough, the police would not be alerted, and the backup protocol—a call from the security company—would not have to be activated. Whoever was in the home would not have to answer the three system security questions that Marat and Johanna had set.

Donovan and Eleri had not messed with anything internal to the system, only piggybacked it to alert them if it went off. So Donovan frowned at the screen. No, he hadn't figured it all out yet.

"Let's go!" Eleri jolted him from his thoughts. She was already gathering her bag and heading to the door in the kitchen that led to the garage. "If we leave now, maybe we can get there before they leave."

"But we can watch the footage," Donovan said, "and get the person later."

"If we catch them in the act, we don't—*Shit*," she said, "we will have to break cover. But we're probably going to have to do that either way. I say we can catch them in the act," Eleri said, "Don't you think we have a better chance of getting them to talk if we are doing so inside the Rychenkov-Schmitt home? Rather than tracking this person down later today or tomorrow?"

"Damn." Donovan had to agree. Before he'd finished the word, Eleri was flying out the door into the garage. He'd been hungry when he walked in. Eleri had interrupted his digging in the fridge to tell him important news. While he agreed the news had been important, he was still hungry. Now he had no idea how long it would before he could eat. Haphazardly, he reached into the pantry as he jogged by and grabbed a fistful of granola bars as he headed out the door. Trailing along behind her, he asked her to please drive.

Climbing into the passenger side of her car, Donovan peeled the wrapper on one bar, shoving half of it into his mouth in one bite as she backed rapidly out of the driveway.

The problem with this scenario was that they were heading to the home in the middle of a break-in, but they still had not seen the intruder—or intruders.

He chewed as Eleri took the turn, exiting Pythagoras Point just a little too sharply. His hand automatically reached up to hold on to what his father had always referred to as the "oh shit" bar as he spoke. "This isn't the same intruder, and we don't know who we're encountering."

"Why is it not the same?" she asked, obviously not following the same line of thought.

"Because the old intruder knew the new code that Johanna Schmitt had changed it to. This one didn't. In fact, this one went so far as to break the glass. So they not only didn't know the code, they don't even know how to hack the system and find the code."

"True," Eleri replied, "but they knew the inside code to turn off the alarm. And it seems they managed to do that quickly enough to not have even alerted the police. They were prepared to use that code. It only alerted us because we had it rigged."

"El," he said, more cautiously, even as she hooked the car around another sharp turn, "this means our intruder knew Marat well. But not Johanna. This person knew *him* well enough to know the alarm code to his house. It's an old code, probably. Johanna never said she reset that one. But this person knows it, most likely because they had been there with Marat. He either trusted them enough to give them the code to his alarm system, or else they were able to watch him put it in."

He imagined the scenario they raced toward. "So they came in, probably thinking they could walk right into the house with the codes. Probably they knew the old code for the digital lock. Obviously, he or she didn't have a good workaround plan, because they wound up breaking the glass. But, once they got into the house, Marat's silencing code worked on the alarm system. Hopefully, it means they think they're okay as it is. No worries until someone finds the broken glass in a home no one lives in."

"Which means they are probably still in the house right now." Eleri took another sharp turn, this time to the left, throwing Donovan against the door. He reached out and pushed the button to lock all of the doors. Even as he pressed up against the side of the car, the clicking sound comforted him. The way Eleri was driving, he wasn't so confident that even his seatbelt would keep him from rolling clear.

"El, I know we want to get there, but we can't get pulled over. None of the police officers know who we are . . . or what we are. We can't be seen driving erratically to get to a stranger's house. We have to look like we just randomly arrived in the neighborhood."

"*Shit,* Donovan," she growled, apparently realizing he was right, even as she slowed the car. "I was in Jivika Das's neighborhood this morning. Just driving around. Can I be 'just driving around' this one, too? Am I showing you something? A house for sale?" Eleri kept asking questions Donovan didn't yet have the answers to. "Why are we there? What are we visiting for? We're not. We have no good excuse. We don't even have our workman's uniforms on. Can we park on the street behind?"

She cranked the wheel for another turn, and he didn't feel the acceleration quite as strongly.

"So you mean like the other intruder did—go to the house on the street behind, hope they aren't home, sneak across and climb the fence?" he asked.

"Something like that. We can't go in the front of Johanna's house, because if they see us—God forbid—the Mazur kids are going to *know* we're exactly what Joule thinks we are. At least right now she's got her mother telling her she's being silly."

"Did Kaya really tell her that? Or did Kaya maybe humor her?"

"*Shit,*" Eleri blurted out again, taking yet another turn, this one looping them around Copernicus Circle.

They were close, at least, he thought. *Maybe the intruder is still there.* But he kept the conversation on the other point. "Kaya Mazur told you that she thinks Joule's idea—that we're FBI agents—is silly. But did she tell you that she told *Joule* that?"

"*Fuck,*" Eleri muttered, "I don't know. I guess I just assumed she did."

"Because if she didn't," Donovan continued, "then it's very plausible that Joule and Cage are staking us out as often as they can."

"So we *have to* go into the neighborhood from the other direction. We can't even go by the front of the Schmitt home."

"Right," Donovan said, "because that path will take us right in front of the Mazur home as well."

They pulled up a little too quickly to the house that sat directly behind Johanna and Marat's. As Eleri pushed the gear into park, Donovan climbed out and looked around, shoving the last of the granola bars into his mouth. Still chewing, he walked up to the front door, and knocked. This time, he didn't hear anything, and he was grateful.

They'd been trained to listen for footsteps from the back of the house, dogs barking, that kind of thing. Anything that would indicate somebody was eventually going to come to the door. His keen ears told him more, and he told Eleri, "No one's here. Let's just quickly go around to the back and hope no one sees us."

They acted as though they were checking the place out, looking for the owner or such. Donovan even motioned as though he heard someone in the back, and they headed around. Once they were behind the house, though, they both bolted for the fence, and he was grateful he was wearing something he could run in. To be fair, his khaki pants and blue button-down shirt weren't the best for fence climbing.

He'd popped himself up and over the fence before he even realized that he'd left Eleri in the dust. Climbing back up to reach over and help, he spotted her fingers loop the tops of the flush pickets. She was small, but she stayed in shape. She knew what the job was, and sometimes the job was this: scaling a fence in the middle of the afternoon, quickly.

He watched as she forced herself up by brute strength, coming up onto her hands, and throwing one leg over the fence. Once she was there, she was over and down on the other side as quickly as he had been. Looking at each other, they didn't speak, but the conversation clearly passed between them. They were going to storm the house and catch the person in the act—even though neither of them had their guns on them. They had their badges, and he hoped it would work.

It was the plan now, whatever happened. Donovan took off running for the back door and busted it in with a well-placed kick.

36

Eleri couldn't have been more stunned by the woman they found in the home. If Donovan was right, and she suspected he was, Jivika Das had *not* broken into this home before.

Had she been one of their recent intruders, she would have known the codes. Besides, as Eleri thought back, those who had broken in before had seemed to know what they were doing. They'd come in strong, they'd snuck around, they'd looked—apparently—for something in particular, and they'd left. Which meant they possibly now had *three* different intruders into this house, with two of them likely working together.

Jivika was doing nothing to indicate any organization at all. In fact, as soon as the back door slammed open and Eleri and Donovan came in, even Eleri could hear her running up the stairs. Their culprit seemed to startle, then she turned and ran down the steps right toward them. She seemed startled again when she saw Eleri and Donovan standing there.

Jesus, Eleri thought. If they had known it was Jivika breaking in, they wouldn't have had to confront her. They would have only needed to follow the tracker on her car later to know what was going on. But that option didn't matter anymore. They'd played this card and they had exposed at least part of the fact that they weren't casual new entries to town. Now they would have to live with the consequences.

Eleri looked to Donovan, and he glanced back at her quickly. His expression said he knew they'd blown their cover and they would have to swear Jivika Das to secrecy—or arrest her. If she couldn't stay quiet about what they were, or if either of them got any kind of feeling that they couldn't trust her, they would likely have to take her out of town just to get rid of her and keep her from spreading the news. Then again, if Jivika was their killer, then they had a whole different set of problems on their hands.

Realizing there was only one thing she could reasonably do, Eleri reached into her back pocket, pulling the folded wallet out and flipping it open, showing it to Jivika. Where the woman had previously looked startled and confused, she now looked wholly surprised. Eleri had been prepared for Das to think she was reaching for a gun, and the way her shoulders had stiffened in surprise wasn't a shock to Eleri. Das's expression changed to defeat as she recognized the badge she was seeing, and her shoulders sagged.

Donovan had pulled his badge, too, so it was clear that Jivika Das was facing a pair of agents. It was likely that she'd just now figured out that they'd been brought in to solve the murders of the people who had lived in the home she'd broken into.

"You better start talking," Eleri said, "*Fast.* Tell us everything."

No one moved, though Jivika's stance certainly changed. She looked to the left and then to the right, and then at last she looked them in the eye and said, "Good."

This time it was Eleri who was startled. For a moment, she braced, waiting for Jivika to reach backward into the waistband of the skirt she was wearing to pull out her own gun.

Eleri's brain flashed quickly to her past dangerous encounters and she wondered, if she was scared enough, could she stop a bullet? She honestly didn't know the answer and worked to quell her heart rate as Jivika began speaking, not reaching for a gun, though Donovan interrupted the woman to say, "Keep your hands where we can see them."

To her credit, the woman looked startled to be even told such a thing, but what she said was, "I'm glad somebody's investigating. Somebody murdered Marat, and they murdered Johanna, too."

"What are you doing in this house?" Eleri asked, maintaining her stance even though she didn't have a gun to train on her newest witness.

"I wanted to find Marat's things," Jivika said. "I wanted to see if they'd been stolen. See if I could figure out who took them."

"What things?" Eleri prodded, grateful that Donovan let her lead the questioning, and knowing that he would jump in if she missed something or didn't see a connection that he did.

Jivika shook her head. "I don't know."

There, Eleri thought. The twitch of her eye. The fleeting moment at which her gaze darted down and to the left. *She lied.* Jivika Das did know what Marat Rychenkov had been killed for. Did that make her the killer?

Thinking that through, Eleri realized she couldn't quite make that connection, given the video they had of previous intruders. Eleri shifted topics, wondering if she could possibly catch Jivika Das off-guard by using a non-linear questioning path.

Most of the time, she would count on such a system, but here, in Curie, she didn't count on much of anything. "How did you know the code to the alarm system?"

Jivika's shoulders straightened and she looked them in the eye. "Marat told it to me."

Not a lie, Eleri thought. *So we have a burglar full of half-truths and bold statements.* "Then why didn't you know the door code?"

The woman shrugged. "The door code didn't work." Jivika was still looking at them, shoulders still square. *Also not a lie.*

"Why not?"

"Johanna must have changed it, or someone did after Johanna died. It's not the code that Marat gave me."

"When was the first time you came back to the house after Marat died?"

"Three days later," Jivika replied, and Eleri squinted at her, wondering if she was, in fact, one of the intruders they'd seen and she'd used the old code for a smooth entry before Johanna changed it. This time, she was forced to break the glass. If that were the case, then they might have only two intruders. Eleri tucked that information away.

"What did you do when you broke in that time?"

"I—I didn't break in! Not that time. I *visited Johanna!* I went to the market and bought her a roasted chicken and potato salad and a side of green beans, and I brought her food so she would have something to eat."

"How did you enter the home?" Eleri asked, realizing she'd made a possibly erroneous leap from a poorly worded question.

Jivika looked affronted by the simple question. "I knocked on the front door, and then Johanna answered and invited me in."

"How many times have you broken in?" Eleri asked.

Now Das looked irritated. "Just this once. Obviously, I did a crap job of it, too." Again, her eyes darted down, but Eleri couldn't tell whether this motion was just self-deprecating or whether it indicated another lie. If it did, this one was definitely of a different caliber.

"Marat Rychenkov called you frequently," Eleri said, and watched as Jivika's eyes widened in surprise. Although, at this point, she figured Jivika's brain had to be churning, too, and she had to have realized she was facing two FBI agents. Surely, she would catch on quickly that they knew things she probably hadn't expected them to.

She shook her head though, as if denying Eleri's statement of fact. "I already told the police what Marat and I were working on together. That's why he called me frequently. He kept asking me questions. I'm a biomolecular mimicry specialist," she said, and again, Eleri watched her stance change to yet another new form. This one Eleri recognized: *Academic, speaking in her field of expertise.* Again, Eleri asked, "Why did you break in?"

"I just wanted to find Marat's notes," Jivika said, and that part was straightforward. But her eyes darted again when she said, "I wanted to find out why someone murdered him and then Johanna, in hopes that maybe I could prevent it from going any further."

No, Eleri thought, *that was another lie.*

37

At two in the morning, Donovan was lying on the couch staring at the ceiling. Fifteen minutes earlier, he'd been lying in his bed staring at the ceiling there, but after a while he'd decided this was a better ceiling to stare at.

At least down here there was a vaulted roof line, thick beams overhead, and wide windows. He could see up into the trees and out in little snippets toward the sky, with the occasional star. Curie didn't produce quite enough light pollution to remove the twinkle from the sky and he wondered if that was one of Marshall Bennett's considerations when buying up the land. Even though he could only see one here and there, for a moment he could pretend he was home in South Carolina, where the whole night sky was often visible.

His body ached with the need to shift and go running, but it wasn't an option. Not only because he didn't know how to get out of town and go do it, but also because he was here as an acting agent. If he disappeared for a while into a form where no one could have access to him, he wasn't being a very good partner to Eleri.

He'd smelled the wolf on Keyoor Vergheese as well. So far, Whitlow's friend was the only one Donovan had scented, and he wondered several things about the anomaly. Did Whitlow know what his friend was? And why was Vergheese here? Just as the Lobomau had been attracted to New Orleans, did no one come to Nebraska?

Certain places were hot spots, while others might be practically repellent.

He wondered where Vergheese went when he ran and if it might be worth it to follow him and find out, since he and Eleri had no idea how long they would be here. Did the wolf drive out into the family-owned farms in between here and Beatrice, or go toward Lincoln? Did he walk out into the cornstalks, leave his clothes behind, then change and run?

The stalks were sharper than people gave them credit for, Donovan knew—not quite the romanticized playgrounds that were always seen in movies. Though he looked out and saw the stars, and for a moment imagined himself underneath them with the cornstalks brushing his fur as he went by, he didn't make a move to get up or leave or actually act on any of it.

The day had been far too complex and—though he hoped Eleri was asleep upstairs—it was still churning in his brain. In a strategic move, they'd let Jivika Das leave on her own from the Rychenkov-Schmitt home. They'd asked her how she'd come in and it turned out she'd parked around front, knocked on the front door, and gone around to the back, much as they had at the other house. They sent her back out the front door and told her, in straightforward FBI orders, that she was to go directly home. They would arrive shortly, and she was to let them in.

Donovan made it clear to Jivika that she was not to flee, because they would find her. They were, after all, the FBI. He didn't mention the tracker on her car and hoped she hadn’t found it. Though higher tech options were available, these were radio sensitive, and a sweep of her car would reveal its exact location.

He and Eleri hadn’t gone to the effort to requisition the FBI for better tracker models. Lord knew the residents of Curie could probably find them anyway. They’d told Das they would give her a little bit of a head start, but they didn't give her more than a one-minute lead time.

The heat had been turned off in the Rychenkov-Schmitt house and Donovan could see that Eleri was starting to get cold. Probably she hadn't noticed it when they first walked in, because they were so high on the adrenaline of finding someone. But as they questioned Jivika, and as her answers both sounded and smelled ever-so-slightly like lies, the room had made them both colder and colder.

His only consolation was that Jivika must have suffered from it as well.

Before they'd all left, Eleri patted the woman down and found nothing on her. So, if Jivika had found something in the house, she'd swallowed it or . . . He didn't want to contemplate it. Once she was gone, he and Eleri considered patching up the back window, but instead opted to use their time going after Jivika.

They'd told Das that she would have a head start, but they lied. They headed straight back over the fence, praying no one had come home to the other house, and jumped quickly into Eleri's car.

Eleri practically barreled out of the neighborhood, taking more sharp turns as she headed toward Kangaroo Court where, this time, they parked directly in front of Jivika's house. Heading up the front walk, they knocked on the door, and when Jivika answered, Eleri threw herself into the woman's arms as though they were old friends. Donovan could hear the words—though a normal person would not have—as Eleri whispered into the woman's ear, "Go with it. We are your best friends now. This is the only way you keep your job and stay in town."

Jivika pasted on a wide, fake smile, probably visible to the people who lived across the street, whoever they might be. Donovan made a mental note to look up the names of all her neighbors. Once they'd gotten home later, he had, but none of the names popped. None matched from any of their lists of Rychenkov's phone calls or from Marshall Bennett's unremembered applicants. Nothing stood out, *nothing*.

Once inside the Das home, Donovan started off with a casual, "You live in Kangaroo Court, yet you only have a cat?"

She'd blinked a little, likely wondering how they knew about her choice of pet, but Eleri had mentioned seeing the cat in the window and with several sniffs, Donovan was aware that the woman had no other animals.

Jivika huffed a little. "I'm a biomolecular mimicry specialist. I choose to live here, in the middle of all the biology. You wouldn't believe the number of times that I've been working on something—some theoretical problem—and somebody's out walking their llama down the street." She waved her hand toward the sidewalk beyond the walls of her home. "And I see their hooves or their fur and it sparks something. Or the llama decides it's time for a skirmish with the kangaroo and it's an interesting little battle. But while I watch, I solve something."

"And the cat?" Donovan asked.

"Never solves anything," Jivika said with a smirk. As he'd hoped, the humor put her a little bit at ease. Seeming to find some level of comfort with them, she offered them tea but both agents declined.

He could tell Eleri was concerned about accepting food from the possible killer. For a moment, Donovan thought maybe he should have accepted and sniffed it to check. But GHB itself was odorless, even to him. If Das was cooking up an alternate version, he might smell that but—since he wouldn't know what he was sniffing for or which way the odor might go—*Bananas? Chemicals?*—he wouldn't know if it was there or not. In fact, it might even smell like tea.

Eleri dove in with the harder-hitting questions, leaving Donovan to play good cop, albeit a slightly creepy version who knew too much about their suspect. As she talked, he took advantage, sniffing at things around the house, making observations, and asking disturbing questions as though they already knew more than they did.

But before he even got to ask about her habits, Eleri asked, "How did you kill Marat Rychenkov?"

Though Jivika had startled and seemed affronted, and though he'd smelled fear, Eleri had made a motion to him that the woman was telling the truth when she simply said, "I did not kill Marat. And, before you ask, I didn't kill Johanna either. I've never killed a person."

Donovan frowned. "What have you killed?"

"Mice. Lab mice. Sadly, tons of them. I occasionally had to sacrifice turtles in college. We did vivisections, and that was the worst. I've killed lots of frogs for neuro labs. I can't tell you how many, only that I had a guillotine. But the rats and the bullfrogs, they're the largest things I've ever sacrificed."

Donovan heard her odd wording, but it made sense to him. She didn't *kill* Marat or Johanna and she had *sacrificed* lab animals. When he was an undergrad, he'd been in labs like the one she had. It didn't strike him as odd, luckily for her.

Eventually, they'd sworn the woman to secrecy about their jobs and their goals in town. They let her know that—given her age—if she let on to anyone who or what they were, it would mean a lifetime in jail for her.

The problem that was keeping him awake now was that, though

she'd answered most of their questions clearly, she'd fudged her comments on what she and Marat were working on. So when he and Eleri left, they'd wracked their brains trying to figure it out.

They'd left Jivika Das at home, but he lay there on the couch now looking up at the stars and his heart felt heavy because he knew something was wrong, even if he couldn't put his finger on it.

38

Eleri had the house to herself that morning. Donovan had, once again, gotten up early and gone to the clinic to see patients. Though she knew that was his position and his cover, she couldn't help but feeling that she'd been left behind to clean up all the mess of the night before.

The feelings were pointless, she reminded herself. It was all part of the odd job they both did. So she started with a call to Marshall Bennett and had him send Kate to set the Rychenkov-Schmitt house to rights again. They had to get the glass replaced in the back window, and it had to be non-obvious to anyone walking by that the place had been broken into.

Eleri suggested Kate put the FOR SALE sign out, in hopes that it might spur their intruders to come back. The fear that the house would get cleaned out soon might press the intruders to try again to find whatever they'd been missing. Eleri was relatively certain—though not one hundred percent—that Jivika Das was not one of their previous intruders.

Jivika had been in the house for something else, and she'd been heading upstairs. Eleri could only assume the woman was aiming for Marat's office. She wondered if Jivika had been after the notebooks. Eleri wanted to believe that, because that would mean Jivika was connected to the crime. It would also mean that Eleri now held the item the killer wanted. But she wasn't sure, and she knew she couldn't trust the desire to have cracked at least one portion of this case.

It was just as possible that Jivika was there solely to figure out why her friend had been murdered, and Eleri held exactly zero cards. She didn't know.

Once she'd cleared things up with Bennett, she'd taken a deep breath and made her second call to SAC Westerfield. He'd answered on the first ring with his gruff, and normal, "What do you have?" eschewing all semblance of a polite greeting.

Eleri desperately wanted to answer with, "Exactly jack shit, but luckily more shit than yesterday's shit, sir." However, she'd told him about the run-in with Jivika Das. As she spoke, the vision came to her of him putting his head in his hand, his phone propped on the desk in front of him, speaker phone broadcasting her small voice, while his other hand fidgeted, a shiny quarter walking across the back of his knuckles. She wasn't sure if that was just what she knew from the time she'd spent with the man, or if it was an actual physic vision of what was occurring right now.

Though the vision itself was interesting—maybe she hadn't lost everything—she couldn't give it any attention. She just wanted to get through this phone call with her emotions intact. She had to tell her boss that they'd fucked up.

"So you broke cover again?" he asked.

"Yes," Eleri replied, not adding, *and this time it was without permission,* because that part was pretty obvious.

"You patted her down? She didn't take anything from the home?"

"Yes. And not that we could find, sir." This was the way the phone calls went when she had exactly jack shit. She let Westerfield lead with his questions.

"Do you need backup?" he asked.

"What would you give us? We already have Wade and we can barely communicate with him as it is." Though they could e-mail, being forced to use FBI servers meant that constant contact was virtually impossible. The fear of being hacked was ever present.

Westerfield continued interrogating her. What did she pick up? What did Donovan smell? And in the end, he concluded that while they hadn't done the right thing, they'd chosen the only valid option available at the time. At last, Eleri hung up the phone, glad that unpleasant task was over.

She next headed out the front door, gathering the mail left in the box from the day before, as was her routine. Luckily, this time she saw Marshawn. As she waved to him, she thought again that Westerfield had put them in the right place. The house next store was relatively busy, even if her visitor wasn't LeDonRic.

"Hey, Marshawn," she called out.

"Eleri!" the big man called back. He was taller but thinner than his brother. Marshawn James had a wide smile and an easygoing demeanor.

"Are the girls here?" she asked with a frown on her face, as it was the middle of a weekday.

"Nah, my girls are in school," he told her, and then pointed to the front door of the house. "Left my jacket and my favorite sunglasses the other night."

Eleri didn't ask why he had a key. It was his brother's home. They lived in the same town. Instead, she asked for his help, always a winning move with friendly people.

"Can you do me a favor? Donovan said he wanted me to pick up some 'lightning tree corn' today. He had some ready when I first moved in. I'm supposed to go back and get more. It was phenomenal."

"Oh, yeah," Marshawn replied. "That stuff is amazing."

"Okay. But what is it? I thought most of the corn grown around here was for livestock. Definitely not fit for human consumption."

"That's true," Marshawn told her, coming part way across the lawn, even though he seemed to have unlocked his brother's door already. The people here, Eleri had noticed, were relatively trusting. It made sense, given that there was little crime—until now, when they were dealing with two murders.

"So what happened," he explained, "is this family had a small plot where they grew their own food grade corn for themselves. They operated a small roadside stand. Like most, the vast majority of the farm produced livestock corn, like you're talking about. But they had a big, old tree in the middle of it that they didn't want to cut down, so it was the right place to do a little crop that was hand-harvested. So they planted some sweet corn around the tree."

"And then the tree got struck by lightning," Eleri guessed.

"Exactly. What they noticed was that the scorched soil grew the best corn. They've been going out and re-electrifying the tree stump ever since, to keep the lightning corn flavor."

"*What*?" Eleri asked. "Are you serious?"

"Oh, yeah. Don and I went out and did it with them the year before last. Apparently, what they'd been doing wasn't quite up to par with the original lightning flavor. See, the first year, they burned the tree stump. It didn't give the corn the same taste. Don had been out buying the corn, and he commented that it was good, but not as good as before. So—you know Don—he asked, did they need fertilizer? And they told him about it, so next thing you know, he and I are out there with some crazy ass, homemade batteries, hooking up this tree and zapping it. Eventually, we put a lightning rod into it, so it gets struck naturally more often, and the corn's been pretty good. They've been selling it going on five years now."

"Wow. There's a story you don't hear every day," she said. "Okay, so the next thing I need to know is: how do I get to there?"

He gave her instructions. "Heading toward Beatrice on Homestead, take a left at Pickrell, at the huge, white farmhouse. The one with the *blue* shutters." As Eleri had learned, apparently the shutter color was the only thing distinguishing many a white Nebraska farmhouse from another. Then he added, "It has four silos on the processing plant."

"Got it."

"And then, of course, once you get on the right street—it's gravel—you'll see the Lightning Tree Corn stand there on the right. And you'll see what's left of the lightning tree itself." He grinned at her.

"Well if you guys go back out with your batteries, then I want to go with you," she smiled.

"I know. It should be a party, right?"

She laughed and thanked him and watched as he headed back inside his brother's. Her agent brain couldn't help but wonder if he was doing something nefarious inside. She stayed near the mailbox, flipping through the mail, sorting the junk mail to the back, and even opening things as she stood there. The weather, though turning colder, was still at least decent enough that she could pretend this was a normal activity.

Marshawn came back out in just a few moments, jacket in hand. He waved at her as he headed back to his car, which was parked in front of the house.

She smiled and called out, "I was up way too late last night, and I saw an infomercial for what I think was your mop."

He grinned and headed over to chat again. They talked for a few more moments, and she told him that Emersyn had told her about her dad's inventions. "She's really proud of you. So what are you working on now?" she asked, still trying to be casual.

"Can't tell. Top secret." He grinned, white teeth flashing, and put a finger to his lips.

His answer made sense. Still, she wanted to ferret it out. She wanted to rule him out as a possible killer. For a moment, she thought about how to find out what his new project might even be.

And that was the problem right there. When they had no leads, everyone was a suspect.

39

Though her interaction with Marshawn had been pleasant, the rest of Eleri's day had been a slog. She'd headed into the *Up N Atom* and ordered yet another new coffee. Though she was out of the house for the sole purpose of interacting with Curie residents, she managed to see exactly no one of any relevance to the case, at least that she could tell.

However, her brain was still turned to suspicion mode and she was evaluating everyone who came through the door. Had Kaya Mazur come in, she would not have felt comfortable sitting at the table with Eleri—not with the looks that were likely crossing her face.

While she drank her coffee and nursed another egg pastry, Eleri found herself watching well over an hour of a four-way split screen, showing the security footage from the Rychenkov-Schmitt home.

Once again, everything came up empty. She started from the time when the two of them entered the home, encountering Jivika, and worked her way through every camera angle, all the way up to live feed of the current time. The only intruders she found were Kate setting out the FOR SALE sign, and the glass repairman she let in who put the back door to rights.

Kate sweeping the glass off the floor was the most interesting thing Eleri had seen on the video. But Kate had left the home several hours before, and even with the glass repaired and the sign like a beacon out front, no intruders had come.

The only upside was that no one had come between the night before when Jivika had entered and now, when the glass was repaired. So if the intruder came back, at least there shouldn't be a flag that someone else had been there in the meantime.

Eleri closed the laptop. Out of the shop and on her way, she'd driven almost aimlessly around Kangaroo Court, though Jivika was at work. She'd decided it was worth risking a hacker knowing what she was looking at to keep track of her one good lead. So she checked the tracking device on Jivika Das's car and found that the car had gone to work in the morning and stayed there in the parking lot.

Eleri had no reason to believe that Das had found the tracker. Still, she also had no reason to believe that Das hadn't. With nothing necessary in her plans for the day—which was as depressing as everything else—she found that she spent the afternoon doing small tasks. She trekked out of town and bought Lightning Tree Corn, then she re-watched the videos from Rychenkov's USB. Once again, she saw nothing of major value.

They'd handed copies of the videos over to the analysts at the FBI, but so far, no one had called them back with any news, good or bad. So she dove into the notebooks again, trailing her fingers along the words, and noticing only the same things she'd found before.

It did appear there were indentations in the pages, but far from being a code or secret message, Eleri discovered that when she followed them, they were merely where the pen had pressed from the page before. Neither the videos nor the notebooks turned up anything of value, at least not that she was able to read. It was frustrating, because she was certain the answer was right under her nose. She'd looked again at the words in the notebook—if they were indeed words—and tried once more to crack Rychenkov's system.

The shortest "words" were two digits, which seemed unusual, as "a" and "I" should clock in at one. And the "words" themselves were longer than average English words. Eleri knew it was possible that he'd not only converted to code but written in a different language. It was her understanding that Rychenkov had grown up speaking Russian. Like many immigrants, he also spoke several other languages. French was apparently in his repertoire as one of his high-fluency languages.

She guessed he wouldn't keep his personal notebooks in a low fluency language, although the man apparently also could communicate reasonably in Spanish, Farsi, and Mandarin. She made a note to get the books checked against those languages, too. Just in case he hadn't been exceptional enough in life, the more she learned about him in death, the more it made her feel once again like the fool who'd been let into the city when she hadn't passed the test.

Giving up on yet another task, she hopped in the car and managed to arrive at Jivika Das's home just before Das did. That had been her intent. With the tracker, she could see when the woman left work. If she arrived afterward, then it would be apparent that she was tracing the woman's movements. Eleri was not yet willing to give away this secret.

Though they'd not executed a search warrant, they had asked the woman if it was okay to search her home the night before. Jivika had waved her hand around and said, "Please look at whatever you like. If it helps solve Marat's murder, I'm all for it."

Eleri could not detect anything in the woman's tone or expression that made her think she had anything to hide. In fact, even if she'd said no, they would have searched the home most likely anyway—either through logical bullying or an immediate search warrant. Eleri was glad the woman had agreed. She'd wanted the opportunity to warn Jivika and then watch her face, to play a game Jivika didn't know she was playing of "warmer and colder."

It hadn't worked. Though Eleri had sensed she was "warmer" in Jivika's office, she'd found nothing of value. So tonight, she came back and waited. Once Jivika arrived, Eleri made herself overly chummy and followed her into the home.

When she asked, "What did you do today at work?" she was met with only, "My job."

"What are your current projects?"

"I have top-level national security clearance. I can't tell you any of that. I'm assuming you're testing me by asking me these questions, but I won't reveal anything until you have the proper paperwork and I've gotten word from my superiors to tell you."

"You can tell me if they were related to Marat Rychenkov's projects."

"No, they aren't," Jivika said, clear and fast. Once again, not a lie. Eleri was hoping to insinuate herself in Jivika's life, interviewing her by brute force whenever possible, until the woman either cracked or slipped up, but tonight Jivika answered all the questions with clear, sharp responses.

So, while Eleri had made headway, she couldn't say she'd accomplished anything. She hadn't expected to make much headway, but as she drove back toward the Frank Lloyd Wright House, thoroughly disappointed, she had to admit that she had hoped.

They were almost a week and a half out on Johanna's murder, which put them two plus weeks out on Marat's. They'd released Johanna's body and a funeral was being held Saturday. That meant she and Donovan would attend and look for their killer at the ceremony, as almost certainly he or she would either have to come as a friend or would show up to see what they'd done.

Still, Saturday felt like a long time away, and Eleri wasn't sure she could wait that long for a break in this case. The lack of progress was killing her.

She headed home as discouraged as she'd ever been. And when she arrived home and checked her FBI laptop, she discovered a message from GJ, a very excited, "Call me!"

Thank God, Eleri thought, *something positive.* Though with GJ Janson, it was hard to tell. Some things that GJ thought were pertinent might turn out to be useless.

Then again, it was entirely plausible that GJ had figured out who the murderer was and, in an hour or two, Eleri would be making an arrest and leaving Curie. Though she'd be glad for the case to be over, she would admit to everyone that she was sad to be leaving the town.

Curie would have been a fun place to hang out, to just be, and not have to be an agent. However, the same things she liked about the place meant she couldn't simply call GJ Janson back. A call like this, which they'd been avoiding as much as possible, required a secure line. They had a bag of burner phones, but Donovan kept them in his room, having brought them when he first arrived. Those phones were not traceable to the local box store or anything of the sort. Still, the signal would triangulate to the area and possibly to this house, depending on how well the cell towers were set up here.

Again, she told herself, *This is Curie, Nebraska. Don't put anything past them.* So she grabbed one of the phones and drove thirty minutes out of town to one of the cornfield lanes. Though she was sitting in her car talking while she drove slowly down gravel roads kicking up dust, she was grateful to finally get in contact with GJ and hear the good news. At least the call wouldn't triangulate back to the house, if anyone came looking.

She'd put so many security measures into place, she thought, surely no one could untangle this. But then again, they hadn't been able to untangle Marat's murder either. Eleri sighed and dialed.

Luckily, GJ answered right away: "I cracked the code."

40

In a huff of excited breaths, Eleri relayed to Donovan what GJ had told her. It was the first good news in the case.

She told him how GJ had sent her pictures—snapshots messaged to the burner phone—which Eleri had looked at before turning the phone off, so it couldn't be traced back to this house.

Once she'd memorized what was there, she smiled. Now she relayed it to Donovan. "It's hexadecimal."

"No, it's not," he replied. "We considered that. We considered standard alphabet transposition codes."

Simple codes, Eleri thought, the kind smart kids played at in grade school, where numbers represented a letter and you simply wrote out the number, or where you took the alphabet and counted down ten spaces, so you'd have a key somewhere at the top of the page where you would write the number "10." Then your A would become a J—the tenth letter—and so on, following down the alphabet.

"You're suggesting it's a simple transposition code, but we already checked for that," Donovan insisted with a frown.

"GJ cracked it," Eleri said. "I've actually been *reading* some of the pages."

"But how is *that* hexadecimal?" He pointed to the open notebook in front of him.

"That's the kicker. It *is* a simple transposition code—"

"Is it in Russian?" he asked.

"No, it's in English. The secret is that Rychenkov used his own version of Hexadecimal. He also transposed the numbers and letters in the system, so instead of zero through nine, it goes A through J, and only uses digits one through six. Look," Eleri pointed.

"No digit above six," he mused. "And no zeroes."

"Right. Just to throw off anyone trying to crack it," she said. "GJ told me it was one of Walter's comments that spurred her to figure it out. They were talking about that issue—that no digits went beyond six—and Walter had said it reminded her of some military coding—and boom, all of a sudden it happened. She figured it out!"

He smiled and Eleri felt it in her bones. *Yes!* A crack in this case that had been a headache, a crazy puzzle, and a challenge to every intellectual ability they had. "And that's it, Donovan. Once we know what the code is, we just read it. It's in English and it's number-for-letter."

"So what are the notebooks about?"

"Okay. Big shock here," she told him. "They're about his drones."

Donovan merely raised an eyebrow at her as though she needed to come up with a better answer, but she shrugged. "That's it. It's about his drones. It's about his drone system and which drones he's flying on which day. A lot of it reads like a lab notebook. He records data from the flights. I think one entry correlates to one of the files we saw on the video, but I'm not sure yet. I really only just got started before you got home."

She gave Donovan the code sheet she'd written out, placing it in between them and scooting one of the other notebooks his way as though he would just grab a pencil and a stack of paper and join her.

He did.

Once again, they could have done this on computer, but paper wasn't hackable. It was steal-able, but not hackable. As they went along, they took pictures on a camera they had that was not linked to the web and loaded images into the FBI-secured emails.

They ordered sandwiches from the *Yellow Submarine,* because it delivered. It was hours later that Donovan threw down his pencil. "This is killing me. My brain is fried."

"Are you working tomorrow?" she asked. She could tell by his expression that he was afraid she would insist he keep working if he said "no." But that wasn't her intention.

"No, I'm off for the next five days. And if I'm lucky, I'll never go back."

"*Holy shit.* That bad?" Her own pencil stopped moving and she set it on the table as she tilted her head. While that actually helped him hear better, for her it was just an old gesture that likely hadn't evolved out.

"I had a sixteen-year-old who had a positive pregnancy test."

Ugh, Eleri thought. "Geez. Smart kids, you'd think."

"Smart kids do it, too," he said. "I guess the upside was that she caught it about a week and a half into the pregnancy."

"Damn, that's fast."

"Smart kids," Donovan reiterated with a half-smile, and this time with a better tone than Eleri had used.

"So it wasn't just strep and flu this time."

"No, but I had someone with the flu, too. He wanted a full-scale explanation—he was a mathematician, mind you—of why antibiotics didn't work. And then he wanted to discuss how chaos theory applied to random mutation and viral load."

"Oh, dear God."

"I *know*." He leaned back in the chair, the notebooks now ignored, and he looked at her. "Can I tell you something?"

"Sure, anything."

"I loved it."

"But you never want to go back?" Eleri was confused now.

"Well, I never want to go back because of the pregnant sixteen-year-old. I mean, I hope I helped, but dear God, that's worse than being a parent." Eleri laughed at him, "But damn, I don't think I've ever had a discussion of chaos theory as it applies to viral load. He pulled out Monte Carlo distributions and we discussed the statistics of antibiotics failing and leading to resistance."

"But you don't want to go back," she repeated.

"I loved it, El. But I had less than twenty minutes to see him. Despite the fact that we live in Curie, it's still a business, and as he discussed his mathematical theories and tried to carry a sequence out into the five thousandths place—just as an example of a very small culture of bacteria—I had to leave. I had patients waiting. Also, as a physician I can't ask him what his address is or see if he wants to meet up for coffee. He seemed excited to discuss the nature of 'P does not equal one' with someone in the medical field. He was really excited about the physical application of it."

She laughed at him. "I've had the same thought. I feel like a stupid fool half the time. But I really like it here. What does that make me?"

"A snobby elitist," Donovan told her with a sharp grin.

"Ugh, that sounds terrible. But I love it."

"I like it here, too," he told her, and then his expression turned downward. "But there's nowhere to run."

"Oh." She felt her mouth form a small, O. It wasn't something she'd thought about since they arrived. "Do we need to get you out?"

"Not yet, but honestly, another week and I'm going to get squirrely."

And here, she'd been reveling in the relative normalcy of this case.

As crazy as Curie was, Keyoor Vergheese had been the only odd type, unknown to the public, that they encountered. All of these people with their crazy high IQs, they *told* other people about their weirdness. It wasn't anything they hid. It wasn't like with Donovan—something others would come after you for or lynch you for. It wasn't the kind of thing that created a mob of hunters who would kill whole families and systematically destroy records. The thought turned her somber.

She'd been sitting here, complacent in her relative normalcy—"relative" being the key word—and forgetting that Donovan needed places to run, spaces to change. She suspected his physical body felt the urge to shift every once in a while. Probably it was driven by the same basic factors that gave her the urge to eat chocolate ice cream directly from the carton sometimes.

It was 6:30, she saw looking up at the clock. "Let's go see a movie," she said. "Let's do something crazy, disturbingly normal. Maybe we'll run into people and we'll have a conversation and we'll find out something wild about Marat Rychenkov, or about Johanna."

"Actually," he told her, "hopefully we *won't* run into anybody we know, and we'll see a movie and we'll like it."

"Valid point," she agreed, "but we're going to tell Westerfield it was a fact-finding mission."

"Anything," Donovan agreed, wadding up the wax paper the sandwiches had come in.

As they headed out to the small local theater, Eleri finally began to relax. When they stopped at a light, she began to laugh. "Look at that license plate, Donovan."

"Troilus?"

She grinned and pointed at the back of the car. "It's on an old Toyota Cressida."

But he didn't seem to get it. So she added, "Chaucer? Shakespeare? Didn't you read Troilus and Cressida in high school?"

He only shook his head at her like she was crazy. Maybe she was. Maybe his high school hadn't gone beyond the most obvious classics. Many didn't. "Well, Shakespeare eventually made a play out of it, but you weren't missing much. Chaucer's version was the Twilight of the 1300s."

Donovan snorted and Eleri kept her mouth shut until they made it to the theater. They picked an action flick, which Eleri analyzed regarding how both the good guys and the bad guys held their guns incorrectly. On the way out, she heard a couple actively complaining about the way the man had bled.

"It was all wrong. That's not what it looks like when you hit an artery!"

She almost laughed. She almost reached out and said something and made a new friend because he was right. But she didn't. She and Donovan managed to pretend they were normal for several hours. Once back in the house, though, when she saw it was late and said goodnight, she texted Avery, grateful when her phone buzzed back quickly. His game had ended. They'd won. Everyone was happy.

But she started to wonder when she would have to tell him the truth about herself. Though she hadn't hidden anything from him per se, she hadn't told her boyfriend the whole truth, either. By not doing so, she'd built a hurdle for herself. Had she thrown it at him earlier, she would have been able to share her surprise at the ancestry Donovan had dug up on her and what it meant. She could have told him about her hunches, and a little of what had happened with Echo and Ember. How she'd really found her sister . . .

She didn't like dwelling on those thoughts, so she turned her mind to better ones. She had the key to the notebooks now.

Eleri woke up the next morning ready to eat cereal next to Donovan and translate more. But the more she translated, the more disturbed she became. "I don't know if these have any value at all,

Donovan. They're lab notebooks, but they just described the same things we saw in the video."

"I know, Eleri," he said, "but I have to tell you, I *feel* it. We're missing something right in front of us. I know you're the one who gets the feelings about things, but I have it this time. I'm telling you, we're holding the key. We just can't see it."

41

Donovan could feel it under his skin, almost like an itch just beneath the surface. He felt that familiar squirm—the need to go for a run.

They had translated all of the notebooks Rychenkov left, and—as Eleri had initially found—they read more like lab notebooks than anything else. There was no page titled "secret formula" and nothing that was obviously worth killing for.

As Donovan read along, he saw that Marat had installed a program he simply labeled "A" on the small black drones. Then he placed them in formation inside the room and had them fly certain patterns. The drones went around the room, with some landing cleanly at the end, some falling. Marat recorded which ones did what and then he did it again. And then again. And the last time, the little drones didn't run into anything. As best Donovan could tell, that was all that had happened.

It didn't look like anything worth even hiding the lab notebooks for.

Donovan kept reading. Marat installed program D.12 in the large, white drones. This set had only twelve drones, not like the more numerous army of the small black ones. This set resembled a small herd rather than a swarm, like the other. In fact, each of these had been given a mark and a name that Marat used to keep track of them.

In the lab notebooks, Rychenkov recorded in detail how he'd

taken these out into the park and flown them around from his central controller. The man always meticulously noted which controller he used, which program he'd installed, which sub-programming he was using, and which pieces of code he had changed.

But none of it meant anything to Donovan. As Eleri had said, what was recorded in the notebooks looked very, very much like the five videos that had surfaced from the USB.

"Eleri," Donovan said, grabbing her attention as she was now flipping through her own set of translated pages, rather than the original notebooks. "Let's go do something today."

"Like what?"

"It's been a full day of nothing. GJ cracked the code well over twenty-four hours ago, and still nothing happened yesterday. I know I did nothing of value. We talked to Jivika, and we can go back tonight to talk to her again."

Eleri had shown up with Donovan the night before, once again sitting there when Jivika got home. That had remained the plan, and Eleri seemed worried by it. "What if we miss her? What if we're out and she comes home? Will we be back in time?"

"Then we miss her. So we'll visit her later in the evening. It will startle her, keep her on her toes."

Eleri seemed to turn the idea over for a moment and Donovan was glad when she seemed to let it settle. "Okay, what do you need to do?"

"I need to run."

"*Ah*. Do you need me to go with you, or do you want me to hold down the fort?" He appreciated that she didn't ask anything more than that, that she didn't even bother to question whether he really needed it, or if he could wait a few more days. She simply asked how she could help.

"Why don't you go with me? You had talked about seeing McKenzie Burke's family when you were here."

"Yes." She nodded, once again frowning slightly as a problem occurred to her. "Is it okay to have both of us out today?"

"Wade's in town, and no one has gone back into the Rychenkov-Schmitt home."

She nodded her head, conceding to the truth. "And if we're out and away, I can keep one of the burner phones on, because it won't matter. It won't let anybody track back to this house or us."

"Good point."

"So, then, let's go out. Do you have an idea on where to run?"

While he'd been pretty sure there was no forest land nearby, he'd double-checked. There wasn't. He'd believed that running through the cornfields was a bad idea, but Donovan was now fully on board, and he told her so. "My only other option is to find a random patch of trees, and I think even that is too far away. It's so flat here. There's nowhere to really hide."

"You think you can go out in someone's cornfield and they won't see you?"

"I think it will be okay. Things run through the corn all the time, as best I can tell. I'm more concerned about what I might run into that's not human."

She laughed at him and said, "So you need me to drop you off? Take your clothes, bring them back?"

"That seems kind of dangerous. We'll just leave them there. As long as no one finds me, they probably won't find my clothes. We'll bring a back-up set in case something goes wrong."

It took a while for them to get ready. Eleri messaged Wade on the secure connection. Donovan wanted to change into clothes that were easy to get in and out of.

He had Eleri hook a tracker to a piece of elastic. Once he changed, he would shove his foot down into it. They'd done this more than once, and he really was not up for a collar. Though he didn't particularly embrace the idea of being traced wherever he went, having had accidents before when he was out, he appreciated having a partner who could come and find him if the need arose. He'd been through broken ankles, human discovery, and more.

Eleri was excellent back up, and if it meant he had to wear a tracker, he'd wear the tracker. Keyoor Vergheese was the only person out here that he might run into like himself. If anyone spotted him, they might be more likely to shoot than anything else. The tracker was a necessity, like it or not.

Eleri changed clothes, too. She was wearing a suit, trying to be more professional for the visit, although she'd opted to look like a relaxed FBI agent and slung the jacket over her arm and undone the top button on her blouse. She also wanted to be accessible while she did a little research of a more personal nature. She was hoping that during Donovan's exercise, she could meet with McKenzie Burke's family.

Donovan called Wade and asked if he had any recommendations, but Wade had not been running yet. "In a few days, I'll be asking *you* for recommendations for somewhere to run."

Donovan wondered why Wade seemed to be able to hold out longer. He seemed to have better control on his need for shifting. Was that because Wade had been raised in a community of people like them, and Donovan had been left mostly alone to discover it by himself?

It took them an hour to get on the road, pull up a map, and find a reasonable spot to let him out. While the urge was still there, he started relaxing, just from knowing that a run was coming.

Eleri drove, of course, and eventually they found an old gravel road with no homes on it, just fields as far as the eye could see. She would leave him here and head off on her research mission: to see the family of a girl who'd been murdered. A girl with links to the disappearance of Eleri's sister, Emmaline, links that she was interested in diving into a little more, if she could.

Donovan wanted to go with her, but more than that, he needed to run.

Discreetly, they pulled the car to the side of the road. Climbing out quickly with his bag in hand, he slipped into the cover of the field even as Eleri drove away. A tall man, he found it hard to completely disappear, but he ducked down and pushed his way between the stalks.

Donovan struggled for a little while to find a spot where he could remove his clothing, stuff it down in the bag, and leave it. The stalks had itched as he passed by, and removing his clothing only made that worse, but he rolled his shoulders, feeling the bones slide across each other and stop in new positions.

He flexed each arm out, first his shoulders, then his elbows and his wrists. Then he curled and opened his fingers, watching as each one curled back into a new position, tendons sliding, muscles tightening, bones shifting. His rib cage changed compression slightly, the intercostal muscles breathing and loosening just a little. He rolled his neck and jutted his jaw until the middle of his face pushed out.

It didn't hurt, but it could. Mostly, he felt the pressure of his bones and muscles moving. But the itching faded away as he went through his normal routine. He shifted his hips, rolling first one then the other. He continued the rolling, feeling down his legs the way he had down his arms, until at last he was on all fours on the ground.

It smelled different down here. It smelled different with his nose open. With the hair having pushed out all over his body—a much thicker version of the way ordinary people got goosebumps—the corn stalks were less of a menace. He took off trotting through the stalks, weaving in and out, letting the sharp leaves grab at his fur. His mind finally wandered, the urge finally quelled as he wound his way through the cornfield.

Though he'd managed to escape the physical confines of his body, he hadn't quite managed to escape the thought processes that had been plaguing him for days, and still they lingered there at the back of his brain.

As he loped through the fields, far away from the case, it nipped at his heels. What was it that he wasn't seeing?

42

Donovan pushed his way through the corn stalks. They didn't leave much room for a nice, long-stride run, the kind he'd been hoping for. Still, he wound his way in and out. The walk was enjoyable and he managed a good jog most of the time.

The shift in his physicality was welcome, a remembered feeling, something he'd gone too long without. The runs did him good, and while his brain never shut down, he let it wander the same kinds of meandering paths his feet did.

What was it here in Nebraska that kept the wolves from gathering? Was it the lack of running land, like he was discovering just now? Given his issues today, that was a distinct possibility. It was something he hadn't considered before, that geography, both physical and human, played a role in where his kind ended up. If they got the itch like he did, they would need more space, and apparently specific kinds of space. This one wasn't really cutting it. South Carolina had drawn him for the national forests, the open land, and the trails where he could run and be himself with relatively little, if any, interference.

He hadn't known any of these things—not before coming into NightShade. He'd known what he was, but not truly what it meant. Being friends with Wade—whom he'd poached as a friend from Eleri—had opened his eyes wide.

Some families raised their children this way. Some of the kids had understood, from early on, that they might or might not change later. Eventually, some became like him and some didn't. It seemed to be some combination of recessive genetics. But more than just the change, the ones like him also experienced a handful of other traits: the excellent sense of smell, the acute hearing, the superior vision.

While those changes were always present at some level, they were particularly apparent in this phase, and he let his nose open up. He smelled fuel on the ground in between the corn, from where the harvesters had come by. It was very faint, but it was there. Something else tickled his nose, and he could only figure, not being able to identify it directly, that it was a fertilizer or a pesticide of some kind. The corn itself was the backdrop, almost overwhelming to all the other scents. Every once in a while, he passed a spot where he smelled a human, and it got him thinking.

In New Orleans, he'd smelled something very, very familiar. He hadn't known it could happen like that—not before then, not before he'd asked Wade what he'd scented—but he'd known it instinctively when he smelled it.

Brother.

The word had shot into his mind, even though at the time he was throwing some punches and taking more. He later told Eleri it was *family,* but he only said *maybe* a brother. It was possible that he was just looking back on it and over-remembering it, but he remembered that word, *brother,* being so clear in his head at the time. And the smell—he'd not ever smelled it before but, on some instinctual level, he'd recognized it.

On the one hand, a brother shouldn't be possible for him—not a full-blooded brother, anyway. His mother had come from Calcutta. His father traveled, found her there, married her, and proceeded to drag her all over the US. To call his father abusive would be a bit of an understatement.

Aidan Heath had been an asshole, a white man who believed that his whiteness and his maleness gave him some kind of superiority . . . Or maybe he believed just his very existence conferred it. Maybe it wasn't tied to any kind of racism or sexism. Maybe it was just plain old narcissism, but Donovan's father believed the world owed him.

He believed he deserved promotions. Aidan Heath didn't believe that his family deserved better than others. None of his wishes spread to anyone else, no matter how close. He didn't believe Donovan had any value. And, as he looked back, Donovan could see the man had thought even less of his mother.

Aidan Heath made it clear he deserved more out of life than he earned. Donovan didn't remember the first time he questioned his father's self-belief of superiority. But it had been early enough that he no longer remembered when it first happened, only that it had always been there. When he was seven and his mother died, his father had only gotten worse.

So the question was—given that time frame, from his father meeting his mother in India to his mother's death—how could he have gotten a brother? He was an only child, something he'd both regretted and lauded. He'd wished he had another person to share his time with, someone to talk to, anyone in this world who understood the experience he'd been through. But that didn't exist, and he was grateful to his parents at the same time, for not having brought another child into what Donovan had endured.

In order for him to have a brother, his mother would have had to have given birth before having Donovan. Then . . . he didn't know. Had she given up the baby? Misplaced the baby? As Donovan thought about it, though it might be plausible for his brother to have been given away, he did not think Aidan Heath would have let a male child go.

Another option was that the brother was younger. During the fight when Donovan had first smelled that *brother* scent, he had not stopped throwing his punches to ask, though the man did look plausibly younger. That meant Donovan's mother would have been pregnant while Donovan was alive.

He had no memories of the sort. It would have happened when he was very, very young—and once again, the baby would have been lost, given up for adoption, and the same rules applied as before. Aiden Heath would not have gone along with that. His child was an object that was supposed to improve his life. He wouldn't have given one away, not a male child.

Given all the tremendous unlikelihoods Donovan was encountering, a half-brother seemed more plausible. Imagining his father cheating on his mother was far too easy. The man had no morals in any other ground, so why would he have any about his marriage? Donovan didn't know what had gone on between his parents, given that he was so young when his mother died. He'd never really considered their relationship as an adult. Looking back was something he'd not done, and he wouldn't be doing it now except for that smell and the clear knowledge of *brother*.

He paused in his thinking then, as he came to the edge, where the field met a gravel road. He peeked out, looking warily both ways down the road, before dashing across the street. The gravel was prickly under his feet, but the pads masked most of it. Only once he was between the stalks again did he feel comfortable enough to slow his pace a little. But a turn revealed the lineup of the cornstalks, and an open lane to run down.

He went for it, picking up his pace, and running full out. He hit the other side of the cornfield much faster than he had intended, and he stayed inside the boundary this time. He ran back, turning, pushing his way through the stalks, feeling the sharp edges brush up against him, and heading to another aisle, not wanting to run back exactly the way he'd come. He was taking diagonals across the field, the longest single shot without running into anything.

This time, he pulled back, launching himself into an all-out sprint, his front and back legs reaching wide, the feeling of stretch in his muscles. *This*. This was exactly what he'd wanted.

For a moment, he forgot about his brother, about his father possibly siring other children all over the US. He forgot about his mother, and the loss that still ached, as she was the only one who'd been kind to him, and then, suddenly, she'd been gone.

He ran until he was tired. The tracker, the elastic that had been a struggle to shove his paw into, had stayed on nicely. That was pleasing. He was panting heavily by the time he'd made five runs back and forth, grateful for the experience.

It was getting close to time for Eleri to come and get him, and he headed back the way he'd come. Carefully, he crossed the road, not wanting any humans to spot him. He'd already seen a raccoon out in the fields and a handful of mice, and he'd smelled many more creatures who'd passed through. He loped through the other field, aiming for his clothes and his meetup point with Eleri.

He hoped she had been successful in her meeting. Maybe the Burke family could shed some light on her sister Emmaline's case.

His clothes were easy to find, his sense of navigation strong from time spent running—and besides, his clothes smelled like him.

He'd changed back, once again feeling the stalks try to cut his almost normal human skin. Getting dressed was harder than getting undressed had been, and he heard the honk of Eleri's arrival before he had his feet in his shoes. Still, he was content. He'd finally gotten his run and he was breathing deep, taking in the scent of the field around him even though the smell was dampened with his nose smaller.

As he stepped from between the stalks and onto the gravel of the road, a thought twitched in his brain. He remembered his brother's face, and it didn't just look like Aidan.

The coloring, the tilt of his eyes, the shape of his face . . . the man had looked partially Indian.

43

Donovan woke up finally feeling more like himself the next morning. The run the day before had done him physically more good than he could count. Mentally, he'd been left with more questions than he started with.

His brother's face had looked like his mother's, and like his own, and that's where Donovan struggled to put the pieces together. Still, now was not the time. This was a mystery for a later day. How his mother had died, what she'd been like—other than being his mother—was something he had avoided thinking about for decades. The last thing he wanted to do was follow up on his father or his mother, as he'd hoped all along that he'd left that life behind. But maybe it hadn't left him.

He and Eleri had gone to Jivika Das's home the night before, exactly as planned. They'd showed up late and sure enough, the woman was nervous by the time they arrived. She gave them the same answer she always did: she had learned nothing that day that would help them figure out who'd killed Marat and Johanna. But this time, they gave her a specific task. Her nothing answers helped no one, and despite professing to want to help, her attitude hadn't changed. If she was the killer or she wasn't, she needed to find them answers. They would all have a better chance of learning anything if she could be useful.

Donovan understood. If Jivika was involved, she was working

with someone. It had been a male who had fought with Johanna Schmitt. They'd not told her they knew this. Though they pressed her a bit, they treated her mostly like a helper rather than a suspect. The more free she felt, the more she'd be likely to slip up. Their interrogation strategy was a delicate balance of pressure and release.

This time, they'd also asked her if she felt she was in danger, if she'd noticed anyone following her, if anyone had been in *her* home. She told them they were crazy. The killer had been after Marat and his work. Jivika thought that was obvious, though Eleri let her know that they would keep an eye on her. It was only half sincere. The other half was designed to intimidate.

They were keeping better tabs on her than they had on Johanna. He and Eleri would not be making the same mistake. In addition to the tracker on her car, they'd hidden one in her purse and they believed she'd not yet found it.

So they pushed while they were here, face to face. Donovan decided to go ahead with two pieces of information. First, instead of asking her if she had any idea why Marat might have been killed, he told her, "Here. On this piece of paper, I need you to write down Marat's top five things he was working on. Or anything in his life that you think might have gotten him and Johanna killed for knowing about it."

It had taken the woman a good twenty minutes. He and Eleri had sat idly by, a skill taught at Quantico training. They waited both outwardly patiently and impatiently and as they did, they gathered what information they could.

Once she'd written the list—putting down only four things—Donovan folded it up and put it in his pocket. He didn't look at it. If they needed more information, they would ask her about it when they came back tomorrow. The show of not even glancing at the list was designed to put the two of them in a position of superior knowledge. They would see how Jivika handled it when they came back tomorrow. They would be back every day, until either she was arrested or the killer was found.

The second thing he told the woman was part of what they understood about how Marat and Johanna had been killed. "It appears they were drugged. And that's why they lost their struggle."

"I figured as much." Her knees were pressed together and so were her lips. Her hands perched on her lap as though she were at an unpleasant tea.

Good.

"Why are you telling me this?" she asked.

"Because you broke into Marat Rychenkov's home. There are very few reasons for you to do that. And because you link back to Marat, then it's reasonable to conclude our killer will link Marat to you—just as we did."

That last part had been a lie. The killer would likely not do it the same way they did, but he or she just might figure it out. "Don't accept any drinks or food from anyone. Buy the snacks you eat out of vending machines, and don't make a habit of buying the same thing every day. If you go out, walk into a restaurant and order, don't linger, don't give anyone the time to alter something for you. And never let your food go unattended."

"I know all of these things," she said, her lips pressing together even harder when she finished her small statement.

It was Eleri who jumped in with the smallest dose of sympathy. "I understand. But I've noticed the people in Curie don't quite keep their doors locked. And maybe it's time you did."

Donovan had planted a listening device in the house, but of course he didn't mention it. They'd left it at that. The next night, he intended to give her a sterner warning, in hopes that with her eyes more open, she'd see something—anything. He only hoped she'd be able to tell them who the killer was, or at least steer them in the right direction.

He wasn't due back to the clinic for several more days, and he was grateful for the break. It gave him a push to try to solve the case before his next shift, though he wasn't sure that would happen.

While Eleri spent her morning researching, and he didn't ask what about, he spent his own doing much the same. It was slightly after lunch that he tapped on the table in excitement and said, "Eleri! Eleri, come look at this. I think I may have found something."

"What?" She slid her chair over so she could scoot in next to him and look at his screen.

As he looked, though it made sense to him now, he was relatively certain it didn't make sense to her. And why would it? He'd gone down a rabbit hole, and it had paid off. "So here's what I was thinking. Marat, at least as far as we know, hid two things."

"He might have hidden more," Eleri commented, "and we just didn't find them."

"True. But we know he hid those two. And those two pertain to the same exact thing."

"His drones," she said, catching on.

"Exactly," Donovan answered. "And we don't understand what we're looking at. It's been nagging me that we were looking at the right thing, but we didn't understand it. So, instead of continuing to look at the thing that we didn't understand, I tried to understand the thing we were looking at."

He wondered if that made sense to her. Luckily, she nodded.

"So I began studying drones."

"That sounds ever so exciting," she commented, her voice deadpan.

"I can't begin to tell you. I mean, it was interesting, and some of it was really hard to untangle. I don't program computers or operate drones. So I had to go back and do some of the basics. But I think I found something, Eleri."

"What?"

"Mapping."

"What?" she repeated.

"Unknown space mapping. It's one of the things that people are looking for drones to be able to do, but the issues haven't been fully solved yet."

"So?" She was frowning at him, and Donovan struggled to explain the culmination of his morning of digging.

"I think that may have been what Rychenkov was doing in those videos. Remember, he took his drones out. And he flew them around the room, and then they landed. The first time he did it, they seemed to almost run into things. They bobbled a little bit. They found the backs of chairs and fell because they couldn't back up. Or the chair was too wide for them to rearrange their course and get around it quite fast enough and down they went. But for the second video—remember, we said it looked almost identical to the first?—he set up the drones the same, and the room was the same. But this time, they flew the entire space, without running into anything."

"Oh yeah," Eleri said. "The videos looked so similar, but the second run seemed like he'd done a better job with them. I assumed he'd improved his programming."

"So had I, but I now think it's plausible that the two runs were on the same day. Nothing had changed. The first run was a *mapping run*. What he was demonstrating on the second video was that the drones were fully able to map the space and come back and work within it while using the map from the earlier run. That's a relatively basic operation, but if the drones are data sharing in a new way, then it might be something valuable."

Eleri headed back to her own computer, grabbing the USB, plugging it in and pulling up the videos once again. She opened up the last two yet another time. This time, it looked like Marat had mapped the interior room of the church.

"And," Eleri gushed, joining his excitement now, "according to the notebooks, some of the entries are one day and then the next, or one day and even just a little bit later that same day. The time stamps are very close. In fact, the last several entries, the time stamps between the first and second runs are within minutes of each other."

"What?" Donovan said, as they began flipping through the transcribed pages.

"Look. Look at this one." She pointed to information now in his own handwriting. "See? He runs them, and then not five minutes later, he runs them again, with *no errors*. And he has notes about recording the maps themselves. "

Donovan pointed to his computer screen, where he still had the articles pulled up, and she began reading over his shoulder. "Successful mapping of unknown areas is considered one of the top robotics problems of our decade. Do you think Marat solved it?"

"I don't know, Eleri" he said. "I don't think it even matters. What if he didn't solve it? If he was close enough that somebody else thinks they could run with it or if somebody even *believed* he solved it, I think," he pointed to the screen again, "that this is reason enough for a murder."

"You think somebody would really kill over this?"

"Eleri, it's one of the top robotics problems. If he can solve it, he can sell it."

"And if he can sell it, then money is involved and that's a valuable motive," Eleri added. She was looking at him, now fully on the same track. "Not only that, but he would have a claim to fame. Which, here in Curie, might be even more of a motive."

44

Eleri spent most of the next day reading up on robotics. It wasn't her topic of choice, but it was fascinating. She followed many of the same rabbit holes that Donovan had as well as many new ones.

Jivika Das had placed Marat Rychenkov's drones as only third on her list of reasons she thought he might have been killed. The dog-like robot they'd spotted in his garage had been her first choice. Marat's patent on a multi-legged, tripodal motion system had come second. The drones had clocked in next. Fourth had been Marat's ability to always flip an omelet without breaking it—due to his well-researched combo of pan and fat. The fifth spot she'd left blank.

Given Jivika's obvious disregard for the task, Eleri had wanted to toss the list into the trash. But that wasn't an option. They had to check everything she'd written, even the damn omelets. Luckily, that one went quickly, as there was nothing to find. So Eleri and Donovan spent a good part of the day researching the topics Jivika had handed them. That way, when they went back in the evening and grilled her again, they would have specifics.

The second thing they checked off Das's list was the dog-like robot. It played no part in anything Eleri could find. The bot was interesting, sure, but he wasn't unique. In fact, Eleri had been seeing robots like that on internet videos for several years.

While the literature was full of these types of bots, there was nothing by Marat Rychenkov, and nothing about the dog in his notebooks and nothing that sounded as though this was anything other than a common bot.

The patent had turned up more interesting bits of information. Rychenkov had designed a centipede-like bot that walked using only a series of footprints. When a leg picked up to make a step, it then put down into the exact footprint that an earlier leg had vacated. This left the multi-legged bot having a tripod-like stance that kept it stable.

"Even so," she looked up to Donovan, "Rychenkov already holds a patent for this system. Tripodal motion in robots isn't that new, and Marat wasn't the only one who'd solved it, or maybe even the best."

"He modeled it on what a variety of animals do. He looked at walking gaits in dogs, horses, elephants, and interestingly enough, even spiders and centipedes." Eleri pulled up a video that showed a centipede walking, but the film was from below on a plate that lit up when touched. "Look," she said as she pointed to it, turning the screen to Donovan. "Even all these multi-legged creatures move in a tripodal fashion."

Donovan agreed. "Do you think he was killed for that?"

Despite how fascinating the topic was quickly becoming, it didn't check the boxes for motive. "No, I don't. Other people had access to this information. Even that patent isn't in his name alone."

Donovan tapped on his own keyboard. "I don't see any money trail from that patent. And the other name on the patent is alive but lives three states away and hasn't traveled here . . ."

"So that makes the patent an extremely unlikely path. The drones, on the other hand . . ." Eleri completely agreed. "So do you think she knows about him and the mapping of the drones?"

"Probably."

"Do you think she killed him?"

"No," Donovan said, "but I'm getting more and more concerned that she might be next."

"Jesus, and what about the kids?"

"We'll put the police on them. They'll have some level of protection. It's about the best we can do without scaring the crap out of everyone involved."

Eleri nodded and called Kate's private cell. It might be tapped, but she couldn't wait any longer. "Hey, Kate, sorry to bother you, but it's necessary." She told the woman what she needed and was assured of a call back shortly.

"So we'll have officers following Jivika Das. Do you think they'll be subtle enough?" Eleri asked Donovan.

"Possibly, but this is Curie, so there's every probability they'll be spotted right away. Even by the kids. But I don't know what to do to solve that problem except pull the police detail, and I don't want to do that."

He told her they might be worrying about nothing. "And there's no reason to believe that another murder will be committed. It may be that our killer already found what they needed and they're gone."

"That's valid," Eleri said. "Who's left town since Johanna's murder?"

"No, not since her murder—since the last unidentified break in."

"Good point."

They began working their way through records, but everyone they were watching had remained in place, without even a weekend trip or a family break among them.

Her phone rang as she was checking off the last person on her list. "Kate!"

"It's done. Officers will be on the Mazur home within twenty minutes. We'll have someone on Das within five."

"Wow." Eleri thanked the woman and hung up, passing the news on to Donovan.

"Small town, smart town," he murmured, as though that explained everything. Maybe it did.

Eleri turned her attention back to the robotics problem, because the more she read, the more she learned that there was more information out there than she could possibly hold onto.

This work, at least, was far more rewarding than the rest. It felt like a one-to-one ratio. She could do X amount of work and get X amount of reward. So she dove in.

It turned out, the problem was multifold. The uses for drones—which Marat had specifically been looking at—often involved unsafe spaces. Chemical hazards, war zones, unknown territories. Even deep-sea exploration.

Swarms of drones needed to be able to fly in and navigate safely *and* return with their information. The ability to not fall or get damaged in the first place, or to get back up once they'd run into something, was critical. They had to report their gathered information, share maps, and communicate with the other drones, all while working in a possibly inhospitable area. Eleri was beginning to understand why this was considered a "grand challenge."

After frowning at her computer screen for a moment, Eleri headed back to the pages she and Donovan had transcribed from the notebooks. She flipped through until she found what she wanted. "Here, Donovan. I think we're even closer to what this is about. Look. This entry says the drones fell and then got back up and rejoined the swarm. He ultimately only had a loss of two, which he says is acceptable."

"Do you think it's a hard number or percentage of the herd?" Donovan asked.

"Probably percentage." But she read on, discovering that other problems facing robotics as big challenges in the coming decade involved AI, human brain interface, and biological alloys—materials that would move more like muscles and skin, allowing the drones to withstand more, rather than cracking in accidents.

"None of these," she said to Donovan, "looks like anything Marat Rychenkov was working on."

"No," Donovan said. "And it's not even really up his alley."

"But," Eleri pointed out, "this one is exactly up Jivika Das' alley."

"What?"

"She's a bio-mimicry specialist. If he's trying to design robot skin that acts like human skin, then she's *exactly* the person you'd want to ask—often—about how human skin functions. It explains all the calls between them."

"Or they might have been working on human-brain interface," he added. "Shit, I hadn't looked at it that way. There are several possibilities that would put them not only in contact with each other frequently, but provide an idea that both of them would want to hide."

Eleri was nodding. "If they could solve either of those two problems, it would put them directly in the crosshairs of companies, patent hounds, and even competitors."

Donovan agreed, grateful that they finally had their questions ready for Das before they headed over again. It was once again time to pay a little visit to Jivika Das, only now they were more heavily armed. And it was time to increase her security.

They would start by showing up in person, this time, which they hoped would startle her. Though she was looking up Jivika's tracker and making sure the woman was accounted for, Donovan's voice startled her. As they pulled up in front of Das' home, they saw that Marshawn James was pulling up behind them, apparently visiting the house next door. They couldn't go unnoticed.

"Hey, Marshawn!" Eleri hopped out, motioning Donovan to do the same. "What are you doing here?"

"Oh, Emersyn's friend lives here. You?"

"We're here to see Jivika." She pointed to the woman's front door.

He smiled that wide grin and Eleri had that moment again, *Small town*. She'd have to watch herself or Marshawn would catch on to her. Hell, Emersyn, might have already, especially if Joule Mazur had told them anything.

When Marshawn emerged from the house with Emersyn a few moments later and saw Donovan and Eleri standing and talking, leaning against the car, he frowned.

"Looks like Jivika didn't make it home yet. She's running a little late," Eleri explained, and then she turned to the teenager. "Hey, Emersyn."

She watched Emersyn's eyes carefully as the girl looked at her with half a smile and waved. Did she look at them differently? Eleri couldn't tell. And even if the girl did know something, would she be suspicious, or would she admire them, thinking the job was cool?

Eleri had no idea, but as they were waving goodbye to Marshawn, Jivika Das pulled up into her driveway, once again stopping just short of the garage door. Eleri and Donovan had checked the garage, and much like the Rychenkov-Schmitt home, her parking spaces were filled with boxes, biological oddities, and objects she claimed were from various experiments. At least Eleri's own biology background led her to believe that statement was true.

They followed the woman inside and went through the usual pleasantries where Jivika offered them drinks or food and they declined. She made the offer every evening, as though she had forgotten they'd told her that the killer's initial move had been to subdue the victim through some kind of drug.

Tonight, they opened with, "Tell us about Marat's breakthrough with the drones, Jivika." Both watched as her eyes went wide.

45

The twitch in Jivika's gaze was her tell, and Eleri watched for it. She was seeing it often. Yes, though Jivika refused to say what she had done when working with the drones, it was becoming more and more clear that—whatever the project was—she and Marat had been working together on it. But was Jivika's part supplying biological information for him to apply to his drones?

Eleri asked that exact question and watched as Jivika's mouth said "no," but the twitch in her eye said "yes." Eleri pushed further, as did Donovan. There was no good cop/bad cop tonight. There was only mad cop/mad cop—two FBI agents who were angry that their one witness had been holding out on them.

"We could arrest you," Eleri said.

"You wouldn't," came the reply. "You haven't done it yet. You're not going to do it now."

"Yes, we absolutely can, and we will. I'm considering you for obstruction of justice right now. We have two murders to solve. We're concerned that more might be coming." Eleri bit her tongue, not adding that she was afraid there were children possibly in danger in this scenario, while Jivika was withholding answers.

She tried another tactic. "If the idea is partly yours, then you deserve the credit. If you're not the killer, we can make sure that you inherit the project. But right now, all you're doing is making yourself look bad."

Eleri's anger had not quite shaped the words the way she would have liked. She should have appeared stone cold about all of it, but she *was* angry. Every time Jivika's eye twitched, Eleri got angrier.

"That's not it," Jivika said.

"Then what is?" Eleri volleyed back, almost instantly.

"That's *not it*," Jivika repeated, more sternly this time, making her answer as clear as her refusal to say more.

Well, crap. The woman wasn't going to answer anything she didn't want to. Eleri kept pushing with the questions though, as did Donovan, and they didn't let up.

Then Eleri played another card that they'd been holding onto. "Tell us about the biological-type skin that you and Marat were developing for the drones."

Jivika shook her head. "I don't know what you're talking about."

Fuck, Eleri thought, *a misplay*. She'd been so certain that this was what they'd been working on, but there had been no eye twitch accompanying the denial. In fact, every time Jivika had covered something up, she'd straight out said, "No," or said she wouldn't tell them. This had been a truly genuine reaction, and Eleri felt her anger and her blood pressure rise.

In the kitchen, something rattled for a moment, and the three of them looked up, startled.

Jivika pointed toward the other room, frowning. "Can I go check and see what that was?"

Eleri quickly nodded. "One minute. Go."

It was Donovan who looked strangely at her as though to ask, *Why would you let her go?*

Eleri replied in low tones, "Me," and pointed at her chest.

Donovan frowned harder and mouthed, "You?" and pointed to her, the question clear.

Eleri reached up toward her face as though to sign that she was angry and that had manifested in the kitchen, but she didn't know sign language, and neither did Donovan. But he got the idea, and his head pulled back just a little bit as if to say, *Wow*.

Eleri wanted to agree, but didn't feel quite the same emotion. It was irritating that she had that power but couldn't control it, because now was certainly not the time to be rattling pots in the kitchen. Jivika was already walking back into the room, shaking her head and shrugging as though she had no idea what could possibly have caused the noise.

Eleri imagined a string of curse words in her head. After several more questions, to which Jivika replied in full sentences that she had no idea what they were talking about, Eleri eventually gave up. She was out of possible cards to play, and they'd been all the wrong cards, anyway.

Though they were right that there was something at stake about Marat's drones—something Jivika had been helping him with—they'd only managed to narrow the large categories. The biological type skin idea was all wrong. The human brain interface, also all wrong.

"You need to leave town," Eleri told her, playing a card from a different deck since the first one had failed them.

"I can't. I'm in the middle of three projects."

"This is your safety we're talking about."

Eleri was becoming more and more convinced that things not playing out the way they'd intended was nothing but a bad sign. If she didn't even know what the case was about, how could she protect the people involved? If anyone else could follow what she and Donovan had followed, they would arrive at Jivika's doorstep, too. Now she said as much to the woman.

"I'm not leaving." Jivika crossed her arms, her expression petulant, almost daring them to make her go. Eleri didn't mention the police detail and neither did Jivika.

"If you don't have anywhere to go, we can set you up with a safe house. Maybe you can work remotely, but no one will know your location."

"That's not good enough," Jivika replied, her eyebrows lowering sharply as she stared at the two of them. "I'm not in any danger. Marat was the one who had the idea. He asked me a few questions here and there, but I don't know that I even helped him."

Another lie, Eleri thought. The rest had been true, but that part—about helping him—that was a lie. Jivika had helped him enough to know she was important to the project.

Eleri leaned forward, hoping her expression conveyed that she could read the woman without specifically saying so. "These are instructions from your local friendly FBI agents. I'm not confident that you're safe anymore."

Jivika volleyed another question back, her gaze darting back and forth between the two of them and landing on Donovan, as though she wasn't convinced Eleri was a reliable source. "Are you convinced that I'm *not* safe?"

Donovan first looked to Eleri, and she was grateful for that show of solidarity. Donovan wasn't going to get played off of his partner, and neither would Eleri. As they looked at each other, she shook her head.

"No. I can't tell you that definitively, but I *can* tell you that I'm worried. And I would rather be safe than sorry."

Jivika waved them off as though the matter was decided, and the interview had quickly come to an end. They still had to walk out the front door and go back to their car as though they were old friends saying goodnight, but Eleri felt her blood pressure boiling. She wondered if anything else in the kitchen was rattling.

They'd told Jivika that she would come to their house for their regular interview the next night. Not surprisingly, Jivika had protested that she'd already told them everything she knew. Now Eleri found she simply didn't care.

They couldn't keep showing up on Das's doorstep like this, especially not after they'd been seen by Marshawn and had learned that Emersyn was often next door. It was already possible that Emersyn had seen them more than once. If she had, it would only lend credence to Joule's theory about them being FBI agents. In fact, Joule's theory held a lot of water—because it was true.

Donovan, clearly the calmer of the two, had swung them by a Chinese place and picked up food while Eleri waited in the car, still stewing that they'd missed the topic on Jivika's collaboration with Marat. If it wasn't the human brain interface or the need for more biological-type parts on drones, then what had they been working on? How would Jivika have helped him solve the mapping problem?

Eleri's brain hurt. But just as she was about to give up, Donovan slid back into the car with a bag of cardboard boxes that smelled good enough to make her forget about Jivika Das and drones and murders.

Eleri went to bed with no new insights about how to solve the case. But at ten a.m. the next morning, she was growing concerned. "Donovan, Jivika should be at work already, but her car hasn't moved from her driveway."

46

Donovan tried to find alternative explanations, because he didn't like the expression on Eleri's face or the growing worry in his own chest. "Did she maybe catch a ride with someone?"

"She never has before, not that I know of. She's always arrived at work well before eight. So I called around eight thirty and left a message and she hasn't responded."

"You texted her again?" he asked, even though he assumed Eleri had done it. He was looking for an easy out.

She nodded. "I've texted twice more. It's now been twenty minutes since the last one and there's no return text, voicemail, or even a missed call."

Donovan sighed. They couldn't wait; they'd already lost somebody on their watch, so he looked at Eleri, "Okay. We should go over and check things out, but what's our excuse? Why would we show up at her door in the middle of the morning on a work day?"

"I don't know, but we need a good reason."

There was every possibility they would go over and find that Jivika had simply taken a sick day. Maybe she was asleep and had left her phone off. That was about the best-case scenario Donovan could come up with—no harm, no foul.

While that was a good outcome safety-wise, how would they explain to Jivika that they knew that she hadn't moved her car? They'd not yet admitted they put the tracker on it or the police detail on her. Donovan tried to stay focused on their excuse. "Why did you text her?"

"I told her I wanted to meet up for lunch today instead of our usual evening interview."

"Good one." However, it didn't quite allow for them to go by the house and knock on the door. Or did it? "So we say we were in the neighborhood and you hadn't heard back from her via text, and we decided to stop by," he finally offered. "It's the best I've got. I don't want to wait any longer."

"Agreed. The last time we didn't hear from somebody, she was dead," Eleri said, the last word coming out flat, mirroring his own feelings.

Apprehension crawled farther up his spine with each passing moment. But he knew, that was no reason to go in without a plan. "Okay, what's near Kangaroo Court that allows us to say we were close enough to drive through her neighborhood?"

"The theater," Eleri blurted out, clearly just as agitated as he was, but Donovan shook his head.

"I don't think we can claim we're going to the theater at ten a.m."

"Valid." Eleri sighed the word, her hands going to her hips as she tried again. "There's a pharmacy on the corner. We can claim we were getting a prescription."

"We don't have any prescriptions to fill."

"I know, and you would write them for us anyway, but at least it works as a first-pass excuse. It would hold up unless someone demands to see the prescription. The cover doesn't have to hold to her, just to everyone else."

"Okay, let's run with it," Donovan agreed, swiping his keys off the counter as he grabbed his jacket from the back of the chair.

Eleri was fast on his heels and running around the car. The speed at which she slid into the passenger side letting him know just how worried she was. They were pulling out before the garage door was all the way up. Had there not been something so dire on the line, he would have found the moment comical.

"Remember," she intoned, as he started to back out, "don't do what I did the other night. We can't drive too fast."

"Good point." Forcing himself to at least pretend to be calm, he took the first turn slowly. "Besides," he added, "chances are, it's nothing." But he didn't like that phrase, and Eleri's lack of response showed how little respect she gave it, as well. He didn't have any bad feelings about it but . . .

"El, do you know something in your gut?"

"I want to say I do, but I don't. Or I do, but I can't tell." She sighed in frustration this time, and he understood. He knew that she wished she could read these feelings better. Even though she'd been having them all her life, it was his understanding that she'd merely taken the hunches as they came. Trying to design them or even to understand them for more than just "I think that felt like a feeling," was something that she was only now trying her hand at. It seemed by her reaction that it hadn't been going well.

Donovan stopped at the pharmacy and ran inside for a pack of gum, telling her that if anybody was watching them—or God forbid, tracking the car—this would need to show up on the radar. He told himself the same thing, though he desperately wanted to get to Das's house.

Once again, he slid back into the driver's side, this time with a pack of mint gum stinking up his car, and he turned the corner, heading into Kangaroo Court. Luckily, with the story they'd concocted, he could now head straight for Jivika's house.

She had two garage doors. Her car sat in front of the door nearer to the house, and he parked right next to her on the far side, hoping it would look normal. Climbing out, they both headed up to Das's front door, knocked, and waited. But nothing happened.

"Do you hear anything?" Eleri asked quietly, but he shook his head. They knocked again and waited quietly. Once again, even with his superior hearing skills, he heard nothing other than the cat probably coming down the stairs.

"Now what?" she asked.

"Code." They'd made Jivika hand over her door codes, despite her obvious reluctance the first night. But the flashed FBI badges and threats of moving her to a safe house had pushed her to finally share them. Donovan punched it in, trying to look normal—whatever that meant.

"Now," he paused, "let's hope she hasn't changed it." The knob turned gently under his hand and they walked in as though they were supposed to be there. That was ninety-nine percent of subterfuge: acting like you belonged.

Eleri headed inside first, and Donovan followed as they peeled their jackets. Only when they got the door closed did Eleri look at him and shake her head. They hadn't hollered out. What if someone was here? What if someone had heard them knocking? Any reasonable person who didn't know what Donovan was, who didn't know his special skills, would have run out the back door, but he hadn't heard that.

"I don't think there's anyone here," he said. And then he sniffed the air and smelled it. "*Shit.*"

"What?" Eleri asked.

"I think I smell . . . come on."

With a motion to her to follow him, he bounded up the steps. The odor was faint but growing stronger, and he knew what it was. It was a human body.

"Son of a bitch," he muttered again, and he threw the bedroom door open, almost stumbling across the body as he entered. She was lying between the foot of the bed and the dresser, arms and legs splayed out ever so slightly. He noticed, of course, the rope marks and the dull eyes staring at the ceiling. Jivika Das was gone.

47

Donovan sniffed at the air again as Eleri pulled blue latex gloves out of her back pocket. She said she was a scientist and always liked to be ready, but Donovan knew they were for cases just like this.

"It's a crime scene," she declared, and he nodded in agreement, thinking he was glad they hadn't touched anything yet. She watched him for a moment. "What do you smell?"

"I smell him. I smell the killer. This is recent enough that . . . "

"Who is it?"

And damn, but he couldn't tell her. He shook his head. "I don't know . . ." Donovan sniffed again. "He was sweating, nervous. It's an interesting hormone combination. I get the feeling that he didn't like doing it."

"That does sound odd," Eleri mused. "Though maybe not surprising. If he's killing for information and he's doing it to get these people out of his way, he may not particularly enjoy the job. He might even regret it deeply."

Donovan took another slow inhale. It was there, a faint scent behind the odor of Jivika's corpse, which was slowly beginning to decay. It pissed him off.

He had an excellent sense of smell. Maybe not by dog standards, but he had to be ten or twenty-five times better than the average human. It bothered him that he could smell the emotion, but not the person.

"It's a man," he told Eleri, though he didn't look back at her. He wished he could identify the individual, but it wasn't there. Even though he'd been making an attempt ever since he got here to remember individuals, it wasn't enough. He could recognize LeDonRic walking down the street to him. He could recognize Maggie if she came up behind him. But that didn't make them anything different than people he regularly knew. He could tell when Eleri had been in a room, but he knew her well enough to track that now.

If he were wearing a blindfold, he could identify each member of the Mazur family, and each of the Jameses. He could ID Whitlow and, of course, Vergheese. This, though . . . it wasn't a person he knew well enough to know the various emotional states and be able to smell the individual identifiers underneath the anger and the fear.

Tamping down his irritation, Donovan walked the perimeter of the room, sniffing into the corners until he almost got a headache. He was hoping that something would have drifted or lingered or there might be a scent of a cologne or an overwhelming soap or deodorant. Instead, he got nothing, and it frustrated the hell out of him.

Eleri, meanwhile, had squatted down near the body. Using her first two fingers, she reached out and touched Jivika's neck. She did it even though Donovan had told her he already knew the woman was dead. No one smelled like that when they were alive.

He'd never gotten a live person on his table when he'd been an M.E., but he'd hoped for it. He would not be the one who was making the Y incision when the person sat up screaming, because Donovan could smell the decay, even when it was just starting to take hold. If the person was even just very, very barely alive and cold, they wouldn't smell like decay.

So Donovan had always leaned over and huffed a faint sniff each time he got a new corpse, and each time he'd been disappointed to find that they were well and truly dead. This time it was doubly so. He wished Jivika would be alive enough that he could bring her back.

"Can you come smell her for drugs?" Eleri asked.

He came over and squatted on the opposite side of the body. Neither he nor Eleri wanted to put their knees or hands onto the floor or touch anything they didn't have to.

He took a slow inhale, probably his last as the odors were wanting to mingle together and his brain was wanting to swim with it. "Yes, it's there."

"Butter and dairy?" Eleri asked, almost with a smile, and he nodded. He understood there was a dead body of a person who'd been in their charge and Eleri was almost smiling about the smell. Though it would seem wrong to anyone else, he understood. She'd compartmentalized Jivika's death—not fully, but for now and until her job was done—and this was the only thing they could smile about. At least they had *something*.

"The ligature marks don't indicate struggle. Even less than Johanna," she said, the frustration having replaced the small amount of humor she'd found.

"Bet if we black light her some things will show up." Donovan suspected she might be covered in unbloomed bruises, the same way Johanna Schmitt had been.

"Maybe, maybe not."

Interesting, Eleri disagreed. He tipped his head and waited until she said, "Notice the ligature marks are less deep."

He hadn't noticed that. He'd been too busy sniffing.

"Which means she wasn't tied up as tightly. Which may mean that she simply didn't struggle as much. And what do you think about the smell? Do you think she was maybe drugged more heavily?"

Hating that it was all he had to go on, Donovan shook his head. "I can't tell. This is fresh, right off the body. The last time I smelled it—off Johanna—it had been several days old and through cold storage."

"I would guess from the ligature marks that he did drug her more heavily."

Donovan nodded, but it didn't matter if he agreed with her or not. Eventually, they would get a tox screen back. They just had to wait for it.

He looked down at the body again. Javika's eyes were open, staring sightlessly at the ceiling. Eleri looked the body over one more time and left Donovan to it as she moved around the room, inspecting it for peripheral clues.

"The bed looks wrong," she announced suddenly.

"What do you mean?" He stood up and turned to look. He'd been at the foot facing toward the body, but now he pivoted to aim toward the headboard, leaving Jivika's corpse on the ground behind him, unmoved though not untouched.

Eleri frowned and waved a blue-gloved hand at the upper right corner of the bed. "It looks like it was pulled back. It looks like it was made and *then* pulled back."

Donovan saw what she was saying. Almost three quarters of the bed was made up neatly. On the left hand side of the bed, the covers were still tucked up under the pillows, but the right hand side was a bit of a mess.

"And nobody's slept in it. So, why would he pull the bed covers back?"

Donovan frowned, seeing exactly what Eleri was talking about. Jivika had not been dragged from bed. The bed had been made and only partly disturbed, but not in any of the normal ways a person would.

"How old do you think this is?" Eleri asked, motioning to the room, and Donovan understood she meant the crime scene and the body.

"Eight, nine hours maybe. I don't think this bed was remade this morning. I think this is from last night."

"*Shit,*" Eleri muttered. He guessed she hadn't felt any gut reactions in regards to the slaying of their subject. No niggling sensation at the back of her brain letting her know their person of interest was already dead. In fact, had she had any warning at all, he knew Eleri would have dragged him over to check on Jivika at midnight rather than waiting until the morning's unanswered voicemail and unreturned texts.

Letting that response lie, they split the room and walked up either side of the bed looking for anything out of the ordinary, anything that might tell them what had actually happened. Donovan had no doubt that the cause of death would be unknown again. And he hated it.

This time he knelt down and looked under the edges of the bed, once again trying to see if maybe she'd been splayed out across the top and tied down the way Marat had. But it looked like this time, the killer had tied her to the feet of the nearby heavy objects—the bed and the dresser—leaving her to die on the floor. Donovan leaned over and sniffed at the bed covers.

"She didn't die here."

"I wouldn't think so. It would be hard—or pointless—to put the bed back afterward and just leave the body on the floor."

His sense of smell concurred with the visible physical evidence. The covers weren't rumpled like the body had been laid on it and again, as Eleri had pointed out, it looked like she'd never been in—or even on—the bed.

When he stood up and looked over, he saw Eleri frowning at a pillow. "What is this?"

"I don't know." There was some kind of dirt on the pillow.

"Pillows get dirty." Though even as he said it, he knew that was the wrong response here.

"No. It's right in the middle of the pillow. And look at the other pillows," Eleri pointed them out.

He followed her instructions. Donovan knew bodies. Eleri knew crime scenes better than he did. So he listened.

"There's something on this pillow and it doesn't belong. When we get the crime techs in, we have to make sure they test it."

"When we get the crime techs in . . ." he repeated her words. "You mean, after we leave because someone will have spotted us here at Jivika's house now and there's a dead body found here? How is Marshall Bennett going to explain that we were here and now she's dead?"

48

Another string of swear words ran through Eleri's head as she stood in the bedroom looking at everything in the room they still needed to check.

"Goddammit, the only way out of this," she said to Donovan, "is for us to call it in."

"Which means," he sighed out the words, his frustrations as clear as hers felt, "we have to explain that we went to the pharmacy just for a pack of gum because we now can't claim a prescription. They'll check it."

He was right. She had no doubt that the Curie PD would check everything. The police officers in town had passed Marshall Bennett's IQ test, just like everyone else. It didn't make them better human beings, but it probably did make them smarter, better-than-average detectives. And it didn't take a genius to figure out that a genius cop would be onto them immediately.

Hell, Eleri was surprised they hadn't been called out already. Or maybe the CPD had already figured it all out and knew they were Bureau agents but were staying out of the way. What came out of her mouth was, "Well crap. Now we have to act normal."

"Okay, let's set a timer. We've got five minutes." She turned back to the body.

Donovan was peeling one glove and reaching for his phone. Then he stopped. "No, we don't even have that. We've already been inside for a while. We have to call the police now."

"Oh, *dammit!*" Eleri swore harder, thinking Donovan was right once again. If their entry got cross referenced to the time of the 9-1-1 call, then they would likely get caught. Normal people might not believe that level of accuracy, but more than one criminal had been caught for mismatching times, even by just a few minutes.

"Okay." She peeled her glove, pulled out her own phone, and dialed dispatch.

The voice on the phone answered, "9-1-1. What's your emergency?" And she almost laughed. There were only about four or five dispatchers in Curie, but Marshall Bennett insisted the city run its own station. Apparently, because of whatever the mayor had experienced in life, he did not trust the surrounding counties' resources—not their sheriffs, not their police, and not even their dispatch.

"Hi, um, I'm at Jivika Das's house, and, uh—" Eleri purposefully inserted in the stutters and pitch changes. "She's dead. She's—I think she's *dead*."

The voice from dispatch calmly talked her through feeling for a pulse and Eleri went with it. She could have just stood there and said yes, there was no pulse, but the safer bet was to follow along. Any smart PD would find discrepancies between Eleri's prints and every point the dispatcher had told her to touch the body.

Peeling the glove quietly, so hopefully the snap of latex did not appear on the recording from the call center later, she put her fingers aside the neck—incorrectly—and then she moved them. Just as an untrained person would.

She babbled her way through the whole charade, regretting the time lost from checking the scene. "Yes, I don't, I don't feel anything. Can somebody come and help? I mean, she's staring at the ceiling. I think . . . she's pale. She's gray. I think, I think she's dead."

"Ma'am. We'll have someone out right away."

"Okay, okay. Thank you. Thank you," Eleri said, and hung up the phone, even as the woman was asking her to stay on the line. Eleri and Donovan had a very limited window of time now to check out the room and the house before the police got here. They could not afford to stay on the phone or get caught rummaging through Jivika's home.

"Office!" Eleri announced, and the two of them bolted to the other room, looking first to be sure the curtains were closed and that no one would see them. Though they had done this before, this might be their last chance. This time they also didn't have Jivika looking over their shoulders. Eleri pulled things out of the drawer and handed them to Donovan to hold, and then punched at the drawer bottom.

She got lucky. Jivika had the same trap bottom to the drawer that Marat Rychenkov did. That made it even more likely that the two were working together. Then . . .

"Holy fuck! Donovan," Eleri muttered as she pulled out a notebook. "Look." She held it up. It was the exact same kind of composition book they'd found at the Rychenkov-Schmitt home, the kind Marat had used to record his drone research.

Eleri quickly cracked it open and scanned. "Son of a bitch." It was written in the same code as Marat's notebooks.

Tucking the books under her arm and quickly hustling everything from Donovan's hands back into the drawer, she issued the edict, "Find more!"

They continued searching the office frantically but were slowed by the need to carefully put everything back in its place. They kept gloves on their hands, making sure that they didn't leave fingerprints in here, so that no one could trace them to this room. They hadn't even touched the doorknob on the way in.

Donovan found one more notebook tucked into the lining in the back of a suitcase that had been shoved into the closet for apparent storage. But then he looked up and said, "Sirens."

Though she couldn't hear them yet herself, Eleri looked to Donovan frantically. "Now what?"

He looked back at her. "We have to hide these. We can't take them with us. It's not like I can stick them down the back of my pants."

"Okay. Where do we put them?"

"Kitchen," he offered. "Up high. If they find them, they'll know it's weird. But they probably won't. Not for a while. Even if they do, at least our fingerprints aren't on them."

Eleri nodded her agreement and they headed down the stairs. Donovan opened a series of cabinets before settling on one. He gently shoved the notebooks into the middle of a stack of old warranties and manuals in the small cabinet above the microwave.

"Good. The sirens are closer, El," he warned her, though Eleri didn't quite hear them until his voice ended. "Back up to the bedroom."

They were running up the stairs as she peeled her own gloves and told him, "Give me yours." She wadded them into a tiny flat pack and stuffed them into the zippered section of her purse, underneath the tampons and other feminine supplies she carried there. Hopefully, anyone who searched her purse would not dig that deeply.

If there was a problem, all she and Donovan would have to do is pull their badges. Her badge currently lay at the bottom of her purse, underneath her wallet. But still, she didn't want to tip off the cops that she and Donovan were anything other than what their cover appeared, if they could avoid it.

They'd just bolted through the house twice as the front door was coming open. The police hollered out to them, "Hello, police, police."

Eleri looked at Donovan frantically. "Move," she ordered softly, and he seemed to catch on. They'd been running through the house. Had they just been sitting by the body as she had suggested on the call, they wouldn't be breathing heavily at all. Though they'd both practiced lowering their heart rates and breathing at Quantico, it was still better to have an explanation than to need one.

She paced the room and worked up a few tears in her eyes. Donovan stood on the other side, leaned on the bed, putting his fingerprints directly onto the knob of the posts. He leaned over, staring oddly at the body. Eleri thought it was strange, but she didn't have time to question it.

As the police came in, Donovan suddenly leaned the other way, bending over as though he were going to retch. Eleri almost laughed. Morbid humor was common for people in her profession. She was standing near the body of a woman she'd known, one she was supposed to protect, but she was fighting back the need to laugh at Donovan acting as though he was going to hack up his breakfast.

She hoped the officers saw the press of her lips as distress, and to be fair, more than once she'd come across people standing over a dead body, laughing hysterically. A break from the normal expected emotions was not uncommon. Any trigger in an extreme situation could make expression of emotion go haywire. So she hoped that if she sucked a deep breath and aimed for a tragic expression, the officers would read it as something correct and normal for the scene in front of them.

"Oh, thank God you're here." She rushed toward them and pulled herself up in a harsh stop, almost skidding as she came close to the body. She had to carefully step around, and she pressed her butt against the dresser, even though she had to pick her feet up and over Jivika's hand—the one that lay near the dresser, the one Eleri suspected had been tied with a rope to the foot of the heavy unit.

She almost threw herself into one of the officer's arms. "Thank God you're here. I'm—I'm going to go in the hall if that's okay."

The officer she'd nearly assaulted nodded at her and looked then toward Jivika's body as another tended to Donovan.

"Sir?" The man put a kind hand on Donovan's back and led him, too, into the hallway before motioning them both downstairs.

Upstairs, several officers examined the room, and Eleri tried to figure out how to explain to Marshall Bennett that they needed to be sure the strange pillow dirt was tested. She hadn't even gotten to drag her finger through the odd stuff. Was it sticky? Dusty?

She endured the officer's questioning and explained how they had come in through the door, called out Jivika's name and gotten worried when they hadn't heard her respond. She explained that they'd gone to the store to pick up a few things and then by the pharmacy and so on.

Donovan continued his act of wanting to yak up his guts—despite being a doctor, he'd not seen a friend dead before, he said. But that allowed her to lay down an initial storyline, so he could match it later. One of the officers was bringing him a glass of water and telling him to take slow sips. She motioned Donovan onto the ground and told him to put his head between his knees.

It was brilliant on Donovan's part, Eleri thought. They weren't getting separated, and they were going to get to keep their stories straight.

She continued with her worried re-telling of what hadn't happened. "But she didn't call out, and I wanted to meet her for lunch. I mean, I called her this morning." That would match with the voicemail when they checked Jivika's phone, and she was grateful that she hadn't said anything else. "So when she didn't reply, I just, you know, we were here already, and I got worried."

She pointed as though to the pharmacy four blocks away and maintained her cover, but every moment she spent with the police, every moment she waited while they interviewed Donovan, only ratcheted her nerves up.

She had to get to Marshall Bennett.

49

Eleri was on the phone with Marshall Bennett within minutes of them arriving home. It had taken an hour and a half for the police to look through the house, decide that Eleri and Donovan were not at fault, interview them, and eventually let them leave.

Of course, Eleri had ultimately been interviewed twice by two different officers, as had Donovan. It made sense, but the whole thing with the one officer being nice to "sick" Donovan the first time had allowed them to coordinate their stories quite cleanly.

Of course, the cops should have separated her and Donovan right away. Then again, it was pretty clear from the way the two of them were treated, despite being found in the home standing over the dead body, that they were not considered suspects.

The officers would know right away that this was either by the same killer or someone trying to create a copycat scenario. However, these killings would be hard to copycat without knowing exactly what the killer had done.

Eleri was frustrated as hell. Hell, even she couldn't copycat this murder because she *still* had no idea what the killer had actually done to kill them.

The drugs found in their systems would not have killed them. Even if the buttery smelling toxin were an alternate form of GHB, as they suspected, it would have left some kind of chemical evidence if it had caused the heart to stop. It couldn't have caused oxygen deprivation, which appeared to be the actual cause of death. There were no fibers or bruising in or around the mouth, which should have happened if the murderer had put a pillow or bag over his victims' faces. Hell, their hair wasn't even messed up—and even if a victim didn't struggle, a smothering almost always messed up the hair.

Eleri felt like she was trying to figure out which glass of wine she could clearly not choose—a la *The Princess Bride*. And she was aggravated as hell. She'd splayed out on the couch and looking at the ceiling as though it might have answers. It didn't.

When Marshall Bennett answered the phone, she tried to use her polite voice. "Mr. Bennett, we need your help. We need it quickly."

"I hear there's been another murder," he said, by way of opening the conversation.

Of course, Eleri's way of opening it had been no better. "Yes, sir. We just stumbled across the body of Jivika Das."

There was a pause, and Eleri understood he needed to process. He was likely trying to frame some acceptable way of asking how they had let this happen. Jumping into the space calmly, she tried to act as though this were a normal conversation when they were discussing a third dead citizen.

"We told her to leave town last night. We offered her an FBI safe house, but shy of arresting her, there wasn't much we could do. If we'd forced her to go, it would have not only blown everyone's cover but it would have been against her very clearly stated wishes."

"She didn't want to leave?" Bennett asked softly, still processing.

"No. We suggested it the first time we spoke to her, but she didn't want to. At the time, we didn't believe she was in danger. It was just an offer. But last night, we suggested it very, very strongly. She refused, despite all our efforts."

Eleri still felt guilty. That one thing—Jivika's stubborn refusal to leave, regardless of all the options they'd thrown at her—was the only thing letting Eleri breathe through this day. She'd been able to focus on the body while she was standing over it, but now she had no physical work to occupy her time.

She desperately needed to get her hands on those notebooks. She needed to get to the body, but the body needed to get to the CDC in Lincoln, first. There was little chance of that happening right away. "Sir, I wish she would have left."

"Me too," he said. They sat in the small silence for a moment, acknowledging the sadness of the call, because Bennett, despite the large stack of names he did not remember allowing into town, seemed to truly love every citizen. In a moment, he spoke again. "How can I help? And how do we stop losing people?"

"I have an idea, and I need your help." Eleri truly hoped that Das was the last, and she thought perhaps they were onto something. "When we were in the Das home, and we found the body, we managed to enact a very quick search. We found two notebooks. Black and white composition books."

She was more grateful than ever now for the cover story that he was a friend of her uncle's and was helping her out. It was the only thing that would make these phone calls seem normal if anyone looked at the records.

"The composition notebooks were in different places. However, Donovan and I placed them in the kitchen, in the cabinet above the microwave."

He didn't ask for further description, and Eleri hoped he had everything he needed. He had to transfer the information to Kate seamlessly.

"I don't believe Donovan and I can go back into the house. The house is a crime scene now and the Curie PD are all over it. I'm hoping that Kate can get in there somehow and get those manuals to us." She paused for a minute. Her brain was always turning, and she thought of an idea. "Does Das have a relative we can reach out to? Can you and Kate claim that this relative requested the manuals, and that other papers are included in that stack? Maybe a living will or such. The sooner we get our hands on those notebooks, the sooner we'll be able to figure out what's really going on, and hopefully stop the next person from being killed."

Bennett agreed. He would take Kate and go out to the Das house right away, and they would attempt to get the notebooks surreptitiously out of the way without the officers knowing. "I'll bet Kate will think of something."

Eleri put in her next request. "Can you have Kate deliver them to us? I don't think Donovan and I should be seen out and about this afternoon. So it would help if she could bring them to us, to the house. Maybe she can bring a food basket or something, put the notebooks in the bottom?"

"Something to make you feel better about the loss of your friend," he murmured. "A way to welcome you to town with something *other than a murder*."

She heard the underlying frustration and sadness in his voice, and she felt it herself. NightShade cases often dealt with the paranormal, the unexplained. This set of murders, though perfectly earthly, was quickly falling into the second category.

She hung up the phone and turned to Donovan who asked, "Now what?"

"I don't know. We've got to get our hands on those notebooks. We've got to figure out why these people have been killed, and how it might lead us to the next person on the list."

Donovan nodded as though he agreed, at least somewhat. But his next questions chilled her. "And if we can't?"

50

Donovan sat at the kitchen table, munching on a stick of organic, Slim Jim-like processed meat. Several discarded wrappers already lay in an arc around him. Eleri had raised an eyebrow at them, but Donovan didn't care.

Eleri had taken a wheel of brie from the basket that Kate had brought and was putting it on some crispy Parmesan crackers. As usual, Eleri appeared sophisticated and Donovan much less so, but then again, they'd each been a product of their upbringing.

Despite her job and willingness to get dirty, she still occasionally gave off glimpses of someone who'd been raised with extreme wealth. It showed in the way she knew the names of all the cheese knives and the cheeses, the way she was spreading them on the crackers and then lining them up to be eaten daintily. Donovan had only barely recognized that the spreaders were, in fact, *cheese knives*, and it was only something he'd learned as an adult.

The expense of the gift basket had seemed extravagant but maintaining their cover story was important. Kate had laughed as she showed up at the door, saying how difficult it had been to find a basket big enough to unpack and repack with the notebooks securely hidden inside. Sure enough, when they'd removed all the sausages, the logs of cheese, the rolls of crackers, and jars of dips, two black-and-white composition notebooks had sat underneath.

"Did they find anything else?" Eleri asked Bennett's assistant, ignoring the food, another thing that Donovan found was a trait of the wealthy.

Even as an adult, he always tracked where the food was located, having gone too many times without as a child. He'd learned as an adult that he didn't have to eat it all *right now,* but he'd never been able to kill the reaction every time he scented it. He placed it, cataloged how much there was, and thought about how long it might last.

A random thought slipped into his head again, as it was doing more and more these days. Did he have a brother? And had his brother done the same thing? But right now there was no room for musings in the abstract. He turned his focus back to Kate, back to a murder that was still slightly less than twenty-four hours old.

"The house is swarming with officers," Kate told them as she picked up a cracker with brie that Eleri had expertly plated. After taking a small bite, she held it to one side and continued. "However, they did only a cursory check of the bulk of the house and are mostly concentrating their efforts on the upstairs bedroom, the staircase, and the front door."

That was exactly why Donovan had chosen the kitchen as his hiding spot for the notebooks. He'd known Kate might be able to come in the back door and grab them without being noticed. "Do you know what they found?"

"Oh, yes," Kate said. She'd sat down at the table with them, not helping, but watching as they continued to open or set aside all the food. "I don't have all the exact details and I don't quite speak crime scene tech, but I do know this: They didn't find any signs of forced entry."

"Typical," Eleri murmured, as Kate told them more, and Donovan agreed. This seemed to be the way that the break-ins had been going —not as actual break-ins at all.

"There are no other notable fingerprints around the home. There are plenty in the living room and in the main room. They want to print you two so they can rule out any prints that are yours."

"Of course," Eleri said.

The two of them were obvious choices for stray fingerprints around the house. The PD knew what a crime scene should look like when found by an amateur, so he and Eleri had left a few stray prints in the place. The techs would not only be ruling out the fingerprints they'd left, but also looking at the locations of their prints. Those would be checked against their stories. Anything else might blow their cover.

Donovan knew he'd have to call Westerfield to tell him their prints were going into the system. He wanted to double check that they would be rerouted to false histories. Otherwise, the national database would tell the Curie PD they had two FBI agents in town. Even having their cover blown to the PD and the crime scene techs would be too many people.

He pulled his focus back to the table, as Kate was still talking. "There doesn't seem to be any sign of forced *anything*, according to the officers."

"Did they use a blacklight?" Donovan asked, wondering if they'd managed to get that far ahead.

Kate merely shrugged. "They didn't say anything about it, and I didn't know to ask."

"Understood. We'll use our own."

"Okay. Anything else?" she asked, starting to stand from her seat, and Eleri merely offered her a very kind, "Thank you. Thank you for taking time out of your day to do this. I'm hopeful the notebooks will give us a big break on this case."

Kate merely smiled and said, "Don't worry about it. This *is* my job. I do whatever Curie needs me to do."

But the moment Kate was out the door, Eleri opened the notebook closest to her and picked up a cracker from her delicately arranged plate. Her stomach had started to not-so-delicately growl. It had been hours since they'd left the house, and they hadn't had lunch.

Donovan, chewing on his meat sticks, opened the second notebook and was looking up at Eleri as she looked at him a smile on her face. "It's the same code. Different handwriting."

He was shaking his head at her. "Mine's in Marat's hand. You've got one from . . . someone else. I don't want to assume it's Jivika's."

"I don't know. I don't really know her handwriting." Eleri frowned as she looked down at the code marching across the page.

"Wait." He dashed upstairs to where he'd filed away the list he'd made the bio-mimicry specialist write for them. Though that had not been their intention, it would certainly serve as a handwriting sample. He came back down the stairs, thinking that it looked like a match.

By the time they laid his list out side by side with the notebook in question, Eleri was agreeing. "So we have three notebooks with Marat Rychenkov's handwriting—one of which Jivika Das got her hands on somehow. And we have another, which is in her own writing, but in the same code."

Donovan began thinking out loud. "This means several things: Either Marat gave her the one notebook or she somehow managed to get her hands on it after the fact."

"Do you think she got into the house before the time we caught her?"

The question hung for a moment while Donovan considered that possibility. "It's entirely plausible. We didn't have video surveillance until after we talked to Johanna."

"So Jivika lied to us about that being the first time breaking into the house. It's possible that she was one of the early visitors and that she stole this notebook, then."

"But she didn't get all three," Eleri interjected.

"No. Maybe she didn't find the others. Maybe she only needed this one."

"So hopefully, once we translate it," Eleri added, "we'll know what it says, and whether it was enough to let Jivika finish the project."

"Also," he added, "the false-bottom drawer was the same as the one we found in Rychenkov's house. That's how we knew to look for it."

"True. There's a lot of information here suggesting the two of them were conspiring on this."

"And, of course," Donovan added, "that she lied to us when she said she didn't know."

"Yeah. She knew. I *knew* she knew. She wasn't telling us enough. I just thought we'd have more time to figure it out."

Not wanting to dwell on the failure of keeping Jivika safe, he changed the subject back. "It also means they made the code together, or at least shared it."

With those puzzle pieces now firmly in place, they turned back to the new information. An hour later, Eleri gasped.

She looked up at Donovan with big eyes. "We have to get the kids in custody."

51

It was only thirty minutes later that Eleri found herself sitting at the large dining room table in the Mazur house. The four members of the Mazur family were all in her immediate sight. She was counting this much as a success.

She and Donovan had called Westerfield as soon as she'd explained her reasoning. It hadn't taken long to persuade their SAC of the need to break cover to these two families—and the importance of getting the kids out of town.

Clearly, the "checking in" the Curie PD was doing was not enough protection. The killer had gotten around them—whether it was easy or not didn't matter—and the victim had lain dead in her home overnight.

We should have known better, Eleri thought, *determined now to not make the same mistake twice.*

They had offered Jivika Das a chance to leave town, a chance to get to a safe house. They were not *offering* the same to the children. Eleri would present the facts to the parents, and she hoped they would readily agree to protection. She hoped they might feel less secure about entrusting their children to a whim of personal safety, than Jivika had felt about herself. But if it came down to it, Eleri decided, she would insist.

Eleri had hung her jacket on a dragon-shaped coat stand just inside the front door and was sitting at the table waiting for

Marshawn James and his two daughters to arrive. She'd not yet said anything to the Mazurs about why she and Donovan had called this meeting. But they clearly had their suspicions.

Kaya had met them at the door with a raised eyebrow asking, "Is LeDonRic coming?" But Eleri had simply told her that no, her neighbor was not on the list for tonight.

She'd instructed Kaya to please clear the table and gather everyone. Kaya had to have been wondering for the past fifteen minutes, since Eleri had called and asked to come over, offering a cryptic "Please make sure your whole family will be there . . ."

Originally standing just behind Kaya, Nate Mazur had merely nodded at Eleri's suggestion and gone to fetch the children. Kaya had seated herself at the table and commenced staring at Eleri, waiting.

Eleri then told her new friend, "We've also called Marshawn James and he and his girls are on their way here. I'm sorry. I hope you don't mind that we called this meeting at your house and invited other people."

"I don't mind you inviting my friends. I'm concerned that we're having this meeting at all." Kaya pushed just as Nate and their two children arrived at the table.

"I understand," Eleri replied. "Marshawn should be here any second now and we'll explain everything then in the hopes that we can explain only once."

It was then she noticed Joule did not look worried like the other family members did. Instead, a small smirk sat on her lips. She nudged her brother who looked at her, the question waiting on his eyebrows. Eleri thought she had a good idea what was passing between them.

She was confident that Joule had the best grasp on what Eleri and Donovan were about to say, and she would give Joule her props. Luckily, just then, a knock came at the door. This time, however, the knob turned and Marshawn appeared, clearly feeling comfortable letting himself in. His daughters appeared in the foyer behind him while they looked at the scene, questions on their eyebrows as well.

Yes, Eleri thought. It was strange that she had called them to come to their friends' home where *she* would meet them. The three stood in the entry space, too confused to remove their jackets and come any further. It was Kaya who waved them over to the table.

Kaya and Nate jumped up, gathering extra chairs, and pulling a small bench up to the table. While they motioned for their own kids to move and take the bench, it was Emersyn and Madisyn who quickly sat down together on it. Eleri hoped it helped that the kids were clearly comfortable in this home. It would make this job easier.

Unfortunately, what she and Donovan had to say was anything but comfortable. Now that everyone was present, she let Donovan start.

"You're probably wondering why we've asked you all to come tonight."

"Not so much," said Joule, and Eleri could no longer fight her own grin.

Donovan, too, smiled. "The short answer is that Joule was right." He reached into his back pocket and as Eleri saw him move, she repeated the gesture herself. Almost simultaneously, they flipped open their badges and laid them out on the table. They slid them across the surface, Eleri aiming hers toward Nate and Kaya Mazur, Donovan pushing his toward Marshawn James.

It was most important that the adults see their credentials first and that they feel they were being spoken to. As much as it was the children who were an issue, the adults would have to legally sign off on FBI custody. Eleri and Donovan had discussed their strategy ahead of time, hoping to aim the most pertinent information toward Nate, Kaya, and Marshawn.

Though this little meeting had happened fast, Eleri had worked hard to coordinate it. It had been important that it happen at the Mazur house. It was the easiest way to begin providing protection for Cage and Joule—even though the family didn't know that yet.

Eleri was not going to have another Johanna Schmitt or Jivika Das on her hands.

"I knew it!" Joule grinned as she watched the badges slide across the table. Cage held his fist up, offering a bump of congratulations to his sister.

"You nailed it, Joule," Eleri said. "As you can see from the badge, I'm actually Agent Eleri Eames and my partner *is* Donovan, but he's Donovan Heath. I've been with the FBI for almost a decade now."

While the men sat back to clearly digest the new information, it was Kaya who leaned forward, looking Eleri in the eyes. Eleri knew she owed the woman an apology, but it was more important that she answer their questions first. So she waited to hear what Kaya would say. Luckily, it wasn't an accusation—at least, not yet.

"This is about Marat and Johanna, isn't it?" Kaya pressed, watching Eleri's face as though—having been lied to before—she needed to be sure she was getting good answers.

"Yes." Eleri nodded and she tacked her apology onto the end of it. "I'm sorry that we lied to you." She looked around the table not attempting to make eye contact with all of them, as that would look forced, but to let them know they were all being spoken to. "Agent Heath and I are under direct orders from our boss. When Joule figured it out, we wanted to tell you, but we were forbidden from doing so. However, new information has come to light and," she looked at Marshawn first, then Kaya and Nate, and she stressed the syllables as the words came out of her mouth. "We would like to put your children into protective custody. You can go with them or not. That's a decision we'll make tonight."

She hoped her next words would push that agenda, even though it was not a blow she could soften for them at all. "We believe your children are in danger."

52

Donovan sat back a little and let Eleri lead the meeting. In part, it was because she was the senior agent. Also, she was better at getting citizens to work with them rather than against them—and she was the one who had had befriended Kaya Mazur under false pretenses. It was up to Eleri to mend that rift and give the two of them the best relationship with these families going forward.

In part, he let Eleri lead the meeting because he was the one who could sniff out fear, concern, and maybe even guilt from these people. He needed to not be talking when he inhaled, in order to best sort the scent information he got.

He had smelled interest initially, then concern from the parents. Now a quick dose of fear had come from the two James girls sitting just to his right.

It was Kaya who spoke up again, the two men letting her take the lead. At least Eleri's apology seemed to have been accepted relatively quickly, though it might be something Kaya would be angry about later, when her children were no longer in danger.

Donovan had trained on this kind of thing at Quantico—as it was always wise to know what your suspect or witness or person of interest wanted and most valued—and, though he didn't have children of his own, protecting one's own children was the strongest instinct a human knew. Kaya was clear in her fierce protection of the children.

Resting his elbows on the table, he leaned a little bit forward, watching the players carefully. In a moment, he would lean back and resume inhaling slightly to seeing what he could detect. When he didn't get anything he could identify, he fought down the frustration and joined the conversation.

"Your children were all friends of Marat and Johanna, particularly you two." He turned and looked at Cage and Joule, and they both nodded. "We found information tonight that makes us believe we know what Marat and Johanna were killed for." He paused, not sure if they knew already. "And it's the same reason Jivika Das was killed."

Pausing, he watched as all of their faces transformed, and he smelled the sudden jolts of surprise, anger, or fear that hit them. Those were all appropriate responses, he thought. Though they were physically closer to him, the James family hadn't taken their jackets off, and he couldn't smell the information from them quite as precisely.

Now, it was masking some of the response. He should have asked them to take the outerwear off. But now it would seem a little odd, and maybe they needed them for comfort in a rough situation.

"Jivika Das has died?" Nate Mazur leaned toward the two of them as though they could tell him something that would help. They knew far more information about Das than they were allowed to share.

Again, Donovan let the conversation bounce back to Eleri, and she merely replied, "Yes. We found her in her home this morning. We'd been watching her and . . ." He heard Eleri lob the hardball across the table, hoping it hit all the parents square in the chest. "We urged her to take protective custody. She had a police detail, but it was only checking intermittently to see that she arrived at the right place at the right time. She was killed in her home last night."

She paused, letting the information sit, not sure how well the Mazurs or the James family had known Jivika Das. But clearly, they'd known enough to be shocked at her death. Kaya looked back and forth, not to the children but to the adult men.

"But Jivika was a biologist and . . . and Marat was into robots. If Jivika was murdered, that would suggest that the two were working on something together. But for the life of me, I can't figure out what that might be."

Smart, Donovan thought. Kaya Mazur had had exactly zero

seconds to sort those puzzle pieces and put them into their appropriate places, and she'd done so quickly and accurately.

"Yes," Eleri replied, "that's exactly the issue. And exactly why your children are in danger. They know about the project that has led to these murders."

Nate's hand suddenly came up and rested on the table, as though he'd intended to reach out and hold onto his child's hand. But he had two children and only one hand near them. The gesture, though not useless, struck Donovan as coming close.

Donovan could not imagine the moment a parent was put into a situation of deciding whether they could protect their child, or whether it was something beyond their grasp. The adults all had looks on their faces suggesting they were wrestling with exactly that.

Eleri jumped in again. "Listen, I know this is a lot to take in, but it's also important that you know Donovan and I are sharing with you information that's classified. I know that the two of you—" she looked to the Mazurs, "hold national-level security clearances. Consider this that kind of information."

She next turned to Marshawn and said, "We're trusting you as a civilian to keep this confidence." And then she looked at the Mazur kids on one end of the table, and then to the James girls on the other. "And for you, while I'm aware that you are minors and will not be held to the same kind of legal ramifications your parents are if something leaks, I need you to know that it's very important that you not tell this information to anyone. We're expecting that, as soon as we get your questions answered, we will take the children to a safe location."

There was another pause, and Donovan added another nail to the coffin. He was not going to lose another person in this town. "If you speak of this, you won't just be breaking a clearance, you'll be letting people know that you know about the project. Three people have already died for this information. Talking about it could be the equivalent of placing a target on your own back."

He let that sink in but noticed that Kaya Mazur's mouth opened as though to speak. Eleri held up the palm of her hand softly, not to quell what she would say, but to ask for just another moment to keep talking. "You parents will be allowed to go with the children, either singly or all of you, and that's a decision we'll make in the next few minutes."

Kaya nodded then, stopping her first question, but immediately jumping in with another one. "Will we all be allowed to stay together?"

Eleri nodded. She and Donovan had already made those arrangements with Westerfield, prepping a safe house for a minimum of four occupants and a maximum of seven.

Kaya asked another question, her eyes darting from one corner of the room to another. "Are we safe here in the house, right now?"

Eleri nodded. "Yes, we are."

"How can you be so certain?" Marshawn asked, peering at them.

"Well, for one, right now you have two armed and trained FBI agents guarding you. It's why we wanted the meeting here: this is the safest location. Secondly, we know because of the methodology the killer used—"

Donovan heard the slight hitch at the end of her words and knew she'd cut the sentence off, as though wanting to tell them what they'd found out but knowing she couldn't. Even though these people were going into protective custody, the two agents were not allowed to set loose any more secrets than absolutely necessary, and the method of murder was definitely on that list.

Slowly, he sniffed the air again. The scents coming from the table were a little bit stranger now. Worry mingled with fear; other emotions flitted through, too light for him to fully distinguish. That didn't surprise him, though. The Mazur family lived almost directly across the street from two of the three murder victims. Their children had interacted with Johanna and Marat much more than Emersyn and Madisyn had, at least from what he'd gathered. The evening's developments would create a disturbing mix of emotion from both sides of the table.

Eleri began speaking one more time and Donovan listened, opening his nostrils. While he wished he could change his face to get the best scent possible, he couldn't, not here. The scientists at the table might welcome him as a fascinating study, but he did not believe these people needed yet another blow tonight.

Once she had nods from all of the children, Eleri leaned forward toward the center of the table, as though telling a deep secret. "Here is what Marat Rychenkov was working on . . ."

53

"Cage tipped us off," Eleri told them all with a smile, noting seven pairs of wide eyes all staring at her.

Cage frowned at her, letting her see that he didn't know what Marat's project was exactly, even though he'd already told her the information she needed. That was what had brought her and Donovan rushing over here tonight.

"Marat Rychenkov was working with his drones," she told them, a fact probably everyone at the table already knew. "He had several different sets. He was working to solve the native mapping program problem." Marshawn's eyebrows squeezed in. It looked like an unexpected response, but then his head tipped in question. It was Cage who picked up the mantle and explained.

"There's a concern about drones, particularly swarms, being able to navigate unknown areas. In order to do so, they need to map while they go, and they need to both retain and relay the information they glean. They need to be able to do so in entirely new places, oftentimes places that humans can't get to." He waved his hands as he spoke, for the first time that night seeming excited about the topic. "These may be places that are very, very tiny, and you would use nanobot type drones. In other situations, you might need a swarm to go into undersea scenarios, or into space. So there are a lot of uses, but also a lot of places that we can't predict the environment they might run into."

That was interesting, Eleri thought. In fact, she'd not considered that some of the things the drones might run into would be anything other than physical objects. But as Cage went on, he discussed the need for drones in space, saying that they might encounter pockets of gas, stars, temperature changes, and any other number of things the drones might need to map. Underwater applications he mentioned included changes in the Thermocline; locations of moveable things, like plants or schools of fish; and locations of more solid objects, like chasms and boulders. Undersea drones would need to map the kind of material the sea floor was made of.

"The drones need to be able to record information about these spaces and return with that information. And they need to be able to work efficiently together as a hive, perhaps at a great distance from the central control location. The distance might be great enough that they lose contact with the hive mind." Cage looked at Eleri and Donovan as though to ask if he'd done a good enough job, and Eleri nodded. He'd done better than she possibly could have.

"And that right there," she added, "is the crux of the problem."

Nate didn't seem to question the information his high-school aged son had just spouted. He only looked at Eleri, an expression of concern on his face. "So Marat solved this mapping problem, and he was killed for it?"

"Almost," Eleri added, "because what Cage just said leads to the issue. The mapping problem is just part of what he wound up solving. So if we go back to Jivika Das, Jivika is a biological mimicry specialist. She looks at various things in nature and she determines how animals, plants, and other natural elements have achieved whatever adaptations they have." This one, Eleri felt more comfortable explaining.

"Spiders spin webs to catch their prey. So we use fisherman's nets that look like spider webs. We build wings on our airplanes with the same shape we actively stole from soaring birds of prey." She continued with several other examples. "Basically, what Jivika does is answer questions for other scientists. Marat had been working on his problem for a little while when he called her up. It seems they had not really known each other very well prior to this project." Eleri wondered if the families caught that piece of info. It solidified the connection between the murders even more.

"Marat promised her a portion of the sales, which might be astronomical," Eleri added, hoping to drive home the need for protective custody for probably everyone in the room. "So she agreed to help him out. However, the other problem—the one that Cage just touched on—is the need for the drones to function fully autonomously, possibly well out of range of the central computer."

"Oh," Cage said. "They need a drone to be the central drone to operate as the hive mind when it's away from the central unit."

"Wait," Nate interrupted, raising his hand. "You're talking about something akin to losing radio control." Only Nate was looking at Cage, no longer at Eleri.

"Exactly," Cage answered his father, his face and actions still fully animated. "Whatever control systems we use—satellite, radio, you name it—there's a limit to that communication once we reach a certain distance. It's a different distance in each case," he added, but Nate was nodding.

"The issue with the drones . . ." Cage continued—and Eleri realized that he knew far more about it than they had guessed—". . . is that we need one drone to be the hive leader. And all the other drones have to follow that command."

"Exactly," Eleri pointed out.

"How is that a problem?" Marshawn asked. "How did Marat solve this? Because this doesn't sound like anything other than normal, everyday robotics. I mean, the man was tinkering in his garage." He looked around the table.

Kaya and Nate seemed to almost offer a laugh. But as Eleri watched, she could see the moment their brains kicked in and reminded them of just how serious the situation at hand was.

"But that's exactly the problem," Cage continued. Eleri listened, ready to jump in with questions if he had anything deviating from what they had read from Jivika and Marat's notebooks. "What if something happens to the hive master?"

"Oh," Kaya caught on. Marshawn nodded, still waiting for more information.

"You need a system of 'abdication of the throne.' If the hive master runs a self-diagnostic, and it doesn't come back clean, he needs to abdicate his status. If he's shot out of the sky, a new hive master needs to come into place. And that needs to happen quickly and seamlessly, the new hive master now communicating with all the other drones as though it were naturally the leader. Also, the sheep drones have to accept the new leadership. You can't have interference, you can't hit nodal points, and you can't have drones vying for supremacy."

"Exactly," Eleri said. "It appears—from Marat's own records—that the AI interfaces he used worked fine, until the lead drone was knocked out. But he and Jivika found a solution."

She fully intended to leave the conversation at that. The solution was worth millions—possibly hundreds of millions—on the open market. It didn't matter that Eleri had decided to hold the information back.

Cage, a grin across his face, continued talking. "She told him about the sinoatrial node."

"Yes," Eleri said to him. "That was what you said to me a while ago." She looked up at the parents. "I remembered Cage told me Marat had talked with him about the sinoatrial node of the heart. That's what made us concerned that your children know enough to possibly be targets."

Kaya and Nate both nodded, the information sinking it. But Marshawn turned to his girls, as though to ask, "Did you know this?" Both girls shrugged, indicating they had not. Or maybe just that they hadn't put it together yet. Eleri became concerned that the James family would be the harder sell on protective custody, so she pushed a little harder.

"I don't think it's necessary to talk about the specifics." This time she said it out loud, but it didn't matter. She was overshot by a number of voices covering hers.

"The sinoatrial node? In the heart?" Emersyn asked, frowning.

But it was Madisyn who was nodding her head, her expression clearly showing that she was putting all the pieces together. "It's a cellular *pacemaker*."

"Right," Cage replied across the table, the conversation still sparking in him. Eleri wondered if this was what Marat had looked like, telling Johanna about his discovery. The videos had certainly showed his joy, even though Eleri and Donovan had not understood why, at first. Cage was lit up.

"The sinoatrial node operates with a cluster of cells working in series. Each one has an inherent rhythmicity, firing at a regular rate, though each regular rate is a little bit different. The fastest one runs the pacemaker section of the heart. But if that cell dies or becomes incapacitated, the next fastest cell becomes the fastest. And it sends out a signal to all the other cells when it triggers. So the first cell—"

"So," Kaya interrupted, her hand up toward her son. "Let me get this straight. The first drone that fires sends out a signal, and because all the other drones received a signal—rather than being the one sending it—they know that they're following the leader, and they're not the leader."

"Right," Joule piped in. Emersyn nodded along from the other side of the table. The whole family getting into a biological discussion—one that Eleri would rather they were not having. The more they discussed this, the more they clarified the solution, the bigger targets they became. Their only hope was that no one had yet realized they'd figured it out.

Would the killer try to take out all seven of them?

Eleri didn't know. She interrupted, but did it loudly this time.

"This was the idea for which Marat Rychenkov was murdered." This time she managed to stop the conversation dead. "And now, you all know too much. And you may be the targets of the same killer." She spoke now to the table at large. "The question is: How many of you are going into custody?"

54

Eleri was pleased. It had taken less than forty-five minutes to decide exactly which people would be put into protective custody.

The final answer had been all four children, and both Nate and Kaya Mazur. Marshawn had decided against it, though Eleri and Donovan had assured him there was a space for him and that he would remain with his children.

He'd been torn by the decision. "I want to stay with my girls, but I have people coming into town for meetings. Things I can't reschedule."

"Dad!" Emersyn had protested. "You have to come!"

"If I don't make these meetings, I don't sell my . . . concrete formula." He turned to Eleri and Donovan. "Sorry, new invention. Also a little bit 'top secret.'" He added air quotes around the words and turned to his oldest daughter. "If I don't show, I'll lose everything we've invested. Besides, I didn't know *any* of this." He looked around the table. "So I don't think I'm at risk."

Eleri only shrugged and said, "I don't know. We can't predict exactly who the next target might be." Westerfield had signed orders for the children, but not the parents. She and Donovan could not force the issue further.

She didn't want to worry his daughters, but he had been sitting in this room. Eleri pointed that out softly. "Simply because of your being here, you may be more at risk."

If the killer knew about this meeting, or found a way to know that they had discussed Marat's work, that might cause problems.

Marshawn, however, seemed to have the old high-schooler immortality clause in his brain—the idea that nothing bad could really happen to him. He'd even said, "What would a killer want with me? I'm a chemist who made a mop. Besides, I'm really strong."

He seemed to believe no one would come after him, or that if they did, he could simply fight them off. Eleri had almost sighed right into his face. Yes, the first two murder victims had been older—not young men in their prime, like Marshawn. And Jivika Das? She'd been a small woman. Again, not like him.

Eleri wanted to explain that the victims had been drugged, and that once Marshawn was drugged, he might be as helpless as anyone else. But she couldn't give out that information, and Marshawn wasn't taking any of the rest of it.

He'd waved her away with one of his patented smiles, as though the FBI agents were silly. She would have thought he was being sexist, but he gave Donovan the same "never gonna happen" shake of his head. She almost asked what sport he'd played in high school, wondering if this belief came from some kind of athletic prowess. Most people grew out of it, but some didn't. Clearly, Marshawn hadn't.

Eleri didn't have the authority to cuff him and force him to go. She was afraid he was going to become another Jivika Das, but there was nothing more she could do, and she wasn't willing to frighten his daughters any more than she already had.

As the meeting wound down, they split up into teams, with the goal of getting all the necessary work done as quickly as possible. She and Donovan had brought two cars for exactly this purpose. So it was Eleri who took Marshawn and his two girls back to their home to pack.

"Wouldn't it look odd," he asked, "that you would show up with us at our own home in a different car? What if someone sees that?"

"I agree," Eleri replied softly, "and I think it's a good reason for you to reconsider and go into protective custody."

But he only smiled. Wide, even, white teeth glowing, as though he could see what she was doing, and he wasn't having it. "So why couldn't we take my car?"

The problem was: What if they put the kids into protective custody, and then didn't catch the killer? How long could they last before the money ran out and the kids were released and sent back to school? How scared would they be? Would this killer just wait them out? Or would Marat's discovery burn out at some point in the meantime and become valueless?

She had no idea. But she didn't want to scare the children any more than necessary. So she'd motioned toward Marshawn—who had taken the front seat, luckily—to drop the idea for now and wait. He seemed to catch on, and she was grateful.

They pulled into the driveway in front of the home, but there was no garage at any of the Shire homes. The cars sat anachronistically along the roads, which were at least paved and not true-to-origin-story dirt and dust.

As they headed inside, Eleri made a point of sweeping the house first. Pulling her gun from its holster, she aimed it at the ground and kept two hands on it. She stepped cautiously through doors and swung wide, leading with the barrel of her gun.

She'd asked if the family had pets, but they didn't. Though they had one of the larger homes in the shire, it still wasn't large by current standards. Eleri found it interesting to try and do standard sweep moves through non-standard circular doors. They did not provide the kind of cover that she was used to. She had to step over the jamb or come through the middle. Still, in the end, it didn't matter. The house was empty.

As the two girls headed to their rooms in the back and began to pack, Eleri looked out the windows at the falling night. Flowers grew directly under the glass, right up into the visual space. The place was warm and cozy, and she had to admit she could see the appeal.

As much as LeDonRic had said he couldn't live in the shire with Maggie, she could see that Marshawn fit into his home. But only barely. When he stood to his full height, his head was closer to the ceiling than should probably be comfortable. Apparently, he had managed to find one of the few shire homes built to a slightly larger scale. He saw her scoping the place out and smiled. "The girls loved the idea. So this is where we came."

Eleri grinned, but as soon as the girls were out of sight, she turned to him and explained what she couldn't before. "Donovan and I have been checking our cars. We're confident that they are not being tracked in any way. This is why we didn't want to drive yours."

"I can't leave it at the Mazur home," he protested. "I do need something to drive. I have to seem normal."

"No, you won't leave it there." Eleri tried to be comforting. "We'll have you keep driving it. But I'll take you and the girls back. You can get your car, and Donovan will take everyone to the new location."

"They won't all fit in his car," Marshawn said, another smile on his lips, as though he were discovering logistical holes in their plan.

"I know. He's calling for a ride. The FBI will bring a minivan."

"Oh, that won't tip anybody off!" Marshawn laughed out loud this time, and Eleri laughed with him.

"No, it will look like a ride share. Like they're going to the airport or something."

As he nodded, he called out to his girls and offered Eleri a drink while they waited. But she refused. As crazy as this day had been, she still couldn't eat or drink. She was definitely on the job right now. But she encouraged the girls to grab a snack, as they would be getting on the road soon after returning to the Mazur house.

While Donovan drove them to the safe house, she would head back to their home to watch any comings and goings at the Rychenkov-Schmitt house and try to translate the last of the new notebook passages. She didn't mention any of this to Marshawn. Not yet.

She did talk to the girls, asking them what they would need. She pointed out that if their devices had wireless, they had to keep them turned off. No checking accounts. Good hackers could trace the user back to the location.

She also took their cell phones from them, much to their dismay. "I'm sorry, but I have to do this. At least you'll be in the house with your friends. And you'll have basic internet access there, and movies, and TV and more. But you won't be able to reach out to people you know."

"Really?" Madisyn moaned, frowning.

"I know. Safehouses suck monkeys," Eleri told the girl, and at least that got a smile. "But it's not safe to get in contact with anyone. Donovan and I are going to do our best to make sure that you're out as soon as possible. The most important thing is to remember that you'll be safe. That's why we're doing this."

Emersyn and Madisyn both nodded. Though their expressions didn't brighten at all, they at least accepted their fate with a level of understanding that made Eleri proud.

Within a few more moments, they were fully packed. Climbing into her car again, they all headed back toward the Mazur home. Marshawn would drive his own car. The Mazur car would stay in their garage. Eleri and Donovan had already promised to take care of the cat, though Donovan had no major fondness for cats.

They pulled up just behind the rideshare van that the FBI had provided, and loaded everyone in. Once they were headed down the road, Eleri and Marshawn were the only ones left to wave them off, and she couldn't help the bad feeling that settled in the pit of her chest.

They were close. She knew it. But she couldn't see it coming.

55

Eleri let herself back into the house, her major task for the evening completed. Still, that didn't mean the day was over. This one had been a mess from top to bottom, and it felt good to be back in her own place—at least as much as this Frank Lloyd Wright-style home was "hers."

She knew work was waiting for her at the table and that she should be doing what she could while she waited for Donovan to return. Though she wanted to climb into bed and sleep everything away, she needed to wait for her partner.

He'd climbed into the airport-shuttle-type minivan with both Nate and Kaya Mazur and the four kids. The agent/driver now waited at the Mazur home, armed and ready, simply staring at the walls until Donovan returned with the vehicle.

It was a good hour's drive to the safe house, Eleri knew, and Donovan would have to take the time to get the family and the kids all settled in. So she didn't expect Donovan to come home any time soon.

Flipping on lights as she let herself in through the garage door, she headed toward the front to hang up her coat. She made the mistake of looking at the table.

The black-and-white composition notebooks still lay open across the surface. They hadn't even taken the time to shut them before they dashed out the door. Their laptops, at least, shut down after fifteen minutes and were password protected upon opening the screen again. But she and Donovan had been so convinced the kids were in danger, they hadn't cleared the table well enough.

What if someone had needed to come with her when she came home? What if they showed up at the door? What if someone had snuck in here while they'd been out? Eleri wanted to believe this was the first time that they'd dicked it up so badly, but it couldn't have been. There had been a number of occasions when they'd run out of the house for various reasons.

Despite the darkness hovering outside the large back window, it still wasn't yet late and it would be against protocol to allow her head to hit the pillow and herself to fall asleep for the night. She needed to at least get Donovan's report on how everyone was settled in, and whether they'd handled the rules and their guard FBI agents well.

Eleri knew basically where the safe house was, though not the exact address. It was a small, single-family home in an unassuming neighborhood full of small, unassuming, single-family homes. The FBI liked it because it came with plenty of bedrooms and just enough space between it and the neighboring houses so as not to draw attention to a minivan full of people arriving like a clown car in the late evening.

Donovan would also have walked them through the standard cover for a family of their means being suddenly gone. The general story was to say they had won tickets on a cruise ship, which is why they would only be answering emails and such periodically. He'd had them each compose a message to a friend. The FBI would dole out the notes over the next several days, so no one would file any missing person's reports.

That cover would hold for at least a week. After that, the two of them would have to reconfigure things. It wouldn't do to have family members upset or trying to get a hold of Nate and Kaya or even the kids, wondering where they were.

With a deep sigh that she hoped would keep her awake, Eleri headed into the kitchen, where she pulled a banana off the counter and began to eat it. Donovan hadn't eaten any of them, and she wondered why she might have ever thought he would. He wasn't much a fan of fruits and vegetables, which shouldn't have been surprising.

She ate the whole banana, not realizing that she was hungry until she'd started to peel it. But the food in her stomach seemed to make her even sleepier. Heading to the fridge, she grabbed a soda before sitting down at the table to begin working through more of the pages in the notebooks.

Cola in one hand and pen in the other, she started flipping through the pages, translating as she went. It got easier and easier to read the code with practice. She began recognizing some of the clusters as words, no longer requiring letter-by-letter translation. A ping on her screen caused her to click over and check her email.

The secure FBI system gave her a readout from the CDC lab test on the pillow case. It took three more clicks and a login to open the results, but even that didn't help. Eleri frowned at the screen.

"Cement dust."

What the fuck?

How had cement dust gotten on the pillow on Jivika's bed? Her eyes blinked and she tipped up the soda can only to find that it was empty. Guzzling sodas was not her usual M.O., but tonight was not normal by any stretch. Heading to the fridge, she grabbed another and popped the tab on it. The fizz hit her tongue and her brain but didn't help solve her problem.

Why would there be cement dust in the bed?

She kept working at the code but didn't let the test results wander far from her thinking. She hoped something would ping in her brain, but it continued to annoy her that she had something so unique and couldn't put it together.

It wasn't twenty minutes later that she heard the knock at the door. It wouldn't be Donovan. He'd still be out and he wouldn't knock anyway. So she did a better job than they'd done before and closed all the notebooks and the screen on her laptop before heading to the front door.

Putting her eye to the peephole, she saw that her visitor was Marshawn. She hadn't needed to hide things from him. He already knew that they were FBI agents, and she wondered if he'd stopped at his brother's house next door. Had he told LeDonRic about her and Donovan? How much? Did maybe even Maggie know? She could only hope he'd held to their agreement. Tomorrow, the PD would be following him, much as they had with Jivika, though that hadn't been able to save the woman's life. Eleri worried for Marshawn and his carefree attitude.

As she opened the door and said his name, she noticed he was holding a good-sized duffle bag, and she frowned. Stepping back, she motioned him to come inside. A bad feeling was settling in . . . but they'd checked him out. He had no motive in the case. "What's going on?"

"I changed my mind," he told her with a sigh and a Marshawn smile. "I want to take you up on your offer for protective custody."

Trying to cover her sigh of relief, she wondered at his sudden change of mind. She then worked to hide a second sigh, this one of frustration. This would have been a lot easier if he could have decided it an hour ago. Her expression must have shown, because he explained.

"I thought about it." He rubbed his hands along the sides of his jacket, a nervous gesture certainly. She would have to hide her irritation a little better. "I watched the girls leave, and I thought I would be okay with that. And I do have this huge project that I'll probably miss out on. But I got home and I had to ask myself what was really more important: the project or my children. They've got to be scared out of their minds."

Eleri understood. Sometimes people didn't know what they wanted until they realized they'd made the wrong decision. She smiled. "They looked like they were holding together pretty well. We'll have to wait for Donovan to get back before we can take you out to the house. So you're stuck with me for an hour or so. Can I get you anything to make you comfortable while you wait?"

He shook his head at first, but then seemed to change his mind. "Do you have anything to drink?"

"Sure." She rattled off the options they had in the fridge.

Marshawn asked for a can of coke, probably having noticed hers, and she headed around the counter to fetch it for him, talking while she went. "We won't wait until morning to take you to the safe house. We'll get you back with your girls as soon as we can. But I can't take you right now. Even I don't know the location."

Handing him the drink, she watched as he nodded his thanks. But there was something in the way he nodded that Eleri couldn't decipher. Was he upset that it would take so long to get to his girls? Or what?

"Here." She motioned him to have a seat at the table. Though she wanted to open the notebooks and continue to do the work, she couldn't. Despite everything she and Donovan had already told the group tonight, Marshawn didn't know anything new. He shouldn't see what she might discover, and she couldn't reveal the coding in the notebooks. So she couldn't work while they waited.

Even so, he reached out to flip the front cover on one, and Eleri had to shoo him away. "I'm sorry, those are FBI property, and I can't let you read them."

Standing up and walking around the table, she carefully tucked them all into her bag, along with her laptop and Donovan's and put all their work aside. "Come on into the living room," she offered, thinking they would have to stare at each other for an hour. She grabbed her can of soda and led him further into the house.

He sank into the couch and talked about the girls, about how good Curie had been for them. About how Emersyn and Madisyn had both gotten advanced placements in their classes, even here, even against the best and the brightest. Eleri could see the pride on his face.

She commented, "Yeah, both your girls tested into the high end classes. That's quite an accomplishment." And that was when she remembered—Marshawn's name had appeared in the stack that Marshall Bennett did not remember accepting into Curie.

For a moment, she frowned but didn't say anything. She was hard pressed to make small talk for a while, but she couldn't send the man away or do research while he was here. He needed to stay within her sight. If he was accepting FBI protective custody, then she was currently the one delivering it.

She stood up to get her holster and her gun from where she'd set them on the table earlier. It would not do to have someone burst in and try to kill him while her gun was across the room.

As she slid her shoulders into the straps, she noticed she felt a little bit wobbly.

That was the first sign.

Oh shit.

Turning, she faced Marshawn, who was standing and watching as she walked across the room. He looked sad.

Eleri felt the rage boil up in her, but it was too late. She couldn't grasp the thoughts passing through her head, but she'd unfortunately solved their case. Just about twenty minutes too late . . .

56

Immediately, Eleri pulled her gun, though her hands weren't steady and her grip didn't feel solid. He'd drugged her. She was going to be his next murder. She couldn't hope that he'd only drugged her but didn't plan on killing her, too.

In the back of her head, the thought slipped by that there was cement dust on Jivika Das's pillowcase. It was important, but she couldn't hold onto it. Instead, her mind slid to the next thought—he'd watched her pack up the notebooks. This fucker knew exactly where all the information was . . . And that she and Donovan had the code cracked and were translating it. They'd done all the work for him!

"Why don't you come back and sit down, Eleri?" he said, motioning to the couch behind him.

But she shook her head at him, raising the gun toward his center mass. She would kill him if she had to. Unfortunately, she didn't have quite enough information to justify pulling the trigger yet.

Dammit!

She needed more evidence, and she probably had less than a minute to find it. Her reflexes might completely give out on her at any moment.

What was the right thing to do? Try to stay calm and have the drug diffuse through her system more slowly, buying her some time now. Or hyperventilate, let her adrenaline wash over her, and see if she could metabolize it faster than normal?

Would it be fast enough? She didn't know. Probably not. But her hands were shaking and she'd already forgotten the first option. She shallowed out her breathing so as not to be obvious about it and sped up her heart rate, choosing the only option she remembered. She flexed her muscles though she didn't move from her stance, grateful for the cooler weather and the long sleeves she wore. She pressed her lips together to look as though she were mad as hell rather than thinking as fast as she could when she couldn't quite function at her usual rate.

"How did you do it, Marshawn?"

"I'm sorry, but it's exactly what's happening now. You know."

But she didn't. She still hadn't really figured out how he'd done it. She was afraid she was going to find out too soon.

"*Why* did you do it, Marshawn? Why did you kill them?"

"It's obvious—because the idea is worth billions and I need it. I have a loan shark after me. It's for my girls. Marat was old. I asked him to share it and he wouldn't. He wouldn't even give me a finder's fee for hooking him up with Jivika."

That hadn't been in the notebooks. Was it real? Or a lie he was telling himself now to justify killing people? Eleri's brain swam. But was it from the cognitive dissonance of this kind man who smiled so often telling her that he had killed an inventor just to steal his project —or was it a result of the drugs? Eleri couldn't tell.

She couldn't shoot him, so she would have to arrest him.

She headed back across the room but found her legs too mushy to work fully. Her voice barked at him to sit down and put his hands behind him. Thankfully, that was rote after all the training the FBI doled out.

But Marshawn just shook his head and refused.

She threatened him with the gun, and she should have pulled the trigger. But even now, she couldn't put the pieces together well enough to justify lethal force.

Her brain slipped again, but this time it told her, he'd just admitted to killing Marat Rychenkov. She had a split second to make a decision. She *did* have enough information.

She pulled the trigger.

57

After finally pulling into the driveway at the safehouse, Donovan stepped out of the van and entered the code for the garage door. Once it slowly lifted, he hopped back in and pulled forward.

Though the space was intended for two cars, the van was almost too long to fit, and he had to finagle it within inches to get the garage door to come down behind them. That was important. He didn't want any neighbors or lookie-loos to see the number of people he was letting out of the van—or even worse, their faces.

The ride over had been relatively quiet once their questions had been thwarted repeatedly by, "I can't tell you that," and eventually, "I'm sorry, that's above your pay grade."

He and Eleri had answered pretty much everything they could back when everyone had been meeting at the Mazur's dining room table. The children's initial glee at being important enough to warrant FBI protection had faded as the drive wore on. It was now late at night. Whether it was past the high schoolers' bedtime or not, Donovan had no idea.

Inside, they all scoped the place out and said hello to the two agents already waiting. The kids were most interested in sleeping arrangements. The house had four bedrooms. Though Donovan had initially started to suggest arrangements, it was Kaya Mazur who seemed to understand what the children needed, so Donovan stepped back.

The two waiting agents stepped forward and shook hands, introducing themselves to Nate and Kaya as Omar and Lisa. Then they stayed quietly out of the way as the family got settled. When Donovan raised an eyebrow that Kaya had left one of the bedrooms empty—seemingly purposefully—Kaya nodded at him and said loudly enough for everyone to hear, "It's for Marshawn, when he comes."

Though Donovan frowned, as Marshawn had clearly decided not to take advantage of the safehouse, he looked to Kaya rather than asking his question out loud.

Pulling him aside, Kaya whispered, "His girls are afraid, and it's important that they believe that he's coming. Who knows? He might change his mind. If we put everybody in all the rooms, we don't leave space for him. It sends a signal."

Donovan nodded. Kaya was wise well beyond any parenting ideas he had, and he pushed aside another pestering thought of his parents and their ability to lose his brother . . .

Donovan looked at each of the kids in front of him as they shuffled in and out of rooms. He could easily imagine them as little bugs, moving their things around, setting up as it were, two of them yawning as they stretched. In a moment of insight, he pulled them together to give them a short pep talk—at least, the best he was capable of.

"Look, Eleri and I will likely not be coming to visit you. We can, if you need us to. But you can and should talk to Omar and to Lisa—Agents Shaw and Dillard. They can reach out to us if you need that. But for the most part, Agent Eames and I are going to be working our butts off to get this case solved so you can come home. So you can go back to school, sleep in your own beds, go back to work, and be yourselves again. Okay?"

He'd asked for any last questions and felt his phone buzz in his pocket again. As he headed out to the garage, he checked the messages. One was from Eleri, just lab results. The results showed the dust on Jivika Das's pillow had been a gray cement dust. The second text, which had come more recently and buzzed his phone just now, said nothing. She'd sent only a blank, empty bubble . . .

Donovan frowned as he climbed into the driver's seat of the huge van. He would have to take it back to the Mazur home, check in with the agents there, and trade them this van for his car.

He waited impatiently while the garage door slowly rattled its way up, but as it did, the newly forming sensation of dread in his chest squeezed.

From somewhere behind him, he heard his name.

"Donovan!"

His head turned sharply, almost involuntarily. It was Eleri's voice, but she wasn't there.

He would have told himself he was crazy. Like everyone, he'd had those inklings over the years, the feeling of being watched, the voice in the back of his head, almost clear enough to make him turn around, but this one *had* made him turn.

And it was Eleri.

In his pocket his phone buzzed at him again, and Donovan pulled it out hoping it was Eleri telling him anything else of value. Then he could put this feeling aside.

But it was Wade, instead. The words were terrifying. "Wasn't sure if you saw the report the analysts just sent. It looks like Marshawn James is in serious debt to some kind of mob boss or loan shark. They found origination points for old debts that were paid. It turns out, they weren't paid by Marshawn. Check your email when you can."

Donovan felt a cold sweat break out. The cement on the pillow! He knew what it was. And he'd left Eleri alone with Marshawn.

Climbing up into the car, Donovan cranked the engine and peeled out of the driveway, not even waiting for the door to come down. His chest felt tight, like he couldn't breathe.

As he took the ramp onto the freeway at top speed, he heard her voice again, only this time it was fainter.

"Donovan."

58

She'd missed.

Eleri couldn't believe it, but she'd shot at Marshawn and missed. She was supposed to be good at this, but her hands were betraying her. She fired two more times at Marshawn as he stood in front of her.

Though he flinched each time, and though he was afraid, she knew as well as he did that she likely wouldn't hit him. The drugs were taking over her system and her chances of making the shot were down to luck.

She didn't hit him either time. She considered firing more and more, but figured she'd hit the point where she was more likely to injure herself than him. Her muscles were losing tone, the jerk of the gun as each bullet left the chamber jolted her arm well beyond her control. No wonder she couldn't hit anything.

She considered pulling the gun back and striking him across the temple as he approached her. Though he was tall, she thought she could reach his head with enough force. But the fact of the matter was, as she pulled her hand back, he reached out and grabbed her wrist.

She never even got to the forward motion of her strike. She felt as if she was in a dream where she was running and never got anywhere. Her efforts at punching or kicking him yielded little to nothing, and she was frustratingly slow compared to her merely average attacker.

She was fucked.

Eleri heard the gun as it clattered to the floor. The sound alerted her that he'd squeezed it from her grip more than she'd felt it falling from her hands. She stood, swaying slightly, watching as he leaned over and unzipped the large duffel bag he'd brought with him.

It had seemed to be heavy when he showed up at the door, but she hadn't thought about it. Now, she saw that he had not packed to go to the safe house at all. He had brought rope and a cinder block.

A cinder block.

It was all coming together, but that didn't matter because she was barely able to stand. In fact, she swayed widely one more time before falling.

Marshawn easily caught her small frame with one large arm around her waist. This was how it was done. She understood. She had inadvertently solved the entire case. Marshawn was stealing Marat's invention, and killing anyone who got in his way. Including her.

Eleri understood. The idea was not only worthwhile, but specifically solved a problem even she had been able to look up as one of the major robotics issues of the era. He might as well have made affordable, flying cars, or found a viable alternate fuel source.

Money was a powerful motive, and it sounded like Marshawn was in serious need of cash. He was at least concerned about his own livelihood, maybe even his safety. Those things mixed together could lead to murder.

Eleri understood.

He'd even said Marat and Johanna were older. He hadn't taken as much from them. Even Jivika hadn't been helpful. His words and tone seemed to say that the loss to the world, or even the individual, wasn't that great. He wasn't *that* guilty.

She opened her mouth to tell him that he was. To explain what he was doing now. "If you kill me, you will have murdered *a federal agent*. Donovan will not stop until you're locked up or dead. And trust me, dead is the better option where either my partner or I are concerned."

But what came out of her mouth was a garbled roll of sound that she wasn't even sure resembled words in any language at all. She was hanging over his arm, her mind fuzzy and her body completely unresponsive, aside from a few twitches that she could feel in her fingers.

Her eyes opened before she even realized she'd let them slide shut, and she looked up at the ceiling. It took another moment of trying to focus, to understand that she was lying on the floor between the two couches. Rope was already tied around one wrist.

She frowned. Like with the other bodies, he wasn't splaying her out.

But why? Why had he laid her—

Oh! The cinder block. It was important that she not be able to move it.

Between the drugs and the weight, she wondered how fast his victims expired. This was certainly not the fastest method.

She started her breathing again. She'd been trying to move her limbs, or to get up—she couldn't quite remember—when she did remember to do her shallow breaths. Once again, she needed to see if she could push the drug through her system and metabolize it just a little bit faster. Maybe fast enough to survive.

The problem, though, was that she knew she would need her muscles, and if she wore herself out hyperventilating, that would just kill her faster. Her brain wasn't quite sharp enough to hold onto the ideas and weigh the pros and cons. She was grateful she had reached into her pocket and hit several buttons on her cell phone before she'd begun firing the gun.

She'd intended to call Wade. Donovan was too far out of town to be of much help—at least not before she died. She didn't know if she'd accomplished a signal connection or not. If she was lucky, her phone line was open right now and Wade was listening in. Still, she knew she could not count on being lucky.

"Marshawn!" she tried to yell it. Though again, it came out only as a garbled "Mmmmm" sound.

"That's okay Agent Eames," he said, offering her his kind smile again. "You won't hardly feel a thing. It's very humane."

Humane? she thought. *At what point is killing me humane? Just because I'm not in pain doesn't mean . . .* and the thought drifted away.

She shallowed out her breath again, breathing faster even though she remembered there was a reason she didn't want to do this. She saw Marshawn reach up to the couch and pull down a pillow. He placed it on her chest, balancing the puffy mass carefully. Had she been able to move much, she could have rolled it off. But in a moment, he pulled the cinder block out.

That had been the weight. That was what put the cement dust on Jivika Das's pillowcase. But Eleri didn't have time to analyze it before she felt the weight on her own chest.

Yes, she thought. She was fucked. She knew exactly what that cinder block would do. This was how his victims had died of no apparent cause. How they had suffocated in open air with no loss of lung function. They had no water or mucous in their lungs to explain it. No kind of damage. No sign of strangulation or petechial hemorrhaging.

He'd simply stopped them from being able to breathe.

Immediately, the weight on her chest was an issue. She breathed in—or tried but couldn't accomplish much. Fighting to get as much oxygen into her system as she could, she searched for what she could remember of tidal volume in the lungs. She considered the need to breathe out to get more fresh oxygen in, versus the need to expand her lungs. If she breathed all the way out, would she be able to pull her lungs open again?

She didn't know.

The thoughts slid in and out of her grasp. So even when she had one she could cling to, she'd lost the thing she needed to connect it with.

Eleri kept her breathing shallow, partly because she couldn't take deep breaths, or even normal ones. She tried to conserve her muscle energy. She needed to remain alive long enough for someone to get here.

How far away was Donovan again?

She didn't know.

She didn't know how long he'd been gone by this point. She didn't know how long he would stay with the families, working with them to get them settled. He had to introduce them and hand them off to the new agents who'd be watching the safe house. Ironically, the Mazurs and the James girls were as safe as they could be.

They'd been less safe at the Mazurs' kitchen table when Eleri and Donovan had been sharing their secrets with the killer himself.

She wanted to rail against herself for not having caught this killer sooner, but this was Curie, Nebraska. And Marshawn was smart. Smarter than both of them, clearly. She knew his murder method—even while she lay there suffering from it—was brilliant.

Even the man's money problems had been well-hidden. Then

again, loan sharks didn't keep regular bank accounts for the FBI to trace. And since Marshawn didn't pay off the debts, it had likely taken a while to find the accounts were even related to him.

As her head lolled to one side, she saw that he'd pulled on gloves. *Of course he did,* she thought and almost laughed. Even his own brother would likely never believe that Marshawn was a killer.

She watched as he stood up and grabbed her bag with the FBI laptops, the notebooks, and the transcribed pages.

Fuck the damn papers! she thought. Paper was un-hackable, until the murderer just picked it up and walked off with it. At least he would have to hack his way into the FBI computers. It would set off alarms as soon as Donovan reported the computers stolen. Marshawn would be found.

But, maybe not! Those papers gave him exactly what he needed. He might never open the computers. If he was smart—and he was—he would toss them as soon as he was out the door.

She took in another breath. She could feel it. She wasn't getting enough oxygen. Though she was already drugged, she felt the sensation of her brain tingling a little as she further lost her focus.

Fuck! she thought again. This was why he tied them down. If they could just push the cinder block off, even for a moment, they could gasp like a drowning man coming up for air. Buy more time. Save themselves.

But she couldn't raise her hand to push it off. She couldn't roll and let it fall. She couldn't do anything except lie there and feel the oxygen leaving her system.

For a moment, she thought about slipping away. Then, she got *mad.*

59

Eleri was a crappy witch. Her surge of anger had produced sparks in the air around her eyes, though she couldn't be sure if that was witchcraft or merely the dying embers of her vision fading as she passed out.

Through the haze of her foggy brain, she blinked and saw she was walking in the woods. Leaves lined the trail—a path through the forest that she now knew well. She ran, bare feet crunching in the leaves, knowing time was of the utmost essence. She turned toward the little square house with the door set at a forty-five degree angle into the odd, triangular porch. She stepped up onto the stoop, which was just big enough for one person to open the door.

Turning the knob, Eleri threw herself against the door and bolted into the house. The circular design meant that going to the right would lead through the living space. Then she would enter a dining area, then the kitchen, and finally come around to a back room. But to the left, the route to the back room was faster. And that was where she needed to be.

She turned and raced through the open archway, down the short hall, and into the back room where she could already hear the creak of a rocking chair.

Eleri had once been surprised to see the goddess Aida Weddo here, but now she knew who she would see. As she dashed into the room, her Grandmére looked up from the rocking chair, up from where she was stitching a tiny poppet by hand.

"*Makinde,*" said the old woman in a warm greeting and Eleri breathed in deeply for the first time, a huge sigh of relief.

"*Grandmére.*" She wanted to say, "You are here! Can you help me?" But it was Grandmére who looked up and shook her head. As though she knew what Eleri wished to say but couldn't.

"This is my house now, child. It was built by my own grandmother a long, long time ago. It is here to keep our secrets. In fact, you found it before you were supposed to, child, but I am here now, and here is where I shall stay."

"Emmaline?" she asked, wondering if her sister was available. She'd seen her sister so many times over the years. Now she realized she'd not seen her sister at all since she'd buried her. But she'd seen Emmaline in this house before, and her hopes stayed high.

Grandmére shook her head softly. "No, my child. Emmaline is free now."

Another great gulp tried to find its way into stilted lungs as Eleri felt the news hit. The pressure inside her screamed to get out. Suddenly, she felt all of the grief that she had not felt before. For she hadn't truly lost Emmaline when she disappeared. Her sister had always resurfaced in her dreams. The girls talked, they played, and Emmaline helped her find truths. But Grandmére was telling her she had lost Emmaline now, it seemed.

"*Gone?*" She pushed the words through leaded lips, and Grandmére merely nodded. There would be no more dreams of Emmaline.

But Eleri shook her head to dispel the crushing sense of loss. There would be no more dreams of *anything* if she didn't get out from under that cinder block. In the Frank Lloyd Wright house, she was lying on the living room floor, her hands and feet tied just tightly enough to keep her from rocking and rolling the crushing weight off, to keep her from pushing at it with her hands. She was too drugged to fight anyway.

"Grandmére," she said again, and watched as her grandmother slowly set the poppet to her side and stood to her full height. Not much taller than Eleri, the old woman was definitely sturdier than her granddaughter. Certainly, she was more so here in this house, where Eleri felt like a visiting wraith and Grandmére felt solid.

Grandmére looked her in the eyes. "I cannot leave this house. I can only help you help yourself."

With that, she placed both her hands across Eleri's collarbones, her fingers creating an electric zap where she touched. She leaned back, not breaking contact, and she said, "Go, *Makinde*. Go with Aida Weddo!" And she pushed her granddaughter backward with a force the old woman should not have been able to generate.

Eleri felt herself pulled through time and space, jolting as she landed flat on the floor in the living room of the house in Curie. Her eyes jolted open, looking up through the window at the wash of stars outside.

She was still stuck—still tied out, ropes around her hands, the cinder block still weighing on her lungs—but she no longer felt as though she were drugged. Had Grandmére sobered her up? What could she do if she were sober?

So, using her oxygen in a way that she should not have been able to do, she screamed a loud noise that had Marshawn turning and looking at her, his eyes wide. Surely none of his victims had reacted this way before.

So she did it again.

"Shut up," he hissed at her, but Eleri refused. She rocked side to side, pulling on the ropes, exactly as she had told Donovan an alert victim would do. The rope was a rough fisherman's-type twine, and it cut at her wrists, making tiny slices in her skin. She could feel it, but the sting didn't stop her. She screamed again.

She only needed to get her chest far enough to the side to get the cinder block to roll off, so she yanked at her left hand and then her right, and noticed as she did that she could pull the couch. Just a little, but it was enough. The tension in the rope loosened a bit, and she pulled again.

Eleri was strong, though whether it was physical strength or whatever magic Grandmére might have imbued her with, she didn't know, and she didn't care. She was not going to let Marshawn suffocate her in open air. If he succeeded, he would remove his cinder block from her dead body and then pack it to take home. He'd put the cushion back on the couch, remove the ropes, and leave her there staring at the ceiling.

She would not let her partner find her dead and feel guilty.

Fuck that shit. This time when she screamed and pulled, the couch moved farther, and Marshawn came closer just as she rocked enough to the left to get the cinder block to begin its slow roll off her chest. It landed on her arm, knocking into her brachial artery and sending a twinge out her arm to her wrist as it hit nerve bundles on the sensitive inside skin.

She could feel the tingle in her fingers, but it would not stop her. She lifted her shoulder and shrugged out from under the heavy weight, as she sucked in air, finally expanding her lungs to full capacity. The oxygen hit her like a high, but she couldn't let Marshawn get the upper hand. The move had left her position awkward and she yanked on the rope, tugging against the couches again at the cost of her wrists.

If she needed to bring the furniture with her to stand to her full height, she would. Marshawn was towering over her now, though he still appeared nervous and she could see he'd begun to sweat. He clearly had no intention of letting her merely push the cinder block away and live.

He picked it up to put it back on her chest, and Eleri took deep breaths as though she had been drowning and broke the surface. She sucked in air, feeling it rush through her starved system. Could she lift the couches? Could she break the sturdy feet that supported them and get loose? She didn't know. Could she break the rope? Did she have any kind of force? But now she had oxygen and she screamed again as Marshawn lifted the cinder block to place it back on her chest.

He stumbled backward with the force of her yell, his eyes growing wider as it became clear that he did not know what he was dealing with.

Donovan had told her that her eyes had gone black when she'd screamed out in battle once. Now, she could feel it, she knew they had, so she stared at him, and used the only thing she had left.

In the lowest voice she could muster, with as much magic as she could put behind it, she said, "Marshawn James, if you kill me, you will have not only the full weight of the Federal Bureau of Investigations upon your head, you will have *me*. If you doubt that I could come back to haunt you, know this: if you kill me, I'll be stronger than I ever was."

60

Donovan was on Wade's tail as he screeched to a halt in front of the house. Seeing Wade bust through the front door had raised his heart rate even higher.

Eleri's blank text message had been a warning. He could feel it now. Drawing his weapon, he followed Wade through the door his fellow agent had left standing open. He swept rooms and followed Wade into the living area, where he could hear Eleri struggling, even if he couldn't see her.

Only as he came close, could he see his partner was tied out on the floor, her wrists bleeding, her ankles still roped. She'd managed to get one hand free. He saw the cinder block lying on the floor ten feet away, dust scattered around it as though it had been dropped there.

A fire of anger flared in her eyes as she looked up at him. "It's Marshawn," she ground out the name even as her left hand reached over toward her right and began working at the rope. Wade holstered his weapon and crouched down, popping open the handy Swiss Army knife he always carried with him. Pushing her hand away, he began to saw at the bindings.

Donovan nodded. Leaning down, he tried loosening the ropes on her ankles. "How long ago did he leave?"

He wanted to ask how she'd done it—how had she gotten out of certain death?—but he also didn't necessarily want to know. It was clear that whatever had happened, Marshawn had used his standard technique. In Eleri's case, the pillow that had been used to soften the weight of the cinderblock and stop evidentiary bruising had been discarded to the side. Normally, it would rest on the victim's chest, weighed down with the cinder block. No heart damage. No lung damage. No liquid in the lungs. No signs of cause of death much at all . . . except an unexplained oxygen deprivation.

It wasn't a quick way to kill someone, but it wasn't too slow, either. One only need not be breathing for a handful of minutes in order to die. Strangulation took longer than most people thought, but the difference between strangulation and this open-air suffocation Marshawn had masterminded would not be all that significant. Given a few minutes, he could sit, watch his victim die, and even wait out the clock with a little time to spare before removing his devices and making sure he left the scene with little to no evidence.

As he lifted his head and sniffed the room, Donovan could smell the tinge of Eleri's anger like an acrid smoke. Just under that, Marshawn James' fear hung in the air, and he recognized it as the same scent he'd found in Jivika Das's home.

Wade moved to where Donovan hovered near Eleri's tied ankles and brushed him out of the way. Wade began sawing on one of the ropes around her ankle, and Donovan—not having gotten very far loosening what apparently were expert knots—checked her wrist for any cuts that might be more dangerous than they initially appeared. He then headed into the kitchen for paper towels and water.

She was going to look like she had attempted suicide, but he wasn't going to leave her cuts exposed—not when they still had a killer to hunt down.

"I don't know where he went." She said it almost as though she'd heard his thoughts.

"How did you get out?" Wade asked the question that Donovan had been holding back on.

"I got angry," she whispered. "I managed to get a little loose and I scared him. Once I had enough movement, I rolled a little and the cinder block tipped far enough to drop off. He picked it up to put it back on top of me, and when he stepped back, startled, he dropped it, and he left."

Donovan held the wet towels over her wrists and watched as she gingerly pressed them against her cuts. He hadn't found any cuts that were life-threatening, but they would sting. Grandmére was not here to make them hurt less this time . . .

He laid out two more pieces for her ankles in case the rope had managed to damage her through her socks. He hoped not. Then he darted upstairs for the first-aid kit that he had haphazardly put together first in New Orleans but built a little more sturdily to carry with them now. Before he was even back downstairs with his kit in hand, Eleri was up. She had her holster on and was tugging her jacket over it.

Wade, already dressed to bolt, was hauling her along to the car. Motioning to Donovan, Wade shoved the two of them and the medical kit into the backseat. As he dove into the driver's seat, it became apparent they had no real idea where to go. But Wade turned the engine, and said, "Let me try."

As they headed out of the neighborhood on a quest for Marshawn's car or the man himself, Donovan bandaged Eleri's wrists one at a time.

"It's been almost twenty minutes since he ran out. I think," she said. "We're probably too late," but she called Marshall Bennett and told him to have the Curie PD lock down every road exiting the city. She gave him Marshawn James' name and had him put the full PD on alert. She couldn't call the Curie police directly without needing too long to explain who she was, letting her badge number get verified, and so on, Donovan knew.

It would be faster to go after Marshawn themselves and have Marshall Bennett take care of the PD.

First, they checked his home. Eleri and Donovan headed up and over the grass mound that housed the James family and around back, in case he tried to bolt as Wade pounded on the door. Donovan would be able to hear the man clearly, even if he was on the backside of the house and the other side of a dirt- and plant-covered building. “FBI. Open up!”

When no sounds came from inside the house, not feet running, not an animal, nothing, Wade tried the doorknob. “Got it!” he yelled, and Donovan tried the knob on the back door. It didn’t give.

Rather than leaving the back unattended, they waited for Wade to get through the place and open the door for them. He greeted them with an, “It’s clear.”

Though Marshawn wasn't there, the unlocked front door was suspicious when coupled with a locked back door.

"He locked up after we came to pack the girls up tonight," Eleri informed them. Despite the relatively casual conversation, the three of them were stalking the place with their weapons out and their eyes alert.

"His room's a mess. Looks like he grabbed things and bolted. Smells like it was very recent," Wade called out.

Eleri pointed to the sink and Donovan frowned as he looked at the dish drainer. Small, pointed vials sat upside down, scrubbed out and clean. There was just enough water to indicate that they'd been washed a while ago but not too recently, not on his pass through here after having failed to kill Eleri.

"That's the stuff," she told him and then turned to check out the girls' bedrooms.

Donovan remembered enough from undergrad and a few rotations in med school. The pieces in the drying rack were exactly what a chemist would need for a small batch of GHB-like drugs. He couldn't have cooked up more than a single dose, given the size of the vials, indicating he'd made it each time he'd "needed" it.

There was no doubt in Donovan's mind that the chem set would yield nothing chemically to prove what he'd been doing. Marshawn was a very smart man. Though he'd left out a burner and a stand with a clamp over it, he was a chemist. The fact that he had chemistry lab materials on his kitchen counter would mean nothing in a court of law.

But Donovan didn't need more. He would have sniffed the air for a trace of the drug, but it was odorless. He hadn't even smelled it on Eleri.

Once they'd declared the James home lacking in any further evidence or clues as to where Marshawn might have gone, they headed across town to an office space that Wade had found Marshawn was renting. There, they found a variety of mops featuring sponges from his patented material. There was nothing odd about the mops, except the way they were lined up in front of a standing cabinet.

Bashing the cabinet lock, they swung the doors wide and found the shelves revealed a set of drones Marshawn was keeping for his own. Though they didn't have much time, Wade insisted they turn them on.

Flicking the switch on a controller kept with the set, the three of them watched as each drone lit up. A tiny light graced the top of each robot and it blinked at a consistent rate. However, each rate of blinking was different.

"Look," Donovan said, recognizing the sinoatrial node set up in the blink pattern. "He already started programming them with Marat's ideas. Watch." And as they stared, one by one, the slowest blinks turned to a steady red light, until at last, only the lead drone blinked at a rapid rate.

Donovan watched, amazed. For a moment, he wondered what to do. Then he reached out, grabbed the lead drone, and flipped it upside down. It took a moment to find a switch and turn it off. Within a heartbeat, the others all began blinking again—likely, Donovan thought, because they'd lost their lead signal. They should reconfigure, he supposed as he waited. But he didn't wait long at all. In seconds, one by one, the blinking again steadied to constant red lights, the slowest steadying first until once again a new hive leader remained.

Donovan looked at Wade and Eleri, her bandaged wrists peeking out from under the cuffs of her sleeves.

"It's worth millions," she said.

"Possibly billions," Wade offered.

As they turned off the drones, Donovan called Bennett to check up. Curie PD had found nothing so far. They had nowhere to check, until at last, Wade looked up and said, "His kids are in protective custody, right? Does he know where they are?"

Eleri and Donovan glanced at each other, and Donovan was glad to be able to shake his head, "No. I know the location of the safe house, but even Eleri doesn't."

"Okay, so he can't get to his kids. We've checked his home and his office. Where else might he go?"

The three of them looked to each other. And said the name simultaneously.

"LeDonRic."

61

Donovan hit the button to raise the garage door at the Frank Lloyd Wright house. It was close to two a.m. when they arrived. He'd been awake for almost twenty-four straight hours and working without a break the whole time. He also wasn't certain that the garage door was not going to wake their neighbors and alert their street in Pythagoras Point that he and Eleri were not the random new Curie recruits that they seemed.

Not that their cover mattered much anymore. He and Eleri and Wade had blown that big time tonight. They had surrounded Marshawn James' home in the Shire neighborhood like the FBI agents they were. There was no way to sneak around a home built out of a mound of dirt, grass, and flowers. They'd gone into the business district on one of the back roads and invaded his office. Though no one lived there, Donovan could not be sure other business owners were not in their shops late at night. If anyone had seen them, their business would be obvious. If anyone recognized them, then the days of being Eleri Miller and Donovan Naman were over.

Now, they were prepping to raid the place next door to their own "home." The only consolation was that they wouldn't have to screech the car to a halt on the street this time and then run up to surround the house.

So Donovan pulled into the garage and almost casually pushed the button to lower the door. The three of them headed into the house through the garage, weapons drawn again, sweeping their own home downstairs and upstairs for the second time that night.

They had to. There was always the possibility that Marshawn had returned to the scene of the crime and made an effort to clean up or remove evidence.

"Clear!" Eleri called out from the bedroom upstairs.

"Clear!" Wade's voice, too, carried down the stairs from the offices to Donovan, who had the job of sweeping the wide-open lower floor by himself. Then, once they'd made sure they hadn't just walked past their fugitive in their own home, they gathered at the back door. Turning the knob, Donovan led them out into the fenced yard, once again clearing the space. Though this time, instead of yelling it out, they used hand signals and stayed in sight of each other.

Still at the front of the small pack, Donovan headed to the side gate, his back dually covered by his partners. They couldn't just go out their own front door. They were already going to be conspicuous, and he was trying to limit their exposure as much as he could.

Opening the gate, he led them across the wall the fence made as it connected the two back yards. Donovan motioned for Wade and Eleri to aim for the back door. He would head to the front.

He snuck along the siding, attempting to stay in the shadows even after stepping up on the porch and into the yellow glow of the insect-reduction light that LeDonRic had hung. Unlike the ones Donovan had tried at his real home in South Carolina, this one apparently worked.

Of course it did, he thought. *Curie.*

When he heard the whistle from the back yard letting him know that Wade and Eleri were in position, ready to apprehend Marshawn if he bolted out the back, Donovan stepped into the middle space of the door.

He knocked loudly—once, twice, three times in rapid succession. It would not do to have any inhabitants get the idea that this might be a friendly visit. In a moment, he heard footsteps inside coming down the stairs in two sets. He knew Wade, in the back yard, could hear them, too. Were the two sets LeDonRic and Marshawn?

He didn't think so, as only one sounded heavy enough to be Marshawn. Hopefully, that would be LeDonRic. Still, Donovan stayed ready for anything.

The older James brother was supposed to live here alone. But that didn't mean he stayed alone most nights. Was it Maggie?

Donovan knocked again. Though the knock masked the footsteps, it helped lend the air of urgency he wanted. When the door opened, it was Maggie, confirming Donovan's more promising thought. Luckily, LeDonRic stood right behind her. Between them, her tiny, pink pig pushed her way through the people's legs.

Donovan couldn't help but glance down as the pig looked up and offered a small squeal at him. Atinlay seemed to know what he was, even if it couldn't communicate that to its humans. The pig was stinking cute, and he smiled at it.

It was then that LeDonRic noticed the weapon at Donovan's side and put his hands up.

"Whoa! I don't know what's going on . . ." LeDonRic made the words clear as he began walking slowly backward into the house. Maggie just stood and frowned.

Reaching into his back pocket made both Maggie and LeDonRic jerk back sharply, probably sure this was a home invasion or worse. But Donovan quickly pulled out his FBI wallet. Flipping it open, he showed it clearly to both of them. With that same hand, he held his finger up to his mouth asking them to stay silent.

Two sets of eyes became wide and round, startled at the badge.

Well, he thought, *at least* they *hadn't figured him out yet. No, that was just the teenagers.*

Motioning them to move back once more, Donavan took a step into the entryway and closed the door behind him. They'd already made quite enough of a scene for any neighbors who might be watching.

He looked back and forth between the two of them. "You can put your hands down. Eleri and I are agents with the FBI." He would have said "Agent Eames," except that name would mean nothing to them. They knew her as Eleri Miller. And if they'd read his badge, they would know he was not Dr. Donovan Naman, but Dr. Donovan Heath, Special Agent. They likely would not notice or understand the small diamonds at the end of the lines that bracketed both the top and bottom of the Bureau ID. To anyone who knew . . . it meant he was with NightShade.

Though he could still smell shock and fear on both of them, it faded slightly, and he had a moment to think. *If you hadn't done anything wrong, what did you have to be afraid of?* But he realized this was Curie, Nebraska and there had been murders. And, to be fair, not everyone trusted the authority of the law. No matter what he said or did, that distrust had been well-earned—not by him, but by others who represented various badges. So it was up to him to put these two at ease and determine whether they could be trusted, too.

"We're looking for Marshawn," he told them. This time, wide round eyes turned to a frown. Their surprise seemed genuine. They seemed to have no idea why the FBI would turn up on LeDonRic's doorstep or why they would be looking for Marshawn.

He motioned the two of them toward the back door. "Agents Eames and de Gottardi are at your back door. I need one of you to let them in. Knock twice before you open the door," he added, even as LeDonRic turned his back and walked away.

It was a good sign, Donovan thought, that LeDonRic trusted him enough to leave Maggie here alone with him, at least for a moment.

Though the layout on this house was similar to the one he and Eleri had been living in, the staircase went up from the left instead of the right and the kitchen was in a separate place. It still had an open design downstairs with the bedrooms and extra bathrooms upstairs—or at least Donovan assumed that. He'd not checked the layout of this house, as LeDonRic had not popped up on any of their flagging systems.

But now, he looked up the stairs, as though he might see something from down here. He had to wonder if Marshawn might be up there hiding. LeDonRic and Maggie might be covering for the man's brother. It was also possible that Marshawn was hiding out in the house and they didn't know.

Eleri and Wade came in the back door, presumably having searched the back yard. There was every possibility now that Marshawn might attempt an escape out a second floor window and run off. But it was a chance they would have to take. There were only three of them, not a full S.W.A.T. team.

As Donovan scanned the back yard for a fleeing brother, Eleri and Wade both pulled out their badges quickly, and this time Donovan watched as LeDonRic and Maggie much more carefully inspected them. It was Maggie who spoke up first. "You're here investigating the murders?"

It was a reasonable question, and Eleri answered her, "Yes. That's why we've been here all along."

"Is Marshawn okay?" she asked.

Donovan realized the two still had not grasped the situation. "Is he here?" Donovan asked bluntly. Both shook their heads.

"He has a key to this house," Eleri commented. "Did you know that?"

LeDonRic nodded absently. "Of course. I gave it to him."

But the two still looked confused as they were asked to sit and stay on the couch while the three agents ran a full search of the house. Donovan once again took the downstairs, only this time, he had two persons of interest to watch. If FBI agent training had taught him anything, it was that anyone could pop up with a gun in hand at any time, so he kept a sharp eye on the two of them.

Though they didn't speak, communication seemed to pass between them while he checked inside closets and opened the garage door. When Eleri and Wade returned, it was Eleri who sat in the recliner the two had left open, Atinlay curling at her feet as though Eleri were welcome and the two wolves could please just not bother her.

"You asked if Marshawn is okay," Eleri started, her hands clasped between her knees. She could not have looked more like an agent had she been wearing a dark windbreaker with bold white letters across it. "Physically, we have no reason to believe he's harmed. But we are searching for him. As of ten p.m. tonight, he's wanted for the murders of Marat Rychenkov, Johanna Schmitt, and Jivika Das."

Donovan noticed she left out her own attempted murder.

"That can't be right. Marshawn wouldn't hurt a fly," his brother protested. But Donovan had been ready for that. Marshawn was one of those happy people who smiled at everyone. Even if he admitted to the murders publicly, some people still wouldn't believe it. Even in Curie, where evidence reigned supreme.

He and Wade stood back and waited out the silence with Eleri.

It only took a moment before it paid off.

Maggie turned to her boyfriend with tears in her eyes and said, "Don, you have to tell them."

62

Eleri felt her heart beating faster as the SUV bounced along the dirt road. She was sweating beneath her helmet and her Kevlar vest. Her hand reached to her hip, automatically checking her weapon, then to her other hip, double-checking her backup ammo.

Donovan sat beside her, outfitted much the same as she was. They were in black, head to toe, except for the glaring "FBI" emblazoned in reflective lettering on the fronts and backs of their jackets. Their SUV was packed full, and three more large vehicles followed directly behind them. She and Donovan took the back seat in the front car. They were in the lead as the agents on this case. Wade sat in the front passenger seat, and an assigned agent drove them forward.

An entire team had been assembled for this raid. They were almost three hours outside of Curie as they approached the tiny family cabin that LeDonRic and Maggie had pointed them toward.

It had taken a while for the couple to accept the fact that Marshawn was, in fact, the killer everyone had been afraid of. Originally, they'd just told the trio about the things LeDonRic's brother had been doing that might make the agents mistakenly think *he* might be their suspect. Eleri had to straighten them out and let the man know that she'd spoken to his brother and he'd confessed, before escaping.

Luckily, when they put it in the proper light, Marshawn's behavior over recent weeks had begun to make sense to the two. When she'd asked whether they'd seen him with composition books like the ones they'd found, they didn't say yes. But the answer wasn't "no" either. It hadn't been Marshawn they'd seen with the book, but Madisyn, though neither knew where that book was now.

As they bounced through a turn onto a gravel road, the ride got rougher and therefore slower. Eleri's thoughts took the same turn. Marshawn had their FBI-issued laptops and the notebooks. He'd grabbed the bag as he ran out.

She hated the way her heart sank at the thought. She'd let him get away with almost all their evidence. At least she hadn't let him get away with one more murder.

Maggie and LeDonRic hadn't been done, though. They'd mentioned that his brother had asked both of them, separately, to invest in a new project. As LeDonRic seemed to look at it now, in this new light, his brother's "top secret project" had not so much been a new idea he would be investing in, but money sorely needed to get him out of massive and dangerous debt.

LeDonRic had sat on the couch with his elbows propped on his knees, his head in his hands. "I refused. I didn't want to make an investment. I've been working hard to save for retirement. If I'd known it was about his *life*, about *saving him*, of course I would have given it to him."

Eleri had shaken her head at him. "I don't know how much you have, but chances are it wouldn't have been enough to save your brother. Please don't feel guilty about this." Truly, she hadn't known that, but she'd said it anyway.

She'd then asked LeDonRic who the guardian of his brother's children was, and LeDonRic had looked up, startled once again, eyes wide.

"Me. I'm their guardian."

It was something that would have to be worked out, since Marshawn hadn't passed away but would hopefully be in FBI custody shortly. But once the two had mentioned the family cabin, Eleri hadn't stayed put to dwell on any of it. They had their information. The house had been searched and Marshawn was not there. Neither Maggie nor LeDonRic had seen him that night, and there was no evidence that he'd been in the home.

Wade and Donovan both agreed they'd not smelled him there, or not recently, anyway. And the timing, it turned out, had been even more important than they knew. The one place LeDonRic and Maggie had believed Marshawn might go was this family cabin, and being so far away, it had taken the coordination of a satellite image and local FBI director in Omaha to gather up this team and get them ready.

The sun was coming up behind them as they headed up the uneven road, and she wondered if there was any way Marshawn could miss the caravan barreling toward him.

Though there were corn fields on all sides of them, the land was excruciatingly flat. The dust cloud raised on the gravel roads could not be missed.

Under her breath, Eleri murmured the prayer she'd learned from Grandmére years ago. "*Bon Dieu*, keep me safe. Bind me from trouble. Aida-Weddo, protect me from this forest I walk."

Donovan surely heard her words, but he didn't say anything.

Eleri wondered what Marshawn might say when he saw her. He'd seen just a little of what she was learning she could do when she fought him off at the house. Whatever he'd seen had scared him enough to make him run, to stop trying to murder her, though he could have picked up the cinder block and put it back on her chest.

He would have been starting her suffocation from scratch, as she'd gotten several deep breaths and restored her oxygen, but it could have been done. Still, he'd run, leaving her there, stuck and frustrated, still tied, long after Marshawn left and before Wade and Donovan arrived.

She was snapped from her angry memories as Wade handed her back a tablet. The satellite images showed the small house ahead to have one warm body inside. She prayed it was Marshawn. Otherwise, they were going to startle the hell out of some unlucky camper.

The cabin sat on an acre of open land in the middle of corn fields. The corn on three of four sides would be their cover going in. Again, Eleri thought their cover only worked if no one in the home managed to notice that a dust cloud the size of Omaha hovered just beyond the edge of the fields and that the corn rustled in all directions around the house. For a moment she longed for forests or city buildings, anything that would provide adequate cover, but it wasn't going to happen.

The SUVs stopped and the agents began pouring out. With two more vehicles coming at the cabin from the other direction, they hoped to encircle the house as much as possible. The lead tactical agent opened a line and let Eleri and Donovan have the floor. As the senior agent, Eleri knew this one was on her.

She spoke to the group at large. "Here's what we're looking at. Satellite images tell us there's a single body inside the home, but we don't know if there are more. Most recent images show the body as moving, so we expect one fully functional adult. Though the suspect has murdered at least three known victims, the murder method is slow and precise. I've yet to see him with a gun or firearm of any kind. He justified his murders, suggesting that he was owed, and that the lives he took were those of elderly people, so he'd not stolen too much from them."

This information was important, she knew, because it meant the FBI was much more likely to try to take Marshawn alive.

"Is there anything else we need to know?" an agent from the other side of the property asked.

She and Donovan looked to each other. There was plenty they could tell about this case, but she only added one thing: "The suspect is highly, *highly* intelligent and an excellent manipulator."

Everyone nodded at her, having gotten the message: *Don't fall for anything.*

On a signal from the operating team leader, not Eleri—as this wasn't her specialty—they fanned out. She'd done her job, and she was no longer the lead. This was now a tactical raid, much like a local SWAT team would do. They rustled through the corn as quietly as they could until each signaled he or she was in place.

She and Donovan were close, centered to the front door. They were mostly here for vocal support, to talk to and negotiate with Marshawn as voices he knew.

She and Donovan were the first ones to step out toward the home, emerging at the edge of the corn field. Two humans dressed in black, head to toe, except for their white FBI letters. Hands up, they moved slowly forward, automatic weapons in their grip, barrels toward the ground. The idea was to make it clear they were not aiming at him but that they were more than capable of taking him out.

Holding up her bullhorn, Eleri spoke clearly, "Marshawn James, you're surrounded by the FBI. Please come out peacefully with your hands in the air."

When there was no response, she looked to Donovan, who sniffed at the air. With a tilt of his head, he held up a thermal imager in one hand, showing her the heat signature from inside the small building. This close, this information was much more precise, even showing an outline of the person inside.

Whoever it was, the build looked like Marshawn, and he appeared to be cooking. It looked for a moment as though he paused and then he went back to work. Eleri shrugged. He was making sandwiches and was either deaf or ignoring them.

She yelled her words out again, only this time she heard back. "No, I will not leave this cabin."

"We have your girls!" she countered.

"Good, Madisyn only did it because I made her. Tell Don to keep them safe."

She didn't like hearing those words. It sounded as though he was confessing, and that actually wasn't a good thing. Not only that, he was confessing for his older daughter, too.

Frowning, she took two steps forward. In her peripheral vision, she watched as the other agents followed her lead, now emerging almost as a unit from the corn fields. Like a cinch, the circle slowly tightened around the cabin.

Eleri lifted the bullhorn to her mouth to speak again, barely catching the sputtering noise that was their only warning.

The world went white.

And she was thrown backward fast enough for the world to go dark.

63

Donovan had come around slowly. It took a moment to realize he was lying on the ground, looking up at morning sky. Overhead, cornstalks reached up toward the blue above him.

His ears rang. More sensitive than most, they'd suffer the blast damage even more than normal human ears would. The first thought through his head was the last words from the team leader: "Is there anything else we need to know about the suspect?"

No, they'd said.

We screwed that up.

Though he and Eleri had told the team that Marshawn James was highly intelligent, they had not anticipated him correctly. They had expected him to manipulate the scene, but not like this. And they had neglected to mention that he was also a brilliant chemist.

Marshawn had not been making something to eat. He'd been planning an exit—a dramatic one—and Donovan and Eleri had not caught it.

Donovan looked first slowly to his left and then to his right and saw no one. At his feet, he saw rows of corn, some upright, some not. He'd been standing in the open space around the house. At least, that was the last thing he remembered.

From the way the stalks were bent, it appeared that he had been blown upward, over the tops of the plants, and dropped here. He'd left a trail of bent corn in his wake, almost like Superman crashing to Earth.

But where was Eleri? Where were the other agents? The thoughts tumbled in his head like rocks. He should worry more about the team, but he was worried about Eleri, and about Wade, who'd come in from the other side of the small house.

"El? *El!*" he hollered out, though it sounded like his head was inside a bowl, and he was screaming only inside his own skull.

The ringing continued, and as he tried to sit up, he felt his stomach roll. That was unlike him. He must have taken a very hard hit. Glancing down toward his feet again, he saw a black plume of smoke reaching toward the sky. He must have awakened quickly. He couldn't have been out long, or the smoke would have spread.

Donovan was grateful for his thoughts solidifying as they did. Even if a slice of his life had been completely removed, and he didn't know how long it had been, he was at least able to back-calculate it.

"El!" he yelled again. But this time, he didn't lie there and wait. Instead, he rolled over, scrambling to his hands and knees, leaving his back to the scene—a thing he shouldn't do, but wasn't quite able to not do. In front of him, the corn he had not disturbed stood up straight and blurred, despite only being several feet away.

As he tried to focus, he found he couldn't. He wanted to shake his head but was afraid that would make him actually vomit rather than just feel like he would. The dirt beneath his hands was not the soft, brown loam of a nicely turned garden, but covered in stalks, husks, and other sharp objects from the field. Slowly, he rocked back on his knees.

"El," he yelled it again. "Eleri!" This time, it seemed as if some of the sound he made escaped the fish bowl around his head. He couldn't hear. The ringing was too intense. He could hardly see. Though he could make out objects, he could not focus on them. But this time, the sound didn't feel as though it immediately bounced back to him.

And he could smell. So he stopped, worked to quell the turning in his stomach, and took a deep inhale. He smelled smoke. He smelled old, drying corn. He smelled chemicals from the burning home behind him. He smelled fuel from the trucks they had driven in. He smelled people, and at last, he found her. He would not be able to find

Wade—at least not immediately, as Wade had been much further away.

He could only pray that his friend was safe. Crawling on his hands and knees, because he was unable to stand fully upright, Donovan made his way, pushing at the cornstalks and sliding between them, one slow, forward movement at a time.

"Eleri," he called out, and at last, as he got close, he was able to hear a moan in response.

That was her voice. He knew it! At least she was still alive. He continued calling out and listening for her groans in response, a sharply painful game of Marco Polo.

When at last he came upon her, he grabbed her face in one hand. Though she batted at him half-heartedly, he turned her toward him and used his other finger as a reference point for her to track as a test. He checked her pupils, making sure they were equal and reactive. This blow could definitely have caused serious mental damage, and for a moment, he wondered how his own eyes were functioning.

"Check me," he rasped out and waited while Eleri slowly sat up. She seemed to have taken the hit a little harder than him, though as he looked around—and found his focus was returning slightly—he could see the cornstalks around her appeared to have the same pattern from where he had landed, as though she too had been picked up and thrown to Earth at a high speed. He was looking at the pattern when Eleri, in turn, grabbed his face and aimed him toward her, waving her own finger slowly in front of him.

"You're good," she said, or at least he saw it on her lips, the ringing in his ears having begun again.

He watched as she flinched, and realized this time, she was hearing it too. But it was different this time. He saw her mouth the word "bullhorn" before he caught on.

The bullhorn was sounding off in long, loud beeps. Someone else was still alive. *Hopefully*, Donovan thought, *they all are*. He and Eleri, he remembered, had emerged from the cover of the cornfields first. Though he knew the cornfields weren't adequate cover in any way other than visually—certainly not against the blast that Marshawn had set off—he hoped the others had been further back and all had survived.

"Wade?" Eleri asked, but he shook his head and shrugged, the motion hurting his shoulder blades, revealing a new way he had not known he'd been damaged.

The ringing stopped for a moment, only to be replaced by three more sharp blasts on the bullhorn. There was no longer a need for silence, he knew. Marshawn James had either managed to flee in some way or would be found among the wreckage. It was most likely that only pieces of him would be found.

It took fifteen minutes, but eventually, the lead agent managed to count heads and find everyone. Many agents were sitting on the ground, leaning over. Some had their heads tucked between their knees. Several had actually vomited. Those who were on their feet, the ones who'd been furthest away to start with, were ordered to search the wreckage.

The lead wanted body parts. He wanted to know whether there was any chance Marshawn James could have escaped under cover of the blast he'd set off. With a sigh that hurt his ribs, Donovan sat, his arms looped over his knees, his weapon close enough at hand, and he listened as he heard the first shout.

"I have a hand."

"Sneaker, foot included." The second voice prompted another turning of his stomach.

So they'd found a body. *It will take more than just a visual check to confirm the ID as Marshawn James,* he thought. But just then, Donovan heard the words, "Get back. Get back! Get back!"

And he watched as all the agents turned and ran.

64

Eleri sat on the couch in the Frank Lloyd Wright house, wondering what could possibly be the right thing to do.

She, Donovan, and Wade had been given five days each of medical leave—possibly longer, depending on how they checked out in the coming days. It had been hard at the scene to push the doctors away, not because it was personally difficult, but because medical attention had been necessary. And in the field, docs were pushy.

Still, Eleri had done it. She'd refused anything beyond a standard field check in solidarity with Wade, Donovan, and several other agents who hadn't wanted medical treatment, despite the fact that they'd been tossed backwards by a blast . . . twice.

Luckily, Donovan and Wade had both tested negative for concussion and so had she; the helmets had done their job. The two men had been adamant about not going to the hospital. Neither Donovan nor Wade liked being X-rayed for any reason, even if they had a need for medical interventions.

The last time Donovan had his ankle checked out in a standard ER, the physician had wanted to write up Donovan's unusual physiology in the medical journals. It had been a hard fight to say no. She'd watched as her partner pulled his badge to make it clear to the doctor that he would not have his medical records shared with anyone.

Though she was confident that doctor had taken Donovan's wariness to heart, if two such anomalies turned up in one hospital check,

Eleri wasn't sure how easy it would be to suppress that information. So, the three of them simply refused any medical treatment further than having themselves checked for concussion. Then they refused it from a second set of EMTs. Then from the first set again.

It was lucky the cabin was rather isolated, or the EMTs might have arrived in time to catch the second explosion Marshawn had rigged.

As they'd watched their suspect inside the house on the thermal imager—during what they hadn't then known were the last minutes of his life—he'd not been making food. Marshawn had been cooking a bomb, and he even rigged another one to go off later. Though she had figured he'd made a timer and everything, they had since found out it was simply a second bomb, and a spark from the house crushing something as it collapsed had triggered it.

It wasn't enough that he killed himself. Marshawn had to show the world how angry he was. He'd heard the bullhorn and waited until they arrived to trigger the first bomb. It had been big enough to rock the waiting cars and concuss some of the agents.

But no one had died, Eleri thought, *and people healed . . .* She was still angry about the papers and computer parts that had been found among the wreckage. She'd seen the results of fires, explosions, and bombs. Eleri knew it was always impressive what burned to a complete crisp, and what survived intact.

Fire and explosives had no rhyme or reason when it came to those things. She'd seen refrigerators explode out of burning buildings, and then found whole pieces of uncooked, untouched bologna in the middle of charred ruins. So she hadn't been surprised to find pieces of paper, somewhat singed, but still clean and legible and almost whole. She hadn't been surprised to find crisp-edged corners of pages with penciled handwriting amongst the wreckage.

They'd been *her copies*—the pages she and Donovan had transcribed from Jivika Das's and Marat Rychenkov's notebooks. Original pieces of coded notes and one black-and-white cardboard cover also survived. Several pieces of black plastic and a single motherboard also appeared to be salvageable.

It seemed he'd taken all of the notebooks, and the two FBI laptops with him to the cabin. He'd blown up all of Marat's, Jivika's, as well as their own work—or at least all of it that he'd gotten his hands on.

What was left was the drive that Eleri and Donovan had taken from the false-bottom drawer in the garage of the Rychenkov-Schmitt home. The one with Marat's videos on it. They'd kept it separately. They also had the photos they'd taken of the notebook pages and sent to the FBI, the ones GJ Janson had used to eventually crack the code.

She and Donovan had been back in the house—the case considered closed—for a day. Eleri had slept a good portion of it, though they'd had an alarm set for every three hours to wake up, check each other, and make sure that they were recovering from their head injuries okay.

Wade had taken one of the office rooms rather than staying alone at his house in C'thulhu Heights.

The Mazurs and the James girls had been brought back from the FBI safe house, though Eleri was unsure what was going on with them. She'd not had enough time to check in with them personally, only to hear from another agent that they'd all arrived safely. But LeDonRic and Maggie next door had not come to check on her and Donovan, either.

It could be because they had their hands full with grieving children, new housing arrangements, and of course, the betrayal that the "nice neighbors" weren't "nice neighbors" at all, but FBI agents. Of the people Eleri had gotten to know in town, too many were now dead.

Johanna and Jivika, who might have come and knocked on the Frank Lloyd Wright door to be sure that they were okay, were both already gone. Kaya and Maggie and LeDonRic might never speak to her again.

She wanted to go to the *Up N Atom* and order the largest, sweetest type two coffee that she could get her hands on, but none of the three of them were yet cleared to drive, and she wasn't quite willing to call a ride service. The need for coffee had come on strong when the three of them had suffered through a call with Special Agent In Charge Westerfield that morning.

"Well," Westerfield had told them then, "at least we still have the photos that you snapped and sent to GJ."

Eleri had been glad that some of Marat's original notebook information had survived. It had been enough for GJ to crack the code, and maybe it would be enough to pass onto someone who could do something with it. Westerfield also informed them the FBI had decided to release the information, or at least what remained of it. "It should go to next of kin," he said.

Eleri had nodded at the phone, though they weren't on any kind of video call. So she blinked herself back into focus and said "Okay, we just have no idea who that would be."

"The analysts will figure it out, but you'll need to debrief the players," Westerfield made a slight turn in subject and ignored her comment about Jivika and Marat's relatives. This time, it was Wade who said yes, as though they were all taking turns, just offering an affirmative to whatever Westerfield told them.

Given the way her brain still felt unraveled, Eleri thought that might be a reasonable solution to the day. It would be another twenty-four hours before any of them was medically cleared enough to drive, which meant they would be stuck eating whatever food they could find in the fridge and pantry.

The analysts had also been given the original applications that Marshall Bennett had set aside. They'd been looking through all of the unexplained ones. Marshawn James' application was in that pile.

"We actually have found fifteen other people who cheated their way in," her boss said. His voice made her open her eyes wider.

Damn, Eleri thought. *Marshawn had actually* cheated *his way into Curie. Interesting*. He was certainly bright enough, and she wondered which portion of the application he had failed, and what it was like to be rejected like that. Had Marshall Bennett created Curie's problems with is exclusionary city policies?

Eleri had seen it—the day trippers who came in, served the coffee, made the tacos, and swept the streets. They seemed to have no love for the strange residents of Curie, and the Curie residents seemed to make no real effort to interact with the outsiders, even though the city would fall apart without coffee, tacos, and clean streets.

Marshall Bennett, she mused, had managed to bake his elitist ethics into an entire city.

"Tomorrow," Westerfield told them, "if you can clear medically, you'll need to hold a meeting both with LeDonRic James, and with the Mazur family."

Again, Eleri nodded to the phone before remembering she needed to speak the words. "Okay."

She was not looking forward to either meeting.

65

Donovan drove them across town toward the Mazur home, shifting subtly in his seat at each light, and noticing Eleri did the same. Everything hurt. Being tossed like a rag doll—twice—and then getting only your own medical care would do that to a body.

He and Eleri had just left the house next door to their own. They'd left LeDonRic and Maggie sitting at the table, and no more words of comfort or charges brought against Marshawn could fix any of the things that were wrong. Knowing they would only make it worse, he and Eleri had answered the couple's questions and then shut up.

The two girls, Emersyn and Madisyn, were somewhere in the house, probably listening in, so Donovan and Eleri had watched their comments about the girls' now-deceased fugitive father. Donovan also did it out of sensitivity for LeDonRic, who was, after all, the man's older brother. LeDonRic was clearly dealing with betrayal layered on top of feelings of failure.

Donovan had not known how to deal with any of that. He could set broken bones, prescribe antibiotics, and turf patients to other wards in the hospital, but he hadn't even been good with that. He'd been best in the morgue, where the patients didn't care what he said, only that he solve their mysteries. So now he'd been extra careful about what he said of Marshawn.

Still, Eleri had made a point before they went in—while they would not be rubbing in any of Marshawn's various crimes, they still had to be clear his death was not on the FBI. He'd destroyed himself, both with the bombs he planted in the cabin, and with his actions earlier, killing Marat Rychenkov, Johanna Schmitt, Jivika Das. He had also attempted to murder Eleri herself.

Even just speaking of it, even just skirting the issue, Donovan had been surprised to discover he was far more shaken than he'd originally believed. Though they'd had others come after them in the past, this was the first legitimate—and nearly completed—murder attempt on either of them. That it had not been him, that it had been Eleri, shook Donovan more than he'd been ready for. Eleri was strong, she was more powerful than even she knew, and she had managed to save herself. Still, Donovan couldn't help but note her diminutive size and be worried.

This was why he hadn't had friends in the past. His high school girlfriend had been literally *destroyed* by his father. His heart, which he had thought had been hardened through the years even at seventeen, had been shredded. Now, here he was with actual friends, a girlfriend, a partner. Even the loss of GJ Janson, or Westerfield, would tear him apart if anything happened to them.

He'd not been ready for this. He'd been slowly weaving himself a spider web of relationships, and as he'd woven them, he'd not considered the consequences. It didn't matter; it was far too late now. He was caught in a web of his own making. His only solution was to keep them all safe. He was reminded now that he might not have the power to do that.

Eleri shifted the topics at the table. "Our FBI analysts have struggled to find any next-of-kin for Johanna or Marat, or even for Jivika Das. Well, aside from her ex-husband, and we all agree he shouldn't be privy to the intellectual properties she had fought so hard to keep during their divorce."

Ultimately, the couple joined in that conversation and it was decided that LeDonRic James and the Mazur family should become the new conservators of the estate of information Marat and Jivika had developed. LeDonRic had agreed to share it and Donovan could only hope that the families could work together better now with Marshawn out of the picture. Then they'd said their goodbyes and left.

He and Eleri pulled up to the house where the Mazurs lived and knocked on the door. Luckily, the door opened right away. Donovan knew Eleri had called ahead and they were expected, but he hadn't been sure what kind of reception they would get.

He didn't flip out his badge or paste on a fake smile as though the Mazurs were old friends who'd invited them to lunch. There was no reason to believe any further crimes were being committed, and the subterfuge was no longer necessary. In fact, he wasn't even sure who around town might already know that they were FBI agents. But as he was welcomed inside, he was surprised.

"What's this?" he asked, pointing to various large boxes around the house. Nate's neat handwriting had labeled them with obvious titles of rooms.

"We're moving," Kaya said, just as Donovan put all the pieces together. "I got an offer at another think tank several months ago, and I decided to take them up on it."

He must have frowned.

"I don't know," Kaya said, shrugging. "I think it's just time to go. I love the *idea* of Curie. I love my friends at work. I love the *Up N Atom* and that the movie theater has obscure films. I love that my children are getting such a fantastic education. But I'm struggling with what else they're being educated in."

That, Donovan understood. It reflected his own thoughts on the town. It seemed, he thought, there was no safe place. The town had a wonderfully diverse mix of people of various colors and backgrounds. Immigrants seemed welcome with open arms. Women were paid equally. Fathers stayed home with children as much as mothers did and appeared to be respected for it. It seemed like a utopia until you heard an argument between a highly intelligent person—trying to explain to someone how to cut their pizza into sixteenths so that each slice had one half of one kind of pizza and one half of another—and a server trying to explain that the restaurant didn't offer such a ridiculous service.

Donovan had listened to more than one argument as patrons became angrier and angrier at a server's inability to follow a complex instruction. He'd heard residents claim that the trash company should come on alternating Tuesdays following the Mars orbit. Donovan had even noted that the pizzas were always cut into precise fractions, and the trash was always picked up at the same time. The taco ingredients were weighed each time one was made. He understood the Mazurs need to leave.

"We already have a house," Nate piped up. "I mean, we bought it online." He held up his phone and Kaya laughed.

"Seriously, same reason we bought this one," Kaya added with a half-smile.

It was Eleri who laughed and lightened the mood. "What's that?"

"Two kids, twins. We need two bedrooms of the same size with comparable extras."

Donovan must have frowned, because Kaya aimed her explanation at him. "This house in C'Thulhu Heights was one of only two in the whole town that had a master bedroom, and then two additional bedrooms of the exact same square footage."

Nate grinned and shrugged. "One boy, one girl, same age. What are you going to do?"

And at last, Donovan laughed along with them. Yes, he thought, he'd seen the blueprint of Johanna and Marat's home. He'd noticed the two offices of equal size and wondered if they'd had the same struggle the Mazurs did. They didn't have kids, but how did you decide who got the bigger office?

"Can we chat?" Eleri asked.

Surely it wasn't a surprise, as that was what they had come for.

"Do you want the kids?" Kaya asked.

Donovan and Eleri looked to each other for a quick moment before Eleri told them, "That's your decision."

Kaya and Nate together, as one, called for Joule and Cage to come to the table.

Donovan pulled Marat's drive from his pocket. "The FBI analysts have copies, but this is video footage of Marat with his drones. Many of his and Jivika's notebooks did not survive, but I know he talked to you—Cage—about what he was doing."

They looked to Joule, then to Nate and Kaya. "You all have some idea of what he was doing. The information has been shared with LeDonRic James, and at LeDonRic's request, also with Maggie Wells. It's now also yours . . . if you want it."

Nate and Kaya looked at each other, concern on their faces, and Donovan understood. There had already been three murders committed over this information. The information was worth a goldmine . . . and possibly death.

"It's safer now," Eleri told them, "because the FBI has this information, too. It is officially designated as belonging equally to your family and LeDonRic James."

It was Kaya who nodded.

"Don will share it with the girls."

Donovan thought it only fair to warn the Mazurs that part of the difficulty of the decision was that the FBI wanted it shared between more than one family, for security purposes. LeDonRic and Marshawn had both known Marat and Johanna. But while Marshawn had killed for the information, LeDonRic had not. However, that meant the information would likely wind up—at least in part—in the hands of the children of the man who'd murdered for it.

Donovan didn't share that Marshawn had enlisted Madisyn to break into Johanna's home and try to find the notebooks and video. The young girl was seeing a court-ordered therapist and it would be decided if she needed to face juvenile charges. That was out of his hands.

Eleri picked up the ball. "I don't know how you want to handle this, since you're moving, but we recommend that you stay in touch. I don't know if you want to go public with this information or not. If anything goes wrong, you're welcome to contact either of us. We're certainly not in any position to mediate into any intellectual property disputes, but we'll be happy to help in any way we can."

Donovan found it interesting that, for the first time, he truly felt the meaning behind those words. It wasn't about finishing up the case. It was about the fact that he liked the Mazurs and would gladly give his own time if they needed it. They were the family he wished he'd had, and nothing like the one he'd been dealt.

They talked a while more and after they left, Eleri persuaded Donovan into going to the *Up N Atom* one last time. He ordered an E=MCsquared with the recommended shot of Dopamine and smiled as Eleri ordered her own drink like a seasoned Curie resident.

Of course she did.

They didn't stay in the shop, though. It no longer was a place to stop and linger. Instead, they headed back to the Frank Lloyd Wright house and their last night in Curie.

But as they left the shop, Donovan felt the old familiar itch under his sore skin. It was creeping up on him again. He needed to go for a run.

66

Donovan had been home for a week, running almost daily in the cold, crisp air of the South Carolina woods as winter approached. He would head outside, switch forms, stretch out long, and lope through the woods.

With his reshaped nose, he'd inhaled the forest air. It smelled like home. Not just comfort, not just familiarity, but for the first time, he was calling it *home,* and he felt it down in his bones in a way he hadn't felt since he'd been small and his mother had waited for him after school.

As he trotted up to the back gate, four paws gripping the hard-packed dirt to the trail that led directly toward his back yard, Donovan heard the screech of brakes and the click of his mailbox before the mail carrier drove off.

Slowly, under the cover of the trees—much less now that the leaves had begun to fall and litter the ground, crunching beneath his feet—he rolled his shoulder blades. Lifting to full height, he stretched against the fence, twisted his ankles, and slowly rolled out his fingers, regaining his full height in human form. As far as he knew, no one had seen him on these runs, and he hoped to keep it that way.

Reaching up and over the gate, he undid the latch that he had hooked before he'd changed and gone off on his run. He walked naked through his back yard, opened the back door, and headed directly to his shower.

Only when he was fully dressed again, his wet hair toweled off, his shoes slid onto bare feet, did he head out the long front driveway to his mailbox, where the country road passed by. He pulled down the door and found an assortment of junk mail, a magazine he'd never subscribed to—though his name was on the sticker—and a small box. It was maybe big enough to hold a shampoo bottle or something similar. He wondered what he had ordered. It wouldn't be the first time he'd needed something, placed an online click, and received it days later, not remembering what he'd done.

But as he pulled the package out from underneath the letters, he almost dropped the whole lot right there on the stone pathway back to his front door.

The box had his address, though it lacked any return label. And the black Sharpie was addressed merely to "Brother."

His breathing quickened, and he looked around. Though he had heard the familiar brake and squeal of the mail carrier who came to his home six days a week, whoever had sent this was not here now and had not been here at all.

Sniffing at the air, just in case, he detected only the faint drip of water from the undercarriage of the mail truck. He sniffed the box directly and found nothing strange, though he held it tight in his hand as he walked back through his front door, almost in a daze.

He didn't notice the buzzing of his phone until it quit and immediately started up again. Flipping it over, recognizing the importance of that second call, he saw Agent Westerfield's face. It took still another moment for him to shake out of the haze the package had plunged him into.

He'd mentioned the possibility of a brother to Eleri once, maybe twice, but he'd not told her the idea had lingered in his thoughts. He hadn't told her he truly believed he had a brother.

Now, with the package, all doubts were gone. The other man had smelled him and recognized him as well.

But Donovan said none of this to Westerfield and had no intention of saying it, at least not until he had to.

So he answered the call and tried to put his best professional voice forward. "Heath," he said by way of greeting.

"I need you and Eames on a plane yesterday," his boss barked out. The stress in his voice brooked no argument, leaving no time to wonder about mysterious packages and possible brothers.

Shit, Donovan thought, he wasn't even going to have time to open the box.

But as he pulled his focus back to the phone conversation, Westerfield's voice sharpened it even more. "We have a death of an oceanic researcher on a research rig off the Gulf."

Donovan shuddered at the thought. He did not like water. But Westerfield's next words stopped him cold.

"It's someone Eleri knows."

ABOUT THE AUTHOR

AJ holds an MS in Human Forensic Identification as well as another in Neuroscience/Human Physiology. AJ's works have garnered Audie nominations, options for tv and film, as well as over twenty Best Suspense/Best Fiction of the Year awards.

A.J.'s world is strange place where patterns jump out and catch the eye, little is missed, and most of it can be recalled with a deep breath. In this world, the smell of Florida takes three weeks to fully leave the senses and the air in Dallas is so thick that the planes "sink" to the runways rather than actually landing.

For A.J., reality is always a little bit off from the norm and something usually lurks right under the surface. As a storyteller, A.J. loves irony, the unexpected, and a puzzle where all the pieces fit and make sense. Originally a scientist and a teacher, the writer says research is always a key player in the stories. AJ's motto is "It could happen. It wouldn't. But it could."

A.J. has lived in Florida and Los Angeles among a handful of other places. Recent whims have brought the dark writer to Tennessee, where home is a deceptively normal-looking neighborhood just outside Nashville.

For more information:
www.ReadAJS.com
AJ@ReadAJS.com

www.ingramcontent.com/pod-product-compliance
Lightning Source LLC
Chambersburg PA
CBHW032242020726
47499CB00012B/321
9781948059893